Seminole Landing

Colleen Affeld

Copyright © 2013 Colleen Affeld

All rights reserved.

ISBN:1482663325
ISBN-13:978-1482663327

DEDICATION

To my wonderful friends and family who have traveled with me on life's journey from childhood to adult. Their memory truly inspires the stories of our lives. I cherish and love you all.

Colleen Affeld

ACKNOWLEDGMENTS

Miss Stewart, Teacher of the Year, which was long overdue when that honor was given to you. You inspired so many of us to just be kids and use our imaginations, from the plays you let us make up and actually perform, to the forts we built in the stand of pines along the playground at George Marks Elementary in Florida. You even let us watch the Pirates play in the World Series. You and I had the same birthday and though we were born many years apart, it was only miles from each other in Western Pennsylvania. I am so grateful you made Florida your home as my family did. We all loved you.

Also, much love and appreciation to Mrs. Best for not just reading, but by being a wonderful storyteller and for everyday after lunch taking a bunch of fifth graders from a small town in Florida to Hannibal, Missouri with Tom and Huck.

Most recently, I want to give my thanks and appreciation to Professors John Ruff and Walter Wangerin for critiquing this work early on. Your comments and suggestions were very helpful to the final draft. I want to thank John Ruff, PhD., Associate Professor of English and Director of Valparaiso University CORE, College of Arts and Sciences, for taking the time away from his own writing to reread and add his kind and encouraging comments to this work. He is one of the many reasons Valparaiso is such a fine institution of learning.

Colleen Affeld

Prologue

July 4th 1947

The young Air Force Lieutenant and his partner glided across the wooden dance floor, oblivious to the smiling faces in the crowd. They were a handsome couple; the soldier standing tall in his starched, crisp uniform and the beautiful, young woman dressed in her finest organza Sunday dress, her soft, black hair caressing her shoulders as she swayed to the music. The soldier was home on leave to announce their engagement. He'd been away for nearly two months at flight school. The room was full of friends from their hometown of DeLeon, Florida. Saturday would be their formal engagement party with family. Tonight was to be a celebration of youth and young love. Their guests were intoxicated by the happiness that filled the room; all that was, except one dark, sullen young man, stumbling through the crowd. His intoxication came from something else. Something that intruded crudely, shuffling along, bumping into the guests and cursing them with foul words. Two other men, not part of the celebration waited in the parking lot for their drunken friend, who had insisted they bring him here to this place. They tried to talk him out of it, told him it was useless. But pumped with liquid courage and filled with anger, he became uncontrollable. The fire in his eyes flamed wildly. They were afraid of him when he got like this. There was no stopping him. As the lone man staggered across the dance floor towards the unsuspecting couple, the crowd simply backed away. The young woman saw him first and her smile turned to a sour scowl. She stopped swaying and stood behind the Lieutenant seemingly more embarrassed than frightened. As the man staggered close, the young woman asked, "What are you doing here? You were not invited."

He stumbled and the words slurred sloppily from his lips, "I came to pay my…respects to the happy couple. I figured you must have lost my invitation. You wouldn't do that would you? Not after all we've been to one another." Then he stepped closer to her and the Lieutenant stepped between them.

"We don't need any trouble here. Why don't you just take yourself outside and sober up," the Lieutenant told him.

These words heightened the anger in the drunkard and he began contorting his unshaven face hideously. He shook a dirty hand, a mechanic's grease-stained hand, at the Lieutenant. The Lieutenant backed away attempting to avoid the nauseating mix of cigarettes and alcohol coming from the man's hot breath. The drunk stumbled and fell forward, picking himself up surprisingly quick.

"Who do you think you are?" He put his face so close to the Lieutenant's that barely a hand could pass between them and whispered, "You'll pay for this." His fiery eyes shifted to the shiny medal attached to the Lieutenant's uniform and with a swipe of his soiled hand he ripped it from the lapel, breaking the clasp, leaving a grey, black stain. A small frayed hole replaced the medal. Immediately, three of the Lieutenant's friends seeing the Lieutenant rear back with, his fist tight, grabbed the intruder jerking him backwards. Picking him up by his trousers and shirt they escorted him to the door, tossing him sprawling onto the blacktop at the feet of his surprised companions.

"Get him out of here, before we call the law!" one of the Lieutenant's friends yelled at the men.

Not wanting a fight with a whole room of men, the drunkard's friends picked him up as he kicked and swung, cursing them all the way to their rusted pick-up truck. The guests watched as the three intruders drove away into the darkness.

Inside, the party continued, but the joyous spirit of the evening had vanished along with the intruders. The young woman was visibly shaken, and her Lieutenant tried desperately to comfort her. The rest of the evening he kept fighting off a terrible nagging feeling. It wouldn't leave him. He tried to shake it. The Lieutenant was susceptible to premonitions. It was what they called a gift, but to him it was a curse, always seeming to know of things to come. He inherited this burden from his mother. People came from all over the county to ask her about a dream or to foretell their future. She was respected by some, such as the Landing community, a group of mediums, and spiritists transplanted here from upstate New York. She annoyed a few others, like the three spinsters who lived just outside Seminole Landing. The three were what were referred to as fakers within the spiritist community. Fakers resorted to trickery, duping naive patrons out of their money. They lived on the Landing road near the river.

At the insistence of the Lieutenant, music filled the room again and guests began, couple by couple filling the dance floor, hesitantly at first, but then seeming to dismiss the earlier intrusion. Soon, laughter and celebration continued. … However, the Lieutenant could not shake his ill feeling, a feeling of impending doom. Unable to ignore the urgency of his mind's alarm any longer, he told his fiancée' they needed to leave. He would have to take her home right away, she would be safe there. He needed to go immediately. Sensing his worry, she gave no argument and they said their goodnights, urging their guests to stay and enjoy the rest of the evening.

Later that same evening, Curtis sat on a pine log that lay along the dark water's edge in the swamp. He would come here sometimes and sit by the canal. Somehow the inhabitants of the forest cheered him up and he felt safe. He liked to listen as the frogs and crickets tuned up for their nightly performance of croaking and clickety clicking. A gator further down the canal usually added a bit of bass to their orchestra. He had wanted to go with his brother to the big party at the armory, but his parents felt he should wait until the family gathering on the weekend. Curtis sometimes didn't fit in with the other young people. He was slower than most and mentally younger than his age. His brother wouldn't have minded, and in fact told his parents so, but their parents protected Curtis just a little too much, afraid for him in the outside world. So he sat here with those that understood him and allowed him to join in with the sounds of the night. Curtis pulled out his harmonica from his shirt pocket. His father had given it to him when he was younger thinking it would give him a way to express himself. His melody floated clear and smooth, melting into the other songs of the swamp. He stopped and listened. The whippoorwill called in her refrain. She always answered Curtis' musical call. It was a comfort to him. He played on and soon the swamp was alive with song. The music was especially wild and raucous tonight. Maybe the fireworks echoing up from the river had stirred the woodland musicians. As the orchestra gave their final refrain and all that was left was a lone cricket or frog plucking a note or two, Curtis was feeling better and started his walk back home. His brother would be home soon and they would sit up late on the porch and he would hear about the party. There was something different tonight as

Curtis came to the edge of the swamp. The smell of smoke filled the air. That always sent a chill of panic to anyone living in the forest. Careless campers leaving an unattended campfire around the springs kept the forest rangers and volunteer fire department busy all spring and summer. Curtis stepped up his pace and his panic turned to fear as the smoke plumed up from the pine tops. His heart raced as he came to the edge of the forest to see flames rising up from his home. He ran towards the red and orange light, but the ring of fire burned across the ground, surrounding the house. There was no way across it. Voices carried from behind the inferno and through a veil of billowing smoke, he caught sight of an old rusted brown pick-up truck parked near the woods..

"What are you doing? I thought we were just going to scare them, have a little fun! I don't want no part of this!" Curtis heard a man's angry voice shout. Shadowy figures moved about, stretching out into the night. Suddenly, the blaze cracked and the inferno shot higher into the night sky. Curtis was confused and frozen. His mother and father were inside, sleeping.

Curtis was so frightened he didn't hear the car come up the road.

"Curtis!" he heard his brother call out.

The Lieutenant picked up a blanket from the backseat of his car and ran to his brother. "Don't move Curtis, just stay back," he said. Then as quickly as he came he slapped the blanket at the ring of flame and ran into the house.

Curtis waited for what seemed forever, watching helplessly. Tears were the only thing in motion in his frozen body, and they streamed down cheeks so hot from the intense heat they evaporated before hitting his chin.

Footsteps…A pain so powerful, knocked Curtis' feet out from underneath him and he fell to the soot covered ground, thick ash floated, white against the black sky above him.

"It's you, you crazy loon!" It was a voice Curtis recognized as a second blow shot pain across the side of his head. Before floating with the ash into unconsciousness his eyes met the dead eyes of his attacker peering out from underneath the blue cap with The Little Engine That Could on its crest. Curtis thought he felt rain pouring down on him, but it had a strong medicine smell, like when he had a cut and his mother poured the clear liquid to clean it. His head felt as though it might explode then he imagined a shiny star falling to the ground beside him. As he slipped slowly into darkness he held tightly to the star believing he must be dying and the star was there to carry him to the heavens.

Colleen Affeld

Seminole Landing

Introduction

1961

To an outsider, that is, someone not actually living in our sleepy, southern college town of DeLeon, Florida, summertime might seem to be about as exciting as going to your ninety year old, sloppy cheek kissing Great Aunt Martha's on a Sunday afternoon. After the college kids with all their money and football and basketball games go on their way, and public school closes after the first week of June, some might figure our little town rolls up the sidewalks, locking up the doors until Fall comes rolling around again. I have to admit that the biggest thing on a Saturday night is going to the Boulevard Drive-in Theatre on the outskirts of town, or the University Drive-in, or U.D., as we locals call the only hamburger joint in town. DeLeon does give the appearance of being pretty boring. Now, don't get me wrong, DeLeon is a fine town with fine people, at least most of them, but we'll get to the other ones a little later on.

My name is Cally Cummins, and I've lived here with my Mom and Dad, Will and Kathryn, my two older sisters, Lynn and Kate, and our big brother Bud for all of my ten years. As I was saying, DeLeon is a fine town and pretty enough to be on one of them picture postcards you buy at the five and dime. Some would say it's got classic southern charm, with its boulevard lined with century old moss covered oaks and giant magnolias, their sweet white blossoms scenting the air with pure heaven. Stately brick and wood colonial homes set back from the road, their flowery, cushioned, white wicker rockers on wide front porches invite a body to gently ease into one of them, and sip a glass of fresh squeezed lemonade. As you walk along the carefully edged sidewalks, sprinklers' pulsating rhythms fill the air, turning soft manicured lawns of bahaia and bermuda into plush green carpets with their mist. Alabaster bird baths and glorious pink and white blooms of azalea, camellia, and jasmine adorn the lawns. In a few yards, such as my Great Aunt Ruth's, you might spot one of those shiny blue or gold garden globes, resting atop a concrete pedestal, reflecting brilliant blinding rays back at the summer sun. They look just like one of them crystal balls fortune tellers use. To most, those globes simply enhance the beauty of our town. That is, most people me excluded. Lord how I hate those things. The only whipping I ever got from my Grandpa Cummins was due to Aunt Ruth's big gold globe....

We kids were playing a game of tag when my contemptible cousin, Donny, gave me a shove and I fell right into the globe, sending it flying from its pedestal, becoming a shiny golden blur, smacking with a shattering crash into the side of Auntie's house. Of course, this caused my Grandpa to come outside to see what the commotion was all about. There I lay, sprawled out over the lawn, pieces of globe scattered all around me. Grandpa's face took on a real scary look, and without not one word in my defense allowed, he blew his stack. Grabbing me up by my arm he whipped me and marched me over to his old blue convertible parked in front of the house.

"Now, you just sit there until the rest of us are ready to leave," he ordered. As soon as Grandpa disappeared back into Auntie's house, Donny began taunting me mercilessly, that is until my brother, Bud, collared the scoundrel and made him stop. That's why I've never much liked those globes or Donny, for that matter, since. But, like them or not, the globes, nestled amongst masses of pastel flowering blooms, are all part of the beauty and charm of our picture perfect town. Except for the globe incident, we kids have had wonderful, seemingly endless summers, running and playing in the sprawling lawns of DeLeon. We especially love the warm summer evenings when we gather up old mason jars with holes poked in their lids and collect fireflies. We retreat to front porch swings where we sit and listen to ghost stories my big brother Bud and Cousin George tell us. Not a boring life at all in my estimation. With my big family, boring isn't something we know too much about. Actually, I don't know too many people living here in DeLeon that would ever say it was boring. Fact is, this so-called quiet, and as some refer to it, quaint, little town has a whole different side. Every once in a while, unbeknownst to most outsiders, that is of course, unless they read the back pages of some newspaper somewhere, things just happen here, terrible things that get the whole town all stirred up. Things can be going just fine and then all heck breaks loose. No one seems to be able to explain this dark, mysterious side of DeLeon. My Grandpa Will says it's just all part of living in these crazy times. "There's nothing so mysterious about it," he says. "It's just them contemptible Democrats. They'll be the ruination of this Country...Liberal so and so's..." I'll leave out all that, it's not fit language for children, or so my

Mom says and I'm not about to have another introduction to the taste of Lifebuoy soap for repeating it.

As you can tell, my Grandpa doesn't much care for Democrats. He was especially riled up ever since we elected our new President, Mr. John F. Kennedy. Not only is JFK a Democrat, he's a Catholic too, which riles Grandpa all the more. Grandpa says Catholics like Kennedy are trying to rule the country for years to come. What, with all those brothers of his and all their kids, Grandpa says they have enough kin to stay in office for the next quarter century or more.

"Who do they think they are royalty or something? Why they're already calling Washington, Camelot," he spouts. Grandpa could go on and on about it. My Mom's forever reminding my Dad not to mention politics when Grandpa is around for fear of getting him started up again. I think my Mom likes President Kennedy, and she even told Mrs. Beck she thought he was quite handsome. I can't quite connect how President Kennedy caused all the strangeness of our little town. Why he probably never heard of DeLeon, other than the fact that it was named for Ponce De Leon, that Spanish explorer.

My friend Connie Louise Parker has a very matter-of-fact explanation of what happens to our usually quiet town. Although Connie can be pretty out there some times, her version of our calamities seems to make more sense, for what goes on here in our little part of the country. At least it makes much more sense than the Democrats causing it all.

"It's strictly a cosmic phenomenon," Connie said to me and our friend Patty Boyd one afternoon. "It's all very simple really. DeLeon is the only town sitting on the edge of ancient Indian burial grounds and the mysterious and mystical spiritualist community, Seminole Landing."

Whenever Connie gets started on all her mystic stuff, our friend Patty Boyd gets almost as riled up as my Grandpa does over the Democrats.

"Here you go again with all that mumbo jumbo, supernatural bologna," Patty told Connie one day when Connie started in about it.

Well, that set Connie into a huff. "Scoff if you will Patty Boyd, but my

Grandmother Agnes says it's so and I believe her. She knows all about that sort of spirit world happenings."

Connie's Grandma Agnes once had her fortune told up at the Landing by one of them psychic women. Connie said the psychic told her she would come into a small fortune, and as fate would have it, she did. Ever since, Agnes has been a regular patron of the Landing and of the medium who calls herself Madame Rosemary. Fact is that the original medium's prediction of wealth for Agnes was no big psychic mystery. Patty couldn't resist reminding Connie of this when they would start their fussing.

"That's no big surprise Connie! Everyone in the County knows of your grandmother's family's wealth, and that she was an only child and stood to inherit all her parent's money when they passed. How hard could that be to predict?" Patty would rain on Connie's theory.

Connie had to have the last word, always, and she'd tell her, "Grandma knows plenty more about such things, she sees Madame Rosemary once a week. She is Grandma's advisor from the stars. You don't know anything about it Patty Boyd."

I just roll my eyes and stay out of it. I'm afraid they would argue about this until they were old as Agnes.

Now, Connie and Patty are my two best friends, but they are as different as any two people could be. Connie is a free spirit who would be willing to listen to or try most anything new within reason. Connie was sort of a chip off her grandma's block. She once came to school with tarot cards Agnes gave her and commenced to tell fortunes out on the playground. Well somebody told our teacher, and I have a feeling it was Patty, 'cause she don't believe in that sort of foolishness, and Miss Rowell took the cards away and gave them to Principal Stone. Connie accused Patty of telling on her, but Patty said if them cards were so good at foretelling the future, how come they didn't warn Connie that Miss Rowell was about to pounce. Connie and Patty didn't speak for days.

Patty isn't the only one who distresses over Agnes' influence on Connie. Mrs. Parker, Connie's mother, believes her mother-in-law is a bit of a flake.

"Every family has one," I heard Mrs. Parker mumble one day, after a visit from Agnes. Nonetheless, Connie believes in a world of mysterious mediums and psychics who conjure up dead relatives from the "other side." I must admit, it all sounds pretty creepy to me too, but she's always lots of fun at pajama parties with her ghost stories and her Ouija board.

My friend Patty Boyd, on the other hand, is a very spiritual girl in the usual religious sense, which is good, although at times she does overdo it a bit. She comes from a very religious household of Pentecost. She's forever lecturing Connie about how she is going to the devil if she keeps messing around with that spirit world stuff. I'm not real sure because I'm just a kid, but I figure Patty is probably right. That hocus pocus, talk to dead people sort of thing sounds a little far out to me too. However, I do wonder about what Connie's grandmother has told her about Seminole Landing. My brother Bud and his friends say strange unexplained things happen there.

Built in the late 1800's, Seminole Landing is a haven for mediums, psychics, and healers. A channel meandering off the St. John's River filters into the crystal springs of the Landing. The actual river is a few miles west of DeLeon. It's flows out where my family had lived for a short while when I was nine years old, and just happens to be the place where one of those terrible events occurred turning our town upside down. It was a time I just as soon not think about. It was best left in the past for now.

The St. John's winds its way through thick pine forests, a home for bobcat, deer, and I've heard a few panthers. I've been told, although I've yet to see one, there are some black bear too. If you were to go through the woods at the back of our Garfield street property and through the orange grove beyond, you would find yourself at the dirt road winding around the backside of the springs. From the dirt road, and looking across the clear blue waters, you can see the white cement block wall that surrounds that strange place, Seminole Landing. Take the road a little further south, just beyond the bend, where swamp and forest meet, you'll find yourself at the pillared entrance to the mysterious place. Past the Landing, the dirt road continues on south and makes its way to the county road, out past the minimum security prison, where they keep all them chain gang fellas. So far, since moving back to our home on Garfield Street a year and a half ago, us kids have only made it as far as the springs. We haven't got up our nerve to venture past our side of the cool waters, where if Bud goes with us, me, and my sisters, Lynn and Kate, go swimming on especially hot summer days. Bud rigged an old tire we found in the woods to a rope tied high on the limb of a sturdy oak that hangs out over the water. We take turns standing on the tire while the other three shove us over the deepest spot, where we dive into the cool blue spring. I love when Bud gives one final "Alley Oop," running and pushing the tire over his head, causing us to swoop high into the air, screaming with delight. It's almost as good as the high dive at the public pool, better maybe 'cause it doesn't cost us nothing.

The boil coming up out of the sandy bottom that feeds the spring is on the other side of the lake near the Temple of Seminole Landing. Story tells it that the boil is where the dead spirits make their entrance into the living world, and into the séances held inside the homes of the mediums. I am sure enough glad the water is nice and clear where we swim so as I can spot one of them spirits if they ever take a notion to swim to our side of the spring. The water in the spring holds at a cool sixty-eight68 degrees and I figure it's all those dead spirits keep the bone-chilling waters bubbling up, out of the boil.

Most of the time, I feel pretty sure a lot of Connie's stories, the ones Agnes tells her, are pretty far-fetched, but something inside me makes me wonder that just maybe, Connie's explanation of our town's peculiarity might be right. Maybe things happen here as a result of being too close to that strange place.

There's one other little detail I haven't mentioned, and don't much like to think about. Fact is, that when all those strange, terrible things happen here, at least for the past couple times, I somehow have ended up smack in the middle of it all. Of course, Connie has an explanation for that too. Lord, she's just about as fanatical on that spirit stuff as Patty is about anything that seems fun for us kids, sending us straight to the devil. I don't think too much about some of Connie's mystic ramblings, except maybe when I wake up in the middle of the night and the house is real quiet and the only noise you hear is the old screech owl out in the woods. You see, Connie claims that…Lord, this gives me chills just thinking about it, but Connie says Agnes told her things happen when I'm around because our house lies, as the crow flies, in a direct shot from the pulpit inside the

Temple of the Landing. She says when those big double doors at the front of the Temple are open, especially when it's warm like now; old Mr. J. Coleman's eyes stare straight out from behind his pulpit.

One night when Connie slept over, it was storming like all get out. As we lay there in bed, watching out my bedroom window as lightning flashed across a starless sky, Connie whispered, "Mr. J. Coleman's eyes can see best on nights like tonight. All that electricity flying around out there feeds his telepathic energy, helping him gaze into the beyond. Those eyes can see right smack through the grove, the woods, and directly onto this very property. Maybe they even can see right into your bedroom window, Cally. When Mr. J. Coleman conjures up all those ghosts and spirits, they take over his body. They see what he sees."

I pulled my covers up tight and I don't believe I slept a wink all night.

How she knows all this is a mystery. I don't believe she's ever set foot on the Landing grounds, but she claims to know everything about that strange place, because Agnes told her. Agnes seems to be a walking, talking encyclopedia, when it comes to anything to do with spirits. Agnes is the one who told her that our property sets on part of a Seminole Indian burial ground. As Agnes tells it, seems it was a Seminole Indian Spirit guide that had led the Landing's founders to their new home. The spirit is supposed to be an inhabitant of the burial grounds.

As I have said, the last time something really big happened around here my family was living out near the St. John's River. It's several miles from our home here on Garfield Street. Now, Connie's explanation as to how those spirits reached us way out there, all the way from the Landing seems sort of a stretch, even for Connie and Agnes. The channel running off the St. John's and emptying into the Landing Springs, on a map resembles a long bony witch's finger pointing east. My parents rented a house near the river from my Dad's friend, Mr. Jack Jackson, when I was nine years old.

Connie says it wasn't just a coincidence that Bud and I were mixed up in all that happened that fall at the Jackson Place. Connie said those spirits inhabiting the burial grounds must have seen me and Bud out helping our Dad clear the Garfield property. She said we must have disturbed part of the once sacred Indian land. Who knows what kind of spirits them mediums from the Landing have conjured up what with the Landing and burial grounds so close together.

"Those psychics calling to the here-after and all them dead Indians, ooh, it gives a body the chills," Connie said convulsing with shivers all over. "You know Cally, Grandma says there's good and bad spirits. Maybe some bad ones didn't like y'all disturbing the land. Those are the ones came swimming from the Landing clean out to the Jackson place along the St. John's looking for you. Then, it was just one of those happenstances, things leading from one to the other. Those spirits accidentally came upon those Klan fellas that held their cross burning meetings at the old haunted hotel that sits along the river near the Jackson place. Agnes says angry spirits need a real, living, breathing human to do their spooking; can't be just any human, they have to have a mean streak about them to carry out their dirty deeds. Them ornery spirits like them kind the best. Anyway, Agnes figures they ended up at the hotel, spotted them Klansmen because they're mean, I'm telling you just plain ugly mean, and the spirits possessed them and that's why they began tormenting your colored friend, Mr. Isaac Washington. They knew you'd get drug into it all, because you couldn't resist helping your friend."

Wow! Connie could come up with some stuff. Agnes' and Connie's wild theories sounded like pure hogwash to me. Lord they do have an imagination, but I didn't like Connie using her amateur psychic garble to make light of that terrible time. Me and Bud's lives were changed forever that fall by the events that happened out there. But, that was another story to be told another time, when I am ready. Bud and I never spoke of it since. We just couldn't. Not yet. It was just too soon. I did get up enough nerve to ask Isaac Washington about Connie's theory when Bud and I went fishing with him one day, out near the train depot. Isaac has been a close family friend ever since those days out along the river. Bud and I were his fishing buddies. They say usually out of something bad comes something good and that was Isaac, a good man. Isaac is a very wise man, too. Not book learnin' wise, just plain livin' wise. He'd lived a whole history book worth of learning in his lifetime and carried the stories from his ancestors before him in his mind. When it came to the Bible, old Isaac could run circles around Patty Boyd. I could count on Isaac for an honest straight answer to my questions.

The three of us, Bud, Isaac, and me, pulled up in Isaac's john boat into a bunch of lily pads dropping anchor. After we'd hooked our worms and dropped our lines, Isaac pulled a pack of Red Man from his pocket. Taking a chew he handed the bag to Bud. We fished a while and then I decided it was time to ask Isaac about Connie's and Agnes' theory. When I got started, Bud began choking on his chew, coughing and spitting tobacco juice all over. Isaac sat quietly, listening, then he spat over the side into the black water. Rubbing a hand across his stubbly chin, and leaning forward, he looked me square in the eyes.

"Cally, I believe what happened out there with them Klan fellas wasn't no spirit possession. Some men are just mean as the devil and that's the way things are. Their hate is what possesses them, not no spirit. What happened was what they call a chain of events, plain and simple. Yes ma'am, Cally, we're living in some unsettled times."

Lord, he sounded just like grandpa.

"The whole world is changing," Isaac said. "DeLeon is just one little itty bitty part of it all. You take the good with the bad and pray to the good Lord there's better. It's all a part of livin'." Isaac sat back now and checked his line that was bouncing a little as something nibbled at it. "Fact is DeLeon is pretty tame compared to the rest of the world. So when bad things happen they stick out more. They're not the usual, Cally." Isaac spit over the side again and wiped a little of the brown juice on his sleeve before going on, "The Klan hates coloreds and just about everybody else. You and Bud just got caught up in all that because you were my friends and I'm mighty grateful you was then and still are. As far as your friend's tales go Cally, I just as soon not get too involved with things of the spirit world. I mean to tell you right now, don't go messing with them neither. You can't be too sure about some of that stuff. I don't believe the good Lord wants you to go messing around with dead spirits. If they're dead and still here walking on earth and not up in heaven, they may not be something you want to tangle with. They're evil, maybe."

Well, Isaac's words about did it for me. I tried real hard not to dwell too much more on Connie's tales after talking to Isaac. That is until the events of this past summer. It was about a week until the end of our fifth year at

Jefferson Davis Elementary, 1961...

1 CHAPTER

The big black and white clock over the blackboard in Foxy's fifth grade class said 2:45 p.m. Thirty more minutes left I thought to myself as a soft, warm breeze from the window beside me lifted my math sheet gently off my desk and onto the floor. Turning in my seat to reach down for my paper, I caught Carl Johns motioning for me to look out the window. Out towards the back of the school property where the backyards along Palm Terrace sat, I spotted what had Carl's attention. It was Doc McWilliams' old Setter, Rusty. Now, I'd had a dog and heard tale of lots others, and there were some real mean ones like Zeus the Doberman down the road. Zeus liked to chew on anything or anyone for that matter that he could run down. There were tiny little ankle biters like Tex the Wiener Dog, who belonged to the Andersons. But never, ever, had I seen a dog as unique as the red Irish setter, Rusty. He was about the weirdest animal around these parts. My big sister, Kate, said he was a derelict, whatever that was. But, it must have something to do with the fact that Rusty stole clothing off clotheslines. Now, not just any clothing—not men's, and not kids—, but old Rusty liked women's clothing. Didn't steal no plain colors neither. The fancier the better—bright colored, frilly, fancy clothing, plus any nylon stockings he could get hold of. He'd crawl on his belly across the backyards of DeLeon, and then when he figured it was all clear he'd make a mad dash across the yard leaping into midair, mouth open, snatching up every woman thing hanging. Well, that is except Mrs. Purdy's. Mrs. Purdy was the Sunday school teacher at the First Methodist Church and was one of the biggest ladies in church. Why, she needed practically a whole pew to herself on Sunday morning. Lewis Russell, a boy in my Sunday school class said his

Daddy told him she once sat on a boy who was misbehaving during prayer one Sunday morning and he suffocated—right there on the spot. I figured his Daddy just told him that because Lewis was always acting up. But truth or not, it was a fact that Mrs. Purdy's clothing was a challenge to old Rusty. My friend Connie lives next door to Mrs. Purdy. She said one day she watched Rusty trying to gather up a pair of bright, grape purple shorts off Mrs. Purdy's line. Poor Rusty, he got them caught up on a mulberry root and tangled himself in all that purple cloth. Hearing the story, I said I couldn't decide which would be the better sight—the purple shorts on Mrs. Purdy, or seeing old Rusty howling and growling trying to free himself from them.

Patty Boyd and I followed Rusty one day after he'd visited the backyard of our neighbors, the Partons. We chased him through the backwoods out past the sink hole, and then lost him where the scrub brush and cabbage palm became too thick. I sure did want to find out where he took all them lady things, but we never could catch him. That is we hadn't caught him yet. I strained my eyes now to catch the four-legged bandit in action.

Wham! I nearly came clean out of my skin as the old Foxy's red ruler slapped the wooden top of my desk. Looking up I seen his two black, beady eyes piercing me through bushy eyebrows. I swear you could braid them things if you straightened all that curly black hair. Foxy had a smirk on his face that made my blood boil. It was one of those, "I've got you now, Cally Cummins," kind of looks. I caught an amused laugh coming from the direction of Robert Lee. I shot him such a look. Turning my attention back to the hideous face above me it was apparent I was in for it. Foxy as we all called Mr. Fox, our fifth grade teacher, was my first male teacher. He was a short and sort of wiry kind of man. Bud said he'd had old Foxy and he pitied me for having to endure a year of his tyranny. Bud said Foxy had what you call the short man's complex. He made up in orneriness and torture for his being shorter than most. He was sort of cocky and always, always right, no matter if he was or not. Yes sir, I was pretty sure I wouldn't be shedding any crocodile tears when Friday, our last day of school for the year, finally came.

Foxy stood there tapping. Then raising the ruler, holding it between two hands, staring at it as if reading all the numerals, he said, "Cally, you evidently know all the answers to the problem we have been discussing at great length on the blackboard. That must be why your attention seems to be outside our classroom window. You must be bored." Moving his bushy eyes from me to the class he said, "We wouldn't want Cally to be bored now, would we class?"

The classroom was silent except for Robert Lee's amused reply, "No Sir." I swear that boy is such a brown noser.

I glanced up at the board, my upper lip sweating.

"Won't you join in the class discussion Cally, and give us all the answers you obviously must know so well," Foxy said.

Staring a hole through the black slate, I might as well be Melissa with the bottle cap eyes. The only thing in front of me now was a big, blank wall. This embarrassing lack of concentration had to be what Connie commonly referred to as a brain fart—nothing but air there. Now, I can do a math problem as well as any kid, but don't go embarrassing me in front of everybody, then expecting me to figure it all in my head. Foxy just stood there waiting, tapping that darned old ruler with Langley Funeral Home written across it in big black letters. After what seemed like an eternity Foxy spoke, "We're waiting Cally. You're holding up the whole class until you give me the answer."

My insides were doing somersaults and sweat no longer seeped, it poured from my upper lip, my back, and my hands. I wondered if I was having one of old Aunt Bess' "'Woman Spells,'" hot, sweaty and feeling like screaming. I couldn't bear another minute of Foxy's tapping and glaring, nor could I stop the words, as they came spilling out of my mouth,... "You can stand there tapping until hell freezes over if you like," I said lying my head down on my desk beginning to ball like a baby amidst the gasps of my classmates.

RRING! RRING!

Mercifully, the school bell rang out. Rubbing my eyes and grabbing my books from underneath my cubby I bolted for the door as fast as my wobbly rubber-band legs could carry me not looking at anyone, including Foxy, who was mumbling something cryptic as I exited.

I ran down the school walkway and hit the sandy playground in record time. The playground seemed a lot farther across today I thought as I entered the pine needle covered path running through the clump of trees at its northwest corner. Making it to Garfield street, I caught a blaze of red fur out of the corner of my eye darting from the Hinkle's backyard. Sure enough it was Rusty, something colorful dangling between his teeth. Shoot, there was no time to chase him now. Crossing the road and running up our shell drive I could hear through an open window, the distinctive ring of the telephone. My heart raced. Foxy hadn't wasted any time. I was doomed. Adults stick together and a kid doesn't stand a ghost of a chance. Reaching the front porch, I leaned against the wrought iron post on the corner to catch my breath. I could hear my mother's voice speaking in that higher pitch she uses when she's all fired up about something.

"Cally said what?" I heard her say, then her voice was very low and I couldn't understand what she was saying until she said, "Thank you for calling Mr. Fox."

"Oh man," I groaned to myself pulling open the screened door and walking into the foyer. I watched as my mother placed the phone back in its cradle. Turning towards me, her face was very serious. She just stood there looking at me, not saying a word, which was worse than having her yell. Not being able to stand this unusual quiet, I jumped right in to plead my case.

"Mom, I'll bet that was Foxy wasn't it?"

"Mr. Fox," she corrected me, still just staring at me quizzically. She was waiting for an explanation.

"Sorry Mom, but you don't know how terrible it was today. He is such a tyrant, tapping away at me like he did. I mean a guy like that can scar a kid for life."

She just kept staring.

I went on, "I could end up like the 'Woo Woo Man,' for crying out loud, chasing kids around DeLeon with a shuffleboard stick because they yell at him."

This caused a stir in her. "Cally Cummins you stay away from Mr. Woo Woo…" Then she stopped, closed her eyes, and shook her head in mid sentence. "Honestly, Cally, I swear you kids can be so cruel sometimes. I'm sure the poor soul has a real name." Mom's face got real serious again as she got back on track and warned, "Cally you get into trouble at school, you will be in trouble when you get home. You don't speak to adults the way you did Mr. Fox. I'm not saying I approve of some of his teaching methods, but he is in charge in that classroom and you have to respect him. If you have a problem at school, you come and talk to your father and me about it. You don't take matters into your own hands. And, from here on out, I would suggest you start paying attention in school and quit your daydreaming. Follow the rules and you won't have any problems with Mr. Fox. Now, your father and I will discuss this tonight, but you might as well count on being grounded the rest of this school week.

"But Mom…?" I said pleadingly.

"It's school, homework, chores, supper, and bed until Friday night. I know your birthday is Friday, and plans are already made for your end of school party however, you better toe the line the rest of the week or I will make you cancel," she said.

"I swear Mom, I'll behave, but I tell you, I'll probably at least have some kind of mental block now when it comes to math, because of old Fox…" I caught myself before finishing.

"Cally!" Mom glared.

I had wasted my breath, the punishment stood. No siree…Foxy wouldn't ever get teacher of the year in my book. At least my party was still on, that was, at least so far.

Bud was in his room doing his homework. He was a junior this year. After next year, before I knew it, he'd be off to college. I didn't like to think about him being so far away. I could talk to him about anything. He looked out for me and always treated me like I was special. I'd get sympathy here. I knocked on Bud's bedroom door.

"Come in Cal," he said.

"How'd you know it was me?" I asked.

"Are you kidding? I could hear you and Mom all the way down the hallway. I figured you'd be in here looking for a little sympathy. What's going on?"

I began to explain the miserable details of my day, including how I even missed another chance to follow old Rusty because of this mess. Bud tried to look serious but I could see he was somewhat amused by it all. I sulked on over and sank into the blue and white striped, overstuffed chair Mom had upholstered. When I had finished my version of the day's events, Bud said, "Cally I know how miserable Foxy can be, but you just can't go around saying what you're thinking all the time, especially at school. That's just trouble."

"Oh Bud, you're taking their side," I said.

"No, Cal, I don't blame you for getting upset, he had no right embarrassing you like that, but knowing Fox, he'll make things harder for you if you give him a reason to. It doesn't take much. But, you can't go around being disrespectful to your teachers, no matter how mean they are. That'll just get you in trouble with Mom and Dad. Just think, after Friday, you don't have to look at those bushy eyebrows and beady eyes again," Bud said, squinting his steel blue eyes and pulling the black hairs on his eyebrows. We laughed. It felt good talking to Bud; he always seemed to make things better.

"Hey, so what happened to old Rusty?" Bud asked me. "What a crazy mutt he is."

"I don't know where he lit off to Bud, but he's the quickest, slyest thing on four legs. He always manages to give me the slip." We both laughed at my choice of words. "Where do you suppose he takes all those ladies' clothes and stockings anyway?"

"I don't know Cal, you just keep at him and I'm sure you'll figure it out. Just don't go too far back into those woods over near the Landing, or go back there by yourself. Some real strange things happen over there."

I picked up one of Bud's new arrowheads on his desk and ran my finger across its bone colored tip. "Where'd you get this one, Bud? It's a beauty, and in pretty good shape." Bud had lots of arrowheads he had collected from the Seminole and Tomoka Indians that had been in these parts years back. Our sister, Kate, had a fit every time he brought one in the house. She'd tell him to wash it right away because it might be contaminated from the decayed body of whoever or whatever critter it had been stuck into years ago. Bud would just laugh but would humor Kate and wash them and polish them up real pretty.

"It's pretty cool isn't it? I found it in the hollowed out base of an old oak over near the Landing. Larry, Bill, and I were quail hunting out near the swamp and I sat myself under the oak to rest a bit, being as the only thing moving in those woods that day were the pine needles in the afternoon breeze. I noticed some squirrel had been storing its acorns inside the hollowed base. Must have been 20 or so of the acorns piled in there. I spotted something shiny, and being as them gray squirrels are pack-rats, I thought it might be an old coin or something else of worth. As it turned out it was just an old Dr. Pepper bottle cap, but when I sifted through the dirt I found this arrowhead. It was just about then I heard a gun go off and Bill and Larry were whooping and hollering 'cause they'd hit a covey of birds. So, I left the tree stump to go see what they'd done."

"Did you ever go back and see what else was in there?" I asked.

"No. I stuck the arrowhead in my pocket and forgot all about it until Mom found it when she did the laundry. She put it on the table with the rest of my collection. I never did go back to where I'd found it."

"Do you think we could go back there and look, Bud? I'd like to find my own arrowhead."

"Sure Cal, we can do that. Usually, where you find one there's lots of other neat stuff. Although, I'm wondering who put them in there, because Indians usually didn't bury their arrowheads inside tree stumps. Usually, they were buried with the Indian as part of their ceremony."

"You don't suppose there's some old dead Indian around that tree do you, Bud? Could Connie's Grandma Agnes actually be right when she said this whole area really was some kind of sacred Indian land? Connie's

Grandma says some of the Indian tribes around here dated back to 800 A.D. Do you think that could be true Bud?

"Could be true Cally, there are lots of stories about the Seminole and the Nocoroco tribes that go way back. Connie's Grandma can be a flake sometimes, but there is some truth to her stories."

"She says lots of them spirits wander these woods by our property at night," I told Bud.

"Well, I wouldn't go that far, but that arrowhead there at least proves they were around these parts," Bud said. Sensing my nervousness about the subject he added, "Don't worry Cal, like I said, I don't think it was an Indian put that arrowhead in the base of that tree and I haven't found any bones around here, just arrowheads. Just remember what I told you about not going too far into the woods. I don't want to scare you, but some say, besides any spirits out there, there is an old witch woman who lives near the Landing. She's supposed to live in a cottage out beyond where the pine and oak get real thick. There's one big tall pine with a huge nest up top, just past the big sink hole, near the cypress swamp. She's supposed to live somewhere near there."

A sudden chill ran up my spine remembering Patty and me chasing old Rusty out near the sink hole.

"Larry, Squeakie, and I tried going out there when we were hunting, but turned back because it was getting dark and it just gets too wild. It's where the still black water runs off the springs. Gators and water moccasins are about all it's good for," Bud said. "There must be another way to get there because that swamp is pretty treacherous and she has to get in and out for provisions."

I said, "Maybe she just conjures up her own. You know roots and berries and such, a few little kids, and…"

Bud laughed, "Cally you do have an imagination. But, that's one of the things I love about you. Just remember Cally, besides the old witch woman, there's some pretty rough people who live out along the river branch that flows into the Landing. Don't go out there unless I'm with you, okay?"

"No problem. Witches, spirits, and gators! Man, I'd rather go to school with old Foxy," I said as I pulled myself up out of the chair.

"If you behave yourself the rest of the week maybe this weekend I'll help you track Rusty," Bud said looking back at his algebra book as I headed to my room.

Later when Dad got home I had to relive my past sins of the day and Mom's punishment stuck. Going to bed that night I decided I'd make the best of the rest of the week and concentrate on breaking my last record of running from school to my backyard. Three minutes and ten seconds was my best time. I practiced at least three times a week trying to improve. This had become an obsession of mine, at least that's what Patty Boyd called it, ever since our new President, Mr. Kennedy started having problems with that gorilla man from Cuba. Castro was his name. I told Patty he must be called a gorilla, because he was so hairy. I never saw such a hairy guy as the man on the six o'clock news. He had a big bushy beard and always wore his shirts open in the front to bear a big hairy chest. He always had a great big cigar sticking out of that bushy face. My Daddy said he'd like to have a box of them cigars. Patty said it wasn't gorilla; it was spelled g-u-e-r-i-l-l-a. I told her it didn't matter how you spelled it, he still was hairy as one. Castro took over the Cuban government after the people overthrew a man called Batista. Castro was real good friends with the Soviets from a place called Russia. They were communists and didn't like us Americans very much. In fact, they disliked us so much that they wanted to drop something called a nuclear bomb on us. Blow us all to bits. Robert Lee said those Commies were red; anyway, that's what his Daddy called them, Reds. You couldn't tell on our television, because we had black and white. Their President, named Khrushchev was always on the news and pounding his fist, just crazy mad all the time. Robert Lee and I decided they were probably red because they were so mad. People in Florida were pretty concerned about that Castro guy and his friend Khrushchev. They were especially worried being as Cuba was only about ninety miles away from the tip of Florida, down by Key West. It wouldn't take long for one of them bombs to blast from down there. Anyway, that's why I ran. How fast I ran could mean a matter of life and death some day. The reason I ran to our backyard was because instead of us getting a big cement swimming pool this year like we thought, our beautiful kidney-shaped pool became another big hole in the ground called a bomb shelter. It was supposed to protect us if any of them red guys attacked us. We kept lots of canned goods down there and there was a pump connected to a big spring that ran way down in the ground. There was also an air filter that would keep us from breathing all that bad fallout stuff from the bomb exploding. Some people thought my Dad was nuts for building it, but if he was, there were an awful lot of nuts in DeLeon, because ours wasn't the only one. There was even a sign outside the Building and Contractor Sales office that advertised, "Bomb Shelters - Built to Code.". People were building them all over the state. All this talk about THE BOMB scared the bejeezes out of me. Why, even in school we had to bring in canned goods that Foxy kept in boxes over by the windows just in case we were in school when they dropped the Big One. Every once in a while the eerie Civil Defense siren would fill the school and we would have to crawl under our desks. Like, a lot of good that would do. No sir, I wasn't about to hang around school and have Foxy be the last face I saw before meeting the Almighty. That's why I had to run like the wind. Billy Houston said you had about five minutes to get out of the big black cloud of fallout that fell to the earth after the bomb exploded. I'm not sure where he got his information, but I wasn't taking any chances. I turned on my side next to my sister Lynn. I was having a hard time falling asleep tonight. Out my bedroom window, heat lightning flashed and thunder quietly rumbled in the not so far off distance. A nasty storm was brewing. I scooted closer to Lynn.

"Cally, will you quit fidgeting around," Lynn complained.

"I can't fall asleep. Can't you hear that storm coming?" I asked.

"Cally, you're probably just feeling guilty about the trouble you got into today," she said.

"Goodnight, Lynn," I said tossing back on my other side. My sister Lynn never got in trouble. We teased her that she was Dad's pet. If we wanted something, we'd have Lynn ask for it. She resembled his mother, Anna, who he dearly loved. Lynn had her auburn hair, fair skin, and clear blue eyes. My eyes were getting heavy. I prayed quietly I wouldn't dream about the big black cloud again or Foxy.

2 CHAPTER

CRASH! "No!" the old woman screamed; her eyes snapping open from her fitful sleep, and her heart racing. Faded green eyes strained at the light still lingering outside her bedroom window. Shadows danced through the glass. Rubbing her eyes, she opened them slowly making sure sleep was not still with her. "Go away!" her voice crackled as she threw back the sheet, dangling her skinny legs over the side of the bed. Realizing she was fully awake she turned her gaze slowly to the window again. There was nothing but darkness now. "It was only a dream," she whispered to no one.

CRASH! She clutched her chest as the wickedness of the storm struck again; lightning flashing its white, hot bolts across a blackened sky. Reaching for the fringed-topped lamp on the nightstand, her nimble fingers clicked at the switch, darkness her only response. Rising, she shuffled carefully across the room and fumbling for the box of matches on the table, opening it, a shaky hand struck a matchstick on the flint. A small yellow, blue flame popped and she lit the half melted candle in its holder. Carefully, she raised the small light and made her way to the door and down the short hallway to the door with the moon and star on it. She hesitated before turning the handle. This dream had been even more disturbing than the last. The dreams had been coming to her every night for the past few weeks. Sometimes, she'd lay there afraid to close her eyes. Her sleep's visitors had become a real nuisance, invading her slumber with unwelcome guests. When the visitors became so persistent she might as well give into them. Those restless kinds don't ever give up. They could keep intruding for eternity. What was it they wanted and why now? It was time. An old woman needs her sleep. Resigning herself, she slowly turned the glass knob and entered the room. Lightning flashed once more, casting its light on the clear glass ball sitting on a table in the center of the room. Taking a deep breath, she seated herself. Placing her wrinkled hands on each side of the now hazy filled crystal she closed her eyes tight, calling into the night, "Restless spirits, walking tonight, why are you crying out to me? Why are you tormenting an old lady's sleep, tugging at my psychic senses? What is your burden? Why can you not rest or let me?" Silent now, she waited. Rain beat hard against the window glass.

"Roar!" an animal's high pitched scream pierced the steady beat of the raindrops.

"Good Lord!" The old woman jumped her heart in sync with the beating rain now. The cry was a familiar one to the woman. Only one animal made that chilling sound. It was the big cat. The cries came again and again mixing with the howling of the wind. The old woman thought her heart might burst as it throbbed with the frenzy of the night's fury. Then she heard it…yes, she was certain. It was the same voice that came with the faceless figure in her dream. Whispering across the winds,

"T H E B O Y," she thought it said. The storm raged on and now the voice was mixed with waves of other sounds, other voices, crying, moaning. No, maybe it was just the storm. It made no sense. The ball's haze on the table had turned to a reddish orange fog. "T H E B OY," a familiar woman's voice caused the old woman to turn towards the window.

"Speak to me," the old woman said. "Gifted one," she rasped. "Tell me what you know." She wished the others would stop. The moaning was interfering with her understanding. She tried to get her wits about her. There… "THE BOY," sang the wind. "Oooh!" Whoosh! "THE BOY…is the…key…" Whoosh!

"Aeeeh!" the wind howled again.

CRASH!

Lightning flashed hard, hitting very close by, startling the old woman causing her to jump knocking the candle on its side, extinguishing the flame.

"OOHHHH! AEEEE!" the moaning took over. The old woman ran from the room and back down the hall to her parlor grabbing her smelling salts from the mantle, snapping them and taking a whiff, and collapsing into a cushioned chair. Frozen there, she listened as the storm passed on across the forest into the distance and sometime before dawn she fell into a deep, peaceful sleep.

Colleen Affeld

3 CHAPTER

Walking into class early before the bell rang; I dreaded having to go apologize to Foxy for what I had said the previous day. I was sure he would enjoy every second of my suffering through it. As I approached his desk, he just sat there not looking up from the paper he was putting red marks all over. I cleared my throat.

"Mr. Fox," I said. "I would like to apologize for my disrespect yesterday during class." There I'd said it.

Without even looking up, he said, "Very well, Cally, just don't let it happen again."

That's it! I thought. I worried about this all night and all morning. He'd made such a big deal out of it, got me grounded, and that's it? "Don't let it happen again." I turned and went over to my desk almost sorry I had apologized, but relieved that I didn't have to look him in those beady eyes. Otherwise, he might have noticed I didn't mean a word of it. The rest of the day I was quite the celebrity for what I had said to Foxy the day before. Even Robert Lee said he wished he'd had the chance to tell him the same thing more times than he could count.

The rest of the week Patty, Connie, and I spent our recesses planning what we would do for my birthday party, which was to be a pajama party. We wanted to spend the night in the bomb shelter, but Mom and Dad said no.

At the end of the week we were sitting out on the jungle gym discussing our plans when Connie said, "I can't believe they won't let us stay down there. It would be like camping out."

"I don't know why either, but I almost had them talked into it, until Bud came in the house all excited saying he'd found some more of the canned goods missing from the bomb shelter, mostly Chef Boyardee Ravioli and Spaghetti. He thinks there's an old hermit stealing the food."

"Why don't they lock it?" Connie said.

"A lot of good that would do them," Patty said. "A bomb gets dropped and they can't find the key to get in. Anyway, who would have thought you'd have to worry about that kind of stuff around here. We leave doors unlocked all the time."

"It's really a little creepy to think someone is messing around your place," Connie said.

"Maybe it's one of your spirits, Connie," Patty laughed, "An Italian ghost."

"Funny," Connie said.

"Well, I think maybe we could sneak out when Mom and Dad go to bed and we could do Connie's Ouija board game out there. That would be fun," I said.

"I'm not messing with that thing, it's evil," Patty said. "I'll just be a spectator and see if I can spot one of your ghosts floating through the room as you all try and scare yourselves silly."

"Come on Patty, everyone in the room has to be involved or it won't work. Grandma Agnes says if there are any non-believers the spirits won't come," Connie said

"Well then I doubt you'll connect with them because the only one that believes all that garbage is you, Connie Louise," Patty said.

"Oh, come on y'all, quit your fussing," I said as the bell rang; time to head back to class.

At 3:15 p.m. when the final bell rang I waited for everyone to clear out of the classroom. Slowly sifting through my cubby in my desk, I waited for the last of the bus kids to go. I didn't like to bring attention to what I was doing for fear I'd be made fun of. The other kids were afraid of the bomb too, but we didn't really talk about it. I had a feeling everyone had their own fears late at night when their houses were all quiet and they let themselves think about the end of our world as we know it. Finally, the last of the bus kids were on their way, so grabbing my book bag I checked my watch, 3:22 p.m.

Down the long cement corridor, I ran across the playground and through the clump of pines by the road. Good. No cars were coming down Garfield Street to slow me down. I reached the big silver door of the bomb shelter. "3:25 p.m., I did it! I broke my record," I shouted, dancing on top of the door. My shirt stuck to my back, wet from sweat. It was a hot one today. Winded, I sat down on the metal door that hugged the hillside. It felt cool, shaded by the giant oak tree's branches sprawling overhead. Satisfied by my recent accomplishment, I lay sprawled on the door, staring up into soft white feathery clouds, an artist's lightest brushstrokes against a canvas of baby blue. A bushy-tailed gray squirrel leaped from branch to branch like one of them acrobats we saw at the Clyde Beatty Circus tent last summer. The warm breeze caressed my face cooling the tiny sweat beads sliding from my brow. Looking into the sky, I imagined I was floating on one of them soft white clouds across a kidney-shaped swimming pool, gliding almost weightlessly, so sleepy...

Foxy was saying, "Cally, what is the answer?" Looking toward the voice, I saw Foxy thumping a bright red ruler on Robert Lee's head as they sat atop an enormous dark cloud. The class was all around me, but I couldn't really see their faces. A big, red dog jumped from behind a passing cumulus. He had a wide toothy grin on his face, like he was laughing at me. Everyone was laughing at me and I could hear Robert Lee's laughter above the rest. All of a sudden, the dark cloud Foxy sat upon started bubbling like the boil from the spring. It got bigger and bigger. Something was ringing. Looking down it was my watch sounding like the school bell. I tried to run, but there was no ground under me. My arms and legs were flailing and instead of being upright my body was facing the ground and it was as though I was swimming and flying all at once, falling through the big black cloud. Turning my head as I swam along, I could see the cloud transforming into a huge mushroom and pieces of it began to fall from its umbrella top hitting my face as I swam harder and harder to get away. Looking down I could see what appeared to be my backyard, but it was all in a gray fog. As I got closer, I could see the silver door opening to the shelter below. There was a blonde headed boy I didn't recognize sitting cross-legged on the hillside beside the open silver door like nothing was going on. I could actually see his unfamiliar face and he was staring at a small, shiny box he held in his hands. Looking up, he spotted me and started to run away towards a giant oak tree. I called out to him, "Wait," but he ran into a cave like opening at the base of the tree and then the gray fog made it all disappear. Turning back to the hillside and the big silver door, I watched as it started slowly closing, and somewhere my brother Bud's voice was calling me, "Cally…" As the door shut his voice got fainter. The cloud was beginning to fall around me. I felt rain, cool rain, on my face. I, too, was now surrounded in the gray fog. I made my way to the shelter door through the glow of the reddish gold dust that was falling on it. Pounding on the door, I cried out, "Let me in!" I heard my sister Kate's voice, "You can't come in you're contaminated."

"Cally! Wake up! You're going to get soaked," I heard Bud calling from somewhere in the fog. My eyes opened only to automatically squeeze shut as a big plop of water hit them.

"Bud!" I said wiping the water from my face coming from the sprinklers my brother had just turned on. "Am I glad to see you. I had the most awful dream. Foxy was in it and…"

"Now that's a bad dream, anything with Foxy. One more day Cal and you'll be done with him and those bad dreams," Bud said.

Maybe I'd be rid of Foxy I thought, but the rest of the dream was hard to forget.

Two dragonflies playing tag buzzed my head and landed where I had been lying. Looking down I noticed footprints that were not my own.

Converse, the imprint in the seeded dirt displayed.

"Hey Bud! Look here. There are footprints all around the door. They head out that way," I said pointing towards the tree line out near the garbage pit Bud and Dad had dug. I ran to see if I could find anymore prints out around the pit and path leading into the woods. Sure enough, there was a couple by the pit set deep in the loose dirt and scattering at the sides as though someone had been running. "Bud I think maybe our Ravioli Bandit comes here through the woods."

Bud and I, as if thinking the same thing ran to the bomb shelter. Bud lifted the door so we could go inside. "Well, I'll be a...," Bud's voice trailed off as he looked over the shelves stocked with canned goods and first-aid supplies. "It looks like we've been hit again. He cleaned out the rest of the ravioli and the soup."

"Who do you suppose is doing this?" I asked.

"I'm not sure Cally, but doesn't look like my theory of a hermit holds. Those footprints are too small to be a grown man's. They appear to be more of a boy's size prints."

A blonde headed boy holding a shiny metal box flashed my mind and a chill ran up my spine.

"You can bet I'm going to find out for sure who's doing this," Bud said. "Think maybe me and Larry will stay the night down here over the weekend and see if we can catch the thief."

Carefully checking out the shelves, we found some gauze and antiseptic missing from the first-aid box too.

When Daddy came home and we were having dinner Bud told him what we had discovered.

"Looks like we're going to be forced to put a padlock on the shelter," Dad said. "I didn't want to; it kind of defeats the whole purpose. I suppose we can hide the key up on the ledge of the cement block column in the carport out back. Everyone will know where it is, except the thief."

"Why don't you wait a few days Dad," Bud said. "I have a plan." Bud explained his idea about sleeping down there a couple nights. Being as they decided the thief was a boy, Dad said he could try it.

"Shoot!" I thought. That will ruin our plans for my party. I finished my dinner and helped Kate and Lynn clear the kitchen table.

"I hope Bud catches that kid," Kate said, stacking the plates on the counter. "It's a real uneasy feeling to think someone is sneaking around out here on our property and stealing from us."

"I don't know Kate," Lynn said. "If all they are taking is food and a few bandages, maybe they're really desperate. Maybe real poor and that's the only thing they have to eat."

"Lynn, there you go wanting to save the world," Kate said. "But, the fact is you can't go around stealing people's stuff. It's just not right. Maybe it's just food now, but maybe later he'll get a little braver and try to break into the house for money or something."

"Oh, thanks so much for that information Kate," Lynn said. "I liked it better when he was just a poor starving kid."

After the dishes were cleared I went to check with Bud about his plans for Friday night.

"Why do you care so much about what I'll be doing tomorrow evening, Cally? You seem awful concerned about when Larry and I will be in the shelter," Bud said.

I decided to level with him. I couldn't pull much over on Bud. "Well, you see Bud, Dad and Mom wouldn't let us spend the night down there because of the bandit. Connie, Patty, and I decided we'd wait for Mom and Dad to go to bed and then we'd all sneak out to the shelter to do the Ouija board game. It will be a lot better and weirder down there than in our living room."

"No problem, Cal. I'll be out with Larry and our dates at the drive-in. We can go to the U.D. afterward for a burger and coke. That should give you plenty of time to talk to ghosts. Just be careful and make sure that kid isn't around first. I'll put a big stick on the door. If it's moved you'll know someone has been messing around. If he shows up later when you're down there I don't think he'll bother you. He'll wait awhile until everyone is out."

"Thanks, Bud," I said, hugging him. "By the way, who's the lucky girl this weekend? When will Gloria be home from boarding school?"

Bud smiled his big, old guilty looking smile. "It's none of your business who I'm going out with this weekend half-pint. It's just a girl from school. As far as Gloria goes, she said she'd be home a couple weeks after school lets out."

I just looked at him suspiciously.

"Cal, I told you before, Gloria and I decided we should date other people while she's away at school. I mean we're too young to get so serious as to not date anybody else."

"I know, I know," I told him. "Just so as it's not Sheena of the Jungle you're going out with."

He threw a pillow across the room at me. "No, it's not her. It's just a friend of mine from school.

Sheena was really a girl by the name of Bette Davis. She was wild about Bud. Patty and I called her Sheena, because she had worn a leopard spotted costume to one of Bud's Halloween parties.

Gloria was a terrific girl and I knew Bud was crazy about her. But, her father was a State Senator and also a widower. Gloria went to boarding school somewhere up in New England because Senator Collier had to be away so much up to the State Capitol and Washington, D.C. I sure hoped that all this other dating wouldn't ruin things for Bud and Gloria. She had more class in her little finger than most of the girls that chased after my brother. My sister Kate says that the girls at school are crazy for Bud. They really went for his tallness and his jet black hair and steel blue eyes. Bud and Gloria made a striking couple as she was fair with dark hair and dark eyes. She reminded me of that Veronica girl in the Archie Comics. Kate thinks I'm weird to compare people to cartoon characters. When I told her about Gloria's strong resemblance to Veronica she said, "Cally, you live in a fantasy world. People can't look like cartoon characters or movie stars. Real life isn't like that."

If you ask me, Kate worries too much. I'm just a kid after all and life should be part fantasy. Maybe that's what's wrong with people when they get bigger, they forget how to use their imaginations and have fun. At least teenage girls like Kate do. Kate is the logical and serious one in the house. She's smart as a whip, but sometimes too smart for her own good. A kid has to have fun once in awhile and just be a kid. Sometimes I drive poor Kate crazy because, as she put it to Mom one day when I was especially getting on her serious nerves, "Cally is just too playful and mischievous. I swear that mind works overtime just thinking of things to get into."

Sometimes it irritated the heck out of me when she was right. It was funny how we could be so different, but as far as looks went we could've been twins, except Kate was older. We both were tall and thin, with narrow faces and light hair. Our sister Lynn had our Grandma's features and was shorter than Kate and I, plus she and Bud had Mom's dark hair. Lynn's had a touch of auburn like Grandma's. All us kids had Dad's blue eyes. Mom's were emerald and had tiny specks of gold, like glitter in them. She looked like a movie star.

4 CHAPTER

"Happy Birthday, sweetheart," Mom said, as I slowly opened my eyes squinting at the bright morning light coming through the lavender curtains of my bedroom.

"Thanks, Mom," I said rolling out of bed.

"What's happy about it," Lynn grumbled crawling back under her covers after Mom left the room.

"It's the last day of school, that's what's so happy about it; freedom, at last, from that big jerk, Foxy. It's the best birthday I've ever had," I said

Mom made my favorites; pancakes and ham for breakfast, and everyone actually sat at one time around the table this morning. After the last of the "Happy Birthday's" and all were on their way to work or school, I kissed Mom goodbye and headed for Jefferson Davis Elementary and Foxy for the last time this semester. Life was good!

Arriving at school, Connie came running up to me, "Cally, I can't wait for tonight. We are going to have a great time. I've got Ouija and all my stuff in here," she pointed to her book bag.

"The plans were nearly ruined," I told her explaining what had happened with our bomb shelter thief and Bud's plan. "Bud was really cool about it all, and everything is still a go."

"Your brother is great," Connie said. "Hey, do you think Larry and your cousin George will come by to pick up Bud? I swear they are so cute. My sister has the biggest crush on George."

"Your sister has the biggest crush on just about every guy in school," I said. "They'll probably come by, but we'll be at the movies by then."

Just then Robert Lee, Tommy Cox, and Cliff Townsley came up and asked Connie what she had in her bag. Connie of course, being Connie and slightly boy crazy told them all about our plans for the evening.

"We are going to do the Ouija board in the bomb shelter. Why don't you boys come by," Connie told them. I poked her hard.

"Connie what the Sam Hill are you doing?" I asked after the boys went into class. If a bunch of boys show up, my Dad will have a fit. Plus they are always so loud, there's no way my parents wouldn't hear them." I secretly wouldn't have minded too much, being as I thought Cliff Townsley was pretty cute, but I knew this boy plan just wouldn't fly with my parents. I didn't have to be one of those Seminole Landing spiritualists to see what would happen if they caught them boys around.

5 CHAPTER

"Ten, nine, eight, seven, six, five, four, three, two, one, zero!" Mr. Fox's entire fifth grade class shouted, all eyes staring at the big, black hand on the clock. Foxy was in a real tizzy not being able to control the excitement running through the classroom. He started tapping on his desk with that old ruler, but nobody seemed to care.

RRING! RRING! The final bell blasted and then came utter chaos, everyone laughing and talking at the same time as we made our final exit out of Foxy's classroom. I swear it felt like someone had taken a big old block of cement off of me. FREEDOM!

Patty, Connie, and I were supposed to meet our friends Jackie, Karen, and Suzy up at the Seminole Grocery that sat along the new Seminole county road. The road headed east and eventually ended up at Seminole Landing as it curved back to the north. There was an old Seminole road, but I wasn't quite sure where it was. Bud said it was just an old dirt road, mostly grown over and ended up at the swamp. Seminole Grocery was just a small neighborhood store that looked like a little white clapboard house with a wooden step up porch. There was a red metal cold drink box on the front porch that kept ice cold, ten cent glass bottles of Coca-Cola, Dr. Pepper, and Grape Nehi pop. The black screen door was plain wore out on its squeaky hinges as us kids entered to stock up on penny candy and beef jerky. My Mom always bought her fresh vegetables the local farmers sold in the open-air produce stand outside. Sometimes if my Mom picked me up from school, she and I would go there, just the two of us, and she'd get a

Hazelnut Bar for us to share. Just thinking about it, I could almost taste the creamy chocolate.

"This is good chocolate," she'd tell me, "not that cheap imitation stuff." We'd sit back on the white wooden bench outside and each take a bite closing our eyes with deep satisfaction at the delicious confection. "Mmmm," we'd both say. It was our special time, just me and her. I never even told Kate, Lynn, or Bud because that would ruin our secret.

Finally, our friends joined Patty, Connie, and I after they had taken care of their duties after school. Suzy was a school patrol and Jackie and Karen had to take down the American Flag and the Florida one that flew beneath it. I loved that Florida flag. It had a beautiful brown Seminole Indian girl on it dressed in one of them buckskin dresses with the fringe. She had bright indigo and red berry colored beads. I wondered what she would have thought of the goings on at Seminole Landing.

My friends' mothers had dropped off all their stuff at my house during the day so they didn't have to lug it around after school. By the time the others had arrived Patty, Connie, and I had already made our sugary purchases to supply us for the evening: Jujubes, Vanilla Turkish Taffy, candy lipsticks, and some of those candy cigarettes. We'd stick the cigarettes in our mouths and walk down the road, blowing fake smoke rings, like those starlets in the movies. One time old Mrs. Lamberson, who couldn't see too well, called my mother after seeing us. "Kathryn, I don't like to be telling tales, but did you know your little Cally was smoking?" Mom just laughed, knowing good and well, what had happened.

Mom was so funny later imitating the old busy body, "Well, I can't believe you find this so amusing, Kathryn. Don't call me when she ends up a juvenile delinquent." Mom told her "Thank you for calling, Esther," and hung up.

Connie, Patty, and I sat outside on me and my Mom's white bench waiting for our friends to decide on their purchases. Sitting there I watched as a boy about our age, maybe a year older approached on his bicycle. His bike was a bit too small for him. It was old and the red metal paint flaked in spots. He looked up and saw us sitting and quickly turned off Seminole Road onto a side street went down by Mr. Ellich's Garage.

"Wonder who that was," I said chewing away at my taffy.

"Who are you talking about?" Connie asked.

"That boy that just road back down by the garage," I told her.

"What boy?" Patty asked.

"Never mind, it's just a boy. I never seen him before," I said. There was something about him… No, I'd remember if I'd seen a cute boy like that I thought. I wondered where he lived. He didn't go to Jefferson Davis.

Just about then, the screen door of the grocery squeaked and out walked the others laughing and looking back towards Karen who followed with her red wax lips across her mouth. She looked like that Betty Boop cartoon character with red lipstick plastered all over her mouth.

The six of us started making our way down the road headed for Garfield Street.

We hadn't walked too far when Jackie stopped dead in her tracks. "Oh my gosh look! It's the Woo Woo Man!" she said pointing towards the curly headed blond man walking along carrying a shuffleboard stick. He really does carry that thing everywhere with him I thought. He was walking north on Garfield Street and had just turned east on the county road in front of us. Sure enough, it was him. I had never been this close to him. Usually, I'd seen him while we were driving through town. I'd heard many a story of how the short, stocky man had caught teenagers who taunted him in town and did Lord only knew what to them with that old shuffleboard stick he always carried. We waited motionless as the man rounded the curve using the shuffleboard stick as a sort of awkward crutch. He seemed to have a slight limp in his right leg.

"Let's follow him and see where he goes," Connie said.

"I don't think so!" Patty protested. "He's crazy. My brother Phil says he lives out in the woods and eats raw squirrels and rabbits. He kills them with that shuffleboard stick. Phil says when he catches those kids that make fun of him he uses that stick on them too. Some never have been heard of again."

We all looked at one another pretty darned amused. I burst out laughing. "Patty, since when do you believe your older brother? If that guy had done in any kids don't you think he'd be locked up over at Raiford in the State Pen?"

"My brother says Woo Woo was locked up for years in a state mental hospital. Doesn't know for what," Patty said.

"How's he know that? It's just talk. Come on Patty, let's just follow him a little ways to see where he goes," I said.

"Y'all go right on ahead," Patty said. "I'll go to your house and wait on you. At least there will be someone to tell the police where the bodies are when you don't show up later." She started walking ahead of us.

"Oh for Pete's sake Patty, don't go spoiling our fun. You know darn good and well if you go to Cally's house without the rest of us there'll be questions. And, knowing you, you'll have to tell them everything and Cally will be in trouble," Connie told her.

Patty stopped. She began walking back slowly, glaring at me all the while. "I don't know how I let you all talk me into these things," she said. "I'll go for just a little while, like Cally says, but if things get too weird, or if he sees us, I'm out of here and the rest of you better be too if you know what's good for you."

Well, thank heaven, I thought. Sometimes Patty could try my patience. My Mom said she was a very sensible girl, but sometimes that could drive other kids crazy. Especially when she made you feel guilty for doing something fun. It was like hanging out with your parents or my big sister Kate or something.

We kept a fairly good distance from Mr. Woo Woo, trying to be as inconspicuous as possible for a bunch of giggling girls.

"Quick, look over there," Connie said pointing over towards the Caldwell house just past the intersection. We all turned.

"Slowly," she said out of the corner of her mouth, "Just keep looking. Didn't you see him slow down and cock his head like he was listening to something." Glancing back towards him, I saw he had stopped and was turning his head in our direction. Quickly, I looked back at the Caldwell's. Holding my hand up, I started waving. "Everybody wave, he's looking," I said.

"And just who the heck are we waving at?" Patty asked.

"Just wave and smile!" I said. "Pretend, Patty!"

"I hope nobody is watching this," Jackie said. "If Jimmy Caldwell is home I'll just die."

"Better to die by embarrassment than with a shuffleboard stick stuck in your head," Connie laughed.

I decided to take my chances and glanced back to the Woo Woo Man. "Oh man, he's gone!" I told the rest.

As if we were all thinking the same thing, we broke into a run down the county road. When we got a ways past Garfield Street we came to a stop. The Woo Woo Man was nowhere in sight. Just a little further, we came upon an old worn pathway, just wide enough for one person to walk down. It appeared to have been wider at one time as the taller growth and stand of pines set back a couple feet on either side. Just a foot trail now, the path was overgrown with tickseed and deer moss. Footprints were imbedded in the soft sand where the path led off the road.

"I'll bet this just might be the Old Seminole county road. I'd hate to have to even ride a bike down it with all those ruts, much less walk," I said. "He must've gone down there. Darn it all!"

"Cally, watch your language," Patty corrected me.

"Don't go preaching at me now Patty Boyd. I can say whatever I want, and what's so darn bad about 'darn' anyhow?"

"Remember what happened the last time you kept saying it and I warned you something bad would happen?" Patty reminded me.

Lord how she could aggravate me. I wondered how come we had stayed friends so long.

"Yes, I remember and I hardly think that had anything to do with any of it. It was just a coincidence that's all." Patty was referring to the terrible trouble back a couple falls ago with all that Klan business.

"Well, we might as well head back to my house now," I said. "Mr. Woo Woo is long gone."

"Aren't you the least bit curious as to where he's gone to?" Connie asked. "I say we go down the path a little farther."

"For all we know, he could be hiding in there watching us," I said. "I'd like to see where this old road goes, but now that I think about it, I'd rather wait until Mr. Woo Woo's out of there. We can wait until later to go look around without the chance of him jumping out at us."

"That's enough for me," Jackie said. "I vote we go back to Cally's."

"Connie, I need to get home before my Mom gets worried. Maybe we can check this path out this weekend," I said.

"Is your Mom making her homemade pizza?" Connie asked.

"You bet! Pepperoni and sausage," I said.

"Forget Mr. Woo Woo," she said. "At least until we've had your Mom's famous pizza."

6 CHAPTER

"That was the best pizza ever Mrs. C," Connie said. "You should open a pizza place downtown DeLeon. You could call it Momma C's Pizza."

Mom smiled as she cleared our paper plates. "Besides the movie, what's on the agenda tonight girls?" she asked.

Everyone looked to me for the answer.

"Ouch," Patty shrieked. Connie, sat next to me and kicked her under the table just in case she had any ideas about telling our plans for later.

"Well, after you take us to the movies with Lynn and Kate…"

"Excuse me?" Kate protested.

"Kate, what's the problem?" Mom asked.

"Fine, I know we have to go with them, but we don't have to sit with them do we?" Kate answered.

"Kate's afraid we'll cramp her style if any boys decide to actually talk to her," I said. "Don't worry Queen Kathryn, you don't have to baby sit us. We'll pretend we don't know you. Maybe you'll cramp our style, too."

"That's what I'm afraid of. Just what exactly do you have planned?" Kate asked.

I just smiled, which I knew would drive her crazy.

"Honestly, you two. You figure it out, but Cally don't go embarrassing your sister, you hear? If you behave, afterwards I'll take you all for shakes and fries up to the U.D.," Mom told Kate and Lynn.

"Great," Kate mumbled. "Not only do I have to endure them at the show, I have to actually be seen with them where every guy in high school will be after the show."

"What's that, Kate?" Mom asked who was clanking glasses at the sink, just out of earshot of Kate's grumbling.

"I said fine, that's just fine," she said defeated. Then she turned to me and said, "I'm warning you. Cally, you better not embarrass me."

"They'll be alright," Lynn said. "Just fill them with candy and popcorn and stick them up in the balcony to torment all the kids making out up there. We won't have to worry about them. It will be worth the extra money if they bother Billy Carson and that Darlene girl."

That seemed to satisfy Kate as she and Billy had been an item until that Darlene girl moved here. She told us to hurry up and help Mom clear the kitchen and get ready to go.

"I can't wait," Patty said. "This is the first movie I've ever been to. I can't believe your Mom actually talked my parents into letting me go."

Patty wasn't allowed to go to movies or dances because of the Pentecostal thing. They didn't believe in it. They only agreed to this one because it was a Disney Movie, The Parent Trap. I mean it wasn't like that new Psycho movie Bud and his friends were going to at the drive-in. Mom asked Mrs. Boyd if Patty watched Walt Disney on Sunday nights on the television. She said, "Yes, we all do."

"Well," Mom explained, "I really don't see the difference then if Patty watches the same thing at the movies."

So they let her go this time. Praise be.

Patty really didn't seem to mind too much that she couldn't do certain things. I, myself, couldn't imagine not going to the show for a Saturday afternoon matinee or dancing in our living room after school with Dick Clark's Bandstand. One time my sisters and I attended the Boyd's Sunday go to meeting evening services. They were talking about talents and asked did we know if we knew what some talents might be. My sister Lynn said right out loud, "Dancing." Well, holy brimstone and damnation you should have seen all those eyes burning right through us. You'd a thought we were the devil himself. Kate was mortified and probably wanted to be swallowed up right there. Lynn was madder than a hornet because she was referring' to the likes of ballet or one of them artsy dances. I was just oddly amused by the whole scene. But, that was the last time Lynn or Kate came along for a Sunday go to meeting.

The movie was great. That Hailey Mills played twin sisters. It would be so cool to have a twin. My friend Jackie and I decided we'd sing that song from the movie, "Let's Get Together," in the school talent show. We both had blonde hair and blue eyes. It was 9:00 p.m. when we got home, all stuffed with chocolate shakes and fries. Kate was even in a good mood. Apparently we hadn't caused her too much embarrassment. According to the local Newspaper Bud's "Psycho" movie wouldn't be over until about 11:00 p.m. It was the second in a double feature at the drive-in movies. After the movie they'd take their dates to the U.D. and so I figured we had plenty of time to get on out to the bomb shelter to do our Ouija game.

"I'll bet you and Dad are awful tired after your busy day," I said as Dad picked up the TV listings on the coffee table and sank into his recliner. I saw Kate roll her eyes, and then disappear down the hall to her room.

Looking over his paper he said, "Your Mom and I are going to watch Tennessee Ernie just like every Friday night, then you yahoo's can have the television and the living room all to yourselves." Then he slipped back behind the paper.

Connie gave me an anxious look.

"Come on," I said. "We can go bother Kate and Lynn for a while until it's over. Kate has the new album, 'Blue Hawaii' by Elvis."

"Why do you keep looking at your watch Connie," Kate asked when

Elvis finished singing. "Oh, no reason; I guess I'm what they call a clock watcher," Connie said uncomfortably.

"Come to think of it you all seem a little edgy. Just what devious little things do you juveniles have planned after Mom and Dad go to bed?" Kate asked. "I'll bet you and Mom are so tired after your busy day," she said mocking me. "Come on, Cally fess up. Dad and Mom weren't born yesterday. Do you really think you fooled them with your concern?"

"That's not very nice, Kate. Mom and Dad worked really hard all day, especially with my party and all."

"Save it, Cally," Kate said turning down her record player volume. "Don't look now but 'The Ford Show' is over."

We all nearly ran over one another leaving Kate's bedroom.

"Sleep tight, Kathryn," I said exiting and shutting her bedroom door behind me as quickly as possible to avoid any flying projectiles, because she hated being called Kathryn. She said Kate was more her style; it was younger, more modern sounding. Kate's role models were Jacqueline Kennedy and Kathryn Hepburn. She said their closest most intimate friends referred to them as Jackie and Kate.

Out in the living room, glasses clinked as Mom picked up her and Dad's empty cold drinks from the coffee table. Dad had already gone to their bedroom at the end of the long hallway.

"Don't be up too late now, Cally, and try and keep the noise down to a decent decibel," Mom requested as she rinsed the glasses in the kitchen sink. Giving me a big hug and kiss goodnight, she joined Dad down the hall to my friends' chorus of goodnights.

"Yes!" Connie said. "Finally, we can get down to some real fun."

"Let's watch some Twilight Zone. That should get us all in the mood for Ouija and we can make sure everyone is staying nicely tucked in for the night. We don't need any more interruptions," I said turning the channel dial until I heard Rod Sterling's calm but creepy voice over the eerie music introducing the television show. "The Long Distance Call" was the title of tonight's episode. We all gathered around, seating ourselves on the hook rug in front of the black and white screen lighting the dark living room.

"This show gives me nightmares," Jackie said.

"I'm not allowed to watch this at home," Patty said, not taking her eyes off the screen.

The little boy on the screen answered the ringing telephone. It was his Grandma, his deceased grandma.

"He's a medium," Connie informed us. "He can contact dead people, like my Grandma's advisor over at the Landing."

"It's just a television show, Connie," Patty said. "You don't actually believe all that hocus pocus evil stuff, do you? If you could talk to dead people they wouldn't really be dead would they? They'd just be misplaced. How could you possibly misplace millions of people? When you die, and if you're good, and believe that Jesus is the only holy spirit, you go to heaven. If you get into all these other unholy spirits, well let's just say if you think Florida's hot, just wait."

"I don't worship them. I just think some people have the ability to contact spirits of dead people, like the little boy in the show," Connie said.

"Well, the only problem with that is when you go messing around with things you don't understand, you might get more than you bargained for. Remember, there are also evil spirits just waiting to be turned loose on curious and unsuspecting little girls. With all them spirits you say are out there, who knows which ones your mediums might conjure up when they open the door to the spirit world," Patty told Connie.

"Okay, I've heard enough," I said, now totally creeped out. Just as the little boy received another call from grandma, BONG! The grandfather clock made us all jump. It was ten-thirty. I clicked off the television. The back of the house was quiet. No sign of anyone stirring. The last flush of the bathroom toilet had been about twenty minutes earlier. "Come on, I think we can go out to the shelter now but, let me check one more thing before we go," I said tip-toeing down the hallway to Kate's bedroom. Peeking in the narrow opening of the bedroom door, I could see Lynn was sleeping alongside Kate tonight instead of our bedroom. Seeing her eyes slightly opened, I backed up, running smack into someone.

"Ouch!" Connie said as I quickly turned to see her holding her nose.

Sheets rustled inside the bedroom and I quickly glanced back in to make sure they were still asleep. Satisfied that all was quiet, I returned into the hallway. "They're sleeping," I said.

"Lynn's eyes are open," Connie disagreed with me.

"Remember, Lynn always sleeps with her eyes open. That's how you know she's in a deep sleep," I reminded my friend.

"Y'all are weird, Cally," Connie shook her head.

"You believe in spirits and ghosts and we're weird?" I asked walking back into the living room to join the others.

"Come on, we better get on out to the bomb shelter, or before we know it Bud will be home," I said motioning for the others to follow as I headed through the kitchen to the back door in the laundry room. As we made our way into the night, across the patio between the carport and breezeway, the air had a damp coolness to it. A light breeze blew across the tree tops causing their leaves to flutter against one another with a soft tapping sound. Our quiet giggles trailed behind us as we ran across the backyard toward the bomb shelter. As we ran, the now faint spotlight of the minimum security prison a mile to the southeast from us scanned the grassy slope of my backyard. On warm summer nights it was great fun to play our invented game of convicts escaping from Alcatraz or Devil's Island, running and dodging the moving light as it swept along.

"I feel like I really am one of those convicts sneaking out here like this," Patty said as she and Jackie ran, barely staying ahead of the streak of sweeping light chasing behind them. The rest of us followed their lead running and finally making one final leap, falling and rolling onto the backside of the grassy slope disguising the shelter underneath. Lying there catching our breath and laughing hysterically, Suzy gave a quick, "Shhh!"

"What?" the rest of us said in unison.

"I hear something rustling over there," Suzy said.

We looked out across the 50 feet or so to the woods and listened.

"It's probably just the wind," Connie said.

"No, listen. It sounds like a sort of whirring sound. Almost a rhythmic breathing like…purring," Suzy told her.

"Probably just that old bobcat, scared the daylights out of my Mom while she was hanging out clothes the other day," I said.

"Bobcat?" Patty said. "Let's get in the bomb shelter."

"Maybe it's the panther," Connie said, her voice edged with excitement.

"What panther? There are no panthers out here," I said. "They live further south near the Okeechobee."

"Grandmother says there's a panther that lives out here, near where the old witch lives," Connie said.

"You know about the witch woman?" I asked.

"I only know what Grandma Agnes told me. She says the witch woman has some kind of control over creatures such as the panther."

"Witch woman, and panthers, I say we go back inside Cally's house," Patty said.

"Oh come on Patty, help me open up this steel door. No panther's or witch woman will bother us down inside the shelter," I said tossing the stick off the latch Bud had placed there.

The door was heavy and we grunted moving it up, gently resting it on the side of the grassy slope. Once inside, we all held the weighted steel door, slowly lowering it closed again, straining not to let it slam. Turning on the small flashlight I had taken from the laundry room shelf on the way outside, we carefully followed the lighted stairway into the coolness below. The smell of cement and dampness surrounded us as we made our way from the stairway into the large underground room. Removing the lantern from the masonry nail it hung on, I took out the pack of matches thats cover advertised, Jean's Spaghetti House and lit the wick. Me and Connie straightened out the legs of the card table and set it in the middle of the room. Taking one of the candles from a white box off the pantry shelf, I placed it in a star shaped holder on the table. Each of us grabbed a folding chair from the stack underneath the bunk beds and seated ourselves around the table. Connie removed the box, with the moon and stars adorning its cover from her book bag. Placing the box in the center of the table everyone stared blankly at it, afraid to touch it, let alone open it, and remove its mysterious contents.

"Good grief, it's not going to bite you," Connie said, sensing our hesitation and removing the lid. We all sat back in our seats.

"Come on," Connie said. "Everyone sit with their knees touching the person seated next to you."

Patty gave Connie a funny, scrunched up face kind of look questioning her reasoning behind this strange order.

"You have to connect with everyone in the room. I think maybe that's what Grandma Agnes calls channeling," Connie instructed.

"Just like the rabbit ears on top of my television set, calling all spooks and spirits," I laughed.

Connie threw her arms in the air, "Okay, if y'all ain't going to cooperate and at least half way act like you know what you're doing, we might as well forget it."

"Okay, okay," I said, "I'm sorry. We'll play the game right."

"It's not a game Cally," Connie said totally serious.

Seeing that she had everyone's attention, Connie continued on with her instructions removing the board from the box along with some kind of pointer on peg legs. "Now everyone must sit very still and concentrate on the Ouija Board," she said. The board looked just as mysterious as its legends. The letters appeared as mystical ancient Arabian markings arching across the parchment colored wood. There were two arches displaying thirteen letters each.

"Unlucky thirteen," I gulped, "and on a Friday night too."

"Shhh," Connie glared.

Numbers from one to nine were beneath the thirteen letters. A large NO was in the left corner and YES was in the right and there were little cut-out moons and stars along the border. Connie took the heart-shaped pointer and placed it in the middle of the board. "This is called the Plandette," she said.

"This is getting really weird," I said.

"What's so weird about it," Patty spoke up. "Plandette just means plank in French."

"Way to spoil the mood, Patty," Connie said.

Lord, that girl could spout out French just about as quick as she could Bible verses. Her grandparents on her Mother's side were from Paris.
Connie cleared her throat annoyed. "Is there anyone who would like to try it; anyone who wants to contact someone from the beyond?"

Automatically, we all turned our eyes towards Jackie who had lost her father about a year earlier to Leukemia. I knew she missed him an awful lot and would give anything to be able to talk to him. There was a sudden spark in Jackie's eyes and it wasn't just the candlelight. I had told myself this was just a game, or was it? I could tell it was more than that now to Jackie as she began, "Daddy, are you out there somewhere?" She paused, staring around the room, eyes wide and hopeful. Prickly goose bumps ran up my arms.

"If you are here Daddy, please let me know."

Not a sound could be heard in the room. Even our breathing was shallow and quiet so as not to disturb her moment.

"Daddy, I love you and miss you very much," she said. Suddenly, the pointer began to glide across the board. It moved back and forth and then just sat there. Jackie's eyes were now filled with tears and I knew something better happen and pretty darn quick. Jackie had been sucked into this strange, mystical game. The plandette began moving again and stopped on the I, then circled around and went to the letter A then immediately over to the M. Everyone's eyes and hands stayed focused as it circled again then moved on to W-I-T-H, circling again, Y-O-U, circling. Tears were now streaming down Jackie's face and everyone's eyes were dewy except Connie and me. Circling... A-L-W-A-Y-S. The circling stopped and all eyes met.

"WHOO! WHOO!!"

"Oh, my Lord!" I gasped, my heart jumping to my throat, as a horrible sound came from around the direction of the airshaft.

"WHOO!"

"The Woo Woo Man!" someone hollered. Screams and clatter of the kind you would not believe began like a chain reaction around the card table.

"Good Lord, it is the Woo Woo Man!" Suzy hollered."

The candle somehow got knocked to the floor snuffing out. We all hung on to whoever was nearest, grabbing tight, and then we heard it! Boy's laughter, coming down the airshaft. We ran to the door and fueled by the enormous flow of adrenaline running through the six of us, shoved the door open surprising the group of devilish night raiders. They turned tail and ran towards Garfield Street laughing and slapping hands in victory as they went. Just before they made the corner of the carport the prison spotlight caught the back of a white jersey, displaying a big number 2 with Lee written above.

"Doggone you, Robert Lee!" I yelled, then remembering my parent's slumbering inside the house I quickly contained my anger.

"I can't believe how really incredibly dumb that was," Patty said laughing. "He wears his baseball jersey to do his terrorizing. Okay, how did they find out about us being here tonight? Connie?"

"I just happened to mention it to Carl Johns and Robert Lee and a couple others that Cally was having a sleepover and we might be sneaking down to the bomb shelter and...," Connie said.

"Way to go," Patty interrupted her confession.

"I hope they didn't wake Mom and Dad or my sisters." Remembering Jackie I asked her, "Are you okay?"

"I'm fine, I think," she answered, the moonlight capturing her moist eyes. "Can you believe it? Isn't it wonderful? I heard from my father."

"Jackie?" Patty started.

"No, I don't want to hear it Patty, I heard from my father and that's all I want to hear," Jackie demanded heading back to the shelter with Karen and Suzy following behind her.

"Are you satisfied now," Patty said. "I can't believe ya'll and your stupid game. She actually believes all that hocus-pocus."

"You believed it too, Patty Boyd. I saw the look on your face," I said.

Patty turned and stormed down the shelter steps with the others.

With the four of them inside the shelter, Connie gave me a shove.

"Hey!" I said.

"Don't hey me, Cally Cummins. I know it had to be you moving that pointer. Now tell me...wasn't it?"

"Well, listen to you Miss Hocus Pocus, talk- to- the- spirits person. You're not so sure about all this are you? But honestly, how could you question what happened in there? I mean it was absolutely spooky," I said turning to join our friends.

"Because, someone was pushing the plank the other way from where I was pushing," Connie whispered to my back.

"Well, what do you know? You're a faker, Connie Parker," I turned to face her. "I thought you had great faith in all that spirit stuff."

"I do, but something was wrong and nothing was happening. I think it was because Patty doesn't believe. But, after seeing Jackie's face, I couldn't just leave things hanging."

"That's exactly what I was trying to do," I told her. "For crying out loud, what were you trying to say anyway?"

"I was going to send her the message "I Love You," from her Dad, but then you started shoving the darned old thing the other way and I thought at first it was the spirits, so I just let it go," Connie said.

"Oh brother," I said, "Come on and let's get back down in the shelter before everyone figures out what we did."

Jackie, Karen, Patty, and Suzy had already seated themselves back at the card table, so Connie gave me a shrug and we joined them.

"Let's try something else a little less intense," Connie said. "Ouija, what boy in our class does Patty Boyd like?"

"Very funny," Patty protested.

"Come on Patty. You chicken or something?" Suzy asked her.

We all watched as Connie repeated the question and the plandette started circling and spelling out A-R-T-H-U-R L-A-N-G, causing riotous laughter. Good thing the light from the lantern was fairly dim as to not show off just how red Patty's face had become. We all knew she had an enormous crush on Arthur.

After the board spelled out Arthur and we'd all had a good laugh, a whistling came down the air shaft and with it came a nasty smell. "What is that?" Patty squinched up her nose. I think some one's been using your hole in the ground over here," she laughed. My hand rested on the Ouija Board pointer and all of a sudden it began to move. Connie spotted it and placed her hand on the other side. The Plandette went to the letter, J and stopped, then moved on to the letter T. We stared at one another in disbelief. All at once the pointer flew off the board. "What are you doing?" Connie asked.

"I'm not doing anything. I swear," I told her picking the plandette off the floor and placing it back on the board.

"Who's J.T.?" Patty asked.

"I don't know," I told her, just as mystified sniffing at the air. It was clear again.

For the next few minutes the questions and the giggling went on until I remembered something, or someone.

"Ouija," I asked, "Who is the mysterious boy from my dream while I rested on the bomb shelter door the other afternoon?"

Before I could finish, the little plandette began to tremble slightly moving rapidly from side to side, and without any possible reason it flew off the board again.

Whoosh! A gushing wind came through the airshaft and the lantern dimmed. Everyone gasped taking their hands away from the table, cradling them to their bodies. I looked over at Connie, who was obviously shaken. If she didn't do it, and I didn't do it...who did?

"Doggone, that Robert Lee!" I said, standing. "Come on and help me get the door. I'm going to knock him clean into next Sunday," I said starting up the stairs.

"Cally, wait," Connie said. "How could he have moved the plandette or dimmed the lantern?"

"I've had enough," Patty said. "Let's go see if Robert and Carl are still out there."

The six of us emerged from the shelter into the darkness. A cloud shadowed over milky streams of moonlight and you could barely see your hand in front of your face. My eyes shifted towards the blackness of the woods behind the shelter. "What in the Sam Hill? What is that?" I said frozen in place. Everyone turned. Two large, catlike eyes stared at us from the edge of the woods, eyes too large to be the small bob-cat that lived out there. We stood still as statues.

Then we heard it, "purr, purr" slow rhythmic breaths. Louder than a cat's gentle purring. This was a cat, but not just any cat.

The second set of rhythmic purrs sent us running towards the house as fast as our legs could carry us. Scrambling through the carport, we all crashed into one another as Suzy stopped dead at the back door. Jackie and Suzy began screaming like maniacs as they came upon none other than my brother, Bud, and his friend Larry, who had just returned home.

"Jeez!" What the...," Bud yelled.

Footsteps could be heard coming from inside.

"Oh great, it's Dad! We woke him up," I said.

"What's going on out there?" Dad's voice boomed through the kitchen."

The back door opened and there stood all six foot three inches of my father. He stepped back, "Bud?" Then, he saw the frightened group behind Bud.

"Cally, what's going on?" Dad asked.

Bud covered and said, "Sorry Dad. Guess the girls here thought I was a burglar or something. I tripped over Cally's bike out back before coming in, next thing you know they were all over me. They've watched too much 'Twilight Zone' or something."

"Well, you girls get on back in the house. I think it's time to start settling down for the night. Some of us have stayed out too late and are going to have a hard time getting up for work tomorrow," Dad said looking at my brother who had to work at Setzer's Grocery on Saturday mornings.

"Yes sir," I said to the back of my Dad as he headed back in the house.

As my parent's bedroom door shut we all gave a huge sigh of relief. Bud and Larry were searching the kitchen cupboard for a late night snack, before going out to the shelter to spend the night.

"Thanks Bud," I said. "You know you didn't have to lie for me."

"Sure I did, Cal. I watch out for my little sister. And, it wasn't really a total lie. I did trip over your bike. You know you really should put it in the carport. I could've run right over it."

"Sorry. You didn't hurt yourself did you?"

"No, I'm fine. Y'all just scared the daylights out of me. What had you so spooked out there?"

"You wouldn't believe what Robert Lee and some other boys did to us while we were doing our Ouija board game down in the shelter. It's bad enough they tried to scare us once, but darned if they didn't come back again just a little while ago. When we came up from the shelter to catch them in the act we saw something at the edge of the woods, something with glowing eyes, watching us, and that's when we came running like a bunch of crazy women to the back door and ran into you and Larry," I told him.

By now the others had joined us in the kitchen and Connie said, "You must have scared Robert and them boys off when you came driving in. Lord, I would've given anything to see their faces."

"There weren't any boys around here when we drove in, Cally," Larry said. "As a matter of fact we saw Robert Lee and Carl Johns about an hour ago clear up by the U.D."

"Oh, good gosh," I swallowed hard. "If them boys were up by the U.D. then what happened down in that bomb shelter? Connie!"

"I swear it wasn't me Cally," Connie said. "I swear!"

"What's the matter with you all? You look as pale as one of them ghosts you've been talking' too," Bud laughed.

"I think we better do what your Dad said and settle in for the night. I for one have had enough spirit stuff to last a lifetime," Patty said. Suzy, Jackie, and Karen followed her into the living room. I told Bud and Larry goodnight and Connie and I grabbed the chips and some bottles of pop and joined the others.

Colleen Affeld

7 CHAPTER

The glorious aroma of pancakes and sausages awakened my senses. Bright beams of Saturday morning light crept between the tiny slit in the picture window curtains, prying my eyes open. Dad, Bud, and Larry's voices carried through the quiet from the kitchen on the other side of the living room fireplace. I gathered from their conversation, there were no visitors to the shelter last night, at least not any living breathing ones. Chairs scooted into place around the kitchen table as Mom's voice repeated morning grace, "Dear Lord, bless this food to our use and us to thy service and keep us ever mindful of the needs of others, in Jesus name we pray. Amen."

"Amen," I said quietly.

Crawling from my sleeping bag I tiptoed into the kitchen trying not to awaken my friends who were still sawing huge logs. I giggled as I caught Patty's mouth wide open like my Dad's when he fell asleep in front of the television. You could drive a truck in there.

"Good Morning," I said to the early risers.

"Well, I didn't expect to see you up so early, Cal," Dad said. "Any more spooks come around here last night? That is besides your brother?"

I gave him a wrinkled up nose as my answer.

"You hungry ,Cally? I got a pancake in there with your name on it," Mom said.

"I'll get it Mom," I said, fixing my plate, and doctoring my cakes with yellow margarine and maple syrup.

Mom said, "Cally, after the girls have breakfast and their parents pick them up I am going to take you into town to Aunt Ruth's. She needs her sidewalks and porches swept off."

"But Mom, that will take most of the day," I started to protest.

"Cally, she's an old woman and Dad and I have things to do here today. You had a nice party last night, now it's your turn to do something nice for someone," Mom used the old guilt thing on me.

"Okay Mom," I said. "But, can Kate or Lynn go with and we can just walk there. It's only about a mile or so. It's going to be a pretty day."

"I suppose, but it's up to your sisters," Mom agreed.

Good, I thought. Then we could take some pennies and stop at the grocery on the way and get some candy. I was hoping Lynn would come because I wanted to cut through the college on the way. Connie said her sister told her they keep babies in jars inside the science building. I knew Kate wouldn't let me go look. It would be disgusting or we might get contaminated or something.

After the last girl had eaten her breakfast and her parents had picked her up, Lynn agreed to walk with me to Aunt Ruth's. Kate had plans with her best friend, Elizabeth. They were going shopping with Elizabeth's mother over to the shopping center in Daytona Beach. Kate and Elizabeth were going through their Jackie Kennedy phase. Kate saved all her babysitting money to buy a suit and hat she saw in Furchgott's Department Store, said it looked just like the one Jackie wore in Mom's Ladies' magazine. I did have to admit as Kate was getting older she looked a little like Mrs. Kennedy, especially when she put on her big dark sunglasses and a scarf over her hair. It was too funny. Whenever Kate and Elizabeth talked to each other they spoke in their most sophisticated, charm school kind of voices and so softly, just like Mrs. K. That is of course until Kate would forget herself or rather her Mrs. Kennedy self, and yell at me for using one of her colognes or hair bands. Then it was good old fussy Kate again.

Lynn and I headed out for Aunt Ruth's. As we walked along, I told her about the events inside the bomb shelter the night before.

"Cally, what would you have done if that hermit or whoever he is had decided to join you?" Lynn asked. "For that matter how do you know it wasn't him scaring the daylights out of you that last time before you woke up the whole house?"

"You know I didn't sleep a whole heck of a lot last night after everyone was snuggled up in their sleeping bags, Lynn. I was thinking the same thing. Maybe it was him. But, it doesn't figure. Nobody could've caused the wind to gush in there like that, or caused that awful smell to fill the room. Yeh, just maybe somebody moved the plandette on the board, but the wind?"

"Maybe it was just the breeze coming through the air pipe, Cally," Lynn said.

"Maybe," I said, still not convinced.

When we got to the grocery there were two men inside, one carrying a carton of Camel cigarettes and the other a six-pack of Schlitz Beer. The one with the cigarettes was a rough sort of looking fellow. He hadn't shaved in a few days by the looks of the dark stubble poking out of his face. The other one was a smaller man, with bushy eyebrows that met right in the middle of his forehead. He seemed the nervous type, and kind of wiry. He reminded me of Foxy, except ill-bred and rough looking. A cigarette tottered, stuck on his lower lip as he followed close on the heels of the other man. As I walked past them to the candy isle, I noticed the cigarette man smelled of smoke and alcohol. It was only ten o'clock in the morning for crying out loud. Just as I was making up my mind on taffy or fireballs the screen door squeaked open and in walked a boy.

"I filled my bike tire. I believe I'll just ride it on back home if it's okay with you," he said to the rough looking man beside me.

It was him. The boy on the old red bicycle I'd seen yesterday. Something about him was so familiar to me, yet I didn't know him from Adam.

"See to it you get straight home boy," the man grumbled back as he paid for his cigarettes and started for the door of the grocery.

"Yes sir," the boy said giving me a side glance of embarrassment on his way out the door ahead of the man who I guessed was his daddy. "Hurry up Earl," the man said to the other one, who quickly paid for his beer and ran out.

Lynn and I waited to hand Mr. Elias, the grocer our pennies. He was busy watching the two men as they left the store. "Who were they, Mr. Elias?" I asked.

Mr. Elias turned quickly realizing Lynn and I were waiting to pay for our candies. He shook his head and said, "That's Jasper Tate and that half-wit Earl Skinner."

"Why do you call him a half-wit?" I smiled at Mr. Elias' description.

"'Cause he's got half a brain, the darn fool," Mr. Elias' wife, Gert, said from behind the deli meat counter. "Jasper Tate owns the other half of it, does most of Earl's thinking for him. If Jasper tells him jump, Earl says, 'How far?' The man's a darned fool."

Lynn and I started laughing.

"Is that his boy who came in and spoke to him?" I asked.

"That's Jesse Tate, poor kid, having a daddy like Jasper," Gert answered for her husband.

I watched out the window as Jasper Tate started up his rusted old truck and backed out onto the county road. As Jasper and Earl drove away, I watched as Jasper's pickup dog tracked down the road. They slowed down pulling up next to the boy on the bike then took off again with a jerk. The boy peddled fast after them.

"Come on Cal," Lynn said. "We need to get on over to Aunt Ruth's."

Remembering the babies I hurried along.

It wasn't long before we were walking along the sidewalks which lined the perfectly trimmed hedges and manicured lawns of the college. There were a few students heading to Saturday morning classes and music drifted outside from the open window of Stoner Hall; named after the family of

Dulsey Mae Stoner, Aunt Ruth's next door neighbor. The Stoner family was one of the oldest DeLeon families and had been on the ground floor of the College when it first opened. Miss Dulsey Mae Stoner was about as high society as DeLeon got and always had a tea for young ladies at her home each summer. It was for girls to learn the proper ways to conduct themselves when in certain social circles. If you asked me it was all just a bunch of haughty, taughty baloney, but some people took it all quite seriously. Kate had done it a few years back and Lynn did it last year. Auntie and Kate always had their heads together trying to figure out ways to get me to be more of a young lady. I told Kate there was plenty of time for all that, but for right now I was just a kid and they should leave me be. Sure, my turn was coming, but I figured maybe Miss Dulsey Mae would either be too old or maybe even dead by then.

The science building was now in front of my sister and me.

"Cally, what are you stopping for?" Lynn said as I came to a halt. "Come on we need to get going."

"Lynn, I just want to go see something. It will just take a minute," I said already running for the brick steps leading up to the big wide veranda of the Hall.

"Cally! Where are you going?" Lynn said running behind me.

Ignoring her, I entered the long corridor to the left like Connie said she did and sure enough, right in front of me… Why I could hardly believe my eyes. Sitting there behind a thick glass case were five tall, wide-mouthed jars with babies in them. Babies that hardly looked like anything, the jars dated, three weeks all the way up to one reading three months.

"This is what you had to come see? Oh Cally! Why? What on earth for?" Lynn said.

"I thought Connie was just pulling my leg, but she was telling the truth. I wish I had never come here now. Lynn, where would they get them? And, who would let them put their dead baby in a jar for everyone to stare at? How awful," I said.

Lynn and I just stood there staring. I was feeling a little sickened.

Lynn broke the silence between us, "Cally, they probably used them for medical research. They were probably babies that died when the mother had a miscarriage or something. Remember when Mom and Dad said Mrs. McGuire lost her baby? Well, she didn't really lose it, it just was born too soon and they can't survive that."

"How sad," I whispered. I remembered how badly the McGuire's wanted a baby.

"There are some people who don't want babies at all and sneak off to secret places to get rid of them," Lynn added.

"What do you mean get rid of them?"

"Well, it's not something people talk about much because it's against the law to do it. We learned about it when this girl from the high school did it at some back street clinic in Orlando. She was just a kid and she was afraid. She nearly died from complications from whatever they did to her there. They actually take the baby out of the mother somehow."

"I don't want to know anymore about it, Lynn," I said. "Do you think that's where they got any of these babies?"

"No, Cally, but it's sad how some people want babies so awful bad, and go through all kinds of stuff to have them, and others would risk their lives to not have one," Lynn said.

"Seems to me there should be a way for the ones that don't want them and the ones that do to get together and help each other out," I said a chill running up my spine. "I'm sure enough glad Mom wanted us."

"Well, it would save a whole lot of trouble and heartache if people not wanting babies didn't get that way in the first place," Lynn said.

"Let's get out of here Lynn. Aunt Ruth will be waiting for us," I said sure I'd never forget what I'd just seen. Lynn and I walked back down the long corridor.

When we got to Aunt Ruth's she indeed was sitting on her porch swing waiting for us. "Didn't think you were coming," she said. I could hear the worry in her voice.

"We wouldn't do that to you Auntie," Lynn said, giving the sweet lady a big hug.

"Well, you girls know where the brooms are. When you're done Miss Dulsey Mae wants us to join her for some pastries and tea," she said giving me an ornery little smile. "I know you wouldn't want to miss that would you, Cally?"

"No ma'am, I sure wouldn't," I answered, not very convincingly I'm afraid. Why I'd just as soon go see Doc McWilliams, the dentist. At least he gave you Novocain to numb the torture he put you through.

When Lynn and I were about finished sweeping the sidewalks of the leathery Oak leaves, and dried up, pink azalea petals, Aunt Ruth called from her front porch, "Cally, Lynn, please come on in now and clean up."

We scurried through the tall hedged lined walk leading from the backyard patio to the front of the house. Auntie stood on her front porch no longer in her flowered house dress, but now all fancied up in a light blue linen dress with matching open-toed shoes. She looked fit for Sunday church. As we scampered up the steps she pointed to the screened door, "Hurry along now and wash your faces and hands. Tuck in your shirts, and for goodness sake Lynn, see if you can't do something with Cally's hair. It's a sight."

"Yes ma'am," we said hurrying along.

"For crying out loud, Lynn, what does she expect? I've really been working. I'm not one of them ladies on the television commercials cleaning away in their pearls and every hair in place."

"Oh, it's no big deal Cally. She just doesn't want Miss Dulsey Mae looking down her nose at you. Let's hurry. Miss Dulsey gets the best pastries from the DeLeon Bakery on the Boulevard. Maybe she'll have some cream horns."

"I'd rather sweep ten more sidewalks than have to sit over there under Miss Stoner's inspection. 'Cally, sit up straight, don't talk with your mouth full. Don't do this and don't do that,'" I said mimicking the old woman. "Lynn, you don't have to worry about it so much. She thinks you and Kate are the greatest thing since sliced bread."

"Mercy sakes, what's taking so long," Aunt Ruth called through the doorway.

"Okay, that's good enough," I told Lynn as she hit a tangle at the back of my head. "I think you got it."

"Oh Cally," Lynn said as she put the brush back on the vanity and we trooped out of the downstairs bathroom to the porch. Visions of cream horns were filling my mind. I guessed I could endure it for one of them.

Miss Stoner was already seated at the white wrought iron table at the corner of her mammoth wood porch. She was a rather large woman, portly; Kate had told me when I said she was fat. Her white hair was always wrapped, very neat and tidy, in a French twist at the back of her head. She had the softest looking white skin and clear light blue eyes and I guessed she was probably quite pretty when she was a young woman. Today she wore a dress with big pink flowers and she smelled of gardenias. Good thing the bees weren't out yet; she looked like a big pink and white carnation. Marva, the colored lady worked for Miss Stoner came through the front door with a pretty peacock blue tray carrying a pitcher of what looked like pink lemonade and, thank the Lord, a plate of cream horns cut in small bite-sized pieces. Marva sat the tray in the center of the table.

"I thought we'd have some lemonade instead of hot tea today. It's simply parching this afternoon," Miss Stoner said wiping her forehead with a lace hanky she pulled from inside her enormous bosom. She motioned for us to take a seat.

Marva poured our drinks into four tall, frosty blue glasses that matched the tray and pitcher.

"Don't be shy girls. Help yourselves to one of those pastries," Miss Stoner instructed.

"This is wonderful," Lynn said after her first bite of cream horn. "It was so nice of you Miss Stoner to ask us over."

"Well, it's good to see you helping out your Aunt. Figured after all that work you could use a treat. Maybe later on this summer, when Marva takes some time off, you girls would like to come sweep my walks. I'll pay you fifty cents each for the week," Miss Stoner smiled ever so slightly. Miss Stoner never gave out with a big old friendly smile, just slight, controlled, upward curves to her lips, like she couldn't let herself get too familiar. She was a Stoner and had position to think about. Anyway, it didn't matter how much she smiled. At least this was going much better than I'd thought it would. Miss Stoner could be neighborly after all.

"So, what do you young ladies plan on doing all summer?" Miss Stoner asked.

"I plan on helping Mom teach Bible School over at the Methodist Church for a couple weeks," Lynn told her proudly. "Then maybe I'll go to camp up in Ocala for a week."

"Well, that sounds very nice dear. How about you Cally? What kind of mischief do you plan on?" she asked studying me over the top of her gold rimmed spectacles.

Well here we go, so much for being neighborly, I thought. Already Lynn is very nice dear, and I'm doing mischief. "Oh nothing much," I said. "I'll probably do some swimming and playing with my friends, maybe a little fishing. You know Miss Stoner, fun stuff."

She raised her eyebrows, "Yes, I know."

"Well now, what did that mean?" I thought.

She continued looking over her spectacles, "How come you're not going to camp with Lynn?"

"I'm not old enough for Lynn's church camp. I am only eleven, and there's no way I'm going to Patty Boyd's church camp again, especially after the last time I was there," I said.

"Well, why not?" she asked, eyebrows up again.

"Oh brother, those Pentecostals are forever going to church. Ten minutes of arts and crafts, then go pray. Ten minutes of swimming, then a buddy check for fifteen minutes and then darned if it isn't time to go pray again," I said.

Miss Stoner's eyes got even wider now, but I continued secretly enjoying the reaction I was getting. "Then at night after supper, which we hurry through, you got to go to church again and there is all kinds of crying and carrying on. It all gives me indigestion."

I heard a gasp coming from Auntie's direction and Lynn was choking on her lemonade.

Miss Stoner, still very controlled, but getting down right agitated, obvious by the twisting of her hands together in her lap and the raise in the pitch of her voice said, "I can't imagine that praying hurts you any. I happen to have friends that are Pentecostal and they are very decent people, and their children are very well mannered. You could learn a thing or two from them, Cally Cummins."

I was listening to Miss Stoner's little lecture, but something else caught my eye as she spoke. There was a weathered old woman slowly making her way down the sidewalk in front of Miss Stoner's yard. She slid her feet along the concrete pulling, an old wire basket on big black wheels behind her. The basket was filled with cardboard boxes. The old woman looked to be pretty near one hundred years old with her dried brown apple cheeks and wrinkles stretching from the bottom of her eyes and ending at the cracks around her mouth. Her salt and pepper hair parted down the middle into two braids that streamed down each side of her head ending clear down at her waist. The woman shuffled along staring straight ahead, her head held high. She looked to be a proud woman for sure.

"Who's that?" I asked Aunt Ruth as the woman walked closer.

"Cally, quit staring and turn yourself back around. Don't make eye contact with her," Miss Stoner scolded.

"How come?" I said looking back at Miss Stoner.? "What's the matter with her? She's just an old woman."

"She's a heathen savage, she is," Miss Stoner whispered. "Some say she's even a witch, living out somewhere near the swamps. Look her in the eye and she'll cast her spells on you."

Seeing my look of disbelief, Miss Stoner pointed her finger and leaned across the table towards me, "Heed my words Cally, she's one of them lying, thieving savages, part of the Seminole tribes. You know they never signed a peace treaty with the United States Government, not even after they caught the likes of that warrior Billy Bowlegs. They're savages they are."

"Mercy me, what on earth are you ranting about Dulsey?" Aunt Ruth interrupted her.

"I'm not ranting Ruth Ann. She's a Seminole and that's a fact. Everyone knows they're godless savages hiding out in the swamps and wilderness. Why, they could massacre us all in the middle of the night."

"Dulsey Mae, stop! I won't have you scaring the daylights out of my nieces." Auntie told her.

By now the old woman had passed on by. Watching her walk away she appeared to be just a harmless old woman. I couldn't quite picture her massacring anybody. But, as my eyes followed her descent her head turned back ever so slightly and for an instant my eyes met her dark glance. Turning quickly back to the table I picked up my lemonade, my hand shaking slightly. She has to be Bud's witch woman. That has to be her. Except for my shaky hand, I didn't feel any different. I hoped she hadn't cast a spell my way in that one little instant. She was so old maybe she couldn't see me from that far away. Maybe she couldn't get a bead on my eyes and missed. A smile came to my lips thinking maybe she missed me and hit Miss Stoner right between her eyes. Just in case I grabbed the salt shaker sat in the middle of the big white table. Tipping it upside down and dumping the salt into the palm of my hand, I quickly tossed a handful over my shoulder.

"Now what in the devil are you doing, Cally?" Auntie said. "You just threw salt all over Miss Stoner's porch."

"I'm getting rid of any evil spell the old woman may have cast my way," I said.

"Connie's Grandma Agnes says to keep evil away take and toss a handful of salt over your shoulder."

"Tsk, tsk, tsk," Auntie clicked her tongue. "Dulsey Mae Stoner, do you see what you've gone and done now? You have her all spooked with crazy Indian witch woman stories."

"I'm crazy?" Miss Stoner's voice shrilled. "You want to talk crazy? Well now, how about that Agnes. Now there's a crazy for you; she hangs out over at the Landing talking to dead people. Why on earth you let your niece associate with the likes of those people. My, oh my, Cally Cummins, you sure have some peculiar friends," Miss Stoner said turning at me.

"Oh great, I knew somehow this conversation would come back at me," I mumbled.

"Miss Agnes is just a little eccentric," I said. "At least that's what Bud says. She is a very sweet, harmless lady."

Miss Stoner shook her head, "Lynn, I think it's high time your little sister starts thinking of her future here in DeLeon society."

"Yes, ma'am," Lynn said meekly.

"You should take up with young ladies of culture, like that dear Lucinda Winthrop. Now there's is a fine young woman," said Miss Stoner.

Lucinda Winthrop. The thought made me grimace. What a snob.

"Lucinda would make much better company than that granddaughter of Agnes Parker," she said.

I could no longer hold my tongue. Agnes may be eccentric but she was my friend and so was her granddaughter, Connie. "Miss Stoner," I said. I caught Auntie rolling her eyes back in her head so I lowered and softened my tone. "Miss Stoner, I don't think it's right you should go judging Miss Agnes or that old Indian woman for that matter. You don't really know them."

"I know enough, young lady," she said.

"I just don't think we should judge people before we get to know them," I told her. "Remember Bud and my friend, Isaac. Well, folks said he was crazy and cut up little kids with a six-inch switchblade, just because he was a colored man. He wasn't anything like what folks said. He is a kind and gentle man and has taught Bud and me a lot, including how to treat other people who are different than us."

"There you have it, Cally. There is proof right there. You do take up with all sorts and it just isn't proper for heaven sakes— - colored men and crazy spiritualists. I'll tell you what it is. It's those liberal Democrat ideas is what it is."

"It ain't got anything to do with no Democrats, Miss Stoner. They weren't in there when we met Isaac. Mr. Eisenhower and them Republicans were. It has to do with what's right and wrong and how to treat people."

Lynn gave me a poke with her finger under the table. "Come on, Cally," she whispered out the side of her mouth.

I was on a roll now and I wasn't finished. "I see you at church every Sunday, Miss Stoner sitting right up front in the pew with your family's name all written in gold on that little plaque stuck at the end of it…"

Apparently seeing where this was headed Auntie looked at her watch, "My, my, look at the time. You girls best be getting on home. Your mother will be worried. I've kept you most of the afternoon."

Lynn quickly stuffed the rest of a cream horn in her mouth. Rising from her chair and wiping her mouth with a little square miniature napkin she said, "Well, I think Auntie's right we need to be getting home now. We still have things to do there, right, Cally?" She pulled on my arm.

I hardly noticed. The nerve of Miss Stoner…why Miss Agnes was no crazier than some rich old woman thinking Seminole Indians were going to massacre us all. I wasn't too sure about the old Indian woman. Maybe she was a witch. I'd give Miss Stoner that for now. I mean there were some creepy people out there and she did look pretty mysterious. Even Bud said he heard there was one out near the swamp. But, she was just one old Seminole Indian woman, hardly a war party, at least unless Miss Stoner was right about them hiding out in the swamp. I didn't go there.

Lynn thanked Miss Stoner for the treats and I joined her at the front steps. Miss Stoner stood up from her chair saying, "Wait just one moment."

"Uh oh," I thought, "she's really going to fly in to me now."

"Before you go I want to show you the elegant bed jacket my son Neil sent me all the way from Paris, France," Miss Stoner said heading inside the house. "I'll be right back."

Why Miss Stoner didn't give two hoots for what I was saying before Auntie broke in. I wasn't sure which made me madder: the fact that Auntie interrupted or that Miss Stoner didn't seem to hear a word I had said.

"Show off," I mumbled. "The only reason she probably wanted us to come over was to flaunt her fancy jacket. Bed jacket! Now whoever heard of wearing a jacket to bed?"

"Cally!" Lynn elbowed me as Miss Stoner returned to the porch holding what truly was a beautiful blue jacket. Actually it was more like a robe that had been cut off above the waist except fancier than any I'd seen. The material was slick and shiny as spring water on a clear summer day.

"It's made of the finest silk from China," the old woman said proudly.

"It's lovely," Lynn said, "How nice of your son to buy it for you."

"It is beautiful isn't it," she said with a sigh and quickly added, "You know he was going to bring it himself, but he had to go to London on unexpected business."

Miss Stoner's son lived way over in Paris and hardly ever came to visit. But, he sent her fancy things all the time. I think she missed him terribly what with being a widow now and all. She always made excuses for his not coming to visit. "He's much too busy. You know he's an international lawyer," she'd say. I kind of felt sorry for her, almost. I wasn't too sure I'd visit her much either.

"Well, we really must be going now," Lynn said hugging Auntie. I followed. After my hug Auntie held me out from her slightly, looking me straight in the eyes, giving me a quick wink.

"Thank you for showing us the lovely jacket and thank you for the snack," Lynn said as we hurried down the walk and headed home.

"Seems like a waste of that beautiful blue material," I told Lynn when we got out of Miss Stoner's earshot.

"What are you talking about, Cally?"

"I'm talking about Miss Stoner's bed jacket. What's the point of having something so fancy and expensive if nobody is going to see it?"

"It's one of those luxury items rich people buy. It's just for the pure pleasure of wearing such a fancy thing. That's what makes it so special and luxurious. The rich people are the only ones can afford to indulge in such fineries. That's what makes them think they're so much better than poor folks," Lynn explained.

"Still seems like a waste to me," I said.

"That's 'cause you're not rich and a member of Deleon's High Society," Lynn mimicked Miss Stoner. "Come on, I'll race you home," she said taking off like a shot.

Bud was shooting baskets out front when we got home. "Where you been all afternoon, Cally?" he said as we walked up the driveway. "I've been waiting for you so we can try and find out where the old red dog goes. He was by here about twenty minutes ago."

"Shoot! Which way did he go?" I said disgusted that I had missed him.

"He headed out past the bomb shelter into the woods. I think he was just chasing after an old gray squirrel that had been chattering at him," Bud said.

"Well, do you want to go see if we can find him, Bud?" I asked.

"I guess. Mom said supper won't be ready for an hour or so. Speaking of Mom, you better go in and let her know you're back. She was about ready to call Aunt Ruth."

"We had snacks over to Miss Dulsey Mae Stoner's fancy house," Lynn told him.

"I'll bet Cally enjoyed the heck out of that," Bud laughed. "She didn't give you too hard a time did she half-pint?"

"I think you're a little confused as to who gave who the hard time, Bud," Lynn said.

"Cally Cummins, you didn't go saying something that's going to come back on you with Mom or Dad or worse yet, Kate," Bud winked.

"Nearly did, but Auntie stopped her before she got in hot water, although, I don't think Miss Stoner paid her any heed anyway," Lynn said grabbing the basketball from a side-tracked Bud and shooting. "Two points," she smiled.

"Oh, I wouldn't be too sure about her ignoring me, Lynn," I said. "That old lady never forgets anything. She just keeps it stored up to use on you later when it can do the most damage."

"If we're going to look for the red dog we best be going," Bud said. "Are you coming Lynn?"

"No, I'm tired from cleaning and trying to keep Cally out of trouble," she said going towards the house.

Bud and I walked out back and up the small hill in the backyard towards the woods. "Here's where he went in," Bud said pointing at the large dog tracks in the sandy soil. "It appears he was chasing a two-legged animal instead of a squirrel." Bud kicked at the footprints at the edge of the woods. "Looks like the same type of print we saw outside the shelter the other day, Cally."

"It is Bud. Look here! This one left part of the Converse print like the other. Come on," I said breaking into a run.

We took off through the woods following the dog and sneaker tracks until the sandy ground gave way to scattered pine needles and grass. Following the open path between the pines and sweet gum, we made our way to the open grove area beyond the woods. The ground became sandy again and we searched the edge of the grove for anymore tracks.

"This way Cally!" Bud called, stopping his running and standing dead still. "Listen Cally, can you hear it?"

The faint sound of a dog barking carried through the woods.

We ran back into the woods about 100 feet to the left of where we had come into the grove. The barking got louder the further into the woods we ran. We stopped to get our direction. The barking had become loud and constant, real close now. It came from just behind a big clump of cabbage palm. Looking upward into the moss draped limbs of a towering oak, I saw him. A boy about my age or a little older straddled across a lower limb. It was the boy from the grocery, the one I'd seen riding his bicycle on my birthday.

"Look there, Bud!" I hollered pointing at the treed boy.

We ran around the palms and at the sandy base of the oak sat the excited red setter holding the boy at bay. Rusty was too busy barking and growling at the boy to notice us. Picking up a stick, Bud began banging it on a nearby pine yelling, "Rusty!" The dog took a lurch backward turning to Bud, but held his ground and continued barking, clearly annoyed with the boy. Something dangled from the boy's grasp as he clung to the tree limb. It appeared to be a piece of shimmery material, a lady's slip or something. I now realized what had the red dog in such a tizzy. It wasn't the boy at all. The boy held the dog's latest heist in his possession.

"What you got in your hand?" I hollered at him.

The boy looked down at his hand, and then seemed kind of embarrassed. "It ain't none of your business. Just get that dog away from me so I can get on out of this here tree. Is he your dog, because if he is he's a thief. You should lock him up or something."

"He ain't my dog," I said.

"I believe if you want down out of that tree you better drop what he wants, or you'll be there all night," Bud laughed.

As they were conversing I moved a little closer so I could take a good look at the bottom of the boy's sneakers. "Well, I'll be darned," I said pointing, "Bud it's the Ravioli Bandit. Take a look at his shoes."

"What?" Bud said, moving in to see what I was pointing at.

"Well now, Cally. This is a most interesting situation," Bud said rubbing his jaw. "We got a thieving dog that caught himself a thieving boy. I think maybe they'd make mighty fine company for one another out here tonight." Bud started to walk away motioning for me to follow.

"Bud, where are you going? You're just going to let him go?" I asked chasing after him.

"He's not going anywhere," Bud said.

All at once there was a commotion and the big red dog ran past, the slip in his mouth. A loud thump came from under the tree and footsteps took off in the other direction.

"Come on, Cally," Bud said high tailing it after the boy who had wasted no time jumping down from the oak and scaddadeling, after tossing Rusty his prize.

We chased after the boy, Bud putting it into high gear ahead of me. "Wait up," I yelled then I heard it, the loud thud of something hitting the ground. When I came up on them Bud had the boy face down in the sand, the boy kicking for whatever he was worth.

"Let go of me!" the boy yelled.

"Not until you quit you thrashing about," Bud yelled.

"You're hurting my arm," the boy kicked.

Bud loosened his grip as the boy calmed down. Bud just sat next to him in the sand. The boy looked away from us.

"I don't want to hurt you," Bud said. "I just want to know what you're running from and if you're the one been stealing from the shelter."

The boy didn't say anything. Looking him over, I saw he had a fading bruise on the side of his face. I winced at what might have caused him to get such a mark. "Bud, maybe he ain't the one," I said.

The boy looked up at me and said, "Yeah, maybe you should listen to your skinny little sister and not go picking on the likes of me."

Skinny little sister, I thought feeling my neck get hot. I'm thin. Kate said you could never be too thin or too rich. Well, at least I was thin.

"I said, maybe! I didn't say for sure you weren't the one," I told him. "If you aren't the thief, how'd you know I was his sister, if you haven't been sneaking around our place? And what were you doing over there today anyway?"

"That dumb old dog stole my mama's slip off the clothesline and I followed him through the woods. About the time I got over near the swamp he headed back toward your place, and that's where I finally got the chance to snag it out of his slobbery old mouth. He chased me from there to that big oak tree. He was mad and moving in on me fast so, I shimmied up to that limb you found me on," he explained.

"That sounds like a respectable reason," Bud said, "But it still doesn't explain your sneakers. The bottom says 'Converse' just like the prints we found all around the bomb shelter. Just about your size too."

The boy lifted his shoe and looking sheepishly at Bud and me, said, "Well, anybody could have a pair of Converse sneakers. It ain't against the law is it? Can't convict someone for that, can you?"

"They do on those detective shows on television," I told him.

Bud let him up, and warned, "You go on and get yourself home, and don't let me catch you back around our place again if you know what's good for you."

"Bud, what are you doing?" I said disgusted.

"He's right I can't prove he's the one…" Bud began but was interrupted as the boy tore off through the woods.

"Doggone it, Bud; now he's gone. We had him and you let him go," I said kicking the sand.

"Cally, calm down and follow me." Bud ran in the direction the boy had gone with me close behind. We followed his steps until we came to the edge of the grove by an enormous tangerine tree. Bud grabbed my arm and pulled me behind the tree with him. Peeking through the v-shaped limbs forking upward from its base, we could see the boy running down the dirt road that led past a group of run-down, houses; their paint peeling from years of neglect. The boy kept running along the canal that brought the river into the springs at the Landing. Rounding the bend in the road, he disappeared behind the willow and cypress trees which ran along the canal. Bud and I stuck close, just out of eyesight. One of the three houses had a small painted sign inside a torn window screen, "Madame Vivian - PALM READER." From there the road wound on along the canal where the kudzu vines hung thick from the trees, and large leafy covered limbs formed a giant canopy over the narrow road, a tunnel of moss and vine. Sunlight was barely visible here among the green and gray cover. We walked slowly down the road until spotting a clearing ahead, just past some giant Magnolia. An old rusted car sat up on cement blocks. The pickup I had seen the cigarette smelling man get in, who had been with the boy up to the grocery sat in front of the rundown house. TATE it said on the side of the mailbox in faded black paint. Bud and I stopped when we heard a loud voice shouting obscenities from the screened porch. Bud grabbed my arm and pulled me back out of sight as we listened, peering through an opening in the Magnolia trees. A woman's voice yelled, "Stop Jasper! Leave him be." The man yelled something else we couldn't understand his speech slurred and rough then suddenly the boy ran from the house and down towards the canal. We jumped back hiding behind the trees as a man came to the screened door, opening it slightly, and then let it slam back against its latch. There were harsh words between the woman and man coming from inside. I couldn't see the boy anymore, but he must have slid down the bank by the water's edge to hide. I hoped there weren't any gators or moccasin where he lit.

"Cally, I think we best be getting home. I don't think there's much we can do here," Bud said.

"I agree, Bud," I said turning towards home glad to leave this place. A worrisome feeling came over me thinking of the boy's safety. I wasn't sure which would be worse, meeting up with the creatures in the canal or the one inside that front porch.

We walked along quietly, not much said between us. A covey of quail flapped, flying from the underbrush. Bud said, "Cally, it's funny I don't feel the contempt for the boy I did before. I mean, I feel kind of sorry for him. He's real poor and I don't think he's got much like you and me. If that's his daddy then it sort of explains some of his disagreeableness. I believe that man to be a mean one."

"I think he's a drunkard, Bud."

"Now Cally, what would you know about that?" Bud asked.

"Well, when I seen him up at the grocery with the boy he smelled of tobacco and had a strong smell of liquor on him. You know like the man who sold Dad his fishing boat. Kate said he was a drunkard, smelled of bad whiskey."

Bud said, "Cally, you could be right. You could hear him slurring his words. He was of bad temper, too. Usually a liquored up man makes for a foul temperament."

I remembered the fading bruise covering the boy's cheek. "I think I understand a little more about the boy, Bud. I wish we could have talked to him more."

"Hold on there Cally. I know exactly what you're thinking. You steer clear of this place. If you do, I promise I'll try and think of a way to help the boy."

I knew he would.

At supper Dad said he was ready to dig up the lower ground south of the house for our summer garden. We'd pretty well picked the spring garden clean and it was time to turn the soil and replant. Dad had the disk ready on the back of the small tractor in the garage. I loved to help work in the garden. The smell of the fresh black soil, and planting the seeds only to watch green stems sprout from the earth was truly satisfying. Nothing could beat the taste of a ripe, juicy, red, beefsteak tomato or the snap of the beans as we sat on the porch with Mom, talking about how good they would taste. Dad would get us started Sunday after church. Bud, Lynn, Kate, and I would plant the rows of seeds and seedlings we'd gotten from Jacob's Seed and Feed.

"Dad," Bud said while we were finishing up supper, "Could I have a word with you out on the porch?"

"Sure son, while we're at it, why don't we go out and pace off the garden. We can stake where we want to toil up the ground," Dad said rising from the supper table.

When they had gone outside, Kate couldn't stand the suspense. "Wonder what was so important Bud had to talk in private."

"Well, I imagine it's none of our business, Kate, or Bud wouldn't have found the need for taking your Daddy outside," Mom reminded her.

"I'll bet I know," I said.

"Oh? And how would you know?" Kate asked.

"I just have an idea. Maybe not, but knowing Bud I'd be willing to bet it has to do with something he and I did this afternoon," I told her, knowing it was driving her crazy thinking I knew what was going on and she didn't. I loved to get Kate going.

"You don't know anything, Cally, you're just trying to make us think you do to make us crazy," Kate said.

"Wouldn't take much," I laughed.

Did I know my sister Kate or what?

About an hour later just as darkness had set in, Bud and Dad came back inside.

"I'll check into that tomorrow after church," Bud told Dad as he walked past Kate, Lynn, and me. We girls were playing old maid at the dining room table. I had two cards left and it was Kate's turn to draw. Before heading down the hallway towards his bedroom he glanced over at me and gave me a nod and a wink.

"I knew it," I said out loud.

"What do you know and what was that all about Cally?" Kate asked.

"Oh nothing," I told her.

"Cally, you sure are acting mighty odd. Mom, I think Cally got too much sun today. It's affected her brain," Kate said over the counter to Mom who was sweeping the kitchen floor. Then she drew her card.

"Old Maid," I laughed and jumped up from the chair before Kate swatted at me. I followed after Bud to his room. The door was open so I peeked in with a tap on the door frame. "Can I come in?"

"Sure half-pint," Bud said from across his desk.

"What's going on?" I asked.

"Cally, I talked to Dad about the boy. Asked him if he didn't think we could use some help in the garden."

"We already have all of us Bud, why would we need anyone else to help?" I asked.

"Well, I had this idea. Now, don't go getting too excited, but I told Dad being as we are digging up all that dirt for our garden, why couldn't we dig up a little more and the boy could keep his own little garden for himself. If he helps us keep our part up too, maybe Dad will give him some pay for his work. Maybe then he wouldn't feel the need to go stealing from the shelter anymore," Bud said.

"That's a great idea Bud. I do believe you are without a doubt the smartest boy I ever did know."

"Like, I said, Cally. Don't go getting too excited. Even if the boy wants to do it and that's going to be might tricky, how do you suppose that father of his will react to our wanting to help him? People like that would as soon cut off their arm than accept any charity, usually just out of pure meanness."

"I'll bet you can convince the boy, Bud. Does his daddy really need to know? I mean he's probably so drunk most of the time he doesn't know what the boy is doing anyway."

"We'll see Cally, but you let me handle it, okay? I'll see if I can't find that boy tomorrow. He's bound to be riding his bike around. If not, maybe he goes fishing at the canal. I'll find him and then we'll see what we can do."

Hugging my brother, I left his room only to run into Kate and Lynn who were obviously eavesdropping outside the doorway.

"You and Bud found out who's been stealing from the shelter?" Kate said. "Did you call the police?"

"No! Kate, we didn't call any police," I told her.

"Well, why not?" she asked.

"Bud has a better idea. Just wait and see," I told her.

"Great! Now we've got thieving boys hanging around our place. That's just what you need, Cally. What's got into Dad and Bud anyhow? They don't know this boy. Why, we don't even know his name," Kate said.

"That's right, they don't Kate, but neither do you," I told her. "I think we should wait and see what happens. The boy might not even be interested in what Bud has to say. And, for your information the boy's name is Jesse Tate," I said, remembering what Mr. Elias had told me.

"Well, let's hope he's not interested" Kate said stomping off to the living room to watch television.

8 CHAPTER

Sunday morning's glorious golden light was trying its best to pry open my eyelids. Just a couple minutes more I thought, turning over to escape the day's downright blinding brilliance. Today was going to be a great day. I could just feel it.

We hurried through breakfast and changed into our Sunday clothes. After arriving at the First Methodist Church and seating ourselves in the pew, I poked Kate in the side of her new Jackie K. suit.

"What is it, Cally?" Kate said annoyed.

I pointed to today's lesson in the church bulletin, *The Good Samaritan*. "I think somebody's trying to tell you something," I whispered.

A blue flash of rolling eyeballs and a quick toss of hair was the only response I got back.

A few rows ahead of us I caught sight of a big white feather waving with every turn of Miss Dulsey Mae Stoner's head, as it plumed out of her purple pill box hat. I wondered if she really listened up there perched in her special pew. I also wondered why she wore feathers in her hat if she hated the Indians so darn much.

I could hardly wait for the last song and benediction so we could head on back home and Bud could go look for the boy. I hoped he would take Bud up on his offer and not be too proud. I decided to say a little prayer about it being as I was in the perfect place to get a hold of the Good Lord. "Dear Lord, Sorry, to interrupt the preacher, but I figure he has a main line to you and I just want to ask you something real quick. Please let Bud find the boy and let him not be too bull-headed so as not to know what's good for him," I whispered during the preacher's final prayer.

"Shhh!" came from Kate as she whispered, "For crying out loud Cally, don't be so rude."

"Thank you Lord. I'd be mighty grateful if you'd help. – Amen, and P.S. Lord, please help my sister Kate to relax," I said in my sister's ear before the preacher finished up.

"Shhh!" Kate said again pinching my arm.

"Ouch!" I said a little too loud. Without even having to look I could feel Dad's evil eye upon me. Not that he was evil or anything, but that's what we called it when he got that piercing stare. It told us, "Behave or else." I scrunched back in my seat and could feel Lynn giggling beside me.

9 CHAPTER

Dad had turned the last of the rich black earth and Lynn, Kate, and I marked with wooden stakes where each row of vegetables would begin. It had been over an hour and still no sign of Bud and the boy.

"Hope your brother gets back pretty soon. We've got lots of planting to do. Until then, what say we take a break and get some of that lemonade your Mom was fixing for us," Dad said. A big plop of sweat dropped from the tip of my nose and without a word I dropped my wood stakes and headed towards the house. Kate and Lynn were right with me. It was a hot one today, sticky hot. As if reading our minds, Mom stepped onto the front porch with a tall pitcher of ice cold lemonade and some paper cups in hand.

"Time for a break," she called to us as we trooped across the two acre tract next to the land our house sat in the middle of.

"Bud not back…?" Mom paused gazing towards the road. I followed her eyes across the garden tract to the gentle upward slope of Garfield Street spotting Bud's red Ford making its way from behind the woods that ran south of our land.

"Well, I'll be doggoned," I said to no one in particular as the car sped closer. "He did it." There sitting in the front passenger seat was the boy. No way would I have ever imagined Bud would have actually found him, let alone talked him into coming along. I wondered if he had to wrestle him again. As the car pulled up the long shell drive, the boy just stared across the yard, careful not to glance our way. All eyes were focused on the red Ford as it came to a stop in front of the garage. I figured that boy wanted to turn tail and run soon as he got a load of us gawking at him so. As if reading my mind, Mom said, "For pity's sake, let's not embarrass the boy half to death staring at him like a bunch of vultures ready to swoop down upon our prey."

"Well, what does he expect?" Kate smirked. "He's lucky we didn't call the Sheriff on him, stealing from the shelter like he did."

"Kate!" Dad hushed her. "That's enough; it took a lot of courage for the boy to come here today. I made an agreement with Bud to give him a chance, so let's see how things work out. I don't want any more talk about what's been done up to now. Understood?" he said.

"Yes sir," Kate said, and then went inside in a huff.

Bud and the boy got out of the car and the boy trailed behind Bud, up to the porch like a new pup following its momma. Bud looked okay and not all tousled up from any sort of scuffle.

"Everyone, I'd like you to meet Jesse Tate," Bud introduced the boy and politely grasped the boy's arm, moving him front and center.

"Hi Jesse," we all greeted a red-faced Jesse Tate.

"Afternoon," he said, not looking up. I could just feel his embarrassment with all of us staring at him.

Bud said, "Jesse here has agreed to help me out in the garden in return for having a small parcel of it for growing his own vegetables. Says he likes the idea of working the soil with his hands and seeing what he can do with his own garden."

"How about some lemonade, Jesse," Mom said. "You too Bud, before you go out there and start digging the rows your sisters marked for you."

Jesse Tate stood silent waiting on Bud to take a cup.

"Come on Jesse. Mom makes a mean lemonade. Best around," Bud told the boy.

Jesse quickly took a cup from Mom. He gulped so fast it was downed in a flash. Without a word Mom filled his cup again. His face reddened slightly realizing what he'd done. "There's plenty more where that came from," Mom smiled.

"Well, I guess we better get started. Looks like Dad got the ground ready for planting," Bud said setting his cup back on the tray.

"The seeds and starter plants are over on the trailer behind the tractor, Bud. Your sisters marked the rows and wrote on each stake what's to be planted there. I think I'll leave you boys to take care of the hoeing and planting while I do some work in the garage. If you need anything just holler," Dad said.

I didn't think Dad had much to do really, but sensing Jesse's nervousness thought he'd be more comfortable with Bud, Lynn, and me for now.

We worked most of the afternoon and Mom brought out more lemonade for us. Jesse worked next to Bud without a word, and after the rows were dug we all four planted tomatoes, beans, potatoes, onions, radishes, cucumbers, and two rows of corn. Lynn and I planted some marigolds around the perimeter of the garden to keep out the bugs. Garden bugs didn't care for the strong odor of the golden flower. When the last seed was planted and Bud had helped Jesse plant his parcel, they hooked up the hoses from the garage to a sprinkler and began watering.

"Oh man, I can just taste those fresh tomatoes," Lynn said standing back surveying the results of all our hard work.

"I hope we get a good rain soon to help with the watering. Gardens do okay with well water, but a good soaking rain works miracles," Bud said. Jesse Tate talked a little to Bud while we were working, but didn't pay no mind to me and Lynn. I thought I'd try and say something to him. I mean after all we'd worked all afternoon together, so why couldn't he at least make conversation.

"I'll bet your momma and daddy will be surprised to see all the fine vegetables you'll be bringing to your supper table when our garden starts producing," I said.

"Momma will be. My daddy won't much care one way or the other," he said.

"I'll bet if we brought them over to see all your fine work he would be proud of all you've done here," I declared.

"NO!" the boy said sharply. Seeing my surprise at his tone he said, "My momma don't do much visiting and my daddy won't care as long as supper is on the table. I best be going now. It's almost suppertime. I still got chores to do at home."

"Well, I sure thank you for your good day's work, Jesse Tate," Bud said. "See you tomorrow?"

Jesse nodded.

"We may as well wait until late afternoon to water. Water too early when the sun is high might burn the plants," Bud said.

"Well, I'll see you then," Jesse said leaving.

"Need a ride home?" Bud called after him.

"No, that's alright. I'll just cut through the woods, it don't take long."

"He sure doesn't say a whole heck of a lot," I told Bud as we watched Jesse disappear into the pine woods.

"Nope, but he sure is a hard worker. Can't get much done talking all day, Cally," Bud said, teasingly.

"How did you ever get him talked into doing this anyhow? He doesn't exactly seem the type to just come along without any argument," I said.

Bud laughed, "He didn't make it too easy, and that's for sure." I spotted him sitting alongside the canal leads from the spring. He was dropping a big old worm in he had on the end of his cane pole. When I pulled up he didn't pay me much mind, just thought I was another fisherman I guess. But, when I walked up beside him he pretty near took off, but I caught him by the shoulder and shall I say, persuaded him to sit himself back down. I told him I didn't mean him any harm. I just came to make him a little proposition, a business deal. He just stared up at me like I was up to something, which of course I was." Bud smiled. "Anyway, I explained to him that I couldn't let him continue to steal from the shelter. I told him if he needed food so bad that he had to take it maybe I could help him do it in a little more respectable and honest way."

"I'll bet he didn't sit still for much more of that," I told Bud.

"He said he didn't need mine or nobody else's help," Bud said. "He said he wasn't no charity case, and maybe he'd just done it to prove that he could, so how about that?"

"Now that's just a plain out and out lie Bud. You saw where he lived. If that ain't poor I don't know what is. Not to mention that Daddy of his. He's just a no account."

"Cally, I didn't want to humiliate him by letting him know we'd followed him home and seen how he lives. I just tried to use a little psychology on him. I told him if he just did it for the sport of it, then maybe he should just come along and I'd take him to see Sheriff Baines. Well, he didn't go for that at all. He changed his tune in a hurry saying, 'Supposing' I am interested in your business deal. What you got in mind?'"

"I told him, he seemed like a good enough kid. I mean he didn't take anything but food and some bandages. He didn't destroy anything. Told him I thought he could use a summer job to help out a little, put good food on the table and maybe give him a little extra spending money. That seemed to get his attention, along with the fact that I mentioned how Sheriff Baines didn't take too kindly to folks stealing from their neighbors."

"I knew it. You had to threaten him again," I said.

"I think he would have come anyway, but time was passing and I was afraid Dad would be upset if I was much longer so I used that last final warning. I think Jesse will work out fine, Cally. He's pretty much a loner and has to depend on himself more than a kid should, that's all. Give him a few days and he'll come around."

"I hope so, Bud," I said running between the garden rows to move the sprinkler. The cold well water felt wonderful as it spattered against my hot skin, running down my legs leaving flesh colored streaks through the dust and black dirt coating them.

"Supper in about ten minutes, you two," Mom called from the porch.

"I'll turn the water off after supper, Cally. Let's go clean up," Bud said. "Last one there's a rotten egg," he laughed taking off towards the house.

10 CHAPTER

Jesse Tate came by every afternoon around four, just like clockwork. He'd water and pull weeds and leave. Bud paid him $2.00 two dollars on Friday for his work. Daddy said we'd pay him for helping Bud keep the garden up each week and he hoped he would buy groceries with the money. I figured they'd probably run out of Ravioli at Setzer's Grocery.

Saturday, after breakfast, Mom took me over to Patty Boyd's house. Patty lived up on Terrace Road, which ran along the nice part of the Black Water Creek that came off the river. Fancy houses with boat docks and swimming pools out behind them, lined the road. Terrace Road ran out of blacktop about a mile past the fancy homes and turned into dirt and gravel as it ran through the forest a ways further to the 'Pepper Pot'. The Pepper Pot was just a hole in the wall kind of place. They served up masses of fresh catfish and burgers there. But mostly it was a beer joint, where all the fishermen hung out telling fish tales and drank until the wee hours of the morning. The Boyds and some other brothers and sisters from the Pentecostal Church tried to get a petition going to shut the place down, saying it was a house of wickedness and evil. But, the town of DeLeon said they weren't really in the city limits way out there, so it wasn't in their jurisdiction. The Sheriff told the Boyds and others they hadn't had any trouble there except for a few wives being up in arms over their husbands staying a little too long tippin' the bottle instead of catching fish.

When I arrived at the Boyd's', Mrs. Boyd had packed Patty and I a picnic lunch to take out on their boat. We were going fishing. The Boyds had a nice motor boat setup with a bait well and little holes to stick our poles along the sides. Patty and I usually did more exploring than fishing and today I had the perfect place for our adventure.

"You all be careful now, you hear," Mrs. Boyd called to us from the dock over the deep gurgling sounds of the Johnson Boat Motor Patty had just pulled the starter cord on.

"Yes ma'am, we will," Patty said turning the motor arm and heading southwest from the dock. I waited until Mrs. Boyd was out of ear shot, before asking Patty, "What do you say we try a new spot out today?"

"That's fine with me. What you got in mind, Cally?" Patty said.

"Head back the other direction, east, and I'll show you," I said.

Patty brought the boat around and we were on our way.

"How much farther is it Cally?" Patty asked, passing by the last home along the canal before the forest. "I'm not supposed to go past the paved road. Gets a little wild up further and I don't just mean the landscape."

"Not much further," I said. "I'll let you know."

"That's what I'm afraid of," Patty mumbled. "What are you thinking, Cally?" she asked slowing the boat down.

"What are you doing?" I asked her. The boat motor gurgled and coughed, stalling.

"I told you I'm not supposed to go up this far. There are crazy drunkards and Lord knows what else up here," she said.

"Oh, for gosh sakes Patty; It's ten o'clock in the morning; the drunkards are still sleepin' it off this time of day. Come on it's just a little further. Where's you sense of adventure?" I asked her.

She cranked up the boat again and pretty soon we were running up alongside the Pepper Pot. The smell of bacon and grease filled the air and a couple john-boats were tied up at the dock.

"See! I told you. Just a couple fishermen having breakfast is all," I said.

It couldn't be much further I thought as I strained my eyes through the scrub woods .and thick vine finally spotting a rusted tin roof of what I thought was the Tate's house. The sides of the canal were steep here, where spindly tree roots stuck out of limestone sand cliffs and drooped towards the water. At this spot, if I stood up in the boat, I could just look across the top of the embankment. Any further and the cliffs sloped up a good fifteen feet high.

"Cally! Sit down! Do you want to fall in and drown? We're just about to the Landing, Cally. I cannot go there. I don't want to go there, and I ain't going there," Patty insisted.

"Okay, okay hold your water," I said. "It's got to be in there," I said pointing past a row of cabbage palm near the canal edge. The creek was much narrower here than back towards the fancy houses. There the creek seemed more like a big lake.

Patty stopped the boat.

I looked for a low spot along the creek. We had come to a curve.

"This is the spot, Patty. I swear it is," I said.

"Now don't go swearing, Cally Cummins," she scolded.

Ignoring her, I said, "I'll bet there's a landing on the other side of this curve. Pick up an oar and we'll just paddle around it. It'll keep from stopping and starting your motor. It's not good for it."

Patty didn't pick up her oar, so I grabbed one and started slowly moving the boat toward the curve. She was bound and determined to not make this easy. She could be so darn stubborn, but so could I.

"What did I tell you?" I said seeing the sloping ground leading down to the creek bed as we made the curve.

I stuck my oar in and luckily the bottom was shallow. I pulled the boat forward towards the slope. A large coquina rock jutted out from the cliff top. As we pulled closer I realized the rusted roof I saw wasn't the Tate's house at all, but was what appeared to be a garage type building set back in the trees. From the sandy landing the ground sloped upward from the creek to a grassy area and on to the back of the building. A narrow walking path stretched across the property from the river channel.

"Shoot! I thought for sure this was the place," I said disgusted.

"Well, I'm not going any further, Cally. We shouldn't even be down this far," Patty grouched.

"We're here now. So let's go see what's to do," I said trying to get her a little excited about our adventure.

"I don't think we should be snooping around. Suppose somebody is up there," Patty said.

"Don't appear to be anyone around. Come on let's just go see what's in that old building. Maybe it's just an old deserted camp site," I said. Taking the oar I poked at the soft sandy bottom making sure it didn't suck the oar down as I pressed. A person had to be real careful around the river. Some places along the bottoms had sand so soft you could sink waist deep in the blink of an eye, quicksand. It felt pretty solid here. The boat rocked and I nearly lost my footing. Patty laughed at the prospect of me soaking wet. Getting my balance and taking off my sneakers, I jumped overboard pulling the boat to shore before Patty turned the motor back on and headed out. Patty joined me as I put my sneakers back on and the two of us walked towards the building. It appeared to be empty, at first.

"What's that over there," Patty said pointing to a covered tarp ran along the far side of the place. Walking over to it, I started to lift the tarp when a strong pungent smell like yeast and some other awful nose burning odor crinkled my nose. "Whoo Wee!" I said throwing down the tarp. "Nothing under here except a bunch of wood barrels and wide mouth jugs all stacked up on wooden pallets." I circled around to the front side of the building. A path like the one ran down to the creek started back up again on this side and curved back through the woods. Sure enough I could just make out the Tate's place through the thick pines. "I knew it, I knew this was Jesse's place," I said.

"Jesse? Who's Jesse?" How do you know anybody lives out in this God-forsaken place," Patty asked suspiciously, kicking at a stinging nettle.

"What's inside that window there Patty?" I said pointing at one of two windows on the side of the building. I didn't want to explain to Patty about Jesse and maybe get a sermon on being judged by the company I kept. Patty was forever sermonizing me, almost as bad as Kate mothered me. A kid couldn't have a bit of fun or adventure between the two of them.

Patty half-heartedly looked through the dirty glass and turned saying, "Nothing but a bunch of mechanic like tools and such. It's just someone's garage and we better get on out of here before they see us."

I wasn't really listening to Patty's ranting because I had discovered what lay inside the second window. "Would you take a look at what's in here," I said peeking through where a piece of jagged screen poked out from its frame. "What in the world do you suppose all this crazy tangled up bunch of pipes and stuff is? Look, there's some more of them jugs and barrels, but these ones got curly-queue pipes coming out of the barrels. Looks like some sort of laboratory or something."

"Not a very sterile one," Patty said peeking in beside me.

Just about then a whirring of an automobile engine could be heard coming from the direction of the Tate's house.

"Somebody's coming!" Patty shrieked.

Hearing it too, I started back around the building. "Let's get out of here," I said. "If it's who I think it is, we don't want to be seen here."

Patty was right on my trail.

"Cally, who are we running from?" she asked.

"Just come on Patty. The man's one of your crazy drunkards, Jasper Tate."

We slipped and slid down the slope to the boat.

"Quick, jump in, and as soon as I get this baby back in the water start her up!" I hollered at Patty.

An automobile was coming down the path leading to the water. Patty pulled hard on the cord…nothing. She tried again, just a sputter. "Come on," I said.

"I'm trying," Patty said giving it another pull.

Rumble, gurgle, and finally…smoke sputtered from the exhaust. "Thank the Lord," she said as I hopped in, the boat rocking and floating towards the middle of the creek. "'Point this thing back west and don't look back," I said as Patty maneuvered the boat back the other way. I dared to peek back as we were rounding the curve at the bank along the creek edge. I spotted the bumper of Jasper Tate's truck. A door shut and as we were safely on our way I could see Jasper Tate standing, looming over the creek, fists shaking in the air.

"Who'd you say that was, Cally?" Patty asked.

"His name is Jasper Tate and he's the father of the boy that stole the food from our shelter," I said.

"How do you know that?" she asked.

"'Cause Bud and I caught the boy out in the woods last week, and now he's working for my Dad and Bud in the garden."

"Well, now I've heard everything. Your Daddy took a common thief and gave him a job?"

"SHHH!" I said, "What's that?"

"What's what?" Patty asked.

"We're coming to the Pepper Pot and I think I hear a truck. Speed it up. I'll bet that Jasper is following us down the creek."

"Oh this is just GREAT! Cally Cummins you get me in some of the worst messes!"

"Just get going or you haven't seen nothing yet," I warned her.

Sure enough the truck pulled into the Pepper Pot as we made our way into the open part of the creek. We were back to the paved road, and the big houses along the creek blocked any view Jasper might have of us now.

"Let's just go back to my house and have a picnic on the dock. It's a lot safer there. No drunkards chasing two nosey girls," Patty said.

"Are you sure? Maybe your momma's a secret teetotaler," I laughed. "She's pretty wild sometimes when she gets going on her churchly stuff."

"Oh, that's very funny, Cally. You take that back," Patty said.

"I'm kidding.. I swear, Patty; you need to develop a sense of humor."

A soft breeze blew across the creek, as we finished our sandwiches and chips underneath the covered end of the dock. We spread out big striped towels covering the wooden planks beneath us and lay staring up to the rafters above while the blue black waters of the creek gently lapped at the dock posts. The gentle rhythm of the water rippling against the pilings as it flowed at its own sweet will lulled me. I watched as a dragon fly buzzed another above me. My eyes grew heavy and I could hear Patty's soft breathing as she fell asleep and I too surrendered to the lazy afternoon breeze.

"Cally!" Mom's voice called out from somewhere in my dream.

"Ouch!" I said rolling over on the hard wooden planks, realizing it wasn't a dream after all. Patty was sitting up stretching and yawning.

"Cally!" Mom's voice came again. Looking back towards the Boyd's house I saw my mother standing on their patio by the swimming pool.

"Oh my gosh, Patty, it's my Mom," I said looking down at my watch. It's three-thirty. Patty, we've slept the whole afternoon."

"Yeh, running away from crazy drunkards makes you tired," she said still yawning.

"Coming Mom," I hollered gathering up my stuff from the dock. I wanted to get home before four o'clock.

I quickly said my good-bye and thank you and asked Patty to not say anything about where we had gone.

"Do you think I'm crazy? Mom and Dad would be furious if they found out," she said.

"You're alright Patty Boyd. I don't care what anyone else says," I teased her.

She looked back at me, "What? Who says?"

11 CHAPTER

As Mom and I pulled in the drive, Bud was already home and he and Jesse were down in the garden. I ran inside dropping my things in Lynn's and my room and nearly ran over Kate coming back down the hallway.

"Where are you off to in such a hurry?" Kate asked.

"Just outside," I told her.

"Oh yes, I do believe Jesse is here," she said with a smugness I didn't much care for.

"What's that supposed to mean?" I asked.

"You've only been watching him every day this week when he comes over. That's all," she teased.

Kate could be so darn annoying sometimes.

"So?" I said. "I'm just keeping an eye on him, making sure he's doing his chores, that's all."

"Yeh, sure," Kate rolled her eyes.

"Better watch that. One of these days your eyeballs are going to stick that way," I said ignoring her remark, going for the front door before she could say anything else. Kate had some nerve. She didn't think I actually liked Jesse. I was just curious that's all. I wanted to know more about him and his family and I especially wanted to know about what Patty and I had seen today. The fact that he was sort of handsome had nothing to do with it. He did have a look that was different from any of the boys I knew from school though. He was boyish, but not so perfect. No Brill-creamed hair or that tucked in look, all starched and tailored. He had more of a freedom about him. I think what Kate called worldly looking. He wasn't just an ordinary boy. Jesse had light, golden brown hair with a sun bleached streak of summer across the top. White t-shirts showed off his tanned arms and face that produced a smile that was pleasant to look at. No, he was not like the boys at school and that was a fact. Well, so what if I thought he was handsome. That didn't mean anything.

Bud and Jesse were admiring the little green sprouts poking from the black soil when I walked up. It was the first time I heard Jesse sounding excited about the garden. "Look over here Bud," he said not seeing me yet. "We're going to have the best darn beef-steak tomatoes ever. Do you think we should put up a scarecrow so as to keep them pesky crows and blue jays out? Maybe even make some kind of alarm with old pie tins and string to scare off raccoons and rabbits."

"Sounds like a good idea Jesse," Bud said. "We can do that Monday. Tomorrow is Sunday and I think besides watering we need a break."

I spoke up startling Jesse, "Yeh Jesse. Why don't you come over tomorrow or better yet, why don't Bud and I come over to your place and go fishing? I hear the catfish are really big over there."

The pleasantness Jesse shared with Bud disappeared. "NO! I can't go fishing over at my place. I told you before it's not a good idea. My Daddy doesn't want anyone coming around, especially kids. Just stay away you hear?"

"Well, alright then. Don't get so darn upset about it. We can fish at the other side of the Landing if you like," I said, upset at myself for pushing the idea.

"Maybe… I'll come by if I can," Jesse said to Bud not me. "I better be going now."

"See you tomorrow?" I said.

"I said maybe," Jesse mumbled not even turning around.

"Why do you suppose Jesse is so all fired against anyone coming around his place?" I asked Bud when Jesse had left.

"You saw where he lives Cally and you heard his old man. Would you want anyone coming around? You should have known better," Bud said.

"I think there's more to it Bud," I told my brother.

"How's that Cal?"

I hesitated. I didn't want Bud mad at me for going down by the Tate's. I told him I wouldn't.

"What do you know Cally? You didn't go down near Jesse's did you?

Cally, you did didn't you?" Bud asked reading my face. "Cally, I thought I warned you not to go down there."

"I didn't exactly go to Jesse's house. I was just real close," I told him cringing at what his reaction would be.

"How close?" he asked.

"Close enough to see Jasper Tate's fist shaking at Patty and me while we narrowly escaped being caught spying," I blurted out.

"What!" he croaked.

"Bud, now don't go getting all mad at me or I won't say no more."

"You will say more Cally if you know what's good for you."

I just stood there.

"Okay, Cally. I'm not yelling. I'm perfectly calm. Now just tell me where you were and what you think you saw, okay?"

I explained how Patty and I had gone on down past the Pepper Pot and come up in the landing spot near the old garage. He was trying mighty hard to keep his temper, but I could see his lips tightening up and his jaw clenching

"What kind of tubes and such were in the garage again?" he asked. "What did they look like?

I motioned my hands around in tiny upward circles describing the curlicue shape of the tubing that was hooked to the metal tank and then curlicued some more into another tank. "There were barrels setting all around in the same room and more of them jugs." A slight knowing grin came to Bud's mouth.

"You say the jugs under the tarp had a strong yeast smell?" he asked.

I shook my head.

"That's very interesting, Cally. Do you realize you could have gotten your fool head blown off if what I think is going on down there is for a fact?" Bud said.

"What is it Bud?"

"I'm not saying for sure Cally, but I think Jasper Tate could be running a still down there."

He read my confused look.

"It's corn liquor Cally. You know, moonshine."

"Yeh Bud, I know, just like that movie, 'Thunder Road.' Moonshiners and gangsters and…"

"Yeh, and Cally I think it's best if you don't go saying anything about it to anyone. I heard there was moonshine around here. It's not just Jasper Tate involved. There's lot of folks connected with something like that and they wouldn't be too nice if their source of liquor got cut off. It's just best to forget about it. Don't mention it to Jesse either. Just stay away from there. If I know anything about Jesse's daddy, Jesse would be in for it good if his daddy thought he'd led us kids to his still. It'll be our secret for now, okay?"

"Sure Bud. Anyway, I guess the only ones they're hurting are themselves."

"Well, I don't know about that, but I would guess that's why Jesse doesn't want anyone over. At least it explains things a lot better," Bud said.

"I wonder if the Pepper Pot is involved, Bud. The Tate place isn't far from there."

"That wouldn't surprise me, Cally. It's a pretty tight group that hangs out there. Now we best be getting inside for supper. Remember, not a word."

Colleen Affeld

12 CHAPTER

Summer was still a week away and already the big red numbers on the patio thermometer read in the nineties. Today was no different as I took off my Sunday clothes and traded them for much cooler shorts and T-shirt. Out my bedroom window, facing our garden I could see the white billowy clouds of earlier had darkened slightly around the edges and the sky was a deep blue. The small palm that Dad had planted last spring bent in the afternoon breeze and the string running stake to stake in the garden rose and fell like a jump rope. Sure to be a storm later I thought, pulling on my sneakers and tying the laces. Mom just about had lunch ready by the yummy smells coming down the hallway. I'd eat then go sit in my tree house and read my latest Nancy Drew. I could wait for Jesse to come by up there. It was just too darn hot to do much else.

After lunch I grabbed my book and headed for the back door. Bud was on the phone with his best friend, Larry Voight. Seeing me leaving Bud put a hand over the receiver. "Cally, I'm going with Larry and Bill to the beach this afternoon so I won't be able to go fishing with you today. We'll do it one other day this week on my day off from Setzer's."

Great, now what do I do with Jesse if he shows up. He won't want to go with me. Besides what would we talk about without Bud there?

Up in my tree house I snuggled down with my book in an old lounge chair Mom was going to throw out because one of the web nettings was busted. I loved reading up here where no one bothered my concentration. I was right there with Nancy as she discovered clue after clue. By the time I got to chapter seven my eyes were getting heavy. Glancing at the cut out window, a green chameleon came slithering across the sill. I reached for its spiny tail. The chameleon leaped to the outside of the window clinging to the wall and scampered away. As I searched down the outside wall for the little creature I spotted Jesse coming through the woods carrying his fishing pole and a can.

"Hey!" I hollered down to him. Jesse raised his hand slightly. Not quite a big "'hi how you doing'" wave, but just a "Oh it's you" one.

"Where's Bud?" he said walking up underneath the tree house.

Here we go. He's going to turn and go back home. "Bud went to the beach with his friends," I said. Seeing his disappointment I asked, "What you got in the can?"

"I dug us up some worms to fish with. You still want to go fishing?" he asked.

I couldn't believe my ears. Not only was this the most words he ever said to me after all this time, but he still wanted to go fishing.

"Sure! I'll go get my gear," I said sliding the escape hatch door in the floor open, dropping down from the rope, landing hard on the ground underneath.

"Don't you think it would've been a lot easier to just come down the ladder?" Jesse asked.

"Yeh, but it wouldn't have been near as much fun as to see your face when I did it," I told him.

Jesse smiled. I believe it was the first time he'd smiled in my direction. He had a nice one.

A southerly breeze caught a pile of leathered scrub oak leaves, scattering them into a tiny, swirling funnel across the sandy path in front of us. As we walked through the woods towards the springs, smoky, gray clouds above had taken over the once blue afternoon sky.

"Hope it don't rain on us before we get a hook in the water," I said. A blue jay cackled and took flight from a nearby tree, and from the rustling in the low weeds and bushes, the smaller forest animals were on the move. "Hope that big cat ain't prowling around out here, restless from the coming storm," I said, getting a little nervous remembering the loud purr the night of my pajama party.

"Have you seen him?" Jesse asked.

"Lord no! Don't care to. I never have seen him, except his amber glowing eyeballs in the dark. I've heard him, though. Loudest purring I ever heard; it wasn't no ordinary cat. Don't know if it's the bob-cat Mom saw while hanging out clothes or if it's maybe even a panther."

"Coo-wa-chobee," Jesse said.

"Coo-wa-who? What's that?" I asked.

"The big cat or, you know…a panther…Coo-wa-chobee is what I call him," Jesse said.

"What kind of name is that?" I asked.

"It's Seminole Indian. My mom is full blooded. Her mother and father were part of the Creek Tribe that came from The Big Cypress down near Lake Okeechobee," Jesse explained. "Co-wa-chobee is the name for a big cat or panther."

"Cool. How did your Momma end up way up here?" I asked.

"They came this way years ago following some Baptist preacher who had a mission down there. Looking for a better life off the reservation I guess; better jobs. But, after her parents and grandparents died all my poor momma found was my daddy. So much for a better life," Jesse said.

"She's got you," I said.

"Yeh, a lot of good that does her now," Jesse said. "Someday I'm going to do right by her. I'm going to be an Airman in the United States Air

Force. Look here," Jesse said pulling an old cap from his back pocket. "This here is a for real Airman's hat. I brought it to show Bud. I found it in a box up in the attic one day. Don't know whose it was, but the darndest thing happened when Daddy saw me with it. Why he nearly took my head off when he seen it. He grabbed the hat and tossed it in the garbage pit out back. I waited until he went to town and went and dug it out. I keep it hid up in my closet."

Jesse put the cap on his head. "One of these days I'll have one of these of my very own with all the little medals on it. My momma will be proud of me then," he said.

"Looks mighty good on you, Jesse," I said. He did look handsome.

The bushes rustled again and I jumped. "You don't suppose that's your Coo-wa-chobee cat in there do you?"

"Don't worry Cally. The Coowhachbee won't hurt you unless you mess with me," Jesse said.

"How you know that? I mean, do you know this panther personally. Is he your pet or something?" I asked.

"No, he belongs to the woods and the wind. He's a wild one, but I've known him ever since I could walk. We kind of grew up together. He won't let me touch him or come too close. He turns and runs. I don't know, but it's kind of strange. It's like he watches over me. My momma says that according to Indian legend, the panther possesses the knowledge of all things, heals ailments, and enhances mental powers of those it connects with. Says this one in particular is special. It's the cub of another cat followed around a boy she knew one time. Said the boy had special powers too. He knew the future."

"What happened to the boy?"

"I don't know. When I asked her she got this sad look and said he'd died. So did the panther. Some low-life shot the cat."

"Jesse, you don't suppose…I mean it sounds crazy and all, but maybe their spirits possess this panther," I said. The thought gave me the creeps.

Jesse just rolled his eyes, "Oh, come on, Cally!"

"Think about it Jesse; with the Landing and all them spirit people around these woods, is it that hard to believe?"

"But, why me?" Jesse laughed.

"I don't know. But you said the cat is always following you. Maybe you remind him of the boy. "

"Cally, you've got some imagination," Jesse said as the bushes rustled along the path causing me to jump again and speed up my step. Maybe Jesse was used to panthers following him around, but I wasn't.

"Aren't you afraid? I know I am," I told him.

"At first I was," Jesse said. "But if he wanted to hurt me he could've by now. Boy, Jasper sure hates him. It ain't a natural hate neither. He's tried to kill that cat many a time. But, old Coo-wa-chobee is just too sly and quick for him. One time Jasper, drunk as usual, tried to beat me for something. I can't even remember what I'd done now that made him so mad; all I know is that crazy cat appeared out of the bushes his sharp teeth just itching for a taste of Jasper, and growling a low, deep, threatening growl. The sight sent Jasper running for his truck and his thirty-thirty. The cat turned tail and ran back in the woods. That's how I know the cat won't hurt me."

"You call your Daddy 'Jasper'? I ain't ever called my Dad by his first name, Will. I'd be in big trouble. Sort of disrespectful don't you think?"

"Your daddy is a good decent man. He earns your respect. Me and Jasper don't get on too well. Never have. It's like I'm a big bother or inconvenience to him, another mouth to feed, I guess. The only time he's halfway tolerable is if he's had a couple. Then he sort of mellows out. But soon as he gets a couple more under his belt, look out. He's mean as a snake then. Lord only knows why my momma puts up with him. Guess she really doesn't have anywhere else to go with most of her family gone."

"I'm sorry," I said.

"It doesn't matter. I guess it's just as well. Least this way I can pretty much come and go and nobody really cares. I mean my Momma does, but she's so busy trying to keep things peaceful, cooking, and cleaning, and keeping Jasper happy, if that's possible. She can't worry herself about me now that I'm bigger and more responsible."

"Yeh, now that you don't go stealing from your neighbors," I thought. Soon as I thought it I was mad at myself. Jesse was alright.

"What's Jasper do for work?" I asked.

"He used to work for the railroad years back. He got hurt in some kind of accident there that put him on disability. He works on a few cars in his garage out back of the house. But, mostly he just gets drunk."

We had been walking along all this time and were beyond the woods and grove now. I could see Seminole Landing and the clear blue waters of the spring. The water had a few white caps as the breeze gently lifted the ripples. Jesse and I headed to the narrow walking path ran along the canal. If you kept following the water south, it broke off into a smaller stream into the swamp.

"You hear that?" Jesse asked stopping and holding a hand to his ear.

"Hear what?" I asked. "All I hear are a bunch of frogs croaking down in the swamp."

"A storm is brewing Cally. Frogs singing means storms are on the way," Jesse said, leaning against a wooden gate post leading to an old burned out homestead. A squirrel ran from the large hole at the base of a towering oak. This particular tree seemed real familiar.

"Hey! I'll bet there's some big old juicy fishin' worms in there," Jesse said peering into the hollowed-out oak. "Let's have a look see."

Dropping my cane pole I ran to join him. "Jesse, I'll bet this is the oak Bud found his arrowhead in. You should see it. It's a beauty. Picking up a stick next to me I poked around in the hole. Bud told me about this place, which must have been why it seemed so familiar. "Oh my gosh!" I said jumping back as a big ugly brown roach ran for cover. Jesse laughed. Looking around for something better to dig with I found a chunk of pine bark just right for the job. Making sure there weren't any more disgusting creatures insight I began scraping away the rotted wood chips and dirt. We'd just about given up after having dug a good eight inches when I spied a shiny spot in the black dirt. "Jesse, poke your stick in there at that shiny place."

Jesse tapped where I pointed and it made sort of a tinny sound. Dropping our wood tools, we both scraped away at the dirt, and sure enough uncovered an old tin box. Jesse dug down around it with his fingers loosening the earth's grasp, pulling it free. He looked at me then back at the tin.

"Open it, Jesse. Maybe there's some buried treasure in there. Daddy knew a man, Mr. Scarboro, who found gold doubloons in a Spanish wreck off the coast. Maybe them Spaniards came here and buried some of them," I said.

Jesse just looked at me like he couldn't believe what I was thinking. "Cally, do you honestly believe some Spaniard came all the way to these woods, a good twenty miles from the sea to bury one tiny little box of gold. Shoot, you might get five of them doubloons in there if you're lucky. Besides how many G.C. Murphy Companies do you think were around back in old Ponce DeLeon's day?" he asked pointing to the imprint on the tin.

I felt my face redden. "Just open the box."

The tin's lid was rusted around the top and Jesse couldn't pry it with his fingers. Pulling a pin knife from his pocket he carefully scraped around the edges then tried again. This time the lid gave and some of the box's contents fell to the ground. First thing I seen was a for real Indian arrowhead. "I knew it, Jesse; this is Bud's oak tree where he found another one just like this one." I stuck it in my pocket and looked at the rest of the contents strewn all around.

"The Babe!" I shouted staring at the slightly faded baseball trading card with Babe Ruth staring up at me from the dirt. "Holy cripe, Bud would love this!" I picked the card up dusting the dirt off. "Look here it's got his number three and says, 'The Called Shot.'. Wow! Jesse, you don't mind if I take this to Bud do you?"

"No, it's just an old baseball card. What else is in here? Jesse reached into the tin. "'OH Boy Gum.'. Two sticks for one penny.' Wonder if it's any good? Cally, who do you suppose put all this in here? By the looks of it it's been here a long time."

Jesse put the gum down and examined the other items in the box. "Hey, maybe there's no gold in here, but might be some cash." He squinched up his mouth purely dissatisfied with the next item, which was a torn Little Orphan Annie Rummy Card and an old color picture of that cartoon guy, Alley Oop. His eyes suddenly lit up. "Look there's a smaller box inside." He opened the little box and there sat a gold locket. "Look Jesse, it's got a little hinge on it. Open it up."

Carefully opening the locket, Jesse turned white as one of Miss Agnes' ghostly spirits.

"Why Jesse Tate, It's you, not once but, twice!" Blinking my eyes, I looked at the picture inside the locket again. "What the Sam Hill...?" I pushed Jesse off his haunches as he sat there still pale as could be. "You put this stuff in here you old joker. And how come you didn't tell me you got a twin? What else haven't you told me Jesse Tate?"

Jesse dropped the box and stood staring like he was in some kind of trance, eyes wider than Melissa with the bottle cap eyes. He was starting to get on my nerves real bad. "What the heck is the matter with you? You act as though you ain't ever seen it before. You can quit your fooling around. I'm on to you good. You're nothing but a sneak Jesse Tate, that's what you are."

"It ain't mine!" he snapped out of his trance. "I never have seen it before Cally. I swear to God!"

If I didn't know he had it in him to be deceiving I almost could believe him by his confused manner. But, knowing what I did I just couldn't quite swallow what he was feeding me. "You're good Jesse, but I wasn't born yesterday, or even the day before."

About then I noticed one last item lying on the ground beside where Jesse dropped the tin. "What's this," I said picking up what appeared to be some sort of pin. The shiny pin was in much better shape than the other things in the box. It didn't seem to be quite as old. Turning it over there was an inscription. "United States Air force," I read. "Aha! This proves it's yours Jesse. You told me you were going to be an Air Force man someday. Now what do you have to say about that?"

Jesse's mouth tightened and he appeared about to burst with anger. "I say you're a darn fool if you believe any of that Cally Cummins. I told you these things ain't mine and I meant it. I'm telling you the gospel truth. If you don't believe me then just get on back home, and good riddance to you."

He was trembling all over and was truly upset. Maybe he was telling the truth. "Okay," I said. "So maybe this stuff ain't yours. So, tell me who they do belong to? Explain how your picture got inside that tin box."

"Cally, I am going to tell you for the thousandth time. It's not me!" He shoved the photo in my face. "Look at their clothes and their haircuts. I ain't no Sears Roebuck catalog model, but I sure don't wear clothes from whenever this picture was taken. And look here," he said pointing to the second Jesse in the picture. "I don't wear my hair like this one."

Jesse was right about that, the boy in the picture's hair was light and not straight like Jesse's or the other boys."

Suddenly I had little goose bumps popping up on my arms. "This is real darn creepy, Jesse. Who do you suppose they are?"

CRASH!!

I nearly jumped out of my skin as a lightning bolt hit somewhere off towards the swamp. Thunder rolled across a blackened sky as a phantom gust of wind came ripping through the pines and nearly took the Babe Ruth card from my hands. Plop! Plop! Huge raindrops scattered instant tiny mud puddles onto my sneakers.

"Quick, put everything back in the tin before it gets wet," Jesse cried gathering up the gum and cards shoving them back in the box. He closed the locket and stuck it in his shirt pocket.

"Let's get back to the tree house," I said dodging the now pounding rain and ducking as another bolt of lightning hit somewhere close by.

13 CHAPTER

Jesse and I looked like drowned rats by the time we made it to the tree house. "Jesse, I think we better go to the carport instead. I don't think sitting up in the tree tops is too good an idea with all this lightning."

CRASH!

"Let's go Cally! That bolt hit just a little too close," he said running for the cover of the carport.

I was soaked to the skin, but it felt good after the stifling heat before the storm. "I'll get us a couple towels to dry off with. You can come in if you like, Jesse."

"No, I'll just wait out here until the storm lets up then I better be going," he said holding his hand over the pocket on his shirt.

"Suit yourself," I said.

Jesse was sitting on the bench at the back of the carport when I returned. He had the locket out, staring at the photo inside. Hearing the door shut he quickly stuck it back in his pocket. That picture sure had him spooked. It had me spooked and it wasn't even my picture. I got an idea. "Hey Jesse, I think I know how to find out who those boys are in that picture."

Jesse kind of squirmed uncomfortable like. "I don't really care who they are?"

Now what? Like he really expected me to believe he didn't care. "I care," I said. "Jesse, they look enough like you to be your brothers. You could be triplets. Come on, you know it's bugging the daylights out of you to know; it is me, too. So, do you want to hear my idea or not?"

"I have a feeling you're going to tell me whether I want to or not. So just go ahead, what's your idea?"

I knew he couldn't resist. "There's this woman. Her name is Madame Rosemary. She lives over at the Landing. My friend Connie's Grandma Agnes sees her once a week for spiritual guidance. Madame reads tea leaves and palms. Agnes says she can feel things and tell things about people by just being in the same room with them. She sees things. Maybe she can take a look at this picture and tell who they are, or tell us something about them."

"Well, that would work real great Cally if they're dead. That's what them mediums do you know, they talk to dead people. They believe life continues after death. That's how those spirits communicate with the living. Anyway, I hear they're a bunch of fakers. Jasper's Aunts are so-called seers and they're fakes. Jasper says they all are. He says they laugh all the way to the bank taking all them suckers' money."

"Not Madame Rosemary. Connie's Grandma says she's for real. Connie says the Landing is the portal to a different dimension."

"That's because she chooses to believe all that mumbo jumbo they concoct in their little crystal ball, or their tea leaves, or whatever. If you ask me they're drinking too much of that locoweed that grows in the swamp in their tea. It puts them under that medium's spell so she can cheat them."

This was going to be tougher than I thought if Jesse was going to take that kind of attitude. He had a way of taking the excitement right out of the moment. "Your aunts live in the Landing?" I asked easing up a little.

"No, they live just down the road from me," he said.

I recalled the three small white houses I saw just before the dirt lane, where Bud and I saw Jesse's place.

"Those Landing nuts don't associate with Jasper's family because they ain't part of their camp. The aunts are good at all the tricks them spiritualists use. They put up their signs and outsiders see them before they get to the Landing. The aunts get the business. Lots of locals come to them too because they tell them what they want to hear, let them think they're talking to their dearly departed."

"Don't they feel guilty taking money for trickery?"

"Heck no, people don't care. Like I said they come looking to the aunts for answers and the aunts give them what they want. The customers are happy and the aunts make a little extra cash. What harm is that? You do what you got to in this world."

"Don't seem right to me," I said disgusted with how Jesse found nothing wrong with the whole scam. "I still say we should see Madame. If nothing else she's been around these parts for a good long time and maybe she knew them. I'll call Connie, and she and I can take the picture to her while you wait outside for us so as not to give her any leads. No hocus pocus, just see what she knows."

Surprisingly, Jesse agreed to try my plan. The storm had finally calmed down. Jesse agreed to meet at two o'clock the next afternoon. In the mean time I would get a hold of Connie and have her meet us.

Later, as I lay in bed next to my sister Lynn, sleep was avoiding me as my mind raced thinking of tomorrow. I had never actually set foot inside the Landing. It seemed like a good idea earlier, but now as darkness surrounded me with nothing but the moon and the Big Dipper as my night light, I wasn't too sure. What if the boys in the picture were dead? What if Madame Rosemary conjured up their dead spirits out of that photo? Goose bumps ran up my arms. "Count sheep," Grandma Cummins said. If you can't sleep picture them soft, woolly, fairy tale kind jumping over a vine covered fence. There went the first... then a second then...What was he doing in the herd? Instead of a cute woolly sheep it was the blonde haired boy in the photo. He came running and jumping over the fence and landed smack dab on the shelter door holding a shiny object in his hands, a tin box.

"Oh, my gosh," I sat up in bed.

Lynn gasped, "What the heck is the matter with you Cally?! You scared the livin' daylights out of me!?"

I stared out the bedroom window expecting to see the boy staring back at me. "I think I saw a ghost."

"Oh, for crying out loud Cally, go to sleep," Lynn said rolling back on her side.

14 CHAPTER

It was another Florida scorcher. The afternoon humidity was heavy enough to cut with a knife. A storm was brewing for sure by the looks of the billowy clouds piling one on top of the other. These summer storms came about the same time each day until the front passed on by us. Connie and I sat on the patio porch swing sipping cherry Kool-Aid, waiting on Jesse. Connie was absolutely glowing just thinking about how all her talk of mediums and hocus-pocus was actually going to be of some use. I didn't have the heart to tell her Jesse thought Madame Rosemary was a big faker. Fake or not it was going to be a little creepy. Just being near that place gave me the heebee jeebees.

Bud came out to the carport on his way to work at Setzer's. Licking his finger and holding it towards the darkening sky, like some sort of weather instrument, he teased, "Uh oh. Is it a storm coming up? No, I do believe it's Hurricane Connie and Hurricane Cally over there planning some sort of havoc on an unsuspecting DeLeon?"

"Nope, just another day in our boring little lives," Connie said smiling a big phony grin.

"One thing you both are not is boring. Fess up," he said. "What are you up to? I can see it in your devious little eyes, so you might as well spill."

"We're just waiting on Jesse to come and we are going…Umph! Hey! What are you trying to do, Cally?" Connie choked as I poked her ribs.

"I knew it." Bud shook his head opening his car door and climbing in. Starting the engine, he stuck his head back out. "Don't do anything I wouldn't do."

"That leaves us pretty open," I said waving goodbye as he backed his Ford from the carport.

"Hey, is that Jesse Tate? He's really cute." Connie said. I turned around to see Jesse coming through the backyard.

"Focus and breathe Connie. You'll embarrass yourself with drool all over your chin." If I knew her, she'd be flirting all over the place and we'd never get anything done today.

"Where's Bud going?" Jesse asked watching Bud's car pull around the side drive.

"He's on his way to work," I said.

"Did you give him the Babe Ruth card yet? I'll bet he went nuts over that to add to his collection," Jesse said.

"Oops! I can't believe I forgot it. I was so into what we discovered yesterday I forgot to give it to him. It's still on my dresser. I'll give it to him tonight. That is providing we survive the Landing today." Looking towards the darkening sky I said, "We'd better be going before that storm comes up."

Connie cleared her throat. Sounded like she had the croup or something it was so loud. I knew what she wanted. "Oh yeh Jesse, this is my friend Connie, our guide to the spirits."

Connie was grinning all over herself. At least it wasn't drool. Honestly, she was so obvious.

"Why don't you show her the photo, Jesse," I said.

Pulling the locket from his shirt pocket Jesse handed it to Connie. Opening it, Connie's head moved quicker than the old hoot owl that sat outside in the big oak at night, back and forth, first at Jesse, then the photo, and back again. Her eyes were big as silver dollars. "This is incredible. You sure enough look like them to be their triplet. Only difference is the one boy has curly hair. I'm sure Madame Rosemary will be able to tell us something. Grandma Agnes says if Madame don't know ain't nobody knows."

"We'll see," was all Jesse said as we started on our hike out past the bomb shelter. It was really funny how ever since I'd met Jesse I hadn't even thought about the Big Bomb or those Commies coming to get us. Except now, I traded in my fear of the Bomb with a much closer threat— -ghosts! As we passed the silver door to the shelter images of last night's dream came to me. A sudden chill ran a wave of goose bumps up my arms. Had it been a dream? Who was that boy who came hauntingly into my sleep last night? Was it the same boy I dreamt of the day Bud turned the sprinklers on as I slept on the shelter door? Were they really one in the same? Yes, I was sure of it. But, it was also Jesse. Was it just a dream, or were they really ghosts; Jesse, too?

"Are you coming?" Jesse called from the edge of the woods.

"No Cally, you're imagining things," I thought. My mind was just playing tricks; that's all. I walked towards Jesse and Connie. Ghosts or not there was something mighty peculiar going on around here. Maybe Madame Rosemary would give us a clue.

My skin felt hot and sticky and the clear blue spring at the Landing looked mighty inviting as the three of us circled it on the dirt road; the very same road ran past the tree where Jesse and I had found our treasure tin. As we came to the stone entrance to the Landing thunder rolled off in the distance.

"Madame Rosemary's is just down this main road and to the left on Mockingbird Trail," Connie pointed.

"Hmmm, Mockingbird Trail. Sounds real nice don't it. Sweet like a quiet, normal little neighborhood," I said trying to convince myself to continue. The streets were deserted. Not a soul out, living or dead. It was even too hot for ghosts. It was odd though. You would have thought somebody would be working in a yard or kids would be playing. It was dead silent. We came to a dead end and there in front of us was a bright yellow house surrounded by a freshly painted, white picket fence, with a neatly trimmed lawn. Mounds of azalea and wild flowers filled the yard. Not what I had expected at all. It was almost fairy tale looking. There was even one of them darned old crystal balls perched on a pedestal rising up from some hollyhocks. I gazed closely at the ball as Connie unlatched the gate and Jesse and I followed her into the yard. "I wonder if she uses that in any of her conjuring up of the dead," I said to no one in particular almost tripping over the first step of the front porch. At least there wasn't anything looking back.

"I thought you were going to wait on Cally and I," Connie told Jesse who was still with us just as she was about to ring the doorbell.

"I'll wait around back," Jesse whispered. "After you two go in I'll try and peek through a window so as to keep an eye on what's happening; make sure she's not pulling any of her trickery." Jesse disappeared around the corner.

"Madame is not a trickster," Connie mumbled after a vanished Jesse.

"Just ring the bell Connie," I said.

Connie pushed on the black button. I sucked in a big breath of air. I had no spit to swallow.

Footsteps could be heard coming to the door. The door slowly opened revealing a very slender, elderly woman with snow white hair peeking out from a vibrant orange and yellow hair wrap, sort of turban style. The scarf framed her tiny and remarkably smooth skinned face, except for what my Mom called crow's feet, embedded in deep crinkly lines around her eyes. She wore a long, silky, sleeveless summer dress baring, skinny, slightly saggy, wrinkled arms sticking out from too large armholes. "Yes, can I help you?" she said softly, standing in the doorway.

"Madame Rosemary, I am Connie Louise Parker, the granddaughter of Agnes Parker."

The old woman's eyebrows lifted and her eyes sparkled at this bit of information.

"This is my friend Cally. We were hoping you could help us with a little mystery we have encountered."

Madame's eyes looked to the darkening sky. "Come in, come in, for goodness sake, before the sky bursts," she said standing to the side and sweeping one long skinny arm across the threshold inviting us to cross over into her parlor.

Once inside the room was yet another surprise. No dusty cobwebbed rooms with white sheets hiding the furniture's upholstery, like in them horror films. No pictures with eyeballs following us around the room either. Instead the room was cheerful and bright with a white wicker couch and chairs covered in pink and green flowered cloth cushions. Little white fringed lamp shades matching the pastels in the cushions sat on glassed topped tables. Madame is certainly colorful. I was beginning to feel much more at ease now. Madame motioned for Connie and I to sit on the couch as she took the chair to our right. Hands in her lap she said in a very controlled and soft tone, "What can I possibly do to assist you young ladies? How is Agnes doing?" The woman suddenly had a worried look, "Agnes is well isn't she?"

"Well, you'd think she'd know that," I thought. She's supposed to know everything.

"Oh, she's fine. My friend and I were hoping you could tell us about something we discovered," Connie said digging in her pants pocket for the locket containing the picture. She held it out to the woman who strained her eyes to see. Pulling to her eyes a pair of rose trimmed spectacles that hung around her neck on a delicate gold chain, she inspected the opened locket. All at once she pulled the glasses from her eyes and let them drop against her chest. She looked as though she'd seen a ghost, although I couldn't figure why that should bother her none.

"Where did you get this?" she asked.

"I found it buried under an oak, stands near where the remains of that old burned out house sits down the road," I blurted out startled by her reaction.

Madame closed her eyes shaking her head slightly.

Oh no, here we go I thought. She's commencing to go into some sort of weird trance or something.

Instead she said, "Sad, very sad. I haven't thought of him in a very long time. Not since the terrible fire."

Connie and I stared at one another confused. "What fire?" Connie asked.

Madame slowly opened her eyes recollecting. "The boys are Caleb and Curtis Malcolm. Their mother's family were members of our community here years back. She had the gift."

"The gift?" we said at the same time.

"Yes, she was blessed with the ability to see what lies ahead. Pity she didn't see what the future held for herself and her boys. Maybe she did. Who knows for sure? The boy, Caleb, the one with the straight blonde hair; he had the gift too. I believe that is what brought him back to their house that night. He knew something terrible was going to happen."

Connie and I sat entranced by her voice and what she was saying. I had a million questions, but I was afraid to speak so I listened carefully trying to follow her every word. Madame Rosemary paused every once in a while as if trying to remember the details.

"The young woman came to see me afterwards. Wanted to know if I could reach him in the great beyond; find out what happened to him." The old woman paused, then as if somewhere far away said, "Very tragic."

"What girl? What was very tragic Madame Rosemary?" Connie asked.

"There was a terrible fire in the home of the boys that summer," Madame began. "Ah yes, as I recall it was mid-summer. Hot. Fourth of July, I believe. Let's see…it was about fourteen years ago. It was terrible, just terrible. All perished including Caleb and his parents. Curtis, the curly headed twin in the picture was the only one to survive, that poor soul. The whole town blamed him for the fire, even the young woman. I never did believe it was him set that fire. He loved his brother and parents so. But, because he was mentally not right he was easy to blame I'm afraid. The community of DeLeon wanted answers and that was the best and easiest solution to it all. They sent him to a mental hospital near Jacksonville for a few years. I hear tell he lives in the County Home now." The old woman shook her head. "I never believed it and neither did many others here at the Landing. But, the Landing gets a lot of bad publicity. Some folks would like us all out of here. Our ways make people nervous."

CRASH!! A bolt of lightning hit a tree real close by causing Connie and I to jump. The old woman just sat there calmly raising a hand in the air to halt any conversation. Her wrinkled tired eyes searched the house like she was expecting one of her spirits to come popping out of the walls, or wherever they came from. This was beginning to give me the creeps.

Getting a grip on myself I asked, "Couldn't you find out what happened when you tried to reach Caleb for the young woman," I stumbled for the words, "in the Great Beyond?"

Madame's eyes glared at me and I was sorry I asked the question.

CRASH! Another bolt hit outside.

Madame slowly stood up her eyes fixed out the side window where Jesse was hiding. "Perhaps you should tell the young man with you to come inside out of the storm." Connie and I exchanged wide-eyed stares. Okay, now I really had the creeps.

"Come now; go tell him to come inside. I won't bite you know, but the witchery of the sky will."

Without a word, I rose from my seat and went to get Jesse. Maybe she saw him being hit by lightning or something. I better hurry. Once outside I wanted to just take off in a run and not stop until I got home, but I was afraid of lightning storms too. The lightning in Florida was vicious. It was some of the worst in the country. One time a friend of Uncle Al's and some men were caught out in a field by a big storm while farming. They were all gathered under a big oak when a thunderous bolt reached from the blackness of the storm and fried his friend but good. My cousin George said he looked like one of them characters in the cartoons on "'Uncle Walt'" when they got a jolt of electricity, like an x-ray, bones all lit up. I think he was making that part up but we got the point. I didn't want to see

Jesse glowing all over the Landing.

I waited for the next big bolt to strike before leaving Madame's porch, figuring I had a few seconds before the next came. Jesse was crouched down by a pink Oleander bush. I pretty near scared the pants off him when I came around the corner.

"Just what in the Sam Hill do you think you're doing, Cally? You're going to give me away."

"Madame knows you are here. I don't know how, but she very calmly told me to come get you out of the storm. Is that too spooky or what?"

"Ain't anything spooky about it. She probably saw me when we got here. Just biding her time to make it seem like it just occurred to her from some mysterious vision," Jesse said.

The skies above opened up and the rain pelted us ruthlessly. "Come on Jesse, before we both end up burnt spots in the grass from all this lightning. Madame has some information for us; it might mean something to you."

Jesse followed me inside and as Madame's eyes met Jesse's she went down into the chair like a ton of bricks, waving her hand like a fan in front of her face. "Quick, get me my smelling salts on the mantle there," she gasped.

Connie ran over and picked up the small vial off the mantle. Opening it, wafting it back and forth under the old woman's nose, Rosemary gave a shake and a cough and appeared to feel a little better, though she still looked quite pale. Her drowsy eyes were glued to Jesse and blinking furiously she asked, "Caleb is that you?" She shook again, taking another good look at Jesse. She sat upright in her chair seeming to snap out of her faint. "Of course, it can't be Caleb." Leaning close to Jesse she asked, "Who in tarnation are you? Speak up young man. Cat got your tongue?" Then she looked at Connie and myself and pressed her mouth tightly, directing her words to Connie. "What are you kids up to? Is this some sort of sick joke?"

Oh no, we'd gone and made Madame mad. I closed my eyes expecting the worst and all at once Jesse spoke up, "My name is Jesse Tate."

I gradually opened my eyes to see her reaction. Her eyebrows raised same as when Connie and I mentioned Agnes, a knowing look, as if she'd had some sort of understanding.

Outside the storm was crashing and thundering just like in one of them horror movies. I wasn't sure whether it was the rain or not, but I was no longer hot and sticky as chills ran cold inside me.

Madame spoke, "Jesse Tate." Then she thought a moment, "Tell me your mother's name." Her voice had a sense of urgency to it.

"Her name is Lila."

The crows' feet tightened leaving just a sliver of green iris showing through her eyelids.

"Lila," she said as if the very feel of the letters coming out of her lips were to be savored and released carefully. She turned at Jesse sharply.

"How old are you, Jesse Tate?"

"I turned thirteen last March," Jesse answered.

Now this seemed to make Madame a little fidgety. She got up from her chair and walked to the window standing for a few moments just staring in deep thought. Then without turning she said, "I think it's time for you children to go now. The storm is passing."

That's it? That's all she had to say? She couldn't just leave us hanging like this?

Visibly upset by this dismissal, Jesse walked right up to Madame's back. "Just like that, you're turning us out? I answered your questions, now I got a few of my own," he said.

Madame continued looking out the window ignoring Jesse.

Jesse stamped his foot. "No Ma'am! We're not leaving. Not until you tell what's got you so curious about my mother and how old I am. Cally and Connie here say you got all the answers. Well I'm here to get them."

Jesse was making me real nervous. We didn't want to rile her up too much for fear she might sick some mean old spirit on us.

The woman turned on Jesse, "I have no answers for you. You need to go home and forget about that picture and all this nonsense. Means nothing," she said.

This made no sense at all. She had started telling Connie and I so much before she saw Jesse. Now she just clammed up.

Seeing Jesse was much more upset than myself, and who could blame him, I gathered up my nerve and pleaded, "Please Madame if you know something that can help us clear up all this can't you tell us? Can't you at least tell us someone who can?"

"You children are making me tired," Madame sighed, walking to the door. Opening it she pointed toward the swamp. "Go see the Indian woman, lives in Black Water Swamp. She can tell you what I cannot. If I were you I would just leave it be."

As soon as the three of us were on her porch Madame shut the door and I could hear the latch turn on the lock.

"Come on, let's get out of here. I knew she was just a big faker," Jesse said stomping through her gate.

Turning back towards the house I caught Madame quickly pulling back the curtains of her parlor.

Jesse was already at the dirt road by the time Connie and I got to Madame's gate. "We got one more stop before going home," he said heading in the direction of the swamp.

"Are you crazy? I ain't going in that swamp, Jesse Tate. Miss Dulsey Mae Stoner says that Indian woman is a witch. My brother Bud told me to stay away from there," I hollered after Jesse.

"You talked me into coming here and now you're chickening out? Suit yourself Cally, but I'm going!" Jesse started down the road.

"Oh shoot Connie; we can't let him go alone. He's right. We talked him into this. What if he never comes back? I couldn't live with myself," I said.

"If he doesn't come back then at least we knew where he went so we can tell the Sheriff," Connie tried to reason. "If we all go we might none of us come back. Nobody would even know what happened to us. No, I want to live to tell the tale."

By now Jesse would already be on the path leading back into the deep woods near the sink hole that came just before the swamp.

I ran after him. "Come on Connie! Maybe we can at least talk him out of it!"

"Cally Cummins, why on earth do I ever listen to you?" Connie hollered back, but then came following me down the dirt path.

The rain soaked sand stuck to our sneakers as we walked leaving deep imprints in the path ran along the edge of the creek.

"Oh my Lord!" Connie ran wiping at her arms and hair. She had walked into one side of a big ugly banana spider's web. The spider maneuvered across the silky strands.

I very carefully inched around the spindly trap. "Lordy, it was a big one. Did you see all those bugs in his web," I said. This made Connie shake like she was having some sort of fit, wiping at herself even more.

I spotted Jesse who was now at the sink hole. The big hole had gotten a little deeper since the last time Patty and I chased the big red dog out this way. Water from the last few storms had filled the bottom a good half foot. My daddy says that sink holes are places where caverns run underground and the springs empty into them. The caverns run across the whole state. Dad says that's where the State had talked about building underground shelters in case those Russians ever attacked. Said we'd not only have safety there, but fresh water to drink and it would be cool because of the low temperatures of the spring. There was supposed to be one big cavern that ran all the way from New Smyrna Beach to DeLeon. If you followed the main street in New Smyrna it led right to the river where a canal emptied into it. I figure one day the whole place would sink.

Jesse stopped and turned when he heard us. "Change your mind?"

"We were hoping you would change yours," Connie said.

"Look there!" I said. "Just like Bud told me, there's the eagle's nest just before the swamp and the witch's place."

Something rustled in the bushes getting all of our attention.

Jesse placed his hands around his mouth, "Coo-wa-chobee!"

"Oh great," I thought, "just what we need, the panther." Witches and panthers, my day's complete.

All of a sudden lickety split, in a flash of auburn fur the big red dog came charging through the bushes with a piece of silky undergarment between his teeth. He hastily darted in the opposite direction when he spotted us.

"Get him!" Jesse cried. The three of us took off after him whooping and hollering, running through vines and tickseed.

"Ouch!" my leg brushed a wild rose bramble. That darn four-legged thief kept running into the thicker woods until he was out of sight.

"Where'd he go?" Jesse circled back around from behind a big cabbage palm. "That is the most disagreeable animal I ever did see. He's slicker than an old greased hog at the county fair."

I noticed the ground here was dark and mucky, no longer the sandy path we had followed. It had sort of a slimy film over it. We were at the swamp. Something croaked across the way. On the bank, a big gator sat sunning himself. He had to be about five feet long and lay there still as a statue. Even though he was facing the other direction I was pretty sure he knew exactly where we were. Jesse hadn't seen him and was walking towards it.

"Jesse, stop, there's a gator!" I cried.

"Whoa!" he said running back towards me and Connie.

Surveying the area, we searched for a path out of this mud hole. The pines were tall and covered in thick vine, making it hard to maneuver. Bud wasn't kidding when he'd said it was wild back here. Luckily, over by the gator, Jesse spotted a sandy trail rising up a little higher than the cattails and muck, leading further into the swamp. "Wish I had some marshmallows to toss that gator's way. They love those things," Jesse said tossing a big rock at the gator. Surprisingly, it slithered on down into the water. We didn't waste any time as he made his dissent. Taking the narrow sand trail to get away from the gator, we came to a natural bridge of pine logs crossing over the swamp to a grassy area. A shadow fell over us and I caught the upward flight of a big blue-gray bird. It was a good 15 to 20 inches long with a pointed wing span longer than a yardstick.

"A Peregrine Falcon," Jesse said. "He's a big one. No wonder there ain't been any song birds around this spring." The bird screeched and flew back towards the open spring.

One by one we crossed over the logs. Through the pines and scrub oak you could just make out the roof of a small house up ahead. "Get down," Jesse said as he ran stooped over to stay lower than the tallest bushes hiding the house. The three of us sat crouched, peering over the branches into the clearing. The house wasn't much to speak of, but it seemed in order and clean around it. Just a graying cypress cottage with a small wooden porch and one out building, looked like a chicken coop. There was some commotion coming from behind the cottage and darned if that crazy red dog didn't come running out. This time without his prize he had stolen from some unsuspecting, now panty-less female's clothesline.

"I hope he don't give us away. Nobody move," Jesse whispered.

"Holy smoke, what do you suppose those are?" Connie sat pointing to the one side of the cottage as Jesse hushed her.

Off to the left side of the cottage in front of the chicken coop place were two white clotheslines strung between wood posts. But it wasn't no pants and such hanging there, instead the line was covered with what looked like tiny pale heads, small blank heads; no eyes, nose, mouth or nothing, not even a strand of hair on them. Next to the posts was a big black iron cauldron.

"Dear Jesus, she is a witch," I said. "Let's get out of here."

"Hold on Cally," Jesse said. "You don't know that for sure. Let's just wait a minute. We've come this far. Let's see what happens."

Too scared to high tail it by myself I sat perfectly still, like one of them store mannequins. We waited for what seemed like hours instead of minutes. I scoped the tall grass around us for snakes and gators.

Pretty soon the screen door creaked open and an old decrepit woman stepped out. I gasped. It was the old woman I'd seen at Miss Stoner's, the Indian, Miss Stoner's witch woman. She held something in her hands wrapped in what looked like butcher's paper and sat it on the porch railing. Reaching in her apron pocket she pulled out a crust of bread.

"Get back," Jesse grabbed my arm. He had warm hands and I was surprised at how his touch made me smile.

Slipping back behind the palm, not a sound could be heard between us. I realized I was holding my breath. It was beginning to get late in the day. The sun would be down within the next hour.

"Ke-hay-ke!"

"Jeez Louise," I said my heart jumping to my throat. "What the Sam Hill was that?"

"Ke-hay-ke!" the chilling sound came again like Miss Rowell's nails sliding down the chalkboard when she wanted our attention last year.

"Ke-hay-ke!" the old woman called out again.

All of a sudden there came such a racket above us, screeching like the banshees that haunted an old Irish castle I'd seen in a movie once. The falcon swooped down out of the treetops towards the woman. The old woman, her hand wrapped in a thick rag, the crust of bread lying across it, held it out as the great winged acrobat dove, wings folded to its side, grabbing the piece of crust in its sharp talons. The bird then soared upward perching himself atop a towering pine.

"I can't believe it. Did ya'll see that?" Jesse whispered. "That wild bird ate right from her hands. It didn't even touch her."

"It's probably scared to death of her and that awful noise she's making," Connie said.

"No. She's speaking one of them Seminole languages. I can't tell if it's Creek or Muskogee," Jesse said.

The old woman moved off the porch toward the place where the big black cauldron sat and called out again. This time I recognized the words.

"Coo-wah-chobee! Coo-wah-chobee!"

I caught movement from behind the cauldron. I gulped and stood perfectly still as the biggest darn cat I'd ever seen appeared stretching and arching it's back slinking forward towards the woman. I'll be darned if it wasn't a Florida panther. Just like the ones I'd seen pictures of in books. They had a big stuffed one down at Hontoon Island Bait Shop perched high on a shelf over the cash register. Now, not more than one hundred feet from where I sat was the real, honest to goodness, living, breathing cat. It was one of the most beautiful creatures I'd ever laid eyes on. The cat was sleek and smooth as Miss Stoner's fur wrap she wore to services on cool Sunday mornings, the one with the little fox's head hanging off the end of it. Somehow I always ended up sitting right behind Miss Stoner and those beady little dead eyes stared at me through the whole service. Lynn said I best sit still because the Lord could watch me through that poor creature's eye. Like one of them spirits from the Landing. Lynn and I both agreed if you stared long enough they appeared to blink. Kate said we were both as loony as the Woo Woo Man.

The panther walked right up to the old woman and rubbed against her, just like a house cat does. The old woman never even flinched. She just patted the soft tan fur and spoke more of her gibberish to it. Deep purring followed.

"Would you look at that," Jesse said.

"That's the same loud purring we heard the night of my party when we came out of the shelter. Remember Connie," I said.

She just shook her head unable to speak or take her eyes off the sight in front of us.

"That's old Coo-wah-chobee," Jesse said, "That's the big cat that follows me, Cally."

The big cat shook and gave out with a low growl as two little panther cubs came bouncing and scurrying around the corner of the cottage, rolling and tumbling one over the other, knocking into the larger cat. The big cat took one huge paw and swatted at them, knocking the cubs onto their backs, as if to say, "Don't bother me now; I'm with my human." The old woman unwrapped the butcher paper and took out the biggest piece of red meat I'd ever seen and placed it on the ground in front of the cat. She took a smaller piece and threw it to the cubs. The three of us quietly chuckled to see the rambunctious cubs bat at one another to get the first bite.

"She must be a witch. Look how those wild things take to her. Why that falcon could have ripped her brown skin apart with one swipe, and I don't even want to think what the panther could do to her," Jesse said.

GRRR! GRRR!

"AEEEE!" Connie let out with a scream that could wake the dead.

"What the...," I said turning to see the darned old red dog crouched down on his haunches before us growling and baring his teeth. The falcon's wings beat hard as it lit out from the tall pine.

"Jeez o' Pete! What's the matter with you," Jesse said to Connie.

"Who's out there?" came the raspy voice of the woman sounding like she'd been with the croup too long. "Chatte Effee!" she cried.

"She's calling the dog," Jesse said. "'Effee' is Creek for dog."

"Chatte Effee!"

With the last cry the dog's ears perked up and he whimpered a little, but then turned back at us again with a snarl.

"Chatte!" She gave out with an even louder cry.

The dog yelped then turned slinking towards the old woman.

"Who's there? Show yourself!" said the woman.

Roar!

The panther let out a squall that nearly caused me to wet myself. Then he reluctantly turned and walked away actually looking sort of disgusted that we were disturbing his meal.

"What do we do now?" Connie said.

"Well, I guess we step out in the open so she can see us. You and your big mouth," Jesse said. He cleared his throat, "We'll come out as long as you keep that red dog off us."

The woman gave some sort of command to the dog and he went over and sat on the front porch of the cottage.

"Show yourselves. Come out in plain sight!" she croaked.

"Come on," Jesse said leading the way into the opening.

"Dear Lord, shield us from whatever evil spell that old witch might cast upon us for disturbing her. Amen," I said looking through the pines towards the heavens.

Carefully, Jesse moved forward with Connie and me following. I whispered to Connie, "Don't look her in the eye."

The woman squinted her eyes, straining to see. Hopefully, she couldn't see too good so as to get a good bead on us. She kept blinking. "You children lost or something?" She spoke harshly now, "What are you doing out here in the swamp? Young Rapscallions!"

Jesse spoke up, "No Ma'am, we ain't lost…" he cleared his throat again. "We're looking for you."

"What for?" she said crossing her arms in front of her.

"My name is Jesse Tate and this here is Cally and Connie." Jesse said moving a little closer.

"Not too close, Jesse," I said.

He spoke again, "The Medium, Madame Rosemary, over at the Landing sent us. Said you might tell us what she couldn't."

The woman wiggled a pointed finger at us, "Come closer."

"We'd like to stand right here if you don't mind," Jesse told her.

"Well, I do mind! If you want to talk to me you come here and talk to me. I like to see who I'm talking to."

"Don't do it Jesse, Connie whispered. "She just wants us closer so as to cast her evil upon us."

"What were you children doing over to the Landing? Your mommas know where you are?" she rasped.

"I knew it!" Connie said. "Jesse, she figures there's nobody who knows where we are. She can cast her spell and stick us in that big black pot over there and we'll be hanging on that clothesline with the rest of all those poor souls."

Jesse whipped around looking Connie square in the eyes saying through clenched teeth, "If you don't stop that foolish talk I'll poke out your darned eyes and you won't have to worry about making eye contact with the witch. I got to know what this photo has to do with me. I know it must. I can feel it. I can't explain it, but I know it does. Your Madame Rosemary's reaction when she laid eyes on me proved it. Now either you're with me or you ain't."

"Ahmm!" the witch woman cleared her throat.

"If you promise to look down and not at her" I blurted out but, before he could get all puffed up about it I said, "Take it or leave it, Jesse Tate."

Jesse breathed out some mumbled curse words in one big unintelligible gush and turned head down, thank the good Lord.

"What's the matter with you three? You ashamed or something?" the woman's voice sputtered. "Is there something wrong with you? You can't walk without looking at your feet?"

"No ma'am," Jesse said. I caught him tilting his head up slightly to give her a sideways glance.

"Well, look here then. Let me see your face boy," she demanded.

Jesse took a deep breath raising his face to the woman's. I shut my eyes tight, afraid to watch.

There came such a flow of some strange language from deep within the woman's soul. Evidently some sort of witch talk. I peeked through squinted eyes to see her step closer to Jesse reaching her weathered hand to his face. I wanted to run, but I couldn't. My feet felt like they were glued solid to the ground beneath me. The woods silenced. Not so much as a cricket clicking. I held my breath. Her one rough, wrinkly palm was touching Jesse's cheek and her other pressed to her heart.

"Tyso yaha," she said. It was as though she was somewhere far, far away. Her red lined eyes turned glassy. Dropping her hand from Jesse's face she waved him towards the cottage, "Come."

"I don't think so," Connie said.

"Wait!" I said. "There's something big going on here. Can't you feel it?"

""Yeh and I want to continue feeling," Connie said nodding towards the clothesline.

Jesse hadn't moved and the old woman was at her screened door holding it open.

"Come," she said again. Seeing our hesitance, her face seemed to transform into one much softer and gentler, "Please."

In a panicked plea Connie blurted out, "No, Jesse! Don't do it! You'll end up like them." She was pointing towards the hideous things dangling from the clothesline.

"Holy smoke, we're dead," I said. "Now would probably be a good time to run."

I was about to do just that when all at once the old woman staring in the direction of Connie's pointed finger, raised her head back and came back down with a seemingly uncontrollable guffaw, baring a pretty near toothless mouth. I couldn't believe it. She was laughing her fool head off bobbing back and forth in hysterics. What could be so darn funny? Jesse stepped back with Connie and I, and the three of us stood dumbfounded as the old woman began writhing in laughter.

"Now you've really gone and done it with your mouth. What the devil is the matter with you Connie? Are you crazy or something?" Jesse said.

"Me crazy? I don't think so. Don't look now, but I think the old woman is a little touched in the head," Connie argued.

The woman realizing we were not joining in her fun regained her composure and left the porch walking towards the clothesline where she reached up taking down one of the heads. She held it out shaking it at us, "Tala doll."

We all jumped back. I was sure this was it, the big curse.

She kept shaking the thing at us laughing again. Jesse got a peculiar look on his face now, sort of a cockeyed smile. He stepped towards the woman, studying what she held in her hand.

She pointed at Connie and I. "Lagana Totolose," she said and Jesse broke into a huge laugh too.

"Don't look now but I think that Jesse has joined the land of witches and warlocks," Connie said.

"No I ain't!" Jesse laughed out loud. "I'm not for sure, but, I think she just called you two a couple of yellow chickens. This ain't any shrunken head," he said taking the object from the woman. "It's just palm leaves all bunched together stuffed to look like a head."

"What in the world for," Connie asked.

"Come. I'll show you," she said. This time Jesse followed unafraid and so Connie and I followed, cautiously.

Once in the doorway the woman held up one crinkled brown hand as if to signal us to stop. "Wait here," she said.

She wasn't gone very long and when she returned, in her hand she held a doll, a beautiful black haired doll wearing a dress with every color of the rainbow, just like hers except hers was worn and faded. It was a Seminole Indian replica just like the ones I'd seen when we took Grandpa Will to Miami. We drove along the Tamiami Trail, and every so often, some Seminole women would have their wares out on tables: blankets, quilts, and dolls like this one with long black braids. The old woman pointed first to the stuffed head Jesse held then to the doll's head. I felt my face flushing crimson. The woman had hand-crafted those palm fibers, stuffed and painted them, transforming the palms into beautiful Indian dolls. The old woman held the door open for us to enter now. Upon entering the cottage I noticed a white feather hanging over the doorway.

"Excuse me, Ma'am," I asked. "Why do you have a white feather hanging over your threshold?"

"White feathers remind anyone who enters here of what is right," she said.

I liked that. Was this the tradition of a witch or a savage?

I was surprised to find the cottage neat as a pin as we entered inside. She led us over to a wooden trunk set underneath a window, unlatching it, slowly opening the lid. Connie grabbed my arm, but released it immediately upon viewing the contents of colorful Indian dolls. Each was just as beautiful as the next.

"You made all of these?" I asked.

She smiled proudly walking over to what looked like a sewing machine in the corner. A basket weaved of swamp sweet grass sat next to the machine. It was filled with colorful material. "When I was a young girl at the reservation missionaries came and brought these hand cranked sewing machines to every chickee. The women learned to sew and they made beautiful rainbow colored dresses and these dolls. My mother taught me. It was a very profitable business on the reservation. Young Seminole daughters, such as me, sold the goods to the tourists and the missionaries.

"And we thought you had shrunk up...," Connie started as I jabbed her. "Ouch! What's the big idea?" she said.

The smile lines deepened around the woman's mouth and the ones around her eyes softened with understanding, "I wash the palmetto husks in my big pot outside. While they are wet I form the heads stuffing them with pine needles or material and hang them on the line to dry. When they have dried I crush and strain berries in one of those fine silk stockings the Effa brings to my chickee, then I paint their faces and dye their corn silk hair with indigo."

"Where do you get all these beautiful fabrics for their clothing?" Connie asked picking up a silky pink fabric from the sweet grass basket.

"I used to use old scraps of material I had from worn clothing, but that's before the Chatte Effa came to my Immokalee. He is truly a blessing. The Lord saw the need and provided."

"Effa? The red dog came to your camp?" Jesse started to laugh like crazy.

"Well how about letting us in on the joke," I said.

In between bursts of laughter Jesse asked the woman, "The crazy red dog brings you material?"

The woman shook her head in agreement.

"Cally, that crazy red dog brings all those lady things here. She thinks he's a messenger or something of goodwill," Jesse said.

"That mutt?... A thief maybe, but a messenger of good will; I don't think so."

The woman's smile disappeared from her weathered face causing Jesse to cut out his laughter. "You call him a thief? Then you must call me one, too. I did not send him to bring these things here. He just happened here one day with a beautiful piece and what was I to do. Scold him? I have no way of returning them to their owners so I put them to good use, for the children. The Creator saw a need and he provided."

She had a point there. How could she possibly return the articles of clothing? "What children are you talking about?" I asked. "What do you do with all these dolls?"

"I sell some at the flea market, but most of them I have my friend take to the children's home at Enterprise. The children love the dolls." Her eyes danced as she talked about her dolls and the children. Those were not eyes of some savage as Miss Stoner would have had us believe. They were the wise and generous, very old eyes of an angel. Suddenly, a deep feeling of satisfaction overwhelmed me and I couldn't stop the smile spreading across my face. I could not wait to speak to Miss Stoner again and tell her just how wrong she had been. A small pang of guilt did run across me for misjudging the Indian woman, but the feeling was fleeting when I thought of how I could get one up on Miss Stoner. I figured it was small minded people, such as Miss Dulsey Mae Stoner, who kept the old woman hidden in the forest. The creatures of the woods only judged her by the kindness she is filled with. The old woman was showing Jesse around the cottage and Connie sat in front of the trunk admiring the dolls.

"Wow! Where'd you get that?" Jesse asked staring at the old rifle hanging above the mantel of the fireplace.

"That was my father's rifle," the old woman told him. "My father being a healer, and peacemaker, didn't care for weapons, but in our chickee, he kept one under his bed used only for hunting game. My uncle taught me how to shoot when my father wasn't around." Her face beamed with pride. "I was a crack shot. I once shot a rattlesnake's venomous head off from three-hundred feet away, just as the reptile was about to strike my pony. I don't much like guns myself, but sometimes they are necessary to rid the world of the devil's creatures."

Thinking ahead to the trip home through the swamp again, rattlesnakes were the last thing I wanted to think about. Remembering Connie, Jesse, and my reason for coming here in the first place, and being as the old woman wasn't no savage going to shrink us up into tiny miniatures, or shoot us, I said, "Excuse me, Ma'am, but seems like we should at least know your name."

"Che - Ee-Cho," she said holding her head high. "I am the daughter of our tribe's Medicine Maker and Chief Priest."

Jesse echoed her words, but this time in English, "Her name is Little Deer."

"How do you know that?" I asked, and then felt dumb remembering Jesse's mother was Seminole.

Jesse seeing Little Deer's confusion explained to her, "My mother is Seminole. Her parents came here to start a new life. They left a lot of their ways in the Big Cypress. She told me that years ago she had an Indian woman friend who taught her about the old ways and the language. Her parents forbid her to see the woman, wanted her to fit in with their new world. After that she'd sneak into the forest to see the woman on the sly. After marrying Jasper, he wouldn't allow her to continue her friendship either. She gets real sad when she talks to me about those times. She hasn't seen the woman in years. Jasper threatened her, said he'd do harm to the woman if she seen her again. But, when Jasper wasn't around she told me about her friend and taught me the words."

I wasn't really looking at Jesse as he talked, but at the old woman. She seemed uncomfortable with Jesse's story, but the final part seemed to please her.

"Little Deer," Jesse said pulling the locket out of his pocket and opening it to the picture. "How did the medium over to the Landing figure you would be able to help me find out about this photo? She was as close-mouthed as they come after seeing me. All she'd say was to come here."

Little Deer's eyes widened and I could tell she was searching for what to say. Looking up towards the sky she spoke, "You should talk to your mother about this first."

"What would my mother possibly know about this old photo? I told you my mother is afraid to tell me anymore about her past, because my daddy, Jasper, gets crazy mad at the mention of it."

Little Deer's face scrunched up and she spat into the hearth, which I found pretty unnerving, not to mention disgusting.

"Jasper Tate!" she said with about as much hate as a person could muster, drawing the name up from deep within her, and spewing it out like the spit from her lips. "The devil himself!" she said to our shocked expressions at her familiarity with the man. Seeing our shock at her response, she said to Jesse, "I'm sorry if you call him your father, but I'm sure you're old enough to know what he is."

Oh man, I thought. Jesse is going to get all riled up and we're not going to find out anything else. After all, even though he had said the same things about Jasper Tate, blood was blood. But, surprisingly Jesse didn't say a word, just gave the woman a knowing look.

"How many years are you, Jesse Tate?" she asked.

"Thirteen," he answered.

Little Deer touched her hands to her mouth. "In Seminole years, you are a man. You talk to your mother as I told you, then you come tomorrow in the late afternoon and I will tell you what I know to be true. How you choose to use that information is up to you."

"Why can't you tell me now?" Jesse demanded.

"Patience," she told him in her crackly tone. "Give an old woman time to remember." Then looking out the cottage window across the tops of the pines at the setting sun she said, "It's time for you to go. Soon it will be dark and you children shouldn't be out here in the swamp this late."

Connie, who was still engrossed with the contents of the woman's trunk, came to life running to the window, "It is almost dark. I'm not walking through that swamp, Cally. We'll be like walking gator bait in the dark."

"You can take the path behind my cottage. It is clear and away from the swamp. It will take you to the county road. Jesse Tate, take one of my lanterns with you from the mantle. You can return it when you come tomorrow," she said walking over and taking a long match stick from a box next to the lantern. Striking it she lit the lantern's wick, handed it to Jesse, and then walked to the cottage door.

We all said our farewells, but before we got out the door of the cottage

Little Deer said, "Wait," and scurried to the trunk pulling out two of her creations. "Please take these and the blessings and luck that come with them," she said handing one each to Connie and me.

We thanked her, hugging our dolls close. Little Deer bid us goodbye telling us we would always be welcome. "It is so good to have young people here again."

Jesse led the way holding the lantern to light the darkened pathway.

"I wonder who the young people were who used to come here," I said as we walked single file behind Jesse. The woods were getting blacker than my dolls indigo hair, and they had taken on a whole different feel as we made our way. Except for the lantern, a body could hardly see their hand in front of them. I got a peculiar feeling, as if someone or something was watching us as we moved along. The light from the lantern illuminated the narrow ditch running along the one side of the path. Dappled spots of gold shimmered in the tall pines like a thousand amber eyeballs watching.

"Look at that," I said as we moved down the path. The spots turned to rivers of light, their streams moving into little pools scattered across the earthen floor. Connie and Jesse saw it now and we all stood staring through the trees at the eerie display.

"Come on, just keep walking," Jesse said. We stayed close, as Jesse lifted then lowered the lantern, the lights moved with it.

"Am I crazy or do those lights appear to be moving with us," Connie whispered.

"The spirits," I said in a breathless whisper. "I knew something was watching us. Run!"

The three of us ran with the lights bouncing right along with us. Jesse stopped. Then the darn fool turned off the wick.

"Hey! What the devil are you doing Jesse," I said.

"Just keep walking straight ahead," Jesse directed. "See there's enough moonlight to show the way. If those are spirits we don't want to make seeing us any easier, do we?"

"Good idea," I said realizing I had hold of Jesse's shirt with Connie hanging on to mine. A whippoorwill's gentle song rang through the stillness from the tree tops. I loved to hear them from my bedroom window at night as I was safely tucked into bed, lying by my sister Lynn. Now it sounded lonely and spooky.

"I hate to even think this, but it sounds like, the Woo Woo Man," I said as softly as I could. "Oh my, gosh, Connie, this is the very path us girls tried to follow the Woo Woo man. Remember?"

"Oh good, Cally, that's what I wanted to hear. We've gone from gators to Mr. Woo Woo," she said clutching my arm tight as the three of us became a walking huddle moving forward through the woods.

"Jasper says that guy is loony as they come, calls him Woo Woo, the crazy loony. He says he killed his whole family, burnt them all up in a fire. Remember the old burned out homestead by the old oak tree where we found our tin box Cally?"

Before waiting for an answer Jesse added, "I'm pretty sure that's the house old Woo Woo and his family lived in."

Madame Rosemary's words came to me, "There was a terrible fire. All perished."

"Let's get out of these woods before I lose my mind," I told Jesse. "Supposing whatever is watching us is Mr. Woo Woo's burnt up family. Suppose that wasn't a whippoorwill we just heard at all, but maybe Mr. Woo Woo's family out to get revenge."

"Cally, relax. Your imagination is working overtime," Jesse laughed. "Anyway, Jasper says they couldn't prove Woo Woo done it for sure, even though most of the town figured he did. Said they sent him away to some loony bin place until about five years ago. Ever since the accident all he does is make that Woo Woo noise and walk the streets of DeLeon with that old shuffleboard stick of his. He's probably looking for more innocent victims."

"Yeh, and what's the deal with that shuffleboard stick anyway?" Connie asked. "Why does he carry a shuffleboard stick?"

"I don't know," Jesse told her. "I've seen him up at the park a lot. You know the one where all the old people play that lawn bowling stuff and shuffleboard. I think he might do some work there. He sweeps the courts after all the people leave. You ain't ever seen him up there?"

"Okay!" Connie stopped, jerking my arm with her. "That's about all I want to know about Mr. Woo Woo right now. Let's hurry up and get out of here before they end up finding us with a shuffleboard stick stuck in us."

The whippoorwill called out again and our pace picked up considerably. The welcoming light from a car's headlights streaked down County Road about fifty yards in front of us. I took in a deep sigh of relief as we reached the road. Headlights glared from behind us, lighting our way.

"Cally!" Bud's voice called as his red Ford pulled up along side us, stopping. "Where in blue blazes have you been, Cally? I've been looking all over for you."

"Bud, am I glad to see you," I said walking towards the car. Connie and Jesse stood silent.

"Mom sent me looking about half an hour ago. Where have you been?"

"We were exploring Bud. We just got stuck back on a trail that was a lot longer than we thought," I explained. Bud was visibly upset and asked where we got the lantern.

"It's mine," Jesse lied.

"Well, if you planned on being home at a reasonable time what did you bring a lantern for?" Bud asked.

We all just sort of looked at one another stammering and stalling.

Bud shook his head, "Come on, get in the car and I'll take Jesse and Connie home, then Cally gets to explain to Mom and Dad."

It was a mighty quiet ride. Nobody said anything until each bid goodnight, getting out of the car as quickly as they could at their stops.

"Okay Cally, you've got mud all over my floor boards from somewhere and Jesse just lied about the lantern. Now do you want to tell me what you been up to, or do you want to tell Mom and Dad?"

"Promise you won't get mad at me?" I asked.

Bud sat leaning on his steering wheel, his head in his hands.

"Promise me Bud."

"Depends," Bud said, sitting up.

I looked pleadingly into my brother's eyes. "I couldn't stand you to be mad at me, but I'm busting to tell somebody what happened."

"I don't think I like where this is going, Cally," he said putting the car in gear and moving us forward. "Tell me what happened right now or I just might make you walk home."

I knew Bud wouldn't do that to me. I could tell he was mighty worried when he found us.

I couldn't contain myself blurting out, "We were at the witch's place."

"What!" Bud screeched the red Ford to a stop.

"Whoa!" I said flying forward catching myself on the front of his dash.

"She's not really a witch, Bud!" I blurted out before Bud could begin his bombardment of questions. The words just kept bubbling up from inside me.

"I'm telling you she ain't a witch, she's just a nice old Indian woman who makes little Indian dolls and feeds the panther and falcon, and minds her own business, and besides that she knows something about the picture Jesse and I found…"

"Slow down and start from the beginning," Bud said pulling the car off onto the shoulder.

I began explaining about Jesse and me discovering the tin box and how Connie led us to her Grandma Agnes' Medium, and how she sent us to the old Indian woman. Bud just sat there like he was in one of Madame Rosemary's trances or something. He hardly blinked an eye. "Cally, girl you just beat all. One of these days you're going to find yourself in one heck of a mess and I won't be there to help you. You know that?" Bud waited for an answer, but there was nothing more to say.

"So you say Jesse is supposed to go back to the woman's cottage tomorrow?" Bud asked.

I shook my head, "Yes, in the late afternoon. What do you suppose she knows Bud?"

"Everything, I'd guess," he said. "She probably knows more about the people around here and what goes on than most."

"Bud, what do you make of that Woo Woo man?"

"I think we better not even speculate on that. We need to do some digging first," Bud said.

Watching the headlights bounce across the road, the memory of the strange lights we'd seen in the woods came to mind. "Bud, there was something else out in those woods tonight that's got me all stirred up inside. We saw some of the most peculiar lights. They looked like a thousand cat eyes scattered all around, and the ditch line on the side of the path appeared to be a river of light. It was pretty much one of the eeriest things I ever did see."

"You saw the lights?" Bud said.

"Yes, have you seen them too?"

"I've seen them a time or two. There isn't much that compares to the fear it puts in a body to experience that sight in the dead of darkness, in the middle of the woods." Bud shook his body like he just had a bad case of the chills. "Man, I'll never forget what happened to Squeakie, Larry, Bill, George, and me out there, especially Squeakie."

I wasn't sure I wanted to hear anything else freaky tonight, but Bud was on a roll now.

"It was last summer when a bunch of kids were up at the U.D. and talk came up about the Landing and those mysterious lights near the swamp. Some of the guys were out there parked with their girlfriends on one of the dirt roads leading off the county road. They heard some strange voices coming through the woods. It was a crackly shrill sound, calling out in some odd tongue."

"Probably Little Deer," I offered.

Bud looked at me strangely.

"Little Deer, the Indian woman," I explained.

"Oh. Well anyway," Bud went on, "The girls got scared and so they all decided to leave, but while they were driving out of the swamp they saw bright lights just come from nowhere in front of the car. When the guy driving swerved to miss them he went right into the ditch. They had some bumps and bruises, but were okay. They were so freaked out they all ran to the county road, hitched to town and got the car towed out the next day. After we heard the story the guys couldn't resist the mystery so we drove out in George's car to where the kids had gone. George, knowing how Squeakie couldn't pass on a bet, bet him ten bucks he wouldn't get out of the car and walk in the swamp alone, while the rest of us waited in the car at the Landing road."

I felt a sick clamminess crawl over me as Bud spoke of it. No way would I want to get out in that swamp by myself. Ten bucks wasn't worth it. I asked Bud what Squeakie did. Although I had a pretty good idea knowing Squeakie what his answer was.

"Squeakie took the bet so we let him out and left him standing in the middle of the dirt road. We did give him a flashlight."

I rubbed the goose bumps that had popped up on my arms. "Like Grandma Cummins says Bud, 'there's a fool born every minute.'."

"You sure you want to hear this, Cally?" Bud asked.

"You know I do, Bud. Finish the story."

"There Squeakie stood with his flashlight. He said he was okay until George's tail lights disappeared around the bend. It was then the fear took him over. I mean there he was in the swamp near the Landing, between the gators and the spirits. Squeakie said when he'd been in the car you could hear all kinds of night noises: crickets, frogs, even the gator in the swamp, croaking, but when he stood there in the middle of the road all alone, it got dead silent. Not even so much as a breeze was blowing. It was then he heard it, a kind of howling sound. At first he thought it was the wind, but then realized it was a voice, calling through the woods. He couldn't make out what they were saying. It was a soft low voice. All at once there was another voice, much clearer one, crackly and definitely an older woman's, calling, in a foreign tongue."

I remembered how strange the Indian woman's language sounded. I'd bet that was what Squeakie had heard. How strange and ghostly it would be in the dark when you stood all alone in the middle of the swamp. But, whose voice was the other?

"Squeakie said his adrenaline started pumping and he lit out for the Landing as quick as he could go," Bud said. "He kept walking, slow and listening for the direction of the strange sounds, then pretty soon before he realized it, he was running. He said he was getting pretty shook up and thought maybe the bet wasn't worth it. He came to the first bend in the road and what he saw sent a fright coursing through him like he'd never known. The woods were lit up in a mysterious glow, little pools of light all around, just like you described, Cally. I don't know if it was the fear setting in or just Squeak's imagination but he said the lights appeared to be moving with him. He picked up his pace and his heart felt like it would bust right out of his chest. He heard the deeper voice calling out what might have been a woman's name, Lilly, or Lila, or something. After the name came a crying sound, and the wind began to howl."

"Lilly...Lila!" I said out loud.

"Lila?" Bud repeated the name, confused.

"Lila is Jesse's momma's name, Bud."

Bud just shrugged, not getting the connection. Goose bumps ran up and down my arms. I wanted to hear this story, but it was giving me the creeps and I clicked down the button lock on Bud's car door. "So what happened next, Bud?"

"Really spazzed out by now, Squeakie turned his flashlight towards the voice. Thought maybe someone was lost out there or something. He didn't realize he had wondered off the path until he sunk down over his shoes in the swamp muck. Panicking he was flashing his light all around trying to find the path again and something told him to turn around and there he was facing an even brighter light blocking his path. Somehow, he found his voice buried deep inside all his terror and hollered out as loud as he could. Stepping forward he ran into something. At first he thought it was a tree. Maybe, maybe not, but somehow he managed to get around whatever it was and that's probably about the time we could hear him whooping and hollering, cussing us all out in between yells. George started up the car and the rest of us rode back down the road towards Squeakie's yelling. I mean to tell you Cally, I was afraid for Squeakie. It was a dumb thing to leave him out there. When our headlights reflected on him his arms were covering his face and you could tell he'd actually been crying."

"Squeakie? Mr. Outdoorsman himself? No way, I couldn't believe it. Squeakie was as big and strong as a bull. He looked like one of them wrestling guys. He was always camping out in the woods and hunting the game roaming the area, eating off the land, making the guys' meals of swamp cabbage and wild hog. "Squeakie Arnold crying?" I repeated.

"Don't ever mention it to him, Cally. He'd pound me for sure telling you all this. He swore us all to secrecy or else he'd get even if it took him the rest of his life. Knowing Squeak I was sure he could and would."

"You know Cally, had the circumstances been reversed and it was me out there in that swamp, I don't think I would have handled it any better. Squeakie looked like he had seen a ghost and I'm thinking maybe he did."

Bud pulled the car in our driveway. "Cally, there's one more thing. You have to promise you won't go back in that swamp by yourself, at least not after dark."

"You think I'm crazy," I said.

I was glad he didn't make me promise not to go back at all.

Bud covered as much as he could for me as Mom and Dad met us at the back door. Said he'd found me on my way home from my friend Shirley's house, who lived across from the county road Grocery. I threw in the fact that we got to playing and didn't realize it was getting dark. Bud said it just took awhile because I was with Connie and Jesse and he drove them home first, stopping to talk to Connie's Mom a few minutes. I felt guilty for Bud's lie and mine. But when you got down to it, we really didn't do anything wrong. It wasn't like I'd been out causing any mischief and it was true me, Jesse, and Connie, were so busy so as not to notice night coming on. It was just the exact location of our day that was a lie. Yeh, that's not so bad, I thought. Mom and Dad were relieved I was okay and hadn't come to any harm. I did get a lecture about being home before dark, but that was about it. I thought about Jesse. I sure hoped Jasper Tate wasn't home, or all corn liquored up when Jesse returned. Jesse's evening wouldn't turn out as well as mine if Jasper got hold of him in one of his miserable drunken states. He wouldn't have Bud there to help him out. Mom had held a plate of dinner for me and I gobbled it down pretty quick. I hadn't realized how starved I was until I smelled her cooking. Mom puttered in the kitchen as I ate, "What exactly have you been doing all day, Cally?" she asked. I had shoveled a pretty big bite in just before, so to avoid answering I kind of grunted pointing to my mouth. You can't talk when your mouth is full. I kept shoveling and Mom didn't press me for anymore. Finishing, I excused myself from the table and quickly placed my dirty dish and glass in the sink.

"Ahhhh!" I let out with a big exaggerated yawn, giving Mom a big hug. "Think I'll hit the sack," I told her.

"Goodnight," Mom said with a suspicious look. I usually never went to bed without being told it was bedtime.

Passing by Bud's room I found him and Kate talking in whispers. I stuck my head in, "What are you two up to?"

Kate stood staring at me like I was one of those criminals you see on the Post Office bulletin board. "Cally, what were you thinking out there in the swamp at night?"

"Bud!" I glared at my brother.

"Don't blame me," Bud shrugged. "Kate knew I was covering for you. I've done it for her a time or two," he added raising his eyebrows at her.

I couldn't imagine Kate ever having done anything that needed Bud's covering for her. Kate was like the perfect child. I wondered what Bud knew that I didn't. I'd have to check her diary soon. Last time Patty and I read it, it was pretty boring. Nothing too scandalous other than so and so had gone out with so and so and so and so found out about it and the first and the last so and so, broke up.

Surprisingly, Kate was more curious about what we had discovered at the Indian woman's cottage and what the Medium had told us about the picture. I was pretty uncomfortable about Kate knowing. She tended to mother me and I was afraid she'd tell. She wouldn't out of meanness really, but out of her need to be the protector of her little sister. But for now anyway she seemed amazingly calm about the whole thing.

"Cally why don't you, Jesse, and Connie go to DeLeon College library tomorrow morning before Jesse goes sees the Indian and do a little research," Kate suggested.

"What kind of research," I asked. I wasn't sure, but I think Kate was actually trying to be helpful instead of being her usual gloom and doom predictor of my life.

"Go to the library and check out the information you got from the Medium at the Landing. She told you enough about the tragedy that happened to that boy in the picture to look up dates and names on that microfilm machine they've got there. Look up the old newspaper headlines from about when the boy died. I mean how do you know that Indian woman knows anything for sure? Maybe she's just trying to trick Jesse into coming back. You know, if she's really a witch they can be very cunning," Kate said.

Kate really was trying to help. Will wonders never cease, I thought, and it actually seemed to be a very good idea. "You're right Kate," I said. "I mean how do we know she really isn't a witch? I mean, just because she gave us a doll doesn't mean she's not one I guess. After all, Hansel and Gretel got pulled in by a witch. Although, I'm pretty sure she isn't one."

Kate rolled her eyes at me.

"No, really Kate, think about it, why would the Medium send us to see a witch? She had that white feather over her door and everything."

I tried to ignore the look of pure confusion that Kate was now wearing. "Feather, what feather? Sounds like more tricks to me Cally."

"Okay Kate, I'll give you that," I said.. "Maybe that was just a trick, one of them hex things, but like you said all this information we have is worth checking out. Maybe we really can find out all we need to know at the library and Jesse won't have to go back to see the old woman."

"Alright then," Bud said. "It's settled. I'll take ya'll to the library in the morning. I have to pick up Gloria first then we'll take you."

Gloria was home for the summer and I should have known, because for the last couple days you couldn't pry the smile off Bud's face with a crowbar.

"Sounds like a great idea Bud. I'll call Connie," I told him.

Later, lying in bed, my mind was racing; everything all jumbled in there, bits and pieces popping out, one thing after another. The boys in the locket had to be connected to Jesse. It wasn't any coincidence. Jesse didn't know everything the Madame told Connie and me.

Whoo, whoo, the old hoot owl cried from the tall pine out my window; it was a strange and haunting cry. A chill crawled up my spine. Maybe we should've left well enough alone. Leave the past in the past. Rolling over, I tried to think of something else. I'll not sleep a wink. Maybe I'm just worrying over nothing. I was glad Bud and Gloria would be taking us to the library tomorrow. Maybe they would come in with us until we found out about the microfilm Kate talked about. Miss Posey, the skinny librarian lady maybe wouldn't let us kids mess with anything so important sounding as microfilm unless accompanied by someone like Bud or Gloria, a senator's

164

daughter. Maybe it would be best to just leave well enough alone. The information would remain hidden on that tiny microfilm forever or at least until Jesse was old enough to deal with it. I had a really bad feeling about it all now. But, I had to help my friend. I'd worry about things when the time came to worry. Miss Posey, the librarian popped into my head. Concern took hold now, as I thought about the last time I visited the College's library. Miss Posey, I am certain, didn't like me too much after the last time Patty and I were there working on our school reports. Even before the unfortunate incident that day, she had kept shushing us every time we would giggle at the pictures in the National Geographic. I swear for someone so religious Patty laughed harder than me at the naked pictures in those magazines. When I got tired of staring at naked tribes of natives and such, I left Patty down in the sunken reading area in the middle of the library. On the landing at the top of the steps, I spotted a new Hardy Boy Mystery in the book cart Miss Posey's assistant restocked the shelves from. It was a new one I hadn't seen before, 'The Secret of the Old Mill'. Picking it up and turning to walk away, I brushed a little too close to the cart.

CRASH!

Startled, I quickly turned around, to my horror, the cart I had just plucked my book from rested on its side at Patty's feet in the sunken reading area. Books scattered all over. Patty was laughing and I just stood with my mouth wide-open realizing what I had done, then nervousness took over. Unfortunately for Patty and I, when I get nervous I laugh. I mean I wasn't being disrespectful and I certainly hadn't done this on purpose. How was I supposed to know the darn terrazzo floor had a slight roll to it? Patty and I began picking up the mess, but Miss Posey, came running over, "Alright, I've had about enough of your disruptive behavior. This is a library not a playground," she squawked.

I was so embarrassed and nervous I couldn't stop my laughter.

"I'm certain I don't see the humor in this," Miss Posey said waving her hand as if to brush us away. "You two have done enough damage here for one day; maybe you should try the city library."

Patty and I hurried out. Patty was furious at me afterwards so I treated her to a coke and some fries at the 'Gold Doubloon,' the Student Center cafe' at the College. It was fun to sit in there and watch the college kids. That seemed to pacify Patty, but she still wouldn't go back to the library with me again. It had been a while, so hopefully Miss Posey wouldn't remember me tomorrow.

15 CHAPTER

Morning came quickly. I felt as though I'd just closed my eyes. Bud was up early and gone before I joined Kate and Lynn in the kitchen for breakfast. Gloria certainly had put a rev in his engine. I never knew Bud to get up so early on Saturday except when he had a paper route or had to go work at Setzer's. Gloria had been a good friend of our family's ever since we had lived out along the river while Dad was building our present home. Gloria lived out there on the Collier's old homestead. She and her father, Senator Eugene Collier, lived in the home that had belonged to her grandfather and his before him. Her father, being a politician and all afforded them the privilege of traveling to Washington, D.C. quite a bit. They lived a very glamorous life. I wondered what it would be like, all those parties and meeting people from all over the world. It seemed a fantasy life. Kate said they were no different than us, just regular folks, just richer.

Bud and Gloria arrived to much hugging and carrying on; everyone glad to see our friend. We began catching up on the past few months since she had last visited, when she was on Spring Break from her boarding school up in New England.

The high pitched squeak of the water spigot on the side of the house signaled Jesse's presence. Getting my hugs in I left the rest to the reminiscing and went to help Jesse water the garden and tell him the library plan. According to the rooster clock above the fridge it was just about nine-thirty. Connie should be on her way over by now.

Jesse didn't look up as I came around the corner. He mumbled what sounded like hello still looking down at the hose and not at me. His baseball cap was pulled down low on his forehead, but I still caught the red mark on the side of his right cheek. As if he could feel my eyes on his face he touched his hand to it. "Jasper was a little tanked last night. Lucky for me he wasn't too steady. It doesn't hurt too badly," Jesse said.

My stomach was sickened to think of Jasper striking out at Jesse that way. "How can he do that to you? You're his son, Jesse."

Jesse gathered up the big coil of hose and walked towards the garden, "Boys and dogs. They're all the same to Jasper. Don't do what you're told; you smack them around until they do, especially when he's liquored up."

"I'm sorry Jesse," I said.

"Don't feel sorry for me. I don't care. I still get to do more than most. Only time Jasper cares if I'm around is to take care of any chores need done. Half the time he's too drunk to notice. Hey, how about running back up to the house and getting me the wider sprinkler," he said changing the subject.

"Sure Jesse," I said. I was kind of glad to have the change in conversation. I just didn't know what to say to Jesse. I couldn't imagine having a Daddy like Jasper or a mother who lived in fear of a man. Sounded like at one time she spent time with Jesse, like when she taught him all that Indian stuff. She must have just given up out of fear. Probably just went along so he'd leave Jesse be and not take everything out on him. Whatever it was I wished she'd take Jesse away from all that meanness. I grabbed the sprinkler and while Jesse was hooking it up I told him about the plan.

"Kate says the library has got something called microfilm files with old newspaper stories stored on them. We can look up the year that Madame Rosemary recalled was the time of the terrible tragedy. Maybe get some names or find out something about the boys in the picture."

"Cally!" Connie waved from the driveway.

"I'll finish the watering," Jesse said. "You go on up with Connie. I just as soon not get into what happened to my face with her right now. Maybe she won't notice when we're all in the car."

A good hour had passed before you could hear the squeak of the shut off valve on the spigot. The watering time gave me a chance to join my family as we caught up on Gloria's last few months away.

Colleen Affeld

16 CHAPTER

Skinny Miss Posey walked towards us holding a long rectangle box in her spindly fingered hands she had gotten from a room behind the circulation desk.

"Follow me," she said leading us to a table in the corner with a sign hanging overhead, "'Microfiche.'".

"You ever notice that if Miss Posey were to turn sideways and stick out her tongue, she'd look like a zipper? My goodness is she skinny," Connie whispered.

"I will load the machine for you young man," she said to Bud. Taking the film roll from the box she carefully unrolled one end and curled it around the spool on the gray and blue machine setting on top of the table. With a flick of a switch the contraption came to life, its big screen lighting up. When she had clamped the film in place with a click of the spindle, she instructed Bud how to move the film through the machine with buttons and dials on its side.

"When you are finished with your search, don't try and take the film off. Come and get me," she said, then hurried over to her desk where an important looking man in a suit was waiting for her.

"I think you all can handle this," Bud said. "Just follow the instructions right here on the machine. Gloria and I are going to take a run over to

Setzer's to pick up my check and do a couple other things."

"Bud, we can walk home from here, it's only a mile," I said.

"Okay, but stay out of trouble and don't forget what Miss Posey told you about getting her to put this away when you're done. Be careful," Bud warned. "We'll see you later." He took Gloria by the hand and they left.

Jesse was busy scrolling through all the papers hidden within that tiny roll of film. It was amazing how much information was crammed in there. "Look at the price on a candy bar from fourteen years ago. Man, I could have two or three for what we pay now," he said as a page with a Setzer's Grocery ad crossed the screen.

"This thing is too slow," Jesse spun the dial. There was a button on the side that said forward so checking to see if Miss Posey was looking, I pushed it. We all jumped back as the film spun in a quick blur. "Hey what did you do?" Jesse said. "Cool. Look here. We're clear to 1946. What year did you say it was Cally? 1947?" Jesse scrolled the knob. "There!"

A shushing sound came from the circulation desk. Jesse lowered his voice, "The story should be in here…"

I pointed to an article moving across the screen now. "Look! Here's a creepy one. 'Man Drowns in River.' 'The body of Lucas…Cane, was found early yesterday morning, July 5 in a ditch near the Pepper Pot. There were signs of blunt trauma on the body'.'…"

"That's pretty sick," Connie said.

I scanned down the page, "He probably got drunk and fell in the river. Wait a minute, Jesse. Go back up to the section before that. I think I saw something as you were scrolling down. Slow it down a little. There! That's it," I said, reading the page "'Fire Claims Three Members of Malcolm Family.'."

"Oh, my, gosh," Connie said in a hushed voice. "The terrible fire Madame talked about; how horrible!"

Jesse read the article under the large headline. "'Intense heat and smoke made DeLeon firefighters efforts impossible as they tried to put out the fire and free the family from the burning home. Caleb Malcolm Sr., his wife, Elizabeth Malcolm and son Caleb Malcolm Jr. lost their lives in a home fire last evening, July 4, 1947.'"

"Fourth of July? I wonder if the fire started from some some off course firework rocket hitting the house," Connie said.

Jesse kept reading.

"When firefighters arrived at the scene the fire was already out of control and most of the structure was destroyed. Fire Chief Strong and local police are investigating the cause of the blaze. Caleb Malcolm Sr. was retired from the Florida East Coast Railway. Elizabeth Malcolm was a homemaker. Caleb Malcolm Jr. was a pilot with the United States Air force earning the Airman's Medal during his tour of duty in the Pacific Theater. The deceased are survived by Caleb junior's twin brother, Curtis Malcolm and Caleb junior's fiancée, Miss Lila…'" Connie and I froze. Jesse stood staring at the words on the screen in front of us.

"Good Lord!" I jumped back as Jesse violently slid back in the wooden chair he'd sat in, tipping it backwards as he ran from the room.

"Jesse!" I called out after him.

"Shhh!" Miss Posey looked as though she might have a stroke or something.

She came running over with a death ray glare in her eyes like something out of one of Bud's comics. The glare changed to one of surprised recognition. "Goodness sakes! It's you. I thought there was something familiar."

"Time to go, Connie," I said grabbing my friend's arm. "We're done here Miss Posey. Thanks for your help," I said pulling Connie out of her chair as she still stared at the microfilm screen. Not looking back I just kept walking as fast as I could without running to the front doors. Jesse was no where in sight when Connie and I made it to the front steps of the library. I could not imagine what must be going through Jesse's mind after reading that article. "Lila, Jesse's mother, was engaged to Caleb Malcolm Jr. at the time of his death,." I said to no one in particular, but Connie picked right up on it.

"That's really sad," Connie said.

I didn't think she realized just how sad.

"Connie, we need to find Jesse. You look over by the science building and I'm going over to the tennis courts. Meet me back here in ten minutes."

When Connie got out of eyesight, I pulled out a piece of paper from the notepad I had brought to write down any important information we may have found on the microfilm. I began figuring on the paper starting with the date of the fire and counting backwards. Not nine had to be about eight, I thought as I moved the pencil around... 1961 minus thirteen... 1948. Oh, my Lord. I was right. No wonder Madame Rosemary and Little Deer were so interested in Jesse's age. I ran back to where Connie and I were to meet. Connie was already standing by the fountain in front of the library.

"No luck either?" I asked.

"No, I didn't see any sign of Jesse. Cally, I know all that stuff we saw on that article was disturbing, but why would Jesse be so upset he'd run off like that?"

Sometimes I couldn't believe how someone so knowledgeable in the ways of the world could miss something as obvious as this. "Connie, don't you get it? Think about it. Jesse and I find a picture of twin boys that Jesse could be the triplet of. Then, Madame Rosemary about faints away at the sight of Jesse and the old Indian woman gets all teary eyed and mysterious after seeing him. To top things off we find out that Jesse's Momma, Lila, was engaged to Caleb Malcolm, one of the boys in the picture."

"So?" Connie shrugged. "That still doesn't explain why Jesse's all that upset."

"Do the math Connie! Jesse was thirteen years old in March this year, 1961. The fire was July 4th 1947." I held up the piece of paper I had done my figuring on. The way I figure it, Lila was pregnant about one month before Caleb died. Eight months later, March 1948, Jesse was born."

Connie just stared dumbfounded. "How did you ever think of all that?"

"Remember when Kate's friend, Roberta, suddenly disappeared from school and about nine months later she reappears with a new baby brother. Well, it really wasn't her brother at all. Her parents shipped her off to some unwed mother home, she had the baby and returned, and suddenly they had a new member of the family. It wasn't exactly some miraculous birth, and she didn't get pregnant from French kissing like Patty said. Kate said she got pregnant by her boyfriend and to save embarrassment to the family and Roberta they sent her away, and then adopted the baby. The way I figure it, Lila was pregnant. Her fiancée was dead, so she married Jasper Tate out of desperation. Lila loved her child, and she kept him. But, you know she'd been better off facing the embarrassment and raising Jesse herself."

"No kidding!" Connie agreed. "You're right though, we need to find Jesse, no telling what is going through his head or what he'll do. You know, Cally; there is one good thing about this whole mess."

"What could that possibly be?" I asked.

"Jesse isn't blood related to that awful Jasper Tate."

Looking at the tower clock, I realized time was wasting. "Let's get going. I think the first place we better check is back at the Indian woman's place," I told Connie.

As we walked along, neither of us spoke. I think we were both trying to grasp all this craziness in our own minds. Jasper Tate treated Jesse so bad; he had to know he wasn't really his daddy. That had to be it. I couldn't imagine a real dad treating his child like Jasper did Jesse. At least it was easier to swallow knowing what I thought I knew. All those ideas Jesse had in his head, like how he wanted to be an Air Force pilot when he got big, just like his real dad. That medal we found must have been his daddy's. How did it get in the tin box after Caleb died? I wondered if Jesse had the gift like his grandmother, Elizabeth Malcolm. The paper said she was a member of the Seminole Landing Temple. There was a lot more to that article than what we had discovered. I had to help Jesse sort it all out. After all, I had talked him into going to the library. I felt responsible for what happened next.

"Wow, what a story," Connie broke the silence. I could see that mind of hers was in third gear ready to run with it all. "You know, Cally; I think I've figured out that dream of yours about the boy with the tin box…Poltergeists!"

"Polter what?" I said.

"A Poltergeist… The spirit from the other world is trying to contact Jesse somehow. Jesse's a child; the spirit comes in child form, a Poltergeist is a mischievous child."

"Oh brother, Connie, where do you get this stuff?"

"No really, Cally. It makes sense. All the tricks in the bomb shelter, the wind and the knocking over of the candles and such. Caleb's boy spirit is trying to get to Jesse through you."

"Why me, I ain't no psychic medium," I argued.

"I don't know, maybe it's because you're more open-minded than most. Close-minded people usually ignore the messages; use their physical bodies, but not their psychic ones. Plus, you're a kid, and so is Jesse. Poltergeists are mischievous and channel better with kids. Think about it, Cally. It's all a strange chain of events; Jesse coming and stealing from your shelter, and you meeting him and becoming friends then finding that stuff. That wasn't no ordinary dream you had. You have to admit that!"

"You're giving me the heebee jeebees. I don't want to hear another word. Even if it's so, and I ain't saying it is, it just isn't right. I can feel it," I said.

"Well, I'm going to ask Agnes about it and we'll just see," Connie said, determined to prove she was on to something. "This is just about the most exciting summer we've had, Cally, probably much better than that haughty taughty Lucinda Winthrop's."

"Connie Louise! Don't you say a word to anyone about what we found out today or what we suspect? Jesse is our friend. We have to keep this our secret!" I warned.

"Just who do you think I am, Cally Cummins? I'm not going to say anything to anyone. Who would I tell anyway?"

"Oh well, let me think," I said, "How about practically anyone who would listen."

"Thanks a lot, Cally," Connie walked ahead of me. We were just approaching the Seminole Grocery.

"Connie," I hollered after my friend, "I'm sorry. I should have known you wouldn't tell anything so private." I had to flatter her, or she would probably tell someone just to spite me. "I've got a dime, how about we get some penny candy for our walk to the swamp." Bribery usually worked every time.

Connie stopped and walked back towards me. "I get to pick," she said.

I agreed handing her the dime. The squeaky screen door was slamming behind her before I could say another word.

I hoped she would hurry. Jesse could be long gone by the time we got out to the swamp. What was taking her so long?

My stomach did a flop as the screen door opened and out walked Connie followed by, of all people, Robert Lee, Carl Johns, and Tommy Cox. The three had their fishing poles with them and had bought some worms from Mr. Elias. Connie was jabbering away, giggling and batting her eyes. Surely, she hadn't said anything to those guys. Jesse would never forgive us.

"Why can't we come with you? Where are you going?" Robert said cramming a wad of Turkish Taffy in his big mouth. Connie caught my look of concern and quickly looked away.

"Where are you two going Cally?" Carl asked. "Connie says she can't say."

Good Connie, I thought. You didn't say anything, yet you told them all they needed to know. Now they won't let it go until they find out what we're up to.

"No where special. Back to my house is all," I told Robert. "Come on Connie," I said glaring at her, "Kate will be waiting on us." Turning to the boys I gave a quick wave, "See y'all later."

"Just keep walking and ignore them and maybe they will go away," I whispered to Connie as we went down the county road. The three followed on their bikes a short distance behind us. "Great. Way to go. Now we'll never get rid of them," I told her.

"Turn like we're going to your house and maybe they'll fall for it," Connie said.

Sure enough the boys kept straight to the County Road as we turned off on Garfield Street, walking just past Mr. Ellich's Garage. Stopping there, we each unwrapped a piece of candy. Checking to see if the coast was clear, we ran back to the corner where the boys were nowhere to be seen. Hurrying, we dashed to the place where the path jutted off the road leading to the swamp. Scoping the area for any sign of the boys we headed into the woods. Walking along the trail you could just make out a few impressions in the sand that appeared to be footprints. The sand was all scattered about as if someone had been running. As we came to the spot where the sand gave way to deep black soil, I knew we were getting closer to the swamp. In the darkened earth there was a familiar print. I could just read the "Con" and a part of a "v" from Jesse's sneaker. We walked along where the big oaks, sweet gum, and pine mixed so tightly together they blocked out most of the bright summer sun. Long gray beards of Spanish moss drooped practically to the ground from the branches and the air wasn't as warm, but moist and cool.

"BOO!" I jumped nearly five feet off the ground. Connie screamed and my heart raced as I turned facing Robert Lee. "Doggone you Robert Lee! What's the big idea scaring a body like that? I ought to knock your fool head off!"

"You and what army," Robert said as he and Tommy and Carl doubled over in laughter.

"You scared the Be-Jesus out of me!" I yelled, my hand to my chest.

"Yeh and you said you were going home! So looks like we're even," Robert said.

"What are you up to, Cally? Don't you know there's an old witch woman lives out here?" Carl asked. Carl wasn't as ornery as Robert Lee and he seemed genuinely concerned about our safety.

"Witch woman? Says who?" I asked.

"Says just about everybody that knows anything about anything around here Cally," Carl said. "I know you've heard of her, so what's with all this sneaking around stuff?"

"Well, we might just ask you three boys the same thing? What are you doing?" I asked.

Robert spoke up for the rest, "There's another trail leads off this one, goes to a real good fishing hole along the canal, before it gets too swampy. Don't want to go any further than that and end up some gator's supper. That's all we're up to. You never did answer why you're out here, Cally. You sure are acting mighty suspicious to me. What's your business here?"

I had to think fast. Carl knew me well enough to see I was lying to them. "There's nothing so mysterious about it. Connie and I was walking along and I was thinking wouldn't it be good to have a big old bunch of mulberries to snack on. My mouth was just set for the taste, so I told Connie I knew where there was a big tree out near the swamp. We decided to take a little detour and get some. Maybe take a bunch home for a pie."

"Oh yeh, and just where are they at, Cally? I could use some of them myself," Robert said.

I grabbed Connie's arm and looked at her watch. "Oh look at the time. I don't have time for berries now. I forgot we're having steak sandwiches tonight and then we're going to a ball game down at Brownly Park. Come on," I told Connie. I turned to Robert and pointed on down the path. "If you boys just keep to the path just around the bend there you should find the Mulberry tree. Don't eat them all." I told them as Connie and I turned back towards County Road. As we walked away Connie asked, "What if they go too far and end up at the Indian woman's cottage?"

Remembering that Carl was allergic to bees, I called out a warning to them, "Carl, you best not be going back there too far. There's a hive of bees in the tree next to the Mulberry tree. I wouldn't want you to get all stung and swollen up. They were swarming something terrible the other day. I nearly got stung myself."

"Darn them boys anyway," I mumbled to Connie. "We need to find Jesse. He must be in a state by now."

"Cally, maybe we should leave Jesse alone for awhile," Connie said. "If what you concocted about his momma is true he might not want us bothering him about it, he might even get mad at us. I think we should give him some time."

"I guess you're right," I agreed. "Jesse has a lot to take in and sort out. I mean, really Connie, Lord only knows why Jesse's momma ever married the likes of Jasper Tate. What was she thinking? I mean I don't know much about that Caleb fella, but he sure seemed to be a decent sort. I mean an Air Force pilot and all. He couldn't have been nothing like Jasper Tate, a drunken bootlegger. You know, a lot of shame comes of having babies without being married. Guess Lila Tate was scared. Jasper asked and she took his offer. That's all I can figure."

"I feel so awful sorry for Jesse, Cally," Connie sighed. "What's he going to say to his momma next time he sees her? I'd be awful mad if I were him."

"Mad is probably just one of the feelings Jesse is having right now. I'd be so mixed up. I hope he doesn't get too awful mad at his momma. I mean she was probably just trying to protect him. She could've just given him away or something."

"Yeh, I guess things could always be worse," Connie said.

We walked on and parted company at my driveway. I made Connie pinky swear to not tell another living soul or something terrible would happen. She swore with some hesitation, but a pinky swear was sacred and I counted on her being superstitious enough not to break it.

Later, after dinner, I took my sweet tea out to the front porch. The orange sun was slipping slowly behind the tall pines that stood in the Jefferson Davis Elementary school yard. The front door opened and Bud joined me. "Are you alright, Cally? You were pretty quiet at dinner. What did you find out at the library today?" Bud asked.

I sat silent trying to find a place to start. As I scanned the darkness, movement down below the garden, near the woods, caught my eye.

"Cally, did you hear me?" Bud asked again.

"Hold on a minute," I said holding up my hand. A figure moved slowly towards the back of our property. It was Jesse. It seemed he didn't see Bud or me as he kept his head down as he walked along. I wanted to call out to him but I controlled the urge.

Bud strained to see what had my attention. "Isn't that Jesse?"

"Shhh!" I whispered watching the figure move into the back woods.

Bud sat quietly and we allowed Jesse to disappear quietly into the night. A bob-white called out from a tree top; how I loved to hear them at night, so peaceful. But, tonight his tune seemed empty, lonely and sad. I turned back to my brother who I knew was waiting patiently, somehow knowing the day had been hard.

"I'm sorry Bud," I said. "It's been quite a day."

"You and Jesse have an argument or something?"

"No, I'm not mad. But, I'm afraid Jesse is probably mad at the world right now. He's carrying more than his share for just a boy."

I began to explain to my brother about what we had discovered. I didn't think Jesse would mind me talking to Bud. At least I felt better telling him. Bud was smart. Maybe he could help Jesse somehow. I'd share my big brother with him. I couldn't say that about just anyone. But Jesse was special somehow and I had a feeling he needed a big brother more than I right now. When I finished telling Bud his usually bright eyes had a sadness to them that was echoed in the bob-white's song. We just sat quietly, listening as fireflies lit up the darkness.

17 CHAPTER

It had been a couple days and Jesse hadn't come around. I was getting mighty concerned about what was happening with him. I hoped he hadn't confronted his mother and maybe Jasper heard him. I prayed no harm had come to Jesse. Bud came home from working at Setzer's just as I was finishing up the watering in the garden.

"The garden is busting at the seams. We should have a real feast come the Fourth. There's nothing better than fresh garden vegetables all sliced up. Just give me a salt shaker and I'll be in hog heaven," Bud said admiring a giant red-ripe tomato just waiting to be picked. "No Jesse today?"

"No Bud and I'm getting worried. Haven't seen or heard from him at all."

"I suspect he has a lot on his mind these days. I just hope his momma was honest with him. He's old enough to know the truth. There's something else I found out Cally that is going to come as quite a shock to Jesse when he finds out. Something you haven't learned yet."

"What's that Bud? What else could there be?"

"Well Cally, I was talking to Squeakie Arnold's Dad yesterday. He's been around here all his life and knows most of the people over to the Landing because he works on their cars and other vehicles."

Seeing my concern Bud added, "Don't worry, I didn't tell him about

Jesse, I just was asking general things; you know, about the fire that night and if he knew the people involved. He had some very interesting information about the Malcolms. Everyone is so concerned about the twin that died, that no one has bothered much with the surviving twin. You know who he is Cally?"

I hadn't a clue as to who Bud was talking about and by my expression he could sense that.

"I believe you refer to him as 'the Woo Woo man,'" Bud smiled.

"Oh Bud, I can't believe I'm such a dope. I made all them other connections and completely forgot about the twin that survived. Caleb Malcolm's twin brother is none other than Mr. Woo Woo, the crazy that walks around with the shuffleboard stick, and lives out in the woods killing squirrels and eats them raw? I feel sickened to think about it."

"Who filled your head with all that craziness? Eats raw squirrel?" Bud laughed.

"It doesn't matter none Bud. Jesse's uncle is the Woo Woo man."

"Right Cal. His real name is Curtis Malcolm. After the fire the talk was that he was jealous of his twin brother and set that fire. They never proved it but Mr. Arnold says what mind he still had he pretty near lost the night of the fire and they sent him up to the State Sanitarium afterwards. It was either pure grief or guilt that put him there."

"Oh my gosh, Madame Rosemary!" I said.

"What about Madame Rosemary, Cally?"

"Madame Rosemary said the one twin that survived was sent to some mental hospital.. She knew all along! Why didn't she tell Jesse? And, if the Woo Woo Man, or Curtis, or whatever his name is, is crazy then why is he out walking around terrorizing people?"

"Mr. Arnold says he's harmless as they come. It's people that made him the way he is today. Always making fun and yelling at him because he's different."

"Harmless? He don't appear harmless to me."

"Now wait a minute, Cally. Who's he hurt? I mean really. Have you ever heard of anyone he has actually done anything to? All those tales about kids disappearing are just tales as far as I know. Think about it. He just walks around town and stays to himself. Only time he gets riled is when some smart alecks scream 'Woo Woo' at him. Mom says she thinks he's just a poor lost soul. Got no one left to care about him. Mr. Arnold says he didn't used to be so bad. He was a little slow, but he talked and was always with his brother."

"Well, you're right about one thing Bud, and that is when Jesse realizes his uncle is Mr. Woo Woo, he's going to be hopping mad. If he believes what the town people say about what happened that night, if I know Jesse, he'll be looking for revenge."

"Hey Bud, how about running up to the grocery and getting me a gallon of milk," Mom called from the porch. "I need it to finish supper."

"Sure Mom," Bud said. "Come on Cal, you can come with me. Maybe we can ask Mr. Elias if he's seen Jesse."

When Bud and I pulled in front of the grocery I spotted Jasper Tate's pick-up sitting next to the building. Bud gave me the money to run in for the milk. Sure enough standing at the counter taking his change from Mr. Elias was Jasper Tate. I looked around quickly to see if Jesse was with him. Not seeing him I got up all the nerve I could and walked right up and introduced myself. "Afternoon Mr. Tate, I'm Cally Cummins."

The man just squinted at me. He was unshaven and smelled of liquor again.

"I'm a friend of Jesse; I haven't seen him around in a couple days. How's he doing?" I asked.

All at once Jasper Tate straightened up and reared his head back, squinting his beady eyes tighter, inspecting me like I was from some other planet or something. He had dull lifeless black eyes. "Cally Cummins," he said in a gravely, smoking man's voice. "So you're the little gal that's been taking up all the boy's time with idle foolishness, taking him away from his work, you and that do-good family of yours. He says he's been working your garden instead of taking care of our place."

"No sir, it's not like that," I said.

"And what is it like, little girl? The way I see it you got free labor over there and I ain't got any."

I was getting mighty hot under the collar and I was determined not to let this mean drunk get the best of me, or talk that way about my family. "Fact is Mr. Tate, my Daddy and brother provided Jesse with his own area for gardening and in return for his work you will get a bounty of fresh vegetables for your table. We just provided the ground. You have been eating some mighty fine green beans and tomatoes from your table lately. Where do you think they came from Mr. Tate?"

"Tates don't need no do-gooder charity. You've been putting foolish ideas in the boy's head. I come in the other night and found him and his mother whispering. Had their heads together all hush, hush like. When I asked what was with all the secrets the boy was downright disrespectful, saying it wasn't any concern of mine. Where do you figure he's come up with all this disrespect, girly? He didn't used to act like that until he started hanging out with the likes of you. No sir, girly, girl, no more. I won't stand for it. I forbid him to come around you again."

"But, Mr. Tate, that's not fair. Jesse has worked awful hard on the garden. He did it for you and his momma."

Mr. Elias, waved his hands at me to stop, shaking his head back and forth. "You all finished here, Jasper?" he asked. "I got to close up soon."

Jasper Tate wasn't paying any attention to Mr. Elias. Something had caught his attention out front of the grocery. He pushed passed me real sudden like and moving to the window hollered out, "Get out of here, you crazy loony!" Then he swayed back to the counter wiping nasty, brown tobacco juice from his mean, ornery, grinning mouth. "What a crazy loon. Can't believe they let him out walking the streets," Jasper told Mr. Elias.

I stretched my neck to see out the window. I caught a peek at the Woo Woo man as he quickened his pace and hurried along. He didn't look our way, but kept his head down, paying no mind to the ignorant Jasper. Mr.

Elias bagged up Jasper Tate's purchases and shoved it towards him without a word.

I heeded Mr. Elias's warning and paid for my milk. But, as I started to leave, Jasper Tate called out to me, "Leave the boy be you hear? Stay away from my boy! I catch him over there again I'll whip the tar out of him!"

I slammed the door and ran to Bud's car, not looking back.

I got in the car beside my brother, "Let's get out of here Bud!" I said.

"What's going on, Cally?" Bud asked.

Right then, Jasper Tate gave the screen door a shove nearly knocking it off its hinges as he stumbled outside spitting a big mouthful of tobacco juice into the dirt with a splat. Bud and I sat and watched him fumble with his keys in the ignition, then grinding gears the pick-up jerked away onto the county road with a loud pop and a puff of black smoke coming from the rusty exhaust.

"Hey Cally, you picked any of them good mulberries lately?"

"Oh, great, could my day get any better?" I said to myself.

It was Robert Lee's smart aleck voice as he hit the brakes on his bicycle sliding the back tire around in a wide circle. Too bad he didn't wreck. I looked over at Bud, who seemed amused, and then I glared back at Robert.

"You ain't picked any because there ain't no mulberry tree back in those woods," Robert said as he rode his bike towards Bud's car. "Hey Bud! You know your sister has been hanging around out near where that old witch woman lives?"

I mouthed for Robert to shut-up. But he kept on, delighted in his little discovery. "Yeh, thanks to Cally and Connie we discovered where the witch's place is. My daddy says she's crafty and works her wile on anyone comes around. She communicates with the animals somehow and has pretty much ruined hunting anywhere near the swamp. She protects them with her spells and such. I hear she even has a panther as a pet."

"Maybe it's not witchcraft at all Robert, maybe you're just a lousy hunter," I laughed.

"We seen that white trash boy you've been hanging around coming out of her place too. I think maybe he's one of them warlocks or something," Robert said.

I laughed right out loud.

"I don't think you're talking about anyone Cally knows, Robert. She doesn't know any white trash. Just a few smart aleck boys don't know much of anything," Bud told him.

"It's that kid that's been working over at your garden. He's not from around our school," Robert defended his comment.

"If you're referring to Jesse, he's as fine as they come and smart too. He goes to school over at Spring Lake. I know you can't be talking about our good friend Jesse now are you, Robert?" Bud said.

No, guess not," Robert answered.

I smiled at Bud.

"Well, we can't be wasting our time around here, got more important things to do," Bud said starting up his car.

"Well, if that kid is such a good friend of yours Cally, you ought to tell him not to be hanging out there much if he knows what's good for him," Robert warned.

"What's that supposed to mean?" I bristled.

"Just ignore him," Bud said, backing out of the grocery onto the county road.

"BBQ panther… We'll teach her to mess with our hunting!" Robert hollered out after us as we drove away.

"Robert and them boys are up to no good. What are you going to do about it?" I asked.

"What am I going to do about it? I think Robert is just a lot of talk,

Cally. I'm sure that old woman has dealt with worse than the likes of Robert Lee in all the years she's been around here. What could they do?"

"I don't know Bud, but Robert can be ornery as they come. If nothing else he'll be a nuisance to the old woman. I wouldn't want to just stand by knowing he and some of those other boys are going to try and hurt her or the animals she loves. We have to find out what they're up to Bud. I wish she was a witch and cast her spell on Robert, turn him into a toad or something."

"Don't worry, Cal. We'll figure out what's going on. Hey! You were worried about Jesse and thanks to Robert you know he did make it out to see the old Indian woman."

"Yeh, but then what happened to him?"

When Bud and I got home I could hear the phone ringing as I came up the front steps to the porch..

"I think they just drove in," Mom said to whoever was on the other end as I walked in the front door.

"Cally, Jesse is on the phone for you," Mom said.

"Thank God," I said taking the receiver.

Mom asked where Bud was with the milk she'd sent us for. I pointed towards the front door not wanting to waste time explaining.

"Jesse? Where are you and where have you been? I've been worried sick," I whispered into the phone so Mom and Dad couldn't hear.

Jesse's voice was hushed and he talked fast. "Cally, listen, I can't talk long. Can you meet me at the bomb shelter at seven tonight?"

"Sure Jesse, of course I can," I said. "What's going on?"

"Just be there and call Connie, see if she can take us to her Grandma Agnes. That's the most important part of it, Cally." The phone clicked.

"That was a mighty quick conversation," Dad said.

About a million things were racing through my head, like why Jesse hung up so fast. What if Jasper heard him? He's not supposed to be talking to me.

I just smiled at Dad and shrugged, "He had to go. Had something to do I guess." I ran back to my bedroom. My alarm clock read six o'clock. I had to call Connie, tell her to call me back and invite me over. I snuck into Mom and Dad's bedroom to use their phone. "Come on Connie pick up the phone," I said into the receiver after the third ring.

"It's your dime," Connie answered almost on cue.

In a hurry, I explained the mysterious phone call from Jesse. Connie said she would call Agnes and call me right back. I hung up and exited the bedroom before being seen. Carefully closing my parent's door, I nearly jumped out of my skin as I felt a tap on my shoulder.

"And why are we being so sneaky?" Kate asked.

"Who's being sneaky? I just was looking for a rubber band to put my hair in a ponytail," I tried to say as convincingly as possible.

"So, where is it?" Kate kept on.

I looked down to my empty hands and shrugged, "Couldn't find one."

Ignoring Kate's suspicious eyes I went directly into my room and started brushing my hair. I heard Kate move on down the hallway. It sure was hard to do anything I wasn't supposed to around here with all the extra pairs of eyes. Bud had mentioned taking Kate and Lynn with him and Gloria after dinner. I hoped the plans were still on. Usually if my older siblings were going somewhere, it didn't take much coaxing to talk Mom and Dad into letting me go to a friends.

"Dinner," Mom called.

Sometimes things just seemed to fall into place. As I entered the kitchen Bud was telling Mom that Gloria was coming over. After dinner they were going up to the U.D. to hang out awhile, and then maybe do some miniature golf. "Gloria wanted to know if it would be okay if Kate and

Lynn could come along," Bud asked.

"Sure, that sounds like fun," Mom gave her approval. Kate ran out into the living room to tell Lynn who was watching the six o'clock news. She hadn't even heard Mom call us to dinner she was so stuck to the tube. Lately, she had taken an unusual interest in the news. I started calling her scoop, because she was a walking, talking TV anchor. She especially liked anything that talked a lot about President Kennedy and the Russians.

"Isn't it something how our Lynn has taken such an interest in current events," Dad would say.

Baloney! I was just guessing, but I think she was scared about the bomb too; or else she had a crush on the young news guy. She told me she thought he kind of looked like Frankie Avalon, the teen singing idol.

Bud must have been in an extraordinary good mood, seeing Gloria and all because he asked Mom if I could come along too. I began to panic. Mom would know I was up to something for sure if I turned down a chance to go with Bud and Gloria. The phone rang. I nearly knocked over my glass of milk to get to it first.

"It's awful nice of you to take Cally along with you all tonight Bud," Mom was saying.

"No problem, Mom. If she gives us any trouble, I'll just stick her in the trunk," Bud joked.

"I think we should just put her in there now and save ourselves the trouble later," Kate said.

I almost hated that I wasn't really going along with them. Kate got so embarrassed by just about everything I said or did in front of her friends. They never seemed to be bothered, but she was so worried I might do or say something that would make her a social leper.

Holding the receiver in my hand, I said, "Don't worry Kate I wouldn't dream of cramping your style. Mom it's Connie, she wants to know if I can come over later and spend the night."

Kate looked relieved.

"If that's what you would rather do, I guess it's okay," Mom looked to Dad for agreement.

"Doesn't matter to me, let's just decide what we're doing here and sit down and eat dinner before it's cold," Dad said.

After eating everyone pitched in and cleaned up the kitchen so we could all get going. The rooster clock in the kitchen read 6:55 p.m. In the commotion of Bud and the girls leaving I used this as an opportunity to go out and say goodbye. Soon as Bud's car turned onto Garfield Street I ran for the bomb shelter. Sure enough Jesse was already there lying on the grassy slope chewing on a piece of tall grass.

"You okay Jesse?" I asked walking up and sitting down next to him. The grass was cool and soft.

"Yeh, I'm okay, but I got about a million things to tell you. Did you get hold of Connie like I asked?"

A knot formed in my stomach. Why was he so darn interested in us going to Connie's? Did he like her or something? The boys always liked Connie. She was very pretty with her auburn hair and dark eyes. She hated her hair but my mom always told her, "Do you know how many women would love to naturally have your hair color. Nothing in a bottle could ever match it."

Answering Jesse I tried to hide my new found jealous streak, but my tone came out with a chill, "Yeh, and she's setting things up with Agnes just for you."

"What's the matter with you, Cally?" Jesse asked. I could feel my face reddening.

"Nothing's the matter; just tell me what all this secrecy is about. What did you find out, and where have you been for the last few days?" I asked trying to get the focus off the green-eyed monster taking me over.

"When can we go? We need to hurry up and get going before it gets too late," Jesse said.

"Well, I'm supposed to stay the night at Connie's, so you will have to meet us there after my parents drop me off.," I said.

"Why don't you just go in and tell them I came by and needed to talk. Tell them I'll walk you over to Connie's house. I don't want to waste any more time. We need to go," Jesse repeated.

Mom and Dad agreed to Jesse's idea and actually were very happy to see him. "We've got a couple baskets of fresh picked vegetables in the garage for you Jesse," Dad said as Jesse helped me carry my overnight bag out the front door. "Stop by tomorrow and Bud can load them in his car for you and take them to your place."

"Yes sir," Jesse nodded. "See you tomorrow."

It was only a few blocks to Connie's house up on Kentucky Avenue, but Jesse and I knew the shortcuts down Oak View Lane, through the Gunther's backyard, then on past the park. A starless sky was bringing an early darkness. Blue black clouds signaled a coming storm. The early evening air hung heavy and still. Hearing a fluttering sound overhead, and looking up, I caught the upward flight of a bat eating the mosquitoes that had already started to swarm around the streetlights. In my upward gaze a long strand of gray moss blew ghostlike in the warm breeze from an overhead tree branch. "Relax Cally," I thought. All a sudden, Jesse grabbed my arm and pulled me back behind the Park sign, as headlights swept across the hedges along the entrance.

"Stay still," he instructed until the car had passed. "Jasper was going out when I left. That one-eyed pick up just turned back there, looked like his. His right headlight is out. I don't want to take any chances."

It was getting pretty dark, but not dark enough that I couldn't spot the nasty bruise on the side of Jesse's face, illuminated by the milky light of the oncoming truck's headlight.

I reached for his face on instinct, "What the Sam Hill happened to your face?"

Jesse flinched, stepping back.

Realizing it would be useless to try and cover up what really happened, Jesse admitted Jasper had used his face for a punching bag a couple nights before. "Jasper caught me and my mom in the middle of a disagreement and smacked me for being disrespectful. It's okay for him to push her around I guess, but I can't have strong words with my own mother."

"What were you disagreeing with her about Jesse?" I asked.

"The other day when we went to the library," he began, and then hesitated... "Sorry for running out on you like that. But, anyway when I left there, I ended up at the old Indian woman's place in the swamp. She was expecting me. I told her I'd been to the library and seen the newspaper article about the fire years ago. I told her about seeing my mother's name in the write-up and it saying she was engaged to the guy that died in the fire. I'd like to tell you it all came as a big shock, but I already had a strange feeling about what I would find. Anyway I had a bunch of questions for the old woman. She told me she'd tell me if I came back."

"Yeh, but she also told you to talk to your mother first, remember?"

"I remember, but I didn't get a chance to because Jasper kept hanging around and wouldn't leave. Anyway the old woman is stubborn as a mule and told me I had to speak to my mother. I pretty much guessed what they've been keeping from me, but I told Little Deer I wanted to hear what she knew. Well, that old woman held her ground and all she'd say was to ask my mother first, then she'd tell me what she knew."

"So did you? Ask your mother, I mean?" I asked Jesse.

"I was pretty disgusted when I'd left and primed and ready for an argument, I guess. I just wanted to know the truth, Cally. When I got home Jasper was out with his friend, Earl, so I went right in and the first thing I did was go get that medal you and me found in that tin box. After that I went in the kitchen and told my momma I needed to talk to her. I did most of the talking. My momma just sat and listened. I shared what I knew with her. I could see right then, in her drawn, pale face, all the years of pain and pure dread she'd been carrying around with her, all the fear she had of this day coming to pass, when I would maybe find out the truth."

"What exactly is the truth, Jesse?" I asked softly.

Jesse started to speak but his voice sort of broke for a second. It seemed he might cry, but then he took a deep breath and went on. "I have to tell you, Cally, as mad and as confused as I was by all the lies and secrets, I just couldn't be angry at her. I felt sorrier for her than I did for myself. She didn't try to deny nothing. She came right out and told me what I wanted to know. The only good thing came out of it all, is the fact that as you probably have figured out by now, just like I did after reading that article, that Jasper Tate is no blood relation of mine. I am the son of Caleb Malcolm."

"Well, I did kind of put two and two together Jesse," I told him. My heart sank inside not even being able to imagine how Jesse must feel.

Jesse looked down at the ground like he suddenly was ashamed of something. "Yeh, old Jasper always calls me a little so and so; so I guess he was right."

"Don't go saying that Jesse! You're no so and so, you're Jesse Malcolm, son of a brave Air Force Pilot."

"Cally, I'm what I am. Jasper's right, it's a matter of biology that's all."

"That's Jasper Tate's opinion and who cares? What he says accounts for nothing. Why he's a drunken, snake in the grass is what he is."

"You don't know the half of it, Cally," Jesse shook his head.

"There's more?" I asked.

"A lot more, and Cally, what I am about to tell you is the worst part and why I came up with Connie's Grandma Agnes. I have an idea and as mixed up as I feel right now, it's about all I could come up with. From what came out through mommas and my talk we believe Jasper Tate is somehow responsible for Caleb Malcolm and my grandparents' death. We think maybe he killed them, Cally!"

I couldn't speak. I couldn't find the words. I just sat staring at Jesse. The night could have just swallowed us up right then and there. It was like there was no air to breath. Seeing I was speechless, Jesse continued. He pulled that medal we found in the tin box from his pocket. "It was this that made me realize the horrible truth," Jesse said dangling the medal in front of me. "I was talking to my mother, not realizing I was turning this medal around and around in my hand, when she laid eyes on it. Why her face turned the color of blackboard chalk when she saw it. It was then I realized I had it in my hand and I held it up so she could get a better look. She took it in her hands and tears welled up in her big brown eyes. She walked to the window and said his name, 'Caleb.' She started running her fingers over Caleb Malcolm's initials scratched on the back of the medal and asked me where it was I got it. I explained how you and I had found it in the tin box with the picture of the boys and all that other stuff. Mentioned how it looked a little newer than the rest of the things in the box. Like someone had added it to the contents later on. By then tears streamed down her face and she kept repeating, 'I knew it, I knew it.' Then she said, 'Poor Curtis....'"

"That's the other boy in the picture, the twin. Remember Cally, from the article? You know who he is, Cally?" Jesse asked me.

"Yes, Jesse. It's the man everyone calls, 'The Woo Woo Man.'."

"Yeh, can you believe it? My uncle is that guy everyone thinks is crazy. Most people think he killed his family in that fire. Well, I'm here to tell you, he may be crazy, but he didn't kill anybody. He took the blame, because he couldn't speak up for himself, his mind being not quite right and all. If my Momma and I are right, Jasper Tate is the real killer and walked away free as a bird. When I think about how Jasper and Earl harass that man every time they see him." Jesse's face was red with anger. "Why they holler, 'Crazy Woo Woo, Loony!'. Of course, they never do it to his face. They always are a good distance or in a vehicle driving by. I'd like to see Curtis Malcolm show those two just how crazy loony he could be, maybe knock the tar out of both of them. I tell you, Cally I'd like to fix them good."

"Whoa! Slow down a minute, Jesse. How could some medal we found out in the woods, prove Jasper had anything to do with the fire let alone murder? I don't understand," I said.

"I'll explain later. You're just going to have to trust me, Cally. We can't waste time right now with explanations. I need more proof and that's the part where Connie's Grandma Agnes comes in," Jesse said.

"What's Agnes got to do with anything?" I asked, curious in his sudden interest in Connie's eccentric grandmother.

"I want her to take us to that Madame Rosemary and try and conjure up my real daddy, and find out what really happened," Jesse explained.

My stomach turned. "Jesse, I'm all for helping you find out what happened, but going to see the medium? I thought you didn't believe in all of that stuff."

"Well, until we come up with a better plan, that's all I got," Jesse said. "Now come on, we need to hurry."

Scared, yet a little relieved to think that was all he needed of Connie, I reluctantly followed Jesse. As we walked under the streetlights, I could see Connie sitting on her screened porch waiting on us. Jesse and I passed by the Pentecostal Church. By the sounds coming from the opened arched windows them Pentecost were just getting warmed up inside the small white building. A loud "'Praise the Lord'" followed by a bunch of "'Hallelujahs'" echoed into the heavens. The Boyd's station wagon sat in the church parking lot. From all the ruckus inside I could tell Patty and the rest were on their way down front, tears streaming and arms thrashing about, once again, just like every Sunday and Wednesday night. That's when they asked the good Lord to save them and reserve a place for their sinful souls in heaven. Holy Rollers was what Bud called them, and that was a pretty fair description I thought after having had firsthand experience when I'd visited a few months ago. When all them Pentecost's including Patty, walked down front to the alter; I went along with Patty. I didn't want to appear to look conspicuous, like I thought I was sin-free or something. I didn't want to be left sitting in a pew all by myself while they were all down there on their knees confessing their weekly bad deeds. My, oh my, how they wailed and carried on. I sat there dumbfounded at first, everyone around me thrashing about, including Patty. Pretty soon I was crying too, not for fear of going to hell over my sinfulness, but because I was scared half to death. I wondered afterwards if it was a sin, not praying for forgiveness while I sat there, but instead asking the good Lord for it to be eight o'clock so I could get the daylights out of there. I was sure glad

Methodists prayed quietly in their seats. That is all of them except old Mr. Cobb. If it was an especially long winded prayer, old Mr. Cobb's head would start bobbing up and down, as he filled the solemn room with snores so loud it rattled the stained glass windows. This lasted just until his wife Charlese would start poking him in the ribs, sending him into fits of coughing and snorting as he awakened. One thing for sure, those Pentecostals paid attention.

Connie must have seen us coming, and, as Jesse and I walked up the Parker's sidewalk she came outside.

"Come on, Grandma Agnes said we can come by," Connie said walking past us to the road. "While we're on our way, ya'll can fill me in as to why you're so darned bent on seeing her tonight."

Connie's mouth never shut as Jesse explained what his plan was. Her vocabulary consisted mostly of "'Oh my Gods'" and, "'you're kidding me.'". Jesse asked her if she thought Agnes would help.

"I have to tell y'all, with or without her help, I'm going to find out what happened to Caleb Malcolm. I owe him that much," Jesse said.

I could see the determination in his face and knew there was no stopping him now.

"You don't know my Grandmother," Connie said. "She'll jump at the chance to delve into all that mystic stuff, however, Madame Rosemary may be a different story."

Grandma Agnes lived in a stately southern home complete with wide front porch and white pillars. Connie unlatched the wrought iron gate leading into the towering masses of pink azalea lining the entrance. "Y'all stay out here on the porch and let me explain to Grandma."

Jesse stood back and took in the enormity of the place. "How rich is the old girl?"

"She's loaded; old money, very old," I whispered to Jesse.

It was taking a long time and I wasn't so sure old Agnes was that excited about taking a bunch of kids out to see her private medium. Jesse sat on the porch steps poking a stick at some carpenter ants ready to make an attack on Agnes' wooden porch. Footsteps could be heard inside the house. Through the fancy, cut glass front doors, Connie's and Agnes' figures shimmered in the foyer's dim light coming towards us. Agnes' shrill voice filled the night, as the doors swung open, "Gather your little friends up, Connie Louise we must be prompt. Rosemary's a busy woman." She kind of sized Jesse up as she stepped around him on the steps and leaning towards Connie, glasses tipped on the end of her nose whispered, "Not bad dear."

Pretty soon the four of us were in Agnes' big white Cadillac in route to the Landing. As we pulled off the lighted county road onto the Landing road, darkness surrounded us except for the headlights of Agnes' car. We had been in such a hurry all night I hadn't really had time to think about what it was we were getting ready to do. Now, as we pulled between the white stone archways of the Landing a fear ran through my stomach causing it to flip flop. My palms were wet and clammy.

Agnes' car stopped in front of the mediums cottage and she turned to the three of us, "Now you children just sit tight. I called Madame Rosemary before we left. She doesn't like drop-in clients you know. I need to make sure she is ready for us."

"Yeh, so she can do some digging into her client's past, I'll bet," Jesse mumbled.

Connie glared at him as Agnes primped in her rear-view mirror and exited leaving us to fend for ourselves in this god-forsaken place. I felt an unearthly dread, sitting there in the dark, looking around at the land of psychics and mystery. Patty's words of warning rang in my head about this spirit calling being the work of the devil. I scanned the white picketed yards and cottages. I didn't see anything lurking, but I could feel something, something evil. I couldn't shake it.

"Oh my Lord!" I threw a hand to my chest, my heart jumping as Agnes opened the car door.

"Rosemary is prepared. Come now," Agnes instructed.

Gulping is difficult without any spit. My mouth was dry as a bone.

"Be prepared to be amazed and astounded with her psychic abilities," Jesse said sarcastically. "I never asked, but is she charging us for her services? All I got is five bucks."

"Yeh, I wonder if she charges like Southern Bell Telephone. Talk about a long distance call," I nervously joked.

"Don't worry. My Grandma Agnes will take care of it, she's loaded you know," Connie boasted.

I gave Jesse a knowing nod.

Agnes led the way along the front walk leading to the little white cottage of Madame Rosemary. This place wasn't at all the kind of place you might think a person who talks to dead people might live. Those kinds of people belong in enormous three story, dilapidated houses, with chipped paint and mysterious wind blowing loose shutters against the outside walls. Their houses had rusty metal and wooden porches where you had to step around rotted floorboards to keep from falling to some hideous pit beneath. Maybe they even had a few bats flying overhead to complete the terrifying picture. This quiet, freshly white-washed cottage with jasmine climbing trellised walls just didn't fit. The whole place didn't, except for the dead silence surrounding us. That seemed to be its most creepy trait so far.

Whoo! A hoot owl seemed to be asking us from a tree top,. "Who are you? What are you doing here?"

What was I doing here? Here we went like lambs to the slaughter. What would my Mom and Dad say? Worse yet what if Patty was right? What if we were facing evil? Patty was much more knowledgeable than me in religious things. She could quote a verse for just about any occasion. Why, she was a walking, talking Bible sometimes. Sometimes it was pretty aggravating, too. Patty could become your conscious when your parents weren't around. What did that mean, 'the wrath of God?' That was one of her favorites. I was sure whatever it was it would be a heck of a lot worse than what Bud called the "Wrath of Dad." Hey, what did I know? I was just a kid. God certainly wouldn't mind me trying to help my friend Jesse, uncover a no good, devil-eyed, murderer; maybe that would make a difference. I wasn't sure of anything right now as Agnes opened the door and waved her arm as an invitation to enter the cottage.

Madame Rosemary was nowhere in sight.

"Should we just be walking into this place without knocking," I asked.

"Madame Rosemary is expecting us," Agnes said.

"Ooh, I don't think I like the sound of that," I said into the stillness of the now chilling cottage, not at all the warm, cheerful place we had visited before. Except for a few candles set around it was pretty dark inside. Agnes picked up a small candelabrum near the door and led the way down a narrow hallway, ending at a closed glass-knobbed door. The door had a yellow moon and star painted on white wood. Agnes reached for the door knob, then turning, pointing her finger in the air said, "Please respect this place and speak only when spoken to once we are inside. Madame Rosemary must use all of her concentration to call on her psychic gifts. Just seat yourselves around the table and wait for Rosemary to speak."

Coldness ran through my body seeing Madame Rosemary seated facing us at a small round table. Her pasty white face appeared ghostly in candlelight. A table fan blew from across the room gently lifting the wispy garment she wore and flittering at the scarf wrapped around her head. The candle's glow cast mysterious shadows on the wall behind her. As I seated myself at the table the uneasy feeling of impending evil swallowed me up. I glanced quickly behind me, but no one was there. At least, no one I could see. After we were all seated, Madame Rosemary lifted something from her lap. My eyes were about to pop from my head as she sat a clear, crystal globe in the center of the table. Except for it's clarity it looked very much like the bigger version from Aunt Ruth's yard that had caused me so much trouble. Not a good sign. I actually could not believe this real live medium person was actually using a crystal ball. I figured that was just something Hollywood had cooked up. Connie, Jesse, and I moved slightly back in our seats as the Madame lifted her wrinkly arms in the air. Loose skin flopped as she waved her spiny long fingers, their tips coated in bright red lacquer, swirling, circling the ball. The room decor was pretty sparse except for a couple pictures hung on the wall. It was too dark to make out what they were. When we entered the room I had noticed on the wall behind my chair, a narrow door that led to who knows where, probably a closet. After a lot of ceremonious waving of her hands Madame Rosemary placed them on the table and closed her eyes. We all followed Agnes' lead closing ours too; first Connie, then Jesse, then I, but not before taking one last quick glance around the room. I closed my left eye, carefully peering from my right, keeping it slightly parted, like my sister Lynn's when she slept. I wanted to keep a close eye on Madame Rosemary all the while. The corners of her thin lipped mouth began to twitch and then she uttered, "Jesse."

All eyes flipped open like Aunt Ruth's window blinds when I pulled the wrong cord while cleaning.

"Yes, Ma'am, that's me," Jesse barely audible, spoke.

"Why are you here before me?" Madame asked.

Jesse took in a deep breath, "To bring up the ghost of someone who has passed on to the other side."

I thought that sounded rather sophisticated coming from Jesse. It just made things seem even eerier.

"Who is it you wish to contact and bring up?" Madame questioned.

Bring up? Now this was getting creepy if she was suggesting bringing up out of the ground. Of course, where else I thought. But, if their dead spirit was still in the ground and hadn't gone on to a better place, as Grandma Cummins always called it, what or who was it she was calling upon? I felt a clammy chill. If the "'better place'" didn't want them yet, I was afraid Isaac was right.

"If they're dead and still walking on earth and not up in heaven, they may not be something you want to tangle with. Evil maybe," I whispered Isaac's warning.

I caught Agnes's glare out of the corner of my eye.

Oh, how I wished Isaac was here now. Of course, that was ridiculous, Isaac wouldn't be caught dead here. So what was I doing here?

Jesse didn't answer yet and Madame kind of squirmed in her chair

Seminole Landing

adjusting her sheer layered cape, surrounding her skinny little arms. "Jesse, please concentrate." She looked around at each of us and her eyes stopped at me. "We must all concentrate," she said sternly. I closed my eyes not really concentrating, just wanting to not look back at her cold stare. Jesse cleared his throat to speak and I relaxed my eyelids just enough to watch Madame's reaction.

"Who is it you wish to contact?" Madame asked.

"I would like you to call upon Caleb Malcolm, my father," Jesse said.

Madame's eyebrows rose slightly. "Do you have something of a personal nature belonging to the deceased?"

Without a word Jesse pulled the picture of the twin boys and the medal from his pocket and handed them to Madame Rosemary.

"Everyone place your hands on the top of the table," she instructed solemnly. Staring for a few moments at the contents in her hands, it seemed her eyes rolled back in her head as she clutched the picture to her chest. She began slowly rocking back and forth in her chair. Her eyes gazed upward, but still just a small crevice of white was all I could see. I guessed she was now in one of those, what they called trances. She lowered her head to her chest and folded her arms at the wrist. There suddenly came a smell I was familiar with, Lilly of the Valley. My Mom wore it on special occasions. It filled the room, quite strong, like the time I had decided to try a little from the small bottle on Mom's dresser and the bottle slipped. I tried to wipe it up, but the smell lingered for days as the oak dresser soaked up the scent. Dad wasn't too happy, "Smells like a hot July morning in church, all this perfume," he grouched. I nearly giggled as I observed Connie busy scrunching her nose trying to avoid the strong smell.

"I feel a cool breeze," Madame said in a whisper. "Tell me Jesse, do you feel it too?"

"Yes, Ma'am," he said.

Well of course he did, we all did. The fan was blowing softly on low speed. Certainly Jesse didn't miss that, I thought.

Madame smiled, "What is that? Yes, I can hear you," she said.

A voice called faintly, whispering, from behind Madame Rosemary, or was it coming from her. She had moved her cape around the lower part of her face. The voice sounded a little like her, yet it was deeper, not the high pitch of an old woman.

"Jesse," It called.

Jesse's eyes opened wide, scanning the room. I held my breath.

"Jesse, this is your father," the voice called softly from somewhere in the unknown.. I kept trying to see through the thin veil of material covering Madame's face. It was too dark to detect any movement around her lips. "What is it you need my son?"

All eyes were on Jesse. "Father, I want to know about the fire the night you and my grandparents died. Was it an accident?"

Madame Rosemary began to sway a little in her chair and Connie and I nearly jumped clean out of our skin at her unexpected movement. Connie grabbed my hand with one of hers and her Grandma Agnes' with the other. The medium started waving her arms in the air, swirling them. Flop, flop. My heart jumped to my throat as a ghostly white light came from behind her. The light moved in long wavy streams, circling and swirling like smoke in the dead air of the room, and then just as quickly as it appeared it disappeared. Madame Rosemary began to moan and groan, then just like the fairy dust that followed Tinkerbelle everywhere in "'Peter Pan'" the medium was surrounded in sparkling light. We all watched in complete amazement and fear as the veil of cloth dropped from her face and her mouth started to move, but robot like, like someone else was controlling her every move. I was too terrified to move. Sweat began to cover my upper lip and palms. Connie gripped my hand tighter. I could jump up and declare this all totally ridiculous and demand Agnes take me home and that would be the end of it. But, I felt like I was glued to my chair and my mouth was so tight it couldn't move. I could barely breathe.

At once warm energy filled the room. It was no longer the cool breeze of the table fan. You could feel the electricity of it. The hair stood up on my arms along with the goose bumps popping up all over me. I had been sure the Madame was creating the atmosphere…that is up until now.

"Oh, the agony," the voice came from deep within Madame Rosemary, her voice much deeper and different now. As if shocked by her own voice, the Madame's eyes popped wide open. I was sure of it now. The voice coming from her this time did not sound like her at all. It was a man's voice.

"It is too painful to speak," the voice croaked again. "I want to spare you the pain. It's cold…so cold…poor Fusee! Save yourself!"

"What is too painful?" Jesse asked timidly. "Please tell me. Nothing could be worse than what I know already," Jesse pleaded. "I have to know if Jasper Tate caused your pain."

CRASH! Lightning lit up the darkened room at the mention of Jasper's name.

"Who is Fusee?!" Jesse demanded.

"Aaeee!" Connie screamed.

Instantly, there was a new odor to the air. A pungent, very foul oily smell, like the dead fish left to lie in the sun along the river bank. It burned my nostrils.

Knock! Knock? Whoooo! All eyes were wide open now, including Madame Rosemary's. A strong wind blew against the house and something seemed to fall outside in the yard. Was there a storm? I had seen the heat lightning from Agnes' Cadillac on the drive here. It seemed to be clear over near Seville then. The crickets were the only sound you could hear as we had made our way in Agnes' Caddie to the Landing. Another wave of wind came from the window behind the medium, blowing out the candles along the walls and knocking the candle in the middle of the table on its side, extinguishing it. The room fell pitch black. Rosemary no longer glowed like, what was it… she reminded me of? Whooo, the wind cried, or was it?

"Who's there? What does this mean?" Madame Rosemary demanded, her own voice returning, as she snapped to attention in her seat. "Who dares to interrupt?"

"It's just the wind, Rosemary," Agnes tried to calm the woman. A storm must have caught us off guard, that's all.

My eyes had adjusted to the darkness, but fear was surging through my body and I thought my heart would jump clean out my throat, it was beating so hard.

"OHHH! WHOOOO!" A moaning came through the window. It sounded like the wind in the middle of a Northeaster blowing in off the Atlantic.

"OOHHH!" It came again and again, pulsing through the darkness. I turned towards the sound and I blinked my eyes to make sure they weren't playing tricks. There appeared to be a small light coming towards the cottage…moving closer and closer like someone coming, carrying a flashlight. The moaning came louder. Madame Rosemary's mouth began to move again, totally out of her control, contorting so, like she was fighting the words, "Pain," it moaned, "Pain, …knows pain. JASPER TATE! Beelzebub…WHOOO!"

CRACK! a bolt of light hit outside, sending a strange flash throughout the room, bouncing around the walls and then exiting from the direction it had come. Uncontrollable chills went through me as I caught Madame Rosemary's frozen stare following the eerie flash as it passed out the window, descending into the woods beyond the cottage. I jumped as the Medium began to shake violently, her voice returning with a piercing cry, "FUSEE! AACHH!" the medium screamed with a pitch I thought sure would curdle my blood.

THUMP! Rosemary slumped to the table, then all went calm. Even the phantom wind had died down,. Not a sound could be heard except five hearts pounding in the eerie silence.

Agnes jumped up and went to Madame Rosemary's side. Jesse moved quickly towards the hallway door clicking on the light.

Madame Rosemary lay still, and Agnes ordered, "Connie and Cally go get the salts from her mantle. She's passed out."

Clutching each other we squeezed through the doorway and into the parlor where we had sat with Madame Rosemary on our last visit. Sure enough on the mantle of her fireplace sat the smelling salts. I grabbed them and still clinging to one another, Connie and I made our way through the dark house to the séance room. Agnes grabbed the salts snapping one open, waving it under the Madame's nose. Tossing and thrashing her head sideways, coughing and sputtering, she finally came to.

"Are you alright?" Agnes shook the Madame's shoulders.

Rising from the table, a look of pure horror had taken over her eyes. The Madame spoke, "I'll never be fine again, I'm afraid." Her old eyes searched the room. "It is gone now."

"What is gone?" Jesse asked her. "What do you mean, IT?"

"The evil spirit; it is a restless one. One from the dark side, destined to walk on earth, never to rest."

I noticed the disagreeable smell the howling wind had carried through the window was no longer present. Just a faint scent of Lilly of the Valley filled the room again, soothing, after that other horrible odor.

"I think it is time for these children to leave this place," Madame Rosemary ordered. Wobbly, she rose from her chair and took Jesse by both shoulders staring straight into his eyes. "You must not pursue this anymore, do you hear me. Do not return here or to any other from my temple. It would be very unwise. You do not understand what you are dealing with here."

"Oh my, oh dear," Agnes said, visibly shaken herself. Grabbing her purse that sat by her chair, she took out several dollar bills. Handing the money to Madame Rosemary, Agnes hurried us out of the cottage and to her car.

No one spoke a word on the drive to DeLeon from the Landing. I could see Agnes glancing in her rear-view mirror at us in the backseat. Finally, breaking the silence she said, "Are you children alright? I feel terrible about taking you out there tonight. I swear I never have had an experience like that when I go for my weekly talks with Connie Louise's late grandfather. I suppose you will have nightmares from this, and your parents will be furious with me. Connie, your mother won't let you come visit me ever again."

Oh, I get it. Agnes wasn't as worried about the psychological damage she and the spooky old woman just did to our young minds as she was worried we were going to tell on her for taking us to see the medium.

"Don't worry, we won't be telling our parents about this. I'd be grounded for the rest of my life if my Mom and Dad found out," I told her studying her worried face in the rear view mirror.

"Turn right here, Ma'am," Jesse told Agnes as we came to the Landing road outside the strange community. "My place is down a ways," he said. When we got to the small white houses of Jasper Tate's aunts, Jesse told Agnes to stop. "I don't want Jasper seeing me getting dropped off from this big fancy car."

I don't know what came over me, but before Jesse could get out of the car I grabbed his hand and gave him a big hug. "Please be careful Jesse. I'll see you tomorrow, okay?"

He just smiled and squeezed my hand.

Back in DeLeon, we arrived at Connie's house. Agnes was still fretting and fussing about our not telling anyone.

"Don't worry Grandma, we asked you to take us there. It's partly our fault too," Connie reassured her.

A rush of panic had settled in on my stomach. I felt kind of sick. Before Connie could open her door I blurted out, "Agnes, I want to go home!" There I said it. I had been thinking it all the way back from the Landing. I didn't want to upset Connie, but I did not want to be away from my family tonight. An uneasy feeling had taken over me, like when you feel someone is watching you and your skin feels all crawly, and cold chills run through you.

"Cally? Why?" Connie whined. "You sound like Patty Boyd."

"Why? What in Sam Hill do you think, WHY? We just visited the village of the evil spirits and you want to know why? That wasn't Jesse's real daddy we just met up with. I believe the Medium concocted him at the beginning, like you and I concocted Jackie's daddy in the bomb shelter. Something else entered that room. Something the Medium wasn't expecting in all her phony hocus pocus. It was one of them evil conjured up spirits, the ones not only Patty, but Isaac had warned me about. I should have listened. We should have listened. I need to go home. Agnes please take me home RIGHT NOW!"

"Oh dear, oh my," Agnes mumbled again, as she put her Cadillac in reverse. "That's okay Cally, I understand," she said backing out of the Parker's driveway. "You just go on home and everything will be fine in the morning. These things always seem worse at night."

Connie was sitting jammed up against the far side of the seat, arms folded and pouting.

As we pulled in my driveway I felt the cold chilling rushes of adrenaline calming inside me. "I'll get my things tomorrow. Thanks, I guess," I mumbled hurrying out of the car. Without turning around I ran straight to the house. I was relieved Agnes kept the headlights on my back until my dad opened the front door.

"Cally?" My dad surprised to see me looked over my shoulder at the car backing out of the drive. "What are you doing home?"

I gave him an enormous hug. It felt safe and he had his familiar smell of Old Spice. "I just decided I wanted to stay home tonight after all. It's not often I get an evening with just you and Mom to myself," I said.

Dad put his large hand against my forehead.

"Cally? I thought I heard your voice," Mom came down the hall. "What are you doing home? Are you sick?"

Dad turned with me still wrapped around one of his big, strong, safe arms. "She says she wanted to be home with us tonight, have us all to herself." An amused smile was on his lips and Mom just sort of squinted her eyes at me, and came and felt my forehead too. Without a word she kind of shrugged and joined in the hug session. "I'm glad you're home.

Let's have some vanilla ice-cream with hot fudge sauce."

That was just like Mom. Even the smallest event, even one where a kid just decided to spend an evening at home, was a reason to celebrate. Much to everyone's great joy it was a time to fill the celebrators up with a yummy treat.

We ate our ice-cream and I tried to forget what I'd seen tonight. But, it was impossible. We watched television, but I just stared at the black and white lights, not really paying much attention. I just hugged close to my mom. Pretty soon Dad began to rattle the living room with snores as he slept in his easy chair, feet propped up on the ottoman. Tired of competing with the roar, Mom awakened him and he retreated to the bedroom. I was afraid that Mom would join him, but luckily she wanted to wait up on Bud and the girls.

"Can I wait up with you?" I asked, not about to head to bed without Lynn being home.

"Sure, what's that show you, Kate, and Lynn like so much, 'Twilight Zone'?" she said turning the channel past Jack Paar's tonight show, which she and Dad usually watched.

"That's okay, Mom," I said. "Let's watch Jack Paar."

"Okay," she said, suspiciously.

Mom and I must have dozed off because next thing I knew I woke to the jiggling of keys in the front door. Kate, Gloria, and Lynn entered the foyer, giggling and talking a mile a minute as Bud followed in after them.

"Have a good time?" Mom asked stretching as she pulled herself off the couch.

Their giggles, chatter, and secret looks let me know boys were somehow involved, but the jest of the evening was that they had fun. "I'm heading to bed," Bud announced and slipped down the hallway.

"Night Bud," Gloria called.

He gave her his killer smile and she blushed.

"I'm too wound up to go to sleep yet," Kate said heading into the living room.

"Me too," Gloria added and joined her.

Luckily Lynn just gave a wave as she headed down the hallway to our room. I was tired and being as she was hitting the sack, I could too. I followed closely behind her. She stopped midway down the hall as if she had forgotten something.

Thump! "Ouch," she said as I ran right into the back of her.

"Cally? Watch out," she grouched. "I have to go to the bathroom."

I started to follow her. "Where do you think you're going?" she grouched again.

"Shhh! you'll wake Dad," I told her.

"Go to bed then and quit following me," Lynn ordered and went in the bathroom, shutting the door.

I stood in the darkened hallway as Bud opened his bedroom door, causing me to nearly jump clean out of my skin. "What's all the commotion out here?" he mumbled.

"Nothing, I'm just waiting for Lynn to come out of the bathroom, that's all."

Bud stared at me through sleepy eyes that turned to mistrust, like old Foxy's, when he thought things weren't on the up and up.

"Why?" He asked.

I just smiled.

"Wait a minute," I thought you were supposed to be at Connie Parker's tonight," Bud came awake. "What happened…Cally?"

"Nothing," I said looking down the hallway. But Bud as usual, instinctively knew I wouldn't have come home from a friend's house unless I was sick. He could read me like a book.

Bud flipped on his light and opened the door inviting me in.

I had to tell him. I had to tell someone I could trust.

"Jeez Louise, what in the Sam Heck were you thinking Cally?" was all Bud could muster after I told him about the evening. "That Agnes, is a case, you know that? What was she thinking taking you kids out there?"

"She was just trying to help Jesse," I attempted to defend her.

"Do you know what would happen if Mom and Dad knew you were out there at the Landing at night, let alone going to see some medium? Good Lord Cally, don't you ever listen to me? I told you not to be going out there."

"Well, I did, so there and that's all there is to it. I'm sorry I did, but it's done and there ain't anything I can do to change it. Anyway, Bud, I don't need your scolding, I was scared half to death tonight and I need to know what in the world it was that we experienced there," I said.

"What you experienced there, little sister is probably one of the most evil things those mediums could conjure up, with all their mumbo jumbo talk to dead people stuff," Bud answered. "If that old medium was as shook up as you say, then I'd say it's probably the first time ever in her whole, fake, con life, she's ever encountered such a thing. Why I wouldn't be surprised if she packed up her things and headed as far away from that place as possible. How could she sleep at night after a visit like that?"

I shivered just picturing the old woman alone in her little cottage.

"While we were leaving she had some kind of potion in a bottle sprinkling it all over the séance room," I told Bud.

"Probably, holy water," Bud said. "Mrs. Ellich is a Catholic and they believe that stuff chases away evil. One time when she and Bill's dad were first married they rented a place out in the country. A lot of strange things happened while they lived there; they heard strange sounds and footsteps at night. One night when Bill was a baby and Mr. Ellich was off at work, she thought the cat was walking around upstairs. Afraid it would go into the nursery, Mrs. Ellich started up to get it and bring it downstairs, but the cat was sitting at the foot of the stairs when she got there. The odd thing was that the footsteps were still walking across the floor above her. Frightened, she took the bottle of holy water off the mantle and sprinkled it all around the downstairs and then went upstairs and did the same. She never heard the footsteps again, but one day when she was about to go down to the cellar to do the laundry, she felt a cold frightening chill as she headed down the steps. It was as if something evil surrounded her. She ran back upstairs and got the holy water. When she had sprinkled before, she had forgotten the cellar. She opened the cellar door and sprinkled from the top of the stairs. When Mr. Ellich got home, she told him she would not spend another night in the house and they found another one to rent and moved."

"Thanks Bud. Thanks for telling me that. I'll sleep real good knowing that tonight."

"Oh Cally, don't be silly. Our house isn't haunted. I just wanted you to know what it was that medium had in that bottle," Bud said.

"Yeh, well, do you think we could get some of that stuff for ourselves? It might come in handy while I try to help Jesse with this. I know darned well, after tonight, he's not going to stop until he finds out what connection that creepy visitor we had tonight has with his father, Caleb Malcolm."

"Don't even think about going back out there, Cally. If you need help just ask. I will help you, but don't you kids go taking on this business by yourselves," Bud warned.

"Okay, Bud. I'm asking. Help us figure out this mess."

"Well, we can't do anything tonight, but we can start tomorrow when I get home from Setzer's. I think a visit to the Indian woman might answer some of your questions. Tell her what you heard tonight see if it makes any sense to her. I only work until noon. Is it a deal?"

"Deal," I said. I heard Lynn head back to the bedroom, so decided it was safe to go to bed now.

"Goodnight," I said.

Colleen Affeld

18 CHAPTER

I poked my finger in the top of my bologna sandwich, two eyes a nose and a mouth stared back at me from the bread. "Don't play with your food Cally and eat your lunch," Mom said.

"Gross Cally, I hope you washed your hands," Kate complained. One poke had been a little too deep and a tiny piece of bologna poked out the mouth looking like a cat's pink tongue. Holding the sandwich between my fingers with the bologna face staring at Kate, I squeezed just enough so a little blob of catsup oozed out the corner of the mouth. "Help me," I whispered.

"Mom!" Kate squealed as I quickly turned my lunch around and took a big bite out of the middle with Lynn cracking up beside me.

"I don't know what you did Cally, but stop it before you give your sister indigestion or something," Mom said sitting down at the table. I could hear Bud's car pull into the carport. The rooster clock said almost one o'clock. Bud was late. Gloria's laughter coming from the garage explained why. I'd hoped he didn't forget our plan. Mom got a couple more plates and glasses out of the cupboard for the two of them as they came into the kitchen. Bud carried a Setzer bag in his arms and sat it on the counter.

"What's in the bag, Bud?" Mom asked.

Setzer's had Fourth of July stuff marked down so I got some black cats, sparklers and a couple other things I'm not quite sure what they do."

Looking over at me he said, "We'll find out though won't we, half-pint?"

I smiled at my brother. I caught Kate rolling her eyes.

We finished up our lunch and Mom went to the back of the house to gather up the laundry.

"Did you remember what we were going to do this afternoon, Bud?" I asked, growing impatient with the dwindling hours of the day.

"Sure Cal," Bud said taking a gulp of milk. "Gloria's coming along. She did a paper on all that spirit stuff up at school this past spring so she thought it would be interesting to see what that Indian woman says about it all."

My tenseness released, but then Kate chimed in.

"Cally, what kind of mess are you dragging Bud and Gloria into now?"

"She's not dragging anybody into anything they don't want to do, Kate. Why don't you and Lynn come along too? We'll make an afternoon out of it. Who knows, you might even enjoy yourself," Bud said.

Kate just gave a blank stare at our brother.

"Come on Kate, let's go," Lynn coaxed. "I'd like to see her dolls."

"Come on Kate. It will be fun," Gloria told her.

"Are we walking or riding?" Kate asked.

"That a girl!" Bud grabbed her by the shoulders. "We're walking."

"UGH!" Kate grumbled.

"Come on, we'll go by the Elias' Grocery and I'll spring for cold drinks and candy for the walk," Bud persuaded.

Clearing the dishes from lunch was a breeze with everyone pitching in and soon we were on our way.

Mr. Elias had just finished stocking the candy shelves from the boxes lined up along the floor. Fresh Vanilla Turkish Taffy was my first pick. Bud gave us each a quarter for our candy and he paid for our cold drinks. I chose a Grape Nehi from the red cooler at the front of the store. It didn't take Lynn and I long to make our decisions and we waited for the others at the counter laying out our taffy, candy lipsticks, and fireballs in front of Mr. Elias.

"Big afternoon planned," Mr. Elias said over his gold rimmed spectacles.

"Oh, nothing much, just going for a walk out near the swamp," Lynn told him.

The grocer stepped back his forehead wrinkling up, "Better be careful out near that swamp, girls."

I smiled at his concern, "Don't worry, Mr. Elias, the gators stay over near the canal and the path is clear enough to spot any snakes that might be sunning themselves."

A groan and the clatter of candy next to my purchases meant Kate was ready to check out too. "There'd better not be any gators or snakes creeping around out there or you can count me out," she sputtered. Mr. Elias winked at Lynn and me.

Bud and Gloria joined us. "Best be careful traipsing around out near the swamp Bud. I was just about to tell Cally and your sisters here it's not so much the gators and snakes out there might ruin your day, but it's more the two-legged kinds of varmints you better keep an eye out for."

"Who's that?" Bud asked.

"I'm pretty sure that Lee boy and his friends are planning to do a little hunting out there about dark. They were in here earlier and I overheard talk about that big cat that's been roaming around out there. They think it's been killing off the small game and dove. They even bought some buck shot from me."

"Why that low-down Robert Lee, it ain't that cat scaring away the game. He's dumber than he looks if he believes that Bud," I turned to my brother. "Little Deer feeds that cat plenty. I'd say probably better than the likes of what Robert Lee gets at home."

Mr. Elias' face was quizzical. Probably didn't know who the heck Little Deer was. The grocer started checking out and bagging our candies, "Well, just the same you best not hang out there too long you hear?"

We each paid Mr. Elias with our quarters and popped the caps off our cold drinks on the cooler's opener as we exited the store. Bud turned before shutting the screen door, "Thanks for the information, Mr. Elias. It's been noted and we'll be real careful."

Kate was already in one of her tizzies when Bud got outside. "Bud, we don't need to be out in those woods with a bunch of trigger happy little boys running around shooting at anything that moves."

"Kate, we need to at least go out and warn the old woman about the boys' plans. If you feel better about going on home, go ahead. I'll go out there myself."

"Not without me," I said.

"I'm going too," Gloria grabbed Bud's arm. "Anyway, the grocer said those boys weren't planning anything until dark. Hopefully, we'll be long gone by then."

"Gloria's right Kate, we'll be gone by then," Lynn chimed in.

I knew Lynn wouldn't back down now. She was like our Uncle Pete's old hound dog on a Coon's trail, except those handmade Indian dolls were her prey. They were beautiful.

The path leading into the pinewoods and the swamp beyond was getting pretty worn. The once tall grasses lay yellowed against the sandy soil. Kate was jittery as a bowl of Jell-O bobbing her head back and forth watching for some imaginary creature lunging from the bushes. She jumped about a mile high as a squirrel scurried across the pine needles.

By the smoke billowing over the treetops we were nearing the cottage. Something smelled mighty fine too as we rounded the bend where the pines grew thick and tall. The tin roof of the cottage shimmered in the afternoon sunlight. As we approached, who should be standing outside the cottage, but Jesse?

"Jesse!" I called out as we came into Little Deer's camp.

Kate stopped dead in her tracks, "Jesse, watch out!" she cried.

Right about then I spotted what had Kate so shook up. Coo-wa-chobee darted from the side of the cottage and straight into the woods.

I threw up my hands, "Kate, have you lost your mind?"

Jesse threw down the large piece of red meat he had in his hand ready to fill the big cat's dish.

"Now look what you've gone and done!" he cried spinning around at Kate, fit to be tied. "She'll probably never come back now!"

"What are you all doing out here?" Jesse hollered

"Sorry, Jesse; Kate didn't know," Bud told him.

"Well, that's pretty clear!" he said.

"Sorry, next time I'll just let that panther make lunch out of you," Kate snapped.

"Jesse, we came out here to see if Little Deer might shed a little light on what you and Cally experienced last night with the medium," Bud said.

Jesse just glared at me, obviously surprised that I told anyone. I felt my face redden.

"I was worried about you and just wanted to help. I had to tell Bud, Jesse," I said.

"He knows everything Cally?" Jesse asked.

Wincing, I shrugged, "Everything."

Now Jesse's face was red.

Kate had that raised eyebrow, confused look. "What haven't you told the rest of us?"

"Not now, Kate," Bud told her. "You don't want to know."

"Like heck I don't," Kate shoved our brother.

"Why not Bud? Pretty soon everyone will know anyway," Jesse said. "Go ahead! Tell them what a no good lying', murdering' snake, Jasper Tate is. When I finally prove he's responsible for killing my real daddy and my grandparents, the whole county will know anyway," Jesse said.

"What?" Kate barely sputtered out, turning white as a sheet. I thought she might have one of Aunt Bessie's spells right on the spot. She walked over and sat down on the old willow bench outside the cottage, mumbling something, I wasn't quite sure what. I did hear my name mixed up in there somewhere.

"Well, you can all just go home. I don't need your help. I'll be just fine. I've taken care of myself for thirteen years, I think I can manage now," Jesse told us.

I swear I was so mad at Kate right now I could just spit. "Jesse, listen to me. Bud and I are in this to the end, no matter what; right, Bud?" I said.

Bud was still watching Kate. Probably afraid she might pass out. "Yeah, uh, right!" he agreed. I wasn't sure he even knew for sure what he'd just agreed to.

Then appearing to come back to us, Bud said, "Jesse we got a more pressing problem I'm afraid. Something we need to stop before it gets started."

"What could be more pressing than catching Jasper in his lies?" Jesse asked.

As Bud explained about Robert Lee's spiteful plan, I could see Jesse's face tighten with anger.

"You mean them boys that are always hanging around the grocery on their fancy new bikes?" Jesse laughed. "So what's the problem? They're nothing but a bunch of spoiled momma's boys."

"A bunch of spoiled momma's boys with shotguns," Bud said. "We need a plan."

The screen door creaked open to the cottage and Little Deer poked her head around it, "Perhaps I can be of some help before you children get your heads blown off."

"Now there's someone that is using their head," Kate said. "I think we should call the police. I'm sure there's a law against kids Cally's age hunting without being with an adult, not to mention hunting after dark."

"It wouldn't stop them from coming out here and causing trouble for Little Deer," Bud told her. "We need to make sure they never come back here. Give them a good scare." Bud said to me and Jesse, "Too bad we couldn't get some of them spirits to come a haunting, eyeballs glaring with their ghostly auras shimmering through the woods like Squeaky seen that time. I'm pretty sure those strange swamp lights would do the trick. Robert Lee and his friends would run like a bunch of scared jack-rabbits."

Bud and I laughed at the thought but Jesse sobered up our lightheartedness. "If we seen anything like we did last night Cally, I have a feeling your Robert Lee wouldn't be the only one leaving these woods in a flash."

Little Deer spoke up again, "I think I have an idea," she said a curious glimmer of mischievousness lighting up the dark eyes.

"Come with me," she said stepping off the front stoop and walking towards the back of the cottage. Without any hesitation we followed.

As we passed the big cauldron I caught Kate's widening eyes as they looked from the black pot to the palm heads hanging out to dry.

"Better hope your face doesn't stick like that," I told her. She shoved me along trying to get by the menagerie as quickly as possible.

The old woman walked slowly, shuffling her reed sandals along in the black soil that is always found near the swamp, great gardening soil. Little Deer had a garden out behind the shed that made ours pale by comparison. "Do you garden all that yourself?" I asked. There's no way she could manage that by herself at her age. I wondered whose skills we were looking at. They surely had a green thumb.

Little Deer didn't answer; she just motioned for us to keep following.

Just past the garden she walked to the swampy ditch line beyond and stopped. Bending over, Little Deer ever so carefully, scooped up a wad of black muck that had the look of tar, in her weathered brown hand. The substance gave off a foul smell as she disturbed it. Looking around I could see the surrounding trees had the same black substance on their bark, like the cresol oozing from between the chips of pine, but darker. "Here is your ghost," she said with her nearly toothless grin. We all just stood there, a bunch of confused lumps.

"Come," she said clasping one hand over her other one, holding the black goop. She seemed like a child who had some new discovery. Her step quickened and again we followed her to the small shed near the garden.

"Go get the lantern over my wood stove," she said to Jesse.

Jesse did as he was told disappearing around the cottage. The old woman instructed Bud to lift the latch on the shed door. Bud obeyed, opening it, revealing not much more than the darkness and damp, mustiness inside.

"I don't think so," Kate put up a hand. "No can do! There are probably scorpions and spiders and Lord knows what else in there."

"We'll wait out here until Jesse comes back," Bud said humoring Kate.

Jesse came running from the cottage holding the lantern out, which he had already lit up. Little Deer nodded for Jesse to enter the shed. He held the lantern in front of him and cautiously stepped inside as Bud held the door open. The rest of us followed, that is all except Kate.

"Close the door young man" Little Deer said to Bud. As the door creaked slowly shut and I tried to adjust my eyes to the darkness enveloping us… THUMP! Something hit the shed wall.

"Hey!" someone shouted as we all jumped knocking into one another.

Thump! Something hit again.

"Bud!" I heard Kate cry from outside.

"What was that?" Jesse shouted swinging the lantern around towards the place the noise had come from.

"Your ghost!" the old woman's voice laughed as we all sucked in our breaths in one huge gasp.

There in front of us in the radiance of the lantern's light was a glowing ball illuminating the wall of the shed. Lynn and I held tight to one another and I noticed Gloria had Bud by the arm.

"What is it?" Bud asked.

"Ooooh!" Little Deer guffawed as the light became misshapen and began to slide down the wall.

Bang! Outside, Kate pounded on the shed door. Little Deer opened the door and Kate fell in and landed in the dirt. "Ugh!" she moaned. Bud and Jesse were over at the wall scraping the black goop from the wooden siding. Bud turned towards us with the stuff all over his hands. "We should have guessed this," he said shaking his head. "We were so full of ghost stories and spirits we couldn't see what was so logical. What is this stuff?"

"Potash and phosphorus; it's all over these swamps. Just minerals mixed with the methane gases from the swamp. Add a little moonlight or artificial light and KHAZAM, ghosts!" Little Deer explained.

"I can't believe I didn't see that at the medium's last night. Remember Cally, the shimmery glow around her?" Jesse asked me. "Jasper used to laugh about how his aunt's used some kind of glowing minerals. They pour the liquid in one of them little spray bottles that ladies use for perfume, hide them up their sleeve and when the time is right, instant spirits in a candle's light. She used one of the oldest tricks in the book on us, Cally."

"Well, that explains the lights in the beginning, but it wasn't no spray bottle caused that light to come from outside and that last voice. No way was any of that fake. For crying out loud, Jesse, the woman fainted dead away from fright," I said.

"That goo explains the lights, but I'd like to know about those strange sounds people say they have heard when the lights appear and what Cally and Jesse heard last night too." Bud said.

"Yeehaw, Opa, Ke-hay-ke!" Little Deer shrugged. Then seeing our confusion she said, "A wild animal, the coo-wa-chobee maybe, or a bird." She smiled, "Perhaps the very wild imagination of a bunch of young people. Who's to say? It may be something else, something unexplainable. In this woods there are very strong connections to the other side, be it black magic, sorcery, or spiritists doing the practices. It can be very powerful, but also very unpredictable and not something to go into lightly, like children playing with Ouija boards and the like."

I swallowed hard.

Bud laughed rolling a ball of the black goop in his hands, "Well, for now we're just going to concentrate on giving Robert and company a night they will never forget. Come on, we have some plans to make. I think we need Larry and Bill's help if you don't mind, Jesse."

"Go ahead, why not?" Jesse shrugged.

"I tell you what," Little Deer said, "You children come back after your big plans and have dinner with me. I will make a feast fit for my young warriors."

"Maybe we can look at your Indian dolls then," Lynn grinned eagerly.

"Yes, that would be my great pleasure. You come for dinner and I promise you can look at the dolls to your heart's content," she patted Lynn on the shoulder.

"Bud, I'm not sure this is a good idea us coming back here later if those boys are out hunting some panther," Kate grumbled as she followed Bud outside. "And, let's just talk about that panther for a moment. Don't they eat meat?"

"Holy smoke!" I said, stepping back towards the front stoop causing

Lynn to knock into me.

"Watch out, Cally," Lynn caught hold of my shoulders trying not to fall over top of me.

My mouth fell slack-jawed, almost as wide as my stare as I stood facing the clothesline near the big black cauldron. There hanging out to dry, its sky blue finery shimmering in the bright sunlight, was a bed jacket exactly like Miss Dulsey Mae Stoner's.

With Little Deer beside her, Lynn must have followed my gaze because she let out with a snort that sent spit down her throat causing her to choke and gasp a resounding, "Oh MY LORD!"

Little Deer seeing what we were staring at, walked over to the jacket, touching its silky material, quite proud of her last gift from the big red dog. "It's a real beauty isn't it? It will make a fine Indian princess' robe don't you think?"

"But...!" Lynn started as I turned glaring daggers at her.

Hastily, I went to the clothesline, removing the now dry garment from the line. After inspecting the tag, which was in French, I knew for sure where it came from. "Little Deer, you can't possibly be thinking of cutting up this fine garment," I said.

"Well, finally you're using your head," Lynn mumbled.

I turned holding the jacket next to Little Deer. "I think you should keep this one for yourself."

"Cally?" Lynn squawked.

"You are so kind to the children, making all those fine dolls, and you take care of the animals, I think you should keep this as sort of a reward. It would be sinful to cut up such a beautiful, and I might say, expensive jacket. I'm sure you deserve it much more than the snooty old rich woman who owned it," I pleaded, delighted at the whole idea.

"Just exactly how would you know anything about who owned that jacket Cally?" Kate asked. "What aren't you telling us?"

"I didn't say I knew anything about the previous owner. We'll never know for sure who that was. That crazy dog is the only one could tell us for sure," I said trying to avoid Lynn's icy stare.

"I think Cally's right, Little Deer. You keep it," Bud said. "You deserve it."

Lynn gave out with a big sigh turning away disgusted by it all.

"I suppose you're right, Cally," Little Deer decided. "It would be a shame to cut up such a beautiful jacket. I shall keep it and wear it only for special occasions, such as our dinner tonight."

I could hardly contain my satisfaction with her decision. A little pang of guilt ran through me remembering how Miss Stoner's son had given it to her, but the feeling didn't last long. She could have one hundred of those jackets if she wanted.

Lynn wouldn't talk to me on our way back to the county road. She kept ahead of everyone. Kate wanted to know what Lynn's hurry was, but she didn't answer and just kept to the path. Kate gave me that look again, the one that said I know you're behind this Cally and I'll find out sooner or later.

By the time we reached the Ellich's, Bud told us to go on back home and he'd meet up with us later. "Kate, better tell Mom about our invite to Little Deer's for dinner."

"Like that's going to go over real big," Kate grumbled.

"She won't mind as long as I'm with you and I'm bringing Larry and Bill along too. I'll need their help to scare those boys off," Bud said crossing the road over to the Ellich's place.

"That should make your night, Kate," I told my sister.

"What?" she asked.

"Larry and Billy boy are coming too," I teased.

Kate tried to hide her smile by acting like she could care less. "Like that's such a big deal," she said.

She and Gloria walked ahead and talked real low, laughing over some little secret passed between them. I knew they were talking about Larry and Bill. Kate and Lynn had crushes on Bud's friends ever since they met and I couldn't much blame them. They were handsome boys. I thought Larry was really dreamy looking with his blonde hair and really nice smile. I'd had a huge crush on him since I could remember. I, of course, was just the little half-pint to those guys, but a kid could dream couldn't she?

Colleen Affeld

19 CHAPTER

"Your brother better hurry up. What time were you kids supposed to be out at Little Deer's cottage for supper?" Mom asked, as I watched out the picture window in the living room for Bud. I shrugged back at her, wishing I would just see some sign of him. He wouldn't forget. This was way too important. He, Larry, and Bill probably just got caught up in something over at the Ellich's garage. They were always messing with their cars, changing plugs or whatever. "Shop talk" they called it. I hoped he came soon before Mom and Dad decided we shouldn't go. They had hesitated a little when Kate told them about it. "How on earth did you kids meet an Indian woman? What does she do out there? What kind of place does she live in? Is it safe out there?" I was certain it was the fact that Bud and the boys would be coming along that persuaded them to agree to let us go.

Kate, Lynn, and Gloria came from Kate's room. They had been back there for at least an hour. I had to admit all that time had transformed them into much older looking teenagers. Kate had on an outfit I was sure Gloria had let her borrow for the evening. It was definitely city-bought designer goods. Kate looked great and she knew it. I saw Mom's raised eyebrows when she saw Kate was wearing more makeup than the usual, but she never said a word, just told them how very nice they looked. She and Dad exchanged looks, but he went back to reading his paper in the orange recliner. Hearing the crunching of a car pulling onto the shell driveway, I ran to the window and watched as Bud and his friends climbed out of Larry's car. Walking by the front window, Larry smashed his lips and nose against the glass.

"Now that's attractive," Kate smirked.

"Now I know how all those marks keep getting on the front window, Kathryn," Dad called over the newspaper.

"Where in the heck have you guys been?" I said as they trooped in.

"Whoa half-pint, is that any way to greet your favorite guy?" Larry asked as Bud headed back to change his clothes.

I felt my face turn fifty shades of red.

"I was afraid you all got tied up at the garage or took off somewhere and forgot," I said.

"No way are we missing out on this," Bill said. Then he bent down and whispered so my Dad couldn't hear, "I can't wait to scare them boys from here clear over to Seville." Then he winked at me and we exchanged smiles as he walked over and began to make over the girls which thrilled them to no end. I wondered if Bill liked Kate just a little. I thought he did, but it would be useless because Bud wouldn't let his friends ask out his sisters. "I know those guys a little too well and they're just a little too wild for my sisters," he told mom one night after she told him she thought Kate had a crush on Bill.

"Is everybody ready?" Bud said joining the rest of us.

We all piled in Larry's car like a bunch of sardines. Bill rode shotgun with Lynn between him and Larry. As the car rolled out of the drive onto Garfield Street, Bill rolled down his window and banged on the roof, "Yee haw!" he cried out in a big rebel yell. "Look out you little sissy boys, 'cause here we come!"

"What exactly have you boys got planned?" Gloria asked. "Is it legal?"

"Just some harmless fun is all," Bill told her.

"Wait until we show y'all," Larry said. "We set up a sure fire cure for some meddlesome wanna be, big game hunters."

Seminole Landing

"I told Jesse we'd pick him up over by the Landing," Bud said.

"And just where do you think you're going to put him Bud?" Kate squirmed in her cramped seat.

"I thought you and me would just climb in the trunk there Katie, honey," Bill told Kate. She sunk in her seat, probably wishing she could crawl under it.

"In your dreams, you big pervert," she said sticking out her tongue.

Bill grabbed over his heart, "Oh you cut me deep, Kate!"

Everyone found this all very amusing except Kate, who pretended to hate it. I could never understand all the silly games between older girls and boys. For crying out loud if they liked each other why didn't they say so? They sure did waste a lot of time. It was such a bunch of baloney, Kate acting like she didn't like all the attention. I mean come on, Patty and I read in her diary about how cute she thought Bill was. Of course, I couldn't let on I'd read it or she'd "Torture me slowly," as she'd said if I ever looked at it. Mom said she was just being coy. Said if you were too eager it would scare a boy off. She was just being Kate, I thought.

Jesse was waiting like Bud said by our hollowed out oak near the remains of the burned out house.

"Looks like you have to sit on Kate's or my lap half-pint," Bud said. Kate shoved me towards my brother, "No thanks, I don't want her bony rear-end on my lap, it hurts." So I climbed on over to my brother and Jesse crawled in the backseat.

"Ready to rumble, Jesse?" Bill greeted him.

"Yeh man!" Jesse answered with a big grin plastered across his face.

"Bud, I'm still not convinced that any of us should be going out near that swamp with those boys running around with guns," Kate said.

"Oh Kate, for crying out loud, we'll be fine," I rolled my eyes.

Bud patted her hand patronizingly, "Kate, you worry too much. It will be okay."

"Well, short of a suit of armor, how do you plan to avoid a stray bullet from some trigger- happy kid, Bud?"

Snap! A sound came from up in the front seat. WHOOO! WHOOO! "Gosh Almighty, what is that?" I said. The awful sound mixed with roaring laughter, Jesse's the loudest of all. I held my ears.

Bill held up a tape recorder that kept screaming that awful noise.

"Shut that thing off! You nearly gave us all heart attacks," Kate smacked Bill from across the seat.

"Success! That's exactly the reaction I was looking for," Bill said snapping off the recorder. "Those boys will high tail it and be long gone when I crank this baby up."

"Yeah, I can't wait to see their faces, especially Robert Lee's," I laughed.

"We'll tell you all about it, when we get back to Little Deer's place," Bud whispered in my ear.

"What do you mean tell me all about it?" I sat up.

"Ouch! You do have a bony butt," Bud hollered as I spun around looking him in the eyes.

"Bud, I thought I was going to get to help," I said. I wanted in and I intended to be there.

"No way Cally, you could get hurt and we'd never forgive ourselves. What would life be without you to harass and tease?" Larry said from the driver's seat, trying to make light of the whole unfair plan.

"You will go to Little Deer's with Kate, Gloria, and Lynn where you're sure to be safe. I can't let you do this, Cally," Bud said firmly.

My neck was red hot and I felt like yelling at somebody, anybody, but I knew it would be hopeless by the tone in Bud's voice. He could be stubborn as Kate some times. It took all the control I could muster, but I just kept all the yelling bunched up inside me. I felt like I might explode. "We'll see," I thought.

Larry pulled the car up along side the county road.

"I think we'd better try and pull back in the path a ways, Larry, just in case somebody comes snooping around," Bud said. "The sand is pretty packed for the first few yards." Larry pulled the car towards the narrow walking path. Low bushes and scrub brush scraped against the bottom and sides of his car, as he pulled it off the blacktop and into the woods. "Somebody's going to do an awful lot of buffing if I get scratches all over my new paint job," Larry complained.

"Just don't get stuck," Kate said.

Bud leaned forward, nearly crushing me against the front seat. "Over there," he pointed to a hidden spot, behind a stand of pines. As the car came to a halt, everyone piled out of our sardine can. Larry opened up the trunk displaying all sorts of things the boys had piled in there to carry out their trap.

Us girls immediately grabbed our noses, "What is that awful stench," Kate said backing away from the trunk. Bill pulled out a bucket filled with that black goo from the swamp. "Here's the culprit," Bill said.

"Man, my car is never going to smell the same again, Whew Whee!" Larry choked. "You can carry that stuff," he told Bill.

We each took something to carry back to the place the guys had set for Robert and his friends. I carried two big spotlights I recognized from Dad's shop. He used them at night while he built our house. They looked like giant flashlights sitting on top of a

big red and blue box battery. Jesse ran up beside me carrying none other than the scarecrow me and Lynn made for our garden. "Hey, what do you think you are going to do with Old McDonald?" I said.

"That's what the goo is for Cally. We're going to cover it with the glowing stuff and put some on its face for eyes. We'll have ourselves an honest to goodness spook," Jesse said.

"Dad's going to skin you if he gets tore up," I warned.

"Is this everything?" Lynn asked, holding a coiled up rope.

"Yeh," Larry said, "everything else is already at the spot."

Dusk was getting ready to set in and we hurried along the path as fast as we could, loaded down with everything. I noticed Kate and Gloria went empty handed. They couldn't be bothered carrying dirty ropes or buckets of mud and ruin their look. Seemed they had a trap of their own, a man trap. They were so funny holding onto each other's arms and tiptoeing along like they might step on some hidden creature.

"Bob-white, bob-white," the tiny birds called from across the hanging limbs above us. Kate and Gloria's pace picked up with every rustle of a mother squirrel or chipmunk rushing about picking up supper for their babies. When we got to the mossy, canopied curve in the path, where daylight became night, Bud moved ahead of us all. "Follow me carefully so you don't walk into our fishing line."

"Fishing Line... You didn't?" I laughed.

"Yes we did and it will be almost as good as the last time," Bud laughed remembering one night last fall. We caught pure heck that night, but it was worth it...

Bud went to school with a girl by the name of Clara Webb. The Webbs were also members of the Methodist Church where we went most Sundays. Clara's mother was the biggest gossip in DeLeon. Why she made everybody's business hers, sticking her nose right in the middle of everything. It was a wonder it hadn't got worn clean off her face. To make matters worse, and to the distress of all the high school kids, Mrs. Webb was employed at the high school as an aide. She'd broken up more romances than the Hatfields and McCoys, not with shotguns, but with her flapping gums. Somehow she always managed to be at the wrong place at the wrong time, catching couples swapping spit between classes or after a football game out in the parking lot. Connie said Mr. Webb probably didn't pay much attention to her so she couldn't stand to see anybody else enjoying the company of the opposite sex either. Anyway, one night after the DeLeon High football game, which we won, all the kids were feeling especially excited. This tends to provoke lots of kissing and stuff with the high school kids especially the football players and their dates. Bud had just came out of the locker room, all clean and ready for a date with this girl by the name of Bette Davis, not the movie star of course. Well that Bette, being a girl without a lot of class and not able to control herself in the presence of handsome boys, came right up and laid a big old kiss on Bud. It was one of those wrong places at the wrong time, because Mrs. Webb just happened to be standing there, too. Bud was mortified when he heard the busy body gasp and she said, "Bud Cummins, you should be ashamed of yourself, carrying on right here in public, in front of God and everyone." With that she turned and marched off to her car. Bud knew exactly what Mrs. Webb would do next, and sure enough when he got home later Mom told him, "Bud I got a strange phone call from Clarece Webb tonight. Said she would stop by tomorrow evening to speak to your father and I regarding our son. You wouldn't happen to know what that's all about would you?"

"Not a clue, Mom," Bud said. Then he got a sly smile on his face, "You know Mom tomorrow is Halloween. It's no big surprise Clarece Webb will be out. What time is her broom due in?"

"Bud!" Mom acted like she was shocked, but I caught a curl to her lips as she turned her head. "Mrs. Webb said she'll be by around eight o'clock when all the trick-or-treaters were done."

"By the way Bud, speaking of Halloween, your dad wants you to put something across the new grass he seeded in the front of the porch. Maybe put some line with red strips of rag tied to it so kids will keep off the area, and come up the drive instead of cutting across the lawn," Mom said.

"No problem Mom, I'll take care of it. Maybe add some garlic to keep Mrs. Webb back, too," he added, quickly kissing Mom's cheek heading off to bed leaving her standing there shaking her head.

I didn't know what Dad was so worried about; we didn't get that many trick-or-treaters, at least not like Mandarin Villas, where there were lots of houses close together. That's where Lynn and I headed and always got the most candy.

Halloween night, Lynn and I had been through Mandarin Villas and all points between here and there, our bags brimming over with great treats. When we came up the drive I noticed Bud's fishing line blockade was still up with a couple red pieces of cloth dangling to stop any would be seed stompers. Trick-or-Treat time was about over and it was pretty much just some big kids left roaming the streets, mostly playing tricks and causing havoc across town. Lynn and me had seen a group of them hanging around down by the stop sign on the corner, so we decided we'd better get home before they stole our candy or something. I could smell the wonderful smells of caramel bubbling in the kitchen as Mom and Kate whipped up more popcorn balls and candy apples for us. The trick-or-treaters had taken the last from the plate Mom had by the front door. I went in and changed my clothes and washed up for bed. While I was in the bathroom I thought I heard some giggling out in the yard. When I opened the frosted glass I didn't see anyone under the light of the big harvest moon in the sky. Then I spotted a big mess on the end of the porch. "Oh man, somebody smashed our two pumpkins. Darn them big kids anyway." Car headlights turned into our drive. I shut the window and ran out to see who it was.

"Somebody is coming up the drive Kathryn," Dad called from the living room. Dad stood staring out the front picture window. He checked his watch, "It's Mrs. Webb. A little late isn't she?"

"Dad, you forget it's Halloween, she's been busy," I laughed. Dad winked.

"That's enough, Cally. Behave," Mom groaned going to the door and opening it. I stood there with Mom watching as the woman got out of her car. I swear she was always wearing that green dress with the high button front and little white starched collar choking her fat neck, so prim and proper. She looked like the Old Maid on my playing cards. Mrs. Webb looked up towards the door and saw Mom and me standing there and instead of coming up the drive walked straight across the lawn towards the door. She was definitely a woman on a mission. Her head cocked high on her neck, pushing forward, her purse tucked under her arm, she was making a beeline for the porch…I just happened to glance down remembering Bud's blockade. "Oh my Lord," I said with a squeak. Somebody had removed the red rags…Just as I started to open my mouth to warn her…

"YEOWWW!" THUMP! She went down like a ton of bricks. She was sprawled across the lawn, dirt all over her, her green dress flipped up above her waist. Her head rested against the big azalea bush next to the porch. What a sight!

"Oh Dear God!," Mom shrieked as Dad ran from the window, both of them passing me by as I stood with my hands clasped tight over my mouth trying not to laugh out loud. Dad grabbed the woman up, all the while her screeching and hollering some language I'd heard a few times coming from the garage when Dad was working on the car and things weren't going quite right. Why, I had no idea such an uppity busy body knew them kind of words, let alone used them. Dad up righted the disheveled woman, who yanked at her dress pulling it back down over her large rear end. Mom tried brushing her off best she could, but quickly stepped back holding her nose. The woman's face was covered with the manure Dad had spread around the azaleas. She was able to stand up on her own and seemed to be okay, at least physically. She was so discombobulated and humiliated she just grabbed up her purse and stormed off to her car. "I will call you about the matter tomorrow, Kathryn," she spouted.

"Bud!" Dad bellowed.

Bud had been in his room, but hearing all the excitement had come to the front door and witnessed the disaster.

"I swear Dad, there were two red flags tied on that line. There!" he pointed to the churned up dirt. There lying on the ground were the two flags. "Somebody took them off, I swear they were on there good and tight," Bud defended himself.

It must have been them kids that smashed the pumpkins earlier," I said helping Bud's defense.

"Everyone just get in the house!" Dad steamed.

"Now Will, it was an accident," Mom tried to calm him.

"Yeh, the biddy will probably sue us over this," he said.

We did as Dad said and went back to our bedrooms, bursting into silent giggles as we hit the hallway. I hoped Dad wouldn't be too mad at Bud; after all, he had tied up the rags. It was an accident. After a while when the house got all quiet I heard Mom and Dad's bedroom door shut to Dad's deep roaring laughter and Mom's soft giggles.

Tonight, Bud and the other boys had the fishing line strung from a lone, tall pine near a thicket of kudzu vine, running it across the path where the other end was wrapped tightly around a moss covered Oak. So as not to repeat Clarece Webb's accident, Bud guided us around it. "Y'all girls go on back a little ways further and you'll run right into Little Deer's cottage. Cally can lead the way. Us guys will stay here and finish getting all this stuff ready for our guests," Bud told us stepping off the path to let us pass.

"You be real careful, you hear?" Kate said as Gloria gave him a hug whispering some sweet nothings in his ear. I wasn't too darn happy about not being there to see Robert Lee get his dues.

We could smell the cottage before we could see it. The aroma was enough to make my mouth water.

"Something smells wonderful," Gloria sniffed at the air.

Little Deer must have been watching for us, because before we even reached the front of her place the door opened and she greeted us with a big smile, "Come in, come in!" She was wearing the bed-jacket over a lovely floor length multi-colored skirt with a wide ruffle at its bottom. Her sparkling eyes and her silver strands mixing in with her once black hair shown radiant against the sky blue of the jacket.

"You look beautiful," I said hugging her. "I hope the boys won't be long, 'cause I'm starving," I told her.

"Cally!" Kate said giving me one of her looks.

Little Deer's table was set with dishes the color of the red clay and a vial the same color held a bouquet of fresh yellow and blue wild flowers. The wood stove was overflowing with pots and pans filled with good smelling things. My stomach grumbled.

"What is all this delicious looking food?" Gloria asked craning her head over one pot with some unknown yellowish, white substance simmering. Little Deer happily pointed out each dish for the evening's meal. The simmering pot contained something called Sofkee, or roasted corn soup made of hominy. Another delicious smelling concoction was Taal-holelke, or boiled swamp cabbage. "I use only the white, tender heart of the palm," Little Deer said with pride. There was sweet potatoes and summer squash and fry bread made with fresh pumpkin. "Hiyo," she smiled and explained, "All this from the bounty of my own late, spring harvest."

"I'm with Cally," Lynn rubbed her stomach, "I'm starved."

Little Deer laughed and quickly brought out a plate she had setting on top of the stove. "Have a piece of fry bread while we wait," she offered. We all, including Kate, hurried to get a piece of the warm bread. The only sounds heard now were the delicate crunches as our teeth sunk into the crispy cinnamon sugar outer shell covering the soft middle of the warm bread inside. Nothing but, "MMM's" and "AHHH's" followed.

"After you have your bread I thought it would be a good time for each of you to choose a doll from my trunk," Little Deer told us.

"Oh yes," Lynn beamed, shoving the rest of her bread in her mouth. She looked like a darn chipmunk, her cheeks bulging.

"Being as I already got to pick one, I think I'll just go sit on the porch and wait on the boys if that's alright with you," I said.

"Don't you go anywhere else, Cally," Kate ordered. I could tell she was more concerned with a doll than me at the moment. It took her forever to make up her mind on the slightest little thing. This would give me plenty of time I thought slipping out the door.

The evening had moved in pretty fast and it was a warm one. Fourth of July was coming up next week and it was definitely going to be steamy. The night was still and the air hung heavy as the bathroom after Kate took her usual twenty minute shower. I peeked in the windows. Kate, Gloria, and Lynn sorted through the trunk, admiring each doll they picked up. The hard weathered lines of Little Deer's face seemed to have vanished and with dancing eyes she looked on with delight. Something stirred in the cabbage palm and red fern on the edge of the clearing. I listened; it was probably just a squirrel or bird. A low purring and squeaking sound brought me to full attention… "Coo-wah-choobee?" I said softly. My heart began to race. Straining my eyes over the streams of moonlight melting over the forest I made out just a glimpse of a long tail disappearing through the bushes, leading to the path behind the cottage.

"No. Coo-wa-chobee not that way…"

Checking inside, everyone still huddled over the dolls. I had to stop the cat from walking right into the sight on Robert Lee's shotgun. Trying to think of something, I ran to the feeding area. Maybe there would be some scrap to entice the cat back towards the cottage. My nose discovered the piece of meat first, the stench causing my stomach to turn. No time for squeamish stomachs now, I thought picking up the scrap and running towards the path. Where was the cat? The further down the path I went, faint voices carried across the light breeze. It was Robert and the other boys. Slowing my pace down, I stooped low so as to stay hidden by the thick lower bushes and weeds. There, crouched behind a dead tree that had fallen, I spotted the back of my brother's head. Slipping into the woods, I stood behind a thick Magnolia's trunk.

"Get ready, here they come," I heard Bud whisper to someone close by.

"I'm telling you this is a crazy idea, coming out here in the dark," I recognized Tommy Cox's voice. "How are we supposed to find that panther anyhow, and how do you know for sure this is where he'll be? These woods are big and it's mostly swamp out here."

"He's out here," Robert said. "The hunting's been slim pickings out here lately, that's how I know where that four-legged devil is. Plus, I got a sure-fire way of bringing him out."

"What's that?" Carl asked him.

They had rounded the curve and were standing in the small clearing in front of me now. I lay down on my belly peering through the bare undergrowth of bushes. Robert held out a sack, waving it in front of Carl and Tommy. "This here ought to about do it," he told them.

"Jeez!" Carl and Tommy both bellowed waving the sack away.

"It stinks worse than Carl's old sneakers, like something died or something," Tommy said.

"Yeh Man, close that thing up. All you're going to attract with that are flies," Carl started gagging. I thought he might just puke his guts up right then and there. I could actually smell it too… "Ugh!" It wasn't that at all. I threw down the rotten piece of meat in my hand and wiped my hands off in the dirt.

Robert took the sack and sat it right in the middle of the clearing. "We'll just lay this right here and wait."

"That's it! That's all we're going to do, sit here in the woods and wait? I could be home eating chips and dip watching…"

"Oh, shut up Carl, you sound like my Grandma complaining," Robert taunted him and with that walked over to a spot under the tall pines propping his shot gun against a tree, sitting down to wait. Carl and Tommy followed.

"Hey, anybody know any good ghost stories?" Tommy asked.

"Oh yeh right! We're sitting out here in the swamp near where they say that old witch lives, not to mention the fact we're real close to Seminole Landing, the land of spooks and spirits, and you want to tell ghost stories?" Carl said.

"Oh, come on sissy boy, you don't actually believe in all that stuff do you?" Tommy asked giving Carl a little shove.

"Hey! Don't go shoving me," Carl told him. "I suppose you don't believe it. That's why you go out of your way to go clear over past the school to Amelia Street and all the way back down to your place, instead of coming down the county road or Garfield after dark? Who's the sissy boy now, Tommy?"

Robert and Carl laughed and taunted Tommy until he got to his feet, hands on his hips trying to look tough. "Why I ought to knock you both into next week. Ya'll two hush up or your sure to scare the cat away if it is around here."

Shoot, I was hoping to see Tommy Cox plant a good one-two punch on Robert Lee.

The boys settled back down and then they waited. We all did. It was real quiet, too quiet. I was afraid they might hear me or one of the others breathing or something. "Bob-white… Bob-white."

I shivered, chills rushing through me, as the night bird called out its name from the tree branch above me. My heart raced afraid someone else heard me, gasp. No one seemed to have taken notice. Moonlight filled the cracks between the trees. Little pools of light scattered across the ground. I nearly began laughing out loud when I saw someone's handy work sculpted on a thick pine behind Robert. The tree's trunk looked like it had two eyes and a hideous looking wide open mouth with white illuminated fangs protruding from it. A wild turkey called from somewhere near the swamp canal. Boys' heads bobbed from underneath the tree. Again, I heard the call. I knew that call. It wasn't any wild turkey, it was Larry. He could coax a covey of quail right out of the bush with his bird calls. The boys always came home with a fine meal of fresh game when Larry went along.

"What's that?" Carl asked.

"It's just a turkey."

I smiled at Tommy's answer.

The forest became a concert of various bird calls and the bushes stirred around us. Robert, Carl, and Tommy were now on their feet, shotguns in hand. I was glad I knew exactly where Bud was. The noise grew louder.

WHOO! WHOOO! WHOOO!

I froze. That wasn't any bird.

The noise had come from my left. I relaxed slightly. It must be Bill's tape recorder.

"That ain't no cat. What is it?" Tommy cried. There was a scurrying around as the three boys stood back to back each peering out in a different direction.

Again a faint WHOO came from the path on the opposite side of the clearing from us.

Very clever, I thought. Make them feel like they're surrounded. I wondered how Bill moved so quickly without being heard. But, then back to my left came a gosh-awful screeching and carrying on, enough to make your blood curdle and a wash of bright light scattered across the ground at the boy's feet. I watched Robert as he followed the light's upward sweep, his eyes wild as he saw what I now saw. There hanging from the treetops was Old McDonald swinging hideously, in the light breeze. Again, Bill's voice came, as he spoke in deep bass tones, "Coo-wa-chobeeeee..." the sound lingering, eerie and haunting.

Robert lifted his gun, swinging the barrel in one direction then the other, "Come on!" he hollered. The other two boys stood behind him guns to their sides, eyes wide. Robert tightened on his grip and all at once...

CRACK! A shot rang through the night, accompanied by a flash of orange-red. I closed my eyes and held my breath. Bark and limb dropped to the ground from the tree tops. Glancing upward my heart gave a leap as I spotted Jesse straddling a branch covered limb above, the scarecrow still dangling close by him. This time Robert pointed his gun upward.

"NO!" I strained to the night.

BLAM! Another shot fired off. Something fell into the brush below. I was afraid to look. Slowly opening my squinted eyes, I gazed up. My stomach dropped from my throat. Jesse was thankfully still lying across the limb unharmed, but Old McDonald was missing his lower half.

"What the...?" I whispered, as a blur of tan fur brushed so close by me I could have reached out and touched Coo-wa-chobee. The cat was quicker than our neighbor, Mr. Parton's, old red rooster after his hens. The cat was running straight for Robert. Robert caught the sleek movement and started to turn towards her, his shotgun cocked and beaded right in at the beautiful, graceful animal. All heck was breaking loose! I watched; hand over my mouth, as Robert met the fishing line fast and furious with Carl and Tommy right behind him.

"UMPH!" Robert flipped in the air. I caught his shotgun's flight as it left his grip; the barrel pointed directly towards the spot Bud lay, behind some bramble at the base of a tall oak.

CRACK!!

Buckshot blasted again; a fireball against the darkness. Coo-wa-chobee fled to the bush. I wanted to call out to see if anyone was on the blast's receiving end. Robert lay sprawled on the ground, eating dirt with Tommy and Carl toppled right over him. By the looks on their faces I'd say they whole-heartedly believed that Satan himself had just snatched them up by their hides. Scrambling to their feet they searched for their guns. The line must have broke on impact cause they stood squawking and staring at the ground, their fearful faces showing they had no idea what trap they had just fallen into.

"I'm out of here!" Carl said dusting himself off. "You stay here and catch that cat if you want. These woods are filled with evil."

"Go ahead, you sissy. Me and Tommy will catch him," Robert said.

I swear that boy was stubborn as they come.

"You're on your own, Robert," Tommy said picking up his gun.

"Well, go ahead! Get on out of here, the both of you," Robert's voice trembled.

Carl cried out pointing behind Robert, "Look out!" Robert spun around to see Coo-wa-chobee moving from the thick cover of kudzu, the cat's amber eyes fixed on Robert. It was as if the crazy cat was daring that darn fool to take another shot. All that was left of Carl and Tommy was their backsides rounding the curve, heading back to the county road. Robert slowly raised his shotgun and I saw Bud move from behind the tree. I started to call out to tell him to get himself back behind the tree when there came a shuffling and crackling of heavy footsteps from the bushes behind Robert. All at once, like some unforeseen lightning strike, he came; not agile and sleek, like the Coo-wa-chobee, but thundering and clumsy. I never heard or seen such a ruckus in my days.

"WOO! WOO! WOO!" cried the bulky man, limping from the weeds, spewing his loud ear shattering cries. It sounded like a freight train jumping its track. Shuffleboard stick and all was moving towards Robert. Fear froze me in place. I wanted to scream or run or something, but I couldn't move a single muscle. This wasn't going to be good.

Kate says I compare everyone to movie stars or cartoon characters, and I swear the Woo Woo man was spinning and swirling, a cloud of sand, dirt and wind, just like that Tasmanian devil. Robert didn't know what had him as the iron fist came clamping down, tight on his shoulder, spinning him around until face to face with the powerful man. Dropping his gun, Robert went down hard, sprawling backwards; staring up into the Woo Woo man's wild eyes, eyes double daring Robert to make one false move. In all the commotion the spooked panther sprung into motion, darting back into the bush, but not before turning his glowing, angry gaze on Robert.

"ROAR!" The panther gave out with a deep, primal warning, a growl, the kind cats give when they are about to fight. It was a warning to Robert, or to anyone who might bring harm to the boy, Jesse. It was amazing. A pine cone fell from the tree where Jesse lie dangling causing Mr. Woo Woo to look upward. Robert seized this opportunity, scrambling to his feet, making a run for it. I never seen him run so fast as he did right now, disappearing down the path hollering and raving, arms thrashing about, propellers in the wind. The Woo Woo man's entrance didn't hold a candle to Robert's exit, a lunatic, escaping. I put my attention back to the Woo Woo man. What in the Sam Hill? He stood there in the moonlight all puffed up like one of them wrestler fellas on television. A rustling and crackling came from the woods around me and I watched as Bud and the others came slowly out of their hiding places. Bark snapped and floated to the ground as Jesse shimmied down the pine. I didn't move. I wasn't crazy. What could they be thinking showing themselves like this? Why that big puffed up man was so crazed right now, he could take them all down in one maniacal charge. One, two, three, they're out; I could hear the wrestling announcer ring the bell. I kept my eyes on Woo Woo. Naturally startled by the four boys, he crouched down turning towards one then the other, ready to either charge or dart away, like a trapped animal. Bud raised his hand in the air with a gesture of peace. It was just like when the white man and Indian meet in the movies. For crying out, who did he think he was Kimosabee?

"Don't be afraid," Bud broke the awkward silence.

Who was he kidding? Bud was the one that was scared half to death. I could hear it in his shaky voice. The Woo Woo man stepped back, standing his ground, his shuffleboard stick at his side like a sword.

"We aren't with those boys," Bud told him. "We were trying to stop them from hurting the big cat. We were waiting on them."

What was my brother doing? Woo Woo doesn't understand him. All at once the man tilted his head, as if studying Bud, but still he didn't flinch. Maybe he did understand.

Bud went on, "We were going to have dinner with Little Deer, our friend."

At the mention of Little Deer's name, Mr. Woo Woo poked his stick towards the path led back to the cottage. No one moved. A grunting noise came from inside him. Sounded as if he said, "Go." He waved and pointed the stick at the path again. "Go!" Yes, I was sure that is what he had said.

One by one, Bud and the others turned towards the cottage, obviously not wanting to aggravate the man any more. Every time one of them nervously glanced back towards Woo Woo, he'd give out with his grunt and they would quickly turn back around. Creeping back behind the cabbage palm's thick fronds waiting for them to pass by, my heart nearly beat out of my chest as the shuffleboard stick welding man came to a stop right in front of me. Closing my eyes tight, I waited to be discovered, praying to myself, "Just make it quick, Lord." The footsteps started up again moving away from me. I took a breath. Slowly opening my eyes, I watched as the boys and their captor went down the path, out of sight, and into the darkness.

"WHOO!" The sound sent a rush of panic right to my core. Oh, thank the Lord it was just an owl calling out near the swamp. I was alone out here…in the dark…near the swamp. Something shook the bushes and a stick snapped behind me. I felt if I didn't get up and run at this very moment, I might be swallowed up by some unknown swamp creature, the creature from the Black Lagoon. "That's it!" I bolted. With every step I felt like something might reach out of the trees and grab me. I wanted to fly, but had to be careful not to run up on the others. Who was I kidding now? At this moment I probably could run up on them, pass them and be in Little Deer's place before they knew what in the Sam heck it was flashing by them. My panic lightened as I caught the soft glow of Little Deer's cottage just up ahead. Warm and inviting, the cottage light guided me. The yummy smells wafting from her fine dinner made me realize just how hungry all this craziness had made me.

Reaching the clearing, I carefully slipped behind an oak when I saw Bud and the others being hustled inside Little Deer's front door by Mr. Woo Woo. Kate's face in the window of the cottage told me I had been missed. The only thing I regretted about not being with Bud and the others is that I'd miss the look on Kate's face when she laid eyes on the Woo Woo man. Where was my Brownie camera when I needed it? I sure hoped we had our facts straight about the Woo Woo man being truly just poor misunderstood Curtis Malcolm and not some crazed, squirrel eating, loony, maniac killer. The door closed and the face disappeared from the window. Listening for screams, nothing came, but a strange silence. This was a little too weird. No whooping and hollering, nothing. Taking a deep breath I moved to outside the cottage door, listening. People were shuffling about and Little Deer's calm voice spoke. I couldn't make out what she was saying. Not able to contain my curiosity any longer I turned the handle on the door. Taking a deep breath, I prepared myself for what was to come.

"Cally Cummins, where have you been?" Kate yelled from across the room. Instantly, all eyes were upon me and Mr. Curtis Malcolm had that wrestler look again. He stood there like a banty rooster, moving nervously back and forth. Little Deer moved to him and took his arm, gently. "It's okay Curtis. These young people are our friends. They came to help me out with those pesky boys that have been hunting around here." Curtis, still pacing, didn't seem too convinced. "Calm down, now," Little Deer patted his arm, taking hold of it, moving him towards the dinner table. "See they have come to join us for dinner," she motioned to the fine looking display of food on the table.

Lynn, standing beside the dinner table, picked up the plate of fry bread and moved cautiously towards the nervous man. She held out the plate. "Would you like some? It's real good."

All at once, his puffed up face softened as he stared into Lynn's big waif like blue eyes, which made her look younger than her thirteen years. Moving his large calloused hand, that dwarfed the platter, he took the piece of bread Lynn held out to him. Bringing the bread towards his mouth he first sniffed at it then took a nibble. Apparently satisfied with its delicious flavor, he shoved in the rest.

"MMM," he smiled at Lynn.

Jesse had been standing, hidden by the bigger boys. He now moved out into the room, clearing his throat. Mr. Curtis Malcolm turned quickly towards Jesse. By his reaction now, I knew he'd not gotten a good look at Jesse outside in the woods, because upon gazing on him now, in the warm glow inside the cottage, Curtis' face lit up with startling recollection. The hoot owl that sat outside my bedroom window at night is what he resembled now, nearly spinning his head clean around, looking from Jesse, back to Little Deer who still stood by the table…back and forth, back and forth. It's a wonder his neck didn't snap and drop off to the floor it moved so fast. Then, Curtis Malcolm let out with such a mix of sounds; at first it was a joyful cry, then turning chock full of woe, a mournful moaning.

"AHHH! EEEE! OOOH! Ooooooh…" he cried. Moving across the floor like an animal pouncing on his prey, he wrapped his massive arms around a surprised Jesse and held tight. As if not believing what his eyes had just witnessed, he pushed Jesse at arms length away from him, then lifted him up, face to face, staring into Jesse's bugged out eyes, and then almost as quickly, released him.

THUMP! Jesse went to the floor. A chorus of loud gasps shot through the room. All at once the giant wrestler turned away like a frightened child, running and cowering in the corner near the cook stove. It was the strangest thing. What must he be thinking? What did he see in Jesse's eyes? Did he see his twin brother, Caleb, when they were boys? He must be thinking he's looking at a ghost, one of them spirits come back to haunt him from the Landing. We all just stood there like the knots in the hardwood floor, frozen in place. Jesse's eyes were as big as saucers as he collected himself.

"Curtis?" Little Deer bent down beside him taking his face in her hands.

"Curtis, it's alright," she said her voice loving and compassionate. "Curtis, it's not Caleb."

"Ca-leb," the man sobbing quietly said.

Little Deer wiped the tears streaming down his cheek, "Curtis, listen to me. It is not Caleb, but Caleb's son. His name is Jesse. He's your nephew." The old woman turned Curtis' face upward so he could see Jesse. "Look at him, Curtis. It is Caleb's young son." Curtis and Jesse stared into one another's tear filled eyes. Not so much as a mouse scurrying could be heard except the crackling of the fire in the stove, and a little sob came from Lynn's direction. There wasn't a dry eye in the house. At this moment, the Jesse Tate I had known, the independent, I don't need nothin' from nobody, tough- talking boy, was just a young, vulnerable, thirteen- year- old boy. Jesse needed to be held by his only connection to his real identity, Mr. Curtis Malcolm, alias the Woo Woo man.

Little Deer took Curtis' hand and led him slowly towards Jesse. As boy and man met, this time Jesse reached out hugging his uncle. Again, there was a sound, a sound coming straight from Curtis Malcolm's heart, a soothing, joyful sound.

"Ahhhheeee…"

A knot about the size of a hickory nut was in my throat as I held in the aching sobs just waiting to escape. I dare not make a sound. I couldn't. This was Jesse's moment and I didn't want to spoil it with all my blubbering. Jesse had finally made a connection to the life denied him. I knew this moment would be fleeting, as Jesse realized he was showing some emotion in front of God and everybody. I felt deeply for my friend. I cared for him more than I cared to admit to anyone, not even Connie. Just as I figured, Jesse composed himself and pulled himself carefully away, wiped his sleeve across his tear-stained cheeks. Curtis Malcolm brushed the top of Jesse's hair, and then unlike his nephew, unashamed of his emotion, turned facing us all. Tears rolled down his cheeks, but now they were detoured by the curled up corners of the warm smile on his face. An uncomfortable silence filled the room. No one knew exactly what to do or say.

"Well, now," Little Deer broke the awkward quiet. "I think we had better all sit down and eat this meal before its scraps are fit only for the animals."

Everyone was grateful for the interruption and gathered around the table talking and laughing. Nervous energy was bursting all over the room. Looking over at Jesse, I nodded for him to join us. He sighed, red-eyed, still a little shaken by the whole thing, but joined the rest of us at the table.

Little Deer bowed her head as did the rest of us as she gave thanks to, Hilis Haya. Jesse whispered to me, "Hilis Haya, the Creator of Good, the Perfect One."

Mr. Curtis Malcolm sure did have an amazingly healthy appetite. His plate was full one minute, then scarfed down the next, only to be filled up again. This pleased Little Deer as she passed him the platters. I thought he might suffocate; he ate so vigorously, never seeming to stop for a breath. Bud and the guys entertained us with their night's adventure. Seems they had found the whole thing pretty darn funny. I couldn't quite share in the humor of it all, especially when Jesse told how the scarecrow's body went flying through the pines as Robert fired off a load of buckshot. It wouldn't have been too doggone funny had it been parts of Jesse flying through the night, or if Bud had been on the receiving end of the blast as Robert tripped over the fishing line. Expressing my concerns, Bud as usual made me laugh. "Cally, you have to admit you enjoyed seeing Robert sprawled all over the ground."

"You know, Bud," I laughed, "It was pretty funny, but I think the funniest thing was when Curtis here, grabbed Robert by the shoulder. The look on his face…"

"Suppose that stray bullet had found you out there," Kate said missing the humor of it all. "Nobody would have even known you were there. You'd have been dinner for some vulture or hawk tomorrow morning, that is providing some evil spirit from the Landing didn't come take you away first."

My body gave a shiver and Kate ranted on, "You know Cally, one of these days you're really going to get yourself in a mess if you don't stop interfering and going where you got no business going."

Leave it to Kate to sober things up. She was forever mothering me. I tried to shake it, but Kate's warning stuck in my craw and the thought of lying out there alone and hurt, dead maybe, scared the devil out of me. It was really frustrating how she was so sensible. Good thing Patty wasn't here. Lord knows she'd be quoting some scripture about foolish acts or something.

"Kate, you don't actually believe in haunted forests and conjured up ghosts and spirits?" Bill teased, changing the tone the conversation had taken. "Not our sensible Kate?"

Kate's face reddened.

"Don't worry Katie, we'll protect you. Besides the only thing haunting these woods are wild imaginations," Bill said.

I looked at Jesse, "I wouldn't be too sure about that Bill," I said.

Bill gave out with his booming laugh, "You know something we don't half-pint?"

"Don't get her started," Kate mumbled.

It just frosts the heck out of me sometimes when Kate is so darn smug. She had no idea what was out in these woods and I decided to tell her so. "Kate if you'd have seen what me, Jesse, and Connie seen last night you wouldn't be acting so high and mighty. You'd be sitting in your room with the covers up over your head."

"Cally, don't be so juvenile," Kate dismissed me. She was trying to impress Bill with her sophistication. "You read too many of those Nancy Drew mysteries," she said, tossing her hair like one of those prissy girls, batting her eyes.

Jesse spoke up now, his face dead serious, "Cally isn't story-telling. What she seen was real. We not only seen it, we felt it. The feeling was evil. It wasn't anything of this world."

"Oh, not you too, Jesse," Kate scoffed.

"Listen Kate, whatever it was scared the fire out of the Medium too. She fainted dead away. We had to give her smelling salts. You can ask Connie Louise's Grandma Agnes. She seen it too," I said.

"Oh, now, that's a real reliable source," Kate said rolling her eyes. "The woman's eccentric as they come. Even Connie's mother, just tolerates all Agnes' nonsensical talk of the spirit world."

Little Deer, who was busy filling a bowl with more cabbage from the stove interrupted, her brow all creased up with concern, "What exactly did you children see, Cally?"

Now, this was more like it. Someone finally took Jesse and me seriously. I began telling of our visit to Madame Rosemary's, and as I talked Jesse helped fill in anything I'd left out. Little Deer and the others surprisingly listened without interruption. At first they seemed suspicious, but became more and more intrigued as we went on. When I got to the most exciting part, where the Medium passed out, I had all their attention. "All of a sudden the Medium's face turned ashen and she screamed out a name or something. It sounded like Fusel, or Fussie or…No, I believe it was Fusee."

CRASH! The bowl that had been in Little Deer's hands fell, cabbage spilling all over the floor.

"Fusee!" she gasped.

Lynn, Kate, and Gloria at once were trying to get to the mess on the floor, but Little Deer halted them, her hand in the air, her voice shaking, "Wait! We will get that later. Did I hear you say, Fusee?"

"Ohhhh!"… That gosh awful moaning came again from Curtis, and his face had gone pale.

"Gosh almighty, I wish he'd stop that, before he gives us all a stroke or something," I said holding my hand to my chest.

Little Deer pressed on, "Are you sure that's what was said, Fusee?"

"Positive," Jesse said. "Do you know what that means?"

A fire came to Little Deer's eyes I'd not seen before and she spat out the name, "Lucas Cane…Lucas Cane!"

"Lucas Cane..." I thought. It sounded familiar. Where had I heard it before? "'Lucas Cane,'", the name flashed across my mind in big letters, big black letters, like on a... That was it, like on a newspaper headline. I hadn't heard it, I'd seen it.

"THAT'S IT!" I shouted.

"Sweet Jesus Cally, what is it?" Kate said holding her chest. "For Pete's sake, you nearly scared me to death, Cally!"

"Lucas Cane! He drowned in the river channel, down by the Pepper Pot. It was the night of the fire that killed Mr. Curtis Malcolm's family," I told them all.

"Well, what's that got to do with some Fusee or whatever?" Kate asked. "What kind of stuff are you concocting now?"

"I'm afraid what she says is not anything concocted," Little Deer silenced Kate and any other non-believers in the room.

"Remember Miss Posey's microfilm newspapers at the Library?" I said turning to Jesse. "Remember, we read about that Lucas Cane fellow just before spotting the story about the fire. Remember?"

A light finally went off in Jesse's eyes. "She's right!" he said. "We did read it, and that's a fact."

"That still hasn't told the rest of us what this all has to do with that Fusee stuff... Cally? Gloria waited for an explanation.

The whole time we talked about this Fusee business Curtis Malcolm had taken to plugging his ears with his fingers.

"It's okay, Curtis, he can't hurt you anymore," Little Deer told him pulling his arms down to release his fingers. Then the old Indian woman said, "Fusee is not a thing, but the nickname the railroad men gave to the keeper of the light. The flares and lanterns burning with a red light were used to guide the trains to their stops or to signal a switch in the tracks. Lucas Cane was such a man. He worked with Curtis' father and Jasper Tate and Earl. Lucas, Jasper, and Earl were the young newcomers to the Florida

East Coast Rail and Mr. Malcolm was close to retiring. Those three younger ones worked together, got drunk together, and created all kinds of trouble. They of course, didn't care for your grandfather, Jesse. Mr. Malcolm was a straight arrow, a good decent man. He didn't fit in with the rest of them wild ones. Mr. Malcolm was respected and didn't give anyone any trouble. That's probably one of the reasons they hated him so. He didn't put up with their shenanigans. Jasper Tate's reasons were more personal for disliking your grandfather."

All eyes and ears focused on Little Deer as she continued, "First off, Mrs. Malcolm had the gift."

"What gift was that?" Jesse asked.

"Jesse, your grandmother had the gift of a true spiritualist," Little Deer told him. "She could communicate with the departed. People came from all around to seek her advice. That's just one of the reasons why the Tates disliked the Malcolms. Mrs. Malcolm was respected in the Landing. Even though the Malcolms didn't actually live within the Landing, she was thought highly of by the community there. Jasper's aunts are what are known as fakers, in spiritualist circles. They use trickery to foil their patrons. Things like table tipping, throwing their voices, and such. When people caught on to their tricks they went to Mrs. Malcolm. Word of mouth spread pretty fast of her talents. Your grandmother had a way with people and animals, too. Caleb and Curtis inherited that from her. The Coo-wa-chobee's mother followed those twins around from the time she was a cub and they were just boys. There was a real bond there."

"Jesse has that bond too, Little Deer," I said. "It seems like every time we are near the forest that cat is close by. Why I believe that cat was there to protect Jesse tonight from Robert Lee."

"That wouldn't surprise me," Little Deer said looking at Jesse, who seemed a little uncomfortable with us talking about him like this. He changed the subject to Jasper Tate.

"Boy, Jasper sure hates that cat and I do believe the feeling is mutual," Jesse told Little Deer.

"If the animals mistrust a man, then he is probably not a man anyone can trust, man nor beast," she said. "There is an Indian folktale about the Panther, the Wind, and the Creator. In it the Panther does indeed have special powers and knowledge. He waits patiently, close to the ground watching all the creatures. He knows who is good and who is not. Jasper Tate hates the Cat because he knows what he is."

"Little Deer, you said there were other reasons why the Tates hated the Malcolms. What else was there?" Bud asked.

Little Deer smiled. "Caleb, Jesse's real daddy, had the attentions of Miss Lila. That was a real source of contempt for Jasper Tate. The green-eyed monster had taken over Jasper, because he was sweet on Lila, too. Jasper hated Caleb. I always knew Caleb and Lila were meant for one another. They were sweet on each other from the time they were about you and Cally's age," she winked at Jesse. This time I blushed. Lynn poked me.

Little Deer continued, "When Caleb went into the Air Force and everyone was so proud of him becoming a pilot, Jasper couldn't stand it no more. With Caleb gone away, Jasper never missed a chance to try and provoke Curtis. Why he would harass poor Curtis mercilessly. Jasper is a real mean spirited man. He'd constantly make fun of Curtis, calling him terrible, hurtful names."

I remembered what happened at Mr. Elias' store as Curtis passed by and Jasper hollered out at him, taunting him so. How could he be so cruel? He was a cold-hearted man. A man like that, if he hated someone, was capable of most anything.

"So, what happened the night of the terrible fire, Little Deer," Bill asked. "Do you think it was intentional?"

Little Deer looked over at Curtis who sat over in a rocker, staring at the fire on the hearth, seemingly oblivious to our conversation. I wondered.

"The week of the horrible fire, Caleb was home on leave," Little Deer began. "He and Lila announced their engagement that weekend. They were very happy."

I thought I caught a wet shininess to Little Deer's eyes now.

"The last time Lila saw Caleb alive was at the dance the night of the fire. It was the Fourth of July. Then, a couple nights later, some old fisherman found Lucas Cane's body floating face down in the canal. It was right down from the Pepper Pot, near Jasper Tate's place."

"Was it an accident?" Bud asked.

"Hard to say," Little Deer answered. "A body in the river a day or two doesn't leave much to examine. Folks were divided on what happened. One theory was that he drowned. At least that was the Sheriff's final conclusion. Figures he and the boys got tanked up on all that moonshine they made..."

Jesse started choking on the piece of fry bread he had picked up off the platter and shoved in his mouth.

"Yes, Jesse, I know all about the spirits over to the Tate's place, and I'm not talking about the ones the mediums conjure up next door at the Landing," Little Deer said.

"Holy smoke!" Kate said. "We've got moonshiners, panthers, and spiritists...what else is here right here under our noses?"

Jesse had downed a glass of the liquid from the pitcher on the table. I walked over to him and tried to touch his arm. "It's okay, Jesse, I knew about it already. It's okay. It's not your fault," I told him.

He pushed away from me and started for the door. "For Pete's sake what don't folks know about the Tates?" he said angrily. "Why didn't you tell me you knew, Cally?"

"Jesse, please don't be mad. I didn't say anything because I was afraid you would be embarrassed. I was right, wasn't I? You are embarrassed and for what? It doesn't make any difference to me or anyone else in here what Jasper Tate is or ain't."

"Isn't" Kate corrected me.

"Oh, for crying out loud Kate, isn't, ain't, who gives a flying..."

"Cally!" Kate cut me off.

"Children!" Little Deer silenced us.

Jesse came back in and sat at the table, his head down, not looking at any of us. "So, I want to hear the other theory. They might as well hear everything," he said.

Little Deer seated herself in a chair by Curtis near the fire, lightly patting his head as she sat next to him. Curtis didn't move, but kept staring into the flames. She turned to us now, "Some folks don't think Lucas just happened to stumble into that canal. Some say he was already half dead before he got there. Somebody finished the job by drowning him while he was unconscious."

"Who would have done such a horrible thing?," Gloria said, sitting down at the old woman's feet.

"No one knows for sure, no one except old Fusee, but people have their suspicions. Some say Jasper or Earl did him in. Maybe he crossed them somehow. I don't know." She looked at Jesse with sad eyes. "You know Jesse, it's just talk. That's all. When something so tragic happens, especially just after that horrible fire, it starts people imagining all kinds of things."

Now the old woman's words were strong and came slow, words of warning. "I told you before that no good comes from seeing those Mediums and trying to bring back the dead. There are evil spirits. Human beings weren't meant to dabble in such darkness. There are some things better left to the Creator to deal with. He tries to protect us from the evil. Mediums and spiritists, if not careful, conjure up what should stay buried. My guess is your Madame Rosemary brought you Lucas Cane's tortured soul, instead of Jesse's daddy."

The room was silent as a cemetery on a full moon night.

"The ones who say Lucas was murdered claim he roams the woods along the canal. His restless spirit is looking to find revenge on his killer. I haven't heard the story in a good long while. Seems to me your Madame, revived his tortured spirit again. My advice is to stay clear of the Landing and all that sorcery."

I jumped as Curtis, apparently hearing enough, stood up and went out to the porch. Through the window a slow, sad melody, floated in on the breeze. It seemed to have the same mournful tone as Curtis' soft whimpers when he held Jesse earlier. We all looked to Little Deer for an explanation.

"It's Curtis," she said and moved to the window. "His daddy gave him that harmonica when he was small. He keeps it in his shirt pocket always. He doesn't say much of anything, so he plays the music. It speaks his mind and heart."

I touched Jesse's shoulder. This time he didn't pull away. "Aren't you proud? Listen to what Curtis Malcolm can do. It's just beautiful," I said.

I was grateful for Curtis' music. Little Deer's warning made me realize how foolish we'd been messing with them mediums. I hated to admit it, but Patty had been right again. "Anyone who practices divination, a soothsayer, or an augur, or a sorcerer, or a charmer, or a medium…whoever does these things is an abomination to the Lord." I suddenly felt very cold.

Bud interrupted our concert. "Little Deer what do you believe happened to Lucas Cane? I mean you've pretty much said, calling Jasper a murderer and all, but why do you believe that?"

"It doesn't matter what an old Indian woman thinks. It won't change anything. What's done is done and life goes on," she said.

"I don't believe you mean that," Jesse said. "It's pretty clear to me you care deeply for Curtis, and my mother. You felt just as strong for Caleb."

Little Deer shut her eyes.

Jesse didn't stop. "My mother told me how you were the one taught her the Creek ways and customs. She loves you like a mother. You know she stayed away because of Jasper. I told you that before. I know the whole story. I can't imagine you believe it doesn't matter what you think. It matters to me," Jesse stopped now, his voice starting to break.

Little Deer blinked her eyes and wiped at them. "You listen to me, Jesse Tate. You listen good. Jasper Tate is a man without conscience. He hates everybody and wouldn't think twice about harming anyone who gets in his way and that includes a boy he knows ain't really his. If I told you what I believe happened way back then, what possible good could come of it? It can only mean more pain."

"Well, I've already lived enough pain for a lifetime and I plan on making Jasper pay for what he's done. I would like to hear about that night when my Daddy died. I have a right to know. What did you see? You must have seen something. You know pretty much everything that goes on around here."

Curtis' melody floated through the cottage and Little Deer resigned herself to tell the story as she knew it.

"It was a glorious summer night," she began. "There were thousands of stars in the sky that night. Did you children know that the stars are campfires of our dearly departed and the Milky Way is their path to the Creator? I was sitting outside having a smoke on my corn cob pipe when I noticed a glow coming across the tops of the new pine saplings. Today, they are the tall pines shading my cottage. That night a glow fell across the forest like the sun setting on the horizon. But, it was too late in the evening for a sunset and I was looking north. Pretty soon the glow rose up turning into orange spires and I knew it was a fire, because I could smell smoke. I grabbed my walking stick in case of any snakes crossing my path and headed towards the light. The further I walked towards the far end of the swamp near the Landing, the thicker the smoke hovered in the heavy night air. As I passed the sink hole, I began to hear the crackle of wood burning. Coming out of the dense forest to the clearing, where the trail starts near the spring, I stood frozen in horror. There in front of me, engulfed in red and orange flame was the Malcolm's home. Quickly getting my senses about me, I began to run towards the house. Just as I got to the giant oaks lining the yard, the heat was most unbearable. Trying to douse the fire would be useless. The top floor had already crashed to the one below. I thought I heard an automobile engine start up, but it was hard to tell for sure with the sounds of the fire. Looking around frantically, just off to my right, at the edge of the path, I saw someone lying face down on the ground. Running to him, I discovered it was Curtis. He was unconscious. There was a smell all around like stale liquor. Upon closer examination, the odor came from his clothes and was all over the ground surrounding him. Curtis doesn't and never has drank. I didn't know what to think. I turned him over. He had a nasty bump on his forehead and there was some blood.

He began thrashing about and out of his hand fell that Air Force medal you children found, which belonged to Caleb. I picked it up."

"I knew it," I thought I heard Jesse whisper.

"It was just about then Curtis began to come to," Little Deer was saying. "He was disoriented at first, and then he figured out who I was. I managed to sit him up. As I sat there with him, something caught my eye, something shiny, the firelight dancing off of it. I went over and picking it up discovered it was one of them flick lighters, the railroad gave to their employees years back. It had a silver locomotive raised up on it. At that moment, I jumped to a conclusion that to this day I'm not proud of. Curtis being the only one around that inferno, and then finding the medal and lighter nearby, I thought he had done a terrible thing. I thought he had used his Daddy's lighter to set the fire. Yet, when I heard the fire truck sirens coming from off in the distance, I knew I had to get him out of there fast. Curtis is different. He is mentally slow. He's never talked very much, but, nothing like he is now. Curtis has been the object of a lot of ridicule for it. You children have heard it."

A pang of guilt chewed away at my insides thinking of how we called him the Woo Woo man.

"I was afraid for him," Little Deer went on. "I gathered him up. His leg had been badly injured during whatever happened before I got there. I let him use my walking stick and I led him away. He was still dazed and reluctant to leave. I'm not sure how I got him moving away from there. That's when I first heard it. I'll never forget."

"Heard what," we all chimed in, mesmerized by her story.

"That strange sound he makes…Woo Woo…you know. He kept saying it and pointing back at the house, then out towards the back of the house where I'd thought I'd heard the automobile engine. He kept saying it over and over, Woo, Woo, Woo, Woo. It was so loud, it's a good thing the fire and sirens made so much noise, or he'd been heard all over the county. I finally got him back to the cottage and cleaned him up best I could. His clothes reeked of the liquor, but, oddly, there was none on his breath. I splinted his leg with a long palm frond wrapped in a piece of cloth. He was plum worn out and lay crying quietly. All he said was that eerie sound, 'Woo Woo.'. He took the harmonica from his pocket and played until he fell asleep, exhausted, the harmonica dropped to the floor. Removing his soiled, rank smelling clothing, I wrapped him tightly with a blanket. As hot as it was that night he trembled and felt clammy, cold, probably in shock. I cleaned his clothes and sat watching him toss and turn fitfully all night. When he awakened early the next morning there came a knock on my door. It was the Sheriff. They took Curtis away. Just like that. Just took him. He didn't speak or cry out, he just went along with them, whispering that woo, woo noise. I was told they took him way up north to the mental hospital near Chattahoochee. It was the last time I saw him, until they released him to the County Home about six years ago."

Little Deer stood up and went to the fireplace where she took a small hand-carved wooden box from the mantle. "Curtis made this box for me out of a piece of poplar," she said opening it, and removing something shiny and golden from inside, setting it down in front of us on the table. It was a golden lighter, had a miniature silver train locomotive medallion on it. We all sat staring at it, like we expected it to do something magical. Finally, not being able to contain myself any longer, I reached across the table to pick it up. Jesse's hand came slapping down on mine and the lighter slid across the table and onto the wooden plank floor boards.

"Now look what you've gone and done, Cally," Jesse said bending down to pick it up.

"Me! If you hadn't got so darned rambunctious trying to snatch it up yourself it wouldn't have fallen."

"Cally!" Kate moaned.

"It was an accident," I said as Jesse emerged from retrieving the lighter, holding it close to his face, examining it.

"What's this?" he said. "The locomotive has been knocked loose." Jesse scraped his fingernail across the black grime trapped underneath the medallion. "There seems to be some kind of writing here."

"What's it say?" I asked him. "I can't see a darn thing with your fingers in the way."

"Look here. There's somebody's initials carved in the metal," Jesse said showing me the lighter.

"I squinted reading the letters, "'J.T.'"

Grabbing the lighter I swung around to show Bud.

"Hey!" Jesse yelled.

"Sorry Jesse. Look it says J.T.," I said as Bud examined it. "See it, J.T. This wasn't Curtis' father's lighter. It says J.T."

"For Pete's sake Cally, you've said J.T. three times already," Kate groaned.

"Kate, who is the only other J.T. we know besides Jesse? And, who would have had access to this lighter back then?" I pounced.

"Jasper Tate," whispers filled the room.

A look of pure astonishment came over Little Deer's brown face. She mumbled something in Indian, then in English said, "All these years. I never once realized that the locomotive slid back and forth."

"It was pretty grimy underneath it," Bud told her. "Probably wouldn't have opened without dropping it."

"I knew it!" Jesse said.

"Knew what Jesse?" Bud asked.

Jesse's eyes locked with mine. "Cally, remember I told you how upset my momma was when she saw me with that medal a few days ago?"

I just shook my head.

"Until then, the last time she seen it was when Jasper pulled it off of Caleb Malcolm's Air Force uniform at the dance, the night of the fire. That's what convinced her and me that Jasper Tate was somehow involved with Caleb and his family's fate."

"How is that so, Jesse?" Kate asked.

Seminole Landing

Jesse answered, "Don't you see? Curtis was in the wrong place at the wrong time, walking up on that fire. Jasper knocked him in the head then dropped that medal by him. Only thing was, Jasper hadn't counted on dropping his lighter, too."

"Aieee!" Little Deer cried holding her hands to her head. "All these years my heart told me Curtis couldn't have done it. I am ashamed that I ever doubted."

With Little Deer's cry, the front door opened and Curtis came in from the porch his eyes full of concern. He went immediately to Little Deer's side.

"Woo Woo Woo!" he began a tirade of that infernal noise, pointing at the lighter I still held between my fingers. The sound was deafening.

"Woo Woo! Woo Woo!"

Lynn, who had been sitting quietly through most of the evening stood up, blue eyes wide, and tossing back her braids she burst, "For crying out loud, Cally, put that lighter out of his sight!"

I quickly shoved it in my pants pocket as Little Deer and Jesse tried to calm Mr. Curtis Malcolm.

"It's all right Curtis. It's just a lighter," Jesse told the hysterical man.

"Woo, Woo! Woo!" came another blast.

"Maybe it would be a good idea not to mention the L-I-G-H-T-E-R anymore," Kate spelled, covering her ears.

"WOO! WOO!" It didn't stop.

"Good Grief, Kate, he's slow not ignorant. He can spell!" I said.

Curtis was wild and Little Deer pulled him over near the fireplace to settle him down. The rest of us stood there helpless to know what to do for the traumatized man.

Lynn turned to us all, her back to Little Deer and Curtis, "Don't you all see that, that ligh…oh dear, she stammered, that thing Cally has in her pocket, is why Mr. Malcolm's entire vocabulary since the night of the fire consists of one thing. Woo Woo," She whispered.

Seeing our blank stares, she went on, "What sound does a locomotive make," holding up her hand before anyone even dared say the words. "Don't say it! Just think! Okay. Now, if Curtis experienced something horribly tragic, so tragic he doesn't speak much at all except to repeat over and over that one word, maybe he's been trying to tell someone something." Seeing she still wasn't getting anywhere she said, "Like maybe he's trying to communicate somehow who the person that actually committed the crime was. Namely one, J-A-S-P-E…"

"Don't say anymore," Bud said shooting a quick look back at Curtis.

"Lynn's right," Bud said. "Curtis truly fears…you know who. He's not afraid of anything or anyone else I've ever seen, so why J.T.?"

"You're right," Larry chimed in. "Lynn, you figured it out."

Lynn beamed proudly from Larry's praise.

"I can't believe the clue has been here all these years. How long did he spend in some mental hospital?" Gloria said. "It's criminal."

"Poor thing," Kate said. "He was blamed all these years just because he couldn't make anyone understand. People ought to be ashamed of how they've treated Mr. Malcolm just because he's a little slow. Why, he understands more than most. Too bad there isn't some way to prove to people he isn't a loony."

"I'm afraid we're the only ones who will know. How could you prove anything now after all this time," Gloria said. "I wouldn't tell Little Deer this," she whispered, "but, if she had turned over that lighter that night, the police may have found the real firebug."

"We need some time to look at all this and find a way to catch the real criminals, make them pay for what they've done. We'll figure something out," Bud said looking at his watch. "I hate to do this, but it's getting pretty late and Mom and Dad will be worried. We'd better be going home."

"Bud we can't just leave things like this," I said.

"Don't worry Cal, we'll figure this out. But, we need more information. We can't just go running to the law until we get more evidence to back up our accusations," Bud said. "Now come on we really need to get on home."

"Not before we help Little Deer clean up from the fine meal she gave us," Gloria said getting up, starting to clear plates. We told Jesse to sit awhile with Curtis while we worked. When everything was cleaned and put away we said our goodnights to Little Deer and Curtis. Jesse asked Curtis if we could take him home. Curtis just stared at Jesse.

"He'll be fine," Little Deer said. "He will stay the night on my cot. I think he needs some time to unwind from all the excitement. I'll tend to him."

"I think Little Deer is right. It has been a pretty wild night. Curtis and Jesse both need time to take it all in," Bud said. "We'll be leaving now, Little Deer. Thank you for your kind hospitality tonight." With that Bud headed to the door and motioned for the rest of us to follow. Lynn ran up and hugged Little Deer, then quickly ran out the door. The rest of us said our goodnights and started back through the woods to the county road. The whole way back, Jesse didn't say a word. No one talked much as we made our way down the road. "Night," was all Jesse said as he got out of the car at the end of the lane before his house.

"Is he going to be alright Bud?" I asked as we watched Jesse disappear around the bend.

"Jesse is strong, Cally. I think he'll be alright. We'll keep a close eye on him."

Bed sure was a welcome sight tonight as I pulled the fresh washed sheets up and lie next to my sister Lynn. I couldn't get our discovery out of my mind. We couldn't just leave it like that. There had to be some way to make Jasper Tate pay for his evil. Jesse and I had to figure out something. I tossed and turned not able to get to sleep. I wondered if Lynn was asleep yet. She'd come straight in when we got home. I whispered, "Lynn, are you asleep?"

"Are you kidding? How could anybody sleep with you tossing and thrashing about? What's the matter?"

"I'm sorry, Lynn. I just can't get Jesse off my mind and everything that we seen tonight, that lighter and all. Lynn, what do you think will become of Jesse? I mean if you were him, what would you be thinking right now? You know he has this tough exterior and all, but he's really just a boy, and he's been through so much. My heart just breaks for him. I can't imagine what I might do in his shoes."

My sister reached over patting my arm softly. "I'm thinking Jesse Tate is thinking right this very moment what a mighty lucky boy he is to have such a good friend as Cally Cummins. That's what I think. Now you better get some sleep, Cally. It's been a long night."

A big tear plopped off my cheek onto my pillowcase, "Thanks, Lynn. I love you."

20 CHAPTER

It was two days before the Fourth of July. The rooster clock read just ten o'clock, and the thermometer on the patio had already climbed to ninety-nine degrees, a real scorcher. There was going to be more than firecrackers heating up the holiday. I couldn't wait. I loved the picnics and the parades. The county was to put on a big pyro display out on the St. Johns River off a barge. Patty's mom and dad were having a big to do at their place and we were invited. It was to be an afternoon of swimming in their pool and a BBQ. After dark, the skies would light up and we could watch it all from their backyard along the river. Jesse hadn't been around for a few days. He'd come and worked in the garden and picked his vegetables, but didn't hang around afterwards. Bud helped Jesse load up the bushel baskets in his Ford and dropped them and Jesse back in the woods as close to the Tate's as he dare without Jasper seeing them. Later Jesse would tote them to his momma when Jasper was gone somewhere. Bud said Jesse didn't say much on those occasions. Said Jesse had a lot on his mind and probably needed time to sort everything out without anybody else's two-cents added in. I told my brother I guessed he was right, but I missed Jesse and couldn't understand him shutting me out.

After Mom fixed us lunch Bud said he'd take us all swimming at the spring. I couldn't wait to wade into the cold water. It was hotter than Hades out. You could take a shower and fifteen minutes later be sweltering again. Days like these were best spent either in doors sipping a cool drink or swimming.

"Don't keep them out there too long, Bud," Mom said handing us a stack of clean towels as we went out the door. "An hour should be plenty, and then you all better get back and rest awhile. I'll have some fresh juice waiting."

Mom worried about polio. We got shots for it, but it was a terrible disease, crippled up a body. These hot, dog days of summer were somehow connected to the illness.

"We'll be back in an hour, Mom," Bud assured her. "I can taste the lemonade now."

Outside, we piled in Bud's car. I was sure glad we were riding today. The perspiration was already sliding down my back.

Bud pulled the car to a dusty halt along the dirt road next to the springs. Stepping into the brilliant rays of sun bouncing off the glassy blue water, I could hardly get my shoes off quick enough. It was tempting to just run and splash, and dive straight under to the sandy bottom, but that would be careless. I heard of a boy once over by Lake Linde carelessly diving into the cold spring water off the dock there. It was a particularly steamy, blistering hot summer day like today. He ran, diving head first and went under. His friends waited for his bubbly return to the surface, but it never came. Thinking he was playing a joke, his friends waited; sure he would surface when he ran out of air. He didn't. Two boys who had been swimming near the spot, seeing the panic that rose in the boy's friends when he didn't come up for air, swam over and dove under in search of the disappearing boy. They must have spotted him, because they came back up for a quick gulp of fresh air and went right back under. When they resurfaced the next time they pulled the boy's limp body up with them. Pulling him to shore, they frantically tried to revive him. All their efforts were useless. The boy died instantly when his overheated body hit the sixty-eight degree water, a heart attack from the shock. I couldn't believe it, a young boy, about my age dying of a heart attack. No sir, no matter how much the cool water tempted, Cally Cummins would wade in.

As I slowly made my way into the clear spring, I couldn't help but think that afternoons like this one were to be the glorious days of my youth. Memories stored away in my mind, like Grandma Cummins photograph album, the one with the pretty lady in the big flowery hat adorning its robin egg blue cover. I would pull them out years from now when I became a very old, southern woman. I'd sit on my front porch swing, sipping lemonade on especially hot summer days, listening to the children laughing and playing in their wading pool next door. Oh, how I treasured these days with my brother and my sisters.

"Cally! Bud!"

Seminole Landing

It was Jesse. Now how could this day be any more complete?

Tossing water with a scoop of my hand I cried, "Come on in. It's too hot to be up there on that dusty road." Jesse laid his bike down and throwing off as much of his clothing as decent, ran to the water's edge. Slowly making his way out towards the rest of us, covering his stomach with his hands, with a shiver he waded in.

"Where you been?" I asked. He smiled that big boyish grin of his. How handsome he was with his white toothed smile against sun-kissed skin and hair.

"I've been busy. Jasper has been making me stick close to home cleaning out his jugs and such. He left for Callahan, yesterday; needed parts for his truck he and Earl been working on. I suspect he'll be making a stop in Seville on the way back to pick up more corn for their brew."

I was surprised at how casually he talked about Jasper and his still.

"Thought I'd take advantage of his absence and come by your place, but you saved me a trip. Better day for swimming anyhow," Jesse waved an arm under the water sending a big splash all over me.

"Hey!" I hollered. I retaliated, giving him a good dunking, sputtering and laughing in pure delight.

"Come on who wants the first Alley Oop!" Bud hollered running to the tire swing dangling from the big oak limb sticking out over the water.

The hour passed quickly, as it always does when you're having a glorious day.

"Duck!" Lynn hollered. "Deer fly!" The darn thing was nearly as big as a deer and I ducked and swatted madly in the air brushing at my shoulder. "Ouch!" I looked down to see my shoulders had become a rosy shade of pink. "Time to go, Bud. I'm getting sunburned."

Kate brushed back my hair, "Somebody is going to be sore tonight. It'll be time for a good tea bath when we get home, kiddo."

"Yeh," Bud said getting a look at my sore shoulders, "Mom will skin me alive if I bring you home looking like a lobster. Better go. Jesse, why don't you come on along? We can stick your bike in the trunk. Mom promised to have some of her famous lemonade when we get back."

Jesse agreed to come and we all piled in Bud's car.

When we got to the house, before going inside, Jesse told me he had something to tell me when we got alone. Said he figured out how to nail Jasper. I could hardly wait to hear. Mom, as promised, had fresh squeezed lemonade ready. She even served it in the white milk glass mugs I loved so, the ones with the grapes carved into their sides. Bud took his and excused himself to the back of the house, probably going to call Gloria. Mom and the girls retreated to the living room to watch that Mr. Anthony guy give away tons of money to some down and out on "'The Millionaire'" television show. If that guy came to our front door, I could help Jesse and his momma get far away from Jasper Tate, where he'd never find them, and have plenty money left to spare.

Jesse and I took our lemonade out to the breezeway, where the only air-conditioning unit in the whole house was. Dad put it out there for mom when she did her ironing. Closing the slider we plopped down on the rattan couch. "Man this feels great," Jesse said. "I wish we had air, especially on days like today."

"Jesse, what was it you wanted to tell me?" I asked impatiently.

Jesse scooted closer to me, which I didn't mind at all, although I could feel my face blush. His voice was low and hushed. "Cally, I think I have a plan to trip up Jasper and prove to everybody what he did to my Grandparents and father, not to mention what I believe he did to Lucas Cane."

"I knew it!" I told him. "I knew you couldn't possibly let this go."

"Fat chance," he said.

"Well, when I hadn't seen you for a few days, I wasn't sure."

"Cally, there's no way Jasper Tate is getting away with murder. I don't believe Lucas Cane just drowned. Do you?"

Visions of the night at Madame Rosemary's came back in a flash, and I nodded my head in agreement with Jesse.

"If we're right, I'd say that old lighter isn't the only thing with old J.T. written all over it. But, Cally, I'm going to need your help to prove it."

"Besides a confession, how are we going to do that?"

Jesse smiled slyly.

"Jesse, Jasper Tate is a slick one. How are we going to trick him into confessing anything?" I asked.

"We're not," Jesse said.

"Huh?" I was confused now.

Jesse laughed, "We're going to let his half-wit, side-kick Earl do it for us. It all came to me the other night at Little Deer's place. The way we scared off those boys you know. We're going to get Jasper Tate with some of his family's own medicine, use a little fakery and a few concocted spirits."

"No way, Jesse, I'm not going anywhere near them spirit calling, hocus-pocus mediums again. Didn't you learn anything by what happened at Madame Rosemary's that night?"

"No, Cally, not real spirit calling. I'm talking the fakery like Jasper's aunts do, and the tricks we pulled the other night, just harmless pranks. Jasper might catch on, but if we get to Earl first and get him all spooked, then he's bound to start fretting and carrying on at Jasper. Earl is gullible enough it should work, and then we'll set up the final trap."

The slider opened as Kate stuck her head in. "What are you two cooking up in here?"

"That's for us to know and you to find out," I said smugly.

"I don't think I want to know," Kate said shoving the door closed.

"If we're going to do this, we need to act this afternoon while Jasper is out of town. He left Earl here to tend to their moonshine they been brewing special for the holiday. Earl is supposed to be taking a bad part out of the truck so Jasper can replace it with the new one he's getting today. It's perfect and we only have another day until the Fourth. That's when all heck is going to break loose."

My heart sank to my toes, "I can't."

"What do you mean, you can't" Jesse jumped up.

"I told you, I'm supposed to go with my family to my friend Patty's out on the river on the Fourth."

He sank back down onto the couch, clearly relieved by whatever I'd just said. "Exactly, that is all part of the plan. You've got to get me invited to their place too."

Well, this sounded better all the time. Spending the Fourth of July with Jesse would be too good to be true. "No problem. So tell me what we're going to do to Earl."

"I'll tell you on the way out to my place," Jesse said.

21 CHAPTER

By the time we'd reached the dirt road leading to the Tates, Jesse had laid out the whole crazy plan. Crazy, but it sounded like it really could work, provided we didn't get our fool heads blown off. When we got to the stand of Magnolia and Dogwood trees just past Jasper's aunts' place, Jesse told me to wait under their shade for fifteen minutes, then come to the garage.

It was nice and cool underneath the fragrant giants. There were some cabbage palms around so if anyone came along I could hide. I waited, hidden under the Magnolia's moss draped limbs for the fifteen minutes, then taking a deep breath I nervously stepped out into the blistering sunlight. My shoulders burned underneath my T-shirt. As I walked towards Jesse's I went over and over in my head what we had rehearsed. I sure hoped Jesse was right about Earl being half-witted. He'd pretty much have to be to hang around with Jasper Tate for all these years. The whining of an engine came from the Landing road. Panic shot through me. Not many automobiles came out this way. Maybe Jasper was coming home early. As the sound moved closer, the whine became more of a gurgle. It was just a motor boat moving up the river run. "Relax, Cally," I said to myself. Walking along the edge of Jesse's property, I thought I caught a glimpse of someone looking out one of the side windows of the house.

"Jesse? Is that you?" A woman's voice called as she stuck her head out the screen- less, window. Stopping dead in my tracks, I wished I had the Magnolia to hide behind now. I dare not look, but I had too. I could feel her eyes upon me. I guessed I better say something to her just in case she hollered out and ruined the whole plan. "No Ma'am, it's not Jesse," I said timidly, walking towards the house so as not to have to talk so loud. "It's Cally Cummins, Jesse's friend."

A warm smile crept across the woman's mouth. Jesse sure did look like Caleb, but his smile was definitely his momma's. She was absolutely beautiful. Not what I'd expected at all, what with her hard life with Jasper and all. She had long dark black hair, shined just like the ebony stone arrowhead Bud kept polished in his collection. Her skin was brown as a berry. She looked like the Indian princess on the Florida State Flag.

"Of course," she said. "I should have known you by Jesse's description. How are you, Cally?"

Jesse described me to his Momma. I wondered what he told her. She sure was smiling a lot. I just stood there fidgeting; primping my hair like Kate did sometimes. "I must look a sight out here in this sweltering heat," I said. "You could fry an egg, right out there in the road," I laughed.

"Oh no, you look fine, Cally. You're just as Jesse said, tall and slender, and you do have the prettiest blue eyes."

I felt my face heat up and I was sure I was red as a beet and it wasn't from the sun. Jesse told his Momma about my eyes. This was one extra glorious day for my memory book.

"Thank you, ma'am," I told her.

"I'm glad Jesse found some friends like you and your family, Cally. I've been meaning to pay a visit to your mother and father and thank them for letting Jesse have such a fine garden. We've had many a delicious dinner with those fresh vegetables."

"Jesse did all the work. He works real hard, Mrs. Tate." Remembering Jesse waiting on me I glanced at my watch. "Well Ma'am, Jesse's waiting on me out back."

Her expression changed to one of concern. "Jesse usually doesn't entertain here Cally, especially out back. Mr. Tate doesn't like anyone out there. Might be a good idea if you tell Jesse to go on over to your place instead."

I nodded. "Yes, Ma'am, we'll do that. It sure was nice meeting you," I said trying to make a gracious exit.

"You too, Cally," she smiled. "Remember, I wouldn't stay out there too long, just in case Mr. Tate gets home soon."

"Yes Ma'am."

Jesse's Momma sure was a pleasant sort. I ached to ask her what in the Sam Hill she was doing staying with a man like Jasper. She must know I knew what he was like. Jesse had told me she was afraid of Jasper.

Glancing at my watch again, I picked up my pace. I sure didn't want to mess around too long and maybe run into Jasper after all. The drive was covered with thick leathery leaves from the scrub oak that crunched under my sneakers, scattering over the sand as I walked. Just up ahead I could see the tin roof of the garage glistening in the sunlight. A smell, the same disagreeable one I'd smelled that day Patty and I were here made my nose scrunch, probably the distilled liquor that sat in the bottoms of those tarp covered jugs. The garage door was open and I could hear voices inside. Here goes nothing I said to myself as about a zillion butterflies flitted around inside my stomach.

"Jesse! Jesse!" I called.

A man's voice inside picked up its pitch and I nearly jumped clean out of my sun-burned skin as I caught Earl's face come to the paned window near the door.

"Cally," Jesse poked his head out. "What you doing way out here?"

I walked into the garage, "Just out taking a walk and thought I'd see what you been up to. I haven't seen you in a while."

"Earl this is my friend, Cally," Jesse introduced me. Earl gave me a sort of sideways look and nod then turned back around clamping a rusted wrench around something under the hood of a beat up Chevy. He spat a nasty, brown wet wad of tobacco juice on the dirt floor next to the truck. "Shouldn't be traipsin' around out here, little girl. Jesse, you know your Daddy wouldn't like you bringing kids out here." Earl twisted the wrench with a squeak, and then spit again. Kersplat! I looked down and my stomach churned at the sight of several big wet mud spots of dried up tobacco mixed in with cigarette butts. I hoped I didn't puke.

"Cally's my friend, Earl, she ain't no trouble."

I just smiled my best innocent looking smile at the disagreeable man. I was surprised to see just how short Earl really was. Why Jesse was nearly as tall as him. Here without Jasper alongside him he wasn't so intimidating, and he did look sort of like what a half-wit should look like. Kind of like when that Red Skelton guy did that stupid looking character on his television show—Clem Kadiddlehopper, a big goof, but Clem had a big heart. I was sure the likes of Earl and Jasper had black holes where their hearts were supposed to be.

Jesse said, "I'm thinking maybe you and I should go try our luck with some cane poles. Do a little fishing? How about it? I know you love to fish the way you talk about that Isaac, you and Bud go fishing with."

"Sure. You want to go down to the run by the spring?" I asked.

"No. Out back behind the garage, where the canal curves around towards the Pepper Pot. Water's dark and cool there. Good fishing'," he said.

"Oh no, not me; not down there," I said trying to be as convincingly frightened as possible.

"Why not?" Jesse said sounding real put out, and then he gave me another wink.

"Why Jesse Tate, I can't hardly believe you ain't never heard the story of the terrible tragedy happened down there. You live right here. I know you must have heard it."

"What story?" Jesse asked.

Before I went on I glanced over at Earl. He'd stopped twisting the wrench and had an ear bent to listen.

"You never heard about that man drowned out there years back. Some say he just got too falling down drunk and fell in the canal and drowned. But, story has it that it wasn't no regular drowning. No sir. Story is he got on the bad side of some really dangerous fellas, some real bad ones that had murder in their eyes. Folks say the bad ones waited until he was good and drunk then hit him on the head and drowned him. They say his ghost never rests. He can't until the persons killed him are found out."

Clank! Earl's wrench dropped to the ground underneath the truck.

"Ouch!" he yelped. He'd hit his head on the hood release and stood there rubbing his wound. "Where'd you hear such a crazy bunch of hogwash?" he said still rubbing at his banged up head.

I looked at Jesse. "Around," I said.

"Around, just around?" Earl reared back giving out with a nervous kind of laugh. He spit again. "Why that's nothing but some whopper them old fisherman sit around dreaming up sitting there half drunk, out on the docks. They can't catch any fish so they gossip like a bunch of old blue-haired women, swapping ghost stories."

"No sir, I'm pretty sure it wasn't drunken fishermen. This was told to me by a real reliable source, a God fearing Pentecostal, Mr. Wallace Boyd," I blurted out at the half-witted man, realizing I probably shouldn't have used Patty's father's name.

"Oh yeh, did those Bible thumpers have a name for this here ghost?" Earl said through tobacco stained teeth. He turned back to the Chevy not even waiting for my answer. He probably was thinking just some dumb kid story.

His ignoring me brought the words out like fire from my mouth, "Lucas Cane!" I said.

Earl spun around before I could finish. I sucked in a deep, courage searching breath and repeated a little less forcefully, "Yes, I do believe that was the name, Lucas Cane." Earl's eyes had turned narrow and piercing as though he was looking right through me. Like X-ray vision, except he wasn't no Superman.

Gulping to swallow the spit that wasn't in my mouth I continued my rehearsed story. "They say this Lucas fellow roams all these woods around here, a restless spirit. He comes out on especially dark summer nights when the moonlight is shy and barely peeking from behind the clouds. He carries an old railroad lantern, searching the darkness for his killer," and then I deliberately added, "Or killers."

"Bull!" Earl started to curse, but his tobacco juice started to drool out the corner of his mouth right in the middle and he spit, wiping his drool on his dirty shirtsleeve.

I took another deep breath, partly from being a little scared, but mostly to keep from losing my lunch and went on. "Some folks say Lucas Cane can be seen most every night, the week of Fourth of July. You see he was supposedly murdered the day after the Fourth." I hesitated slightly to wait on a reaction, but Earl just stood there so I threw in the kicker. "It happened just after another unfortunate tragedy just down the road from here. I'm sure you're familiar with it."

"What's that, Cally?" Jesse asked.

Looking at Jesse, but keeping Earl in the corner of my eye I said, "Oh, it was just awful! Three people died in a house-fire. The Malcolm family was their name. There was something else. That Mr. Malcolm was a railroad man too and worked with Lucas Cane." This is where Jesse's part came in and he didn't miss a beat.

"Hey Earl, maybe you knew them. You used to work for the railroad, didn't you; you and Jasper? You happen to know those people that died?"

Earl's face got real pale and his eyes widened, big as saucers, "I think it's time you and your little girlfriend here quit listening to all these crazy stories about ghosts and fires and let me get back to work. Jasper will be back soon and you better be out of here with your friend by then or we'll all be in trouble." With that he went back to the Chevy and crawled under to get his wrench. Crawling back out, he looked surprised that we were still standing there. "Go on now, get on out of here. I got work to do," he said waving the wrench at us.

"You won't tell Jasper we were out here will you Earl?" Jesse said his voice a little edgy.

"I won't have to tell him nothing, if you don't get on out of here before he gets home. Now go on, the both of you! Skedaddle!"

Jesse grabbed hold of my arm, "Come on Cal, I'll walk you home."

I decided to throw in one more thing for Earl to chew on before we left. "Yeh, I best be getting home before dark. I sure wouldn't want to run into Lucas Cane walking through the woods at night." Jesse pulled me out the door.

Jesse and I walked as fast as our legs could carry us, until we reached the safety of the giant moss covered oak. Its towering shadow was blending into the coming dusk. "Jeez o' Pete, Jesse did you see Earl's face when he whipped around after I first mentioned Lucas Cane?"

"I seen it," Jesse laughed. "Bet he thought he'd never have to hear that name again. I'm sure he knows something. Earl is about as transparent as one of them ghosts."

The two of us walked along the dirt road coming to the path leading back through the grove and woods to my place. The scorcher of a day had turned into a beautiful evening. A warm breeze out of the northwest rustled the leaves in the grove, caressing my sunburned cheeks. It felt good. As we walked along, the fine, white, sandy mounds of grove soil filled up my sneakers crowding my toes, felt like I'd forgotten to take the tissue paper out of new shoes. At the boundary where grove met woods, there lay a decaying tree Hurricane Donna had blown on its side a couple years back. Sitting on the fallen trunk and removing my shoes, about a pound of sand poured to the ground as I tipped them over. Jesse sat down next to me.

"Jesse, do you suppose Lucas Cane really does haunt that canal. I mean Little Deer's story and all and then what happened at Madame Rosemary's."

"It's possible," he said removing his sneakers adding another pile of sand on top of mine. "Too bad we couldn't conjure old Lucas up one more time for Earl and Jasper's sake," he laughed.

"Bite your tongue," I smacked him on the arm.

Just the thought sent goose bumps prickling up my arms. I had a real uncomfortable feeling. "Jesse, all this ghost talk gives me the heebie-jeebies. I don't want to mess around with them spirits ever again. I believe what my friend, Patty, said. "They're evil, just pure evil and the living aren't supposed to go messing with the world of the dead. There's just something not right with that Jesse." I looked him square in the eyes, "Didn't you feel it that night. Why I felt like my body was being possessed by something...something unholy." Rubbing my arms and giving a shiver I told him, "As a matter of fact I feel like someone or something is watching us right now."

"Cally, you're beginning to give me those heebie-jeebies," Jesse said.

I changed the subject. "I met your momma when I was walking past your house earlier."

A look of surprise came over Jesse.

"I think she suspects you're up to something, Jesse," I said. "She asked me as much. Said you usually don't bring friends over 'cause Jasper don't like any kids around, or anyone else for that matter.'"

"She said that?"

"Yeh, she did," I told him.

"Well, I think she's the one acting pretty suspicious lately. She's been asking me a bunch of questions about Little Deer and how she is and all. She's even been disappearing during the day. She told me today she'd be out for awhile before Jasper gets home, which is totally unlike her to go sneaking around."

"Your momma is really nice Jesse," I told him. "She's pretty as can be too. She even told me I looked just the way you said."

Jesse's face actually turned red at this.

Bushes shook behind us and we both jerked around just in time to see the back end of the Coo-wa-chobee slinking back through the tall weeds.

"Jesse, I told you I felt like we were being watched," I said.

"Well, just be glad it's Coo-wa-chobee and not Lucas Cane," he said still watching the bushes where the cat disappeared to.

I got a horrible thought, "Suppose Lucas Cane's spirit has taken over the cat..."

Jesse looked at me like I had four-eyes or something. "Cally, don't get crazy on me now," he said. "That cat ain't evil; I told you how it protected me that time when Jasper was smacking me around. You saw what happened out in the woods with your friend Robert Lee."

"He ain't my friend, Jesse Tate," I protested.

"Well, whatever, I'm telling you that cat ain't evil and he sure doesn't like Jasper. At least that should give the creature some credibility. Remember? If an animal doesn't trust a human, then that human probably isn't someone you can trust either."

"Well, it's just spooky the way that cat is always around you," I said. "You know, as a matter of fact I have a question for you."

"Shoot!" Jesse said curious.

"On my birthday, I had a pajama party and we went down in the bomb shelter to do Connie's Ouija board game. Some really creepy things happened that night, things I can't explain. I think we may have had a visit from a real spirit. It wasn't anything good that's for sure, but one of the strangest things was that big cat. When we came out of the shelter thinking Robert Lee and the other boys were trying to scare us, we heard that loud purring and seen the amber eyes glowing in the woods."

"So?" Jesse had a sly smile on his lips.

"So! Why was the cat there? You were there, weren't you?"

Jesse had this stupid grin on his face. "You all ran like a bunch of scared rabbits," he started to laugh.

"I knew it!" I said smacking him good on his arm this time.

Jesse nearly fell off the tree trunk laughing. "I'd had you good and scared if that strange wind hadn't come up and started howling out of nowhere. I ran for it. At first it sounded like somebody coming from behind me, and then all of a sudden whoosh, that wind came up. I could hear the cat staying with me all the way through the woods until I made it home. I don't mind telling you whatever brought that wind put a fear in me."

"Lucas Cane!" I said.

"What!" Jesse laughed.

I explained, "Before I knew, I had this strange dream while napping on the shelter door. There was a boy holding a shiny box in my dream, but he ran away from me. When I seen you I thought you were that boy, but I think it was your daddy, Caleb. Anyway, that night at the Ouija board I asked who the mysterious boy in my dream was and that's when all heck broke loose. The wind began knocking things down and there was that terrible stench, like dead fish. We ran out of there lickety split. I don't know, maybe like Madame Rosemary, we conjured up Lucas Cane instead. You know him out wondering around the woods and all. Who knew? We were just a bunch of kids messing with things we ought not to. "'Amateurs,'" Patty warned us. She said spirits could be conjured up by either the power of God or by the devil. Well, guess what we got? Lord, Patty knows her scripture. Deuteronomy…"

"Who?" Jesse asked confused.

"Never mind, it's from the Bible. You know, scripture…, "Let no one found among you practice divination or sorcery,' and so on and so forth it goes on to say not to consult the dead as a medium. I should have listened. Every time I ignore her, trouble follows. Jesse, this whole thing, it's like a big puzzle. It's like somebody knew we we're going to meet, like it was all part of a big strange plan. The strangest thing is, that cat was there watching out for you again. I don't get it."

"I think I do, Cally," Jesse said, and then he held out his hand to me, "It's getting late. Come on, I'll walk you on home.

Taking hold of Jesse's hand, he helped pull me up. His touch was warm and pleasant.

"Cally," Jesse said as we walked, "Remember the Indian folktale Little Deer spoke of when she talked of the panther the other night?"

"Uh huh," I answered.

"Well, my momma told me that story a few years ago."

"Tell me the story, Jesse, while we walk. It'll occupy my mind, so as to keep dead spirits out of it."

Dark had begun to settle in the woods and the bob-white were twittering their nightly greetings. Jesse squeezed my hand and began the Seminole story of the Creator and the panther, the story that was told to children on the reservation in the Big Cypress.

"Seems of all the creatures of the earth, the Creator loved the panther most of all, so much so that he chose the panther to first walk the Earth. He put all the animals in a big shell and as time passed the roots of a giant tree cracked the shell, and the Creator sent the wind to whip around the shell faster and faster so the crack would grow larger. The wind, knowing the Creator wanted the panther to be first, helped the animal from the shell. Then all the other creatures followed, and each took their proper place on earth. The Creator rewarded the panther with special powers like the power of all knowledge of all living things. The panther also had great mental and healing powers. The panther and the wind travel together all the time. Little Deer says the panther sits and watches patiently and knows all truth. She says the Coo-wa-chobee crawls on four legs, close to the ground watching the woods and knowing all the creatures inhabiting it, animal or man."

A chill ran up my spine, as this story wasn't helping my uneasiness at all. All it brought me was a disturbing memory. I interrupted Jesse, "Jesse, the wind had snuffed the candle that night in the bomb shelter. It put an end to our foolhardy, messing with dead spirits and such, and had warned you to leave. Coo-wa-chobee was there to protect you."

"Yes, Cally," Jesse said stopping and turning to me. "Don't you see?, I think the cat has brought us together to find out the truth and set me, my mother, and Curtis Malcolm free from Jasper Tate.?"

"Jesse, it's almost like your real father's, Caleb's, spirit, is the one guiding the cat. The cat is like your guardian angel, Jesse. I believe the Creator in the story is God and I do believe he sent your Daddy here to guide you; he's trying to set you free."

Jesse squeezed my hand again and we kept walking silently. The only sounds were the light wind and the swishing of the pine needles above. My uneasiness seemed to fade as we walked hand in hand, just me and Jesse and it occurred to me that this must be pretty much as close to heaven as we get here on this Earth.. The closer Jesse and I got to my place, the more I wished the path would never end. But, soon the lights from my house faintly crept across the grass as we reached where wood and yard met. "I guess I'll be alright from here, Jesse. You better get back home before it gets too late. Thanks," I said.

"I'll just watch until you get to your backdoor Cally."

Smiling up at Jesse in the soft light, my tummy seemed to have a million butterflies fluttering in it, and without giving it another thought, I gave him a quick, awkward hug and then ran to the house. At the back door I turned as Jesse gave a wave, and then disappeared into the woods.

22 CHAPTER

The Fourth of July was finally here, hotter than Hades. "There's a storm coming soon," Dad had said last night. "Anytime it gets this sticky hot we're in for a real doozy."

I hoped not, at least not until after the fireworks. Dad must have been mistaken because the sunshine streaming in my bedroom window said it was sure to be a glorious day. Mom was going to bring plenty of her lemonade to the Boyd's cook-out. Dad said to bring an extra jug because he didn't want pop. "Pop doesn't quench your thirst out in that hot sun. A good cold Miller beer would hit the spot, but Lord knows there won't be any of that on the Boyd's premises," he'd told Mom. Dad wasn't a big drinker, but he liked a cold one now and then. On Friday nights when he got paid sometimes he'd take us to the Spaghetti House in Orange City. He always got an icy cold Miller High Life with the pretty dark haired girl sitting on a sliver of moonlight across the label. I preferred their breadsticks, crisp and garlicky on the outside, but soft in the center. I had a taste of Dad's Miller one time. It looked so good, all fizzy and cold. Boy was I surprised. I can't figure how Jasper and some of those men down at the Pepper Pot could drink enough of it to become so drunk. I mean it wasn't too terrible, but I didn't think I'd ever become the alcoholic Kate said I'd be if Dad gave me sips. She had me on some place called Skid Row by the time I was in High School, just for a tiny sip. I'd probably blow up from all the gas the fizziness caused in my stomach first. The smell of southern fried chicken filled the bedroom. Mom was taking it to the Boyd's. Kate, Lynn, and I had made a triple layer devil's food cake last night to take along.

I looked over at the alarm clock, "Oh my, gosh, Jesse! I almost forgot," I said sitting straight up in bed.

"Cally, what are you doing?" Lynn said pulling her pillow over her head.

"I'm supposed to meet Jesse at nine o'clock," I told her.

"Lynn pulled her pillow from her head. "You spend more time with Jesse Tate than you do Connie or Patty these days."

"So," I said not really seeing the problem.

"So, I think somebody has a sweetie," she said making little kissy sounds and pulling the covers over her head. Her foot stuck out at the bottom and I reached down and pinched her big toe.

"Ouch!" she kicked her foot at me, "Must have struck a nerve."

There was no time to argue so I ignored her remark and hurriedly got ready then headed into the kitchen stuffing some Snap, Crackle, and Pop down me.

"I'll be back in a little bit," I told Mom.

Before I could get across the kitchen, Dad said, "Cally, what's the rush?"

"Jesse's coming by in a few minutes. We're going to Little Deer's. She asked him to stop by this morning. I won't be long. I promise."

"Well, make sure you're not. You'll need to get back here and help your Mom and sisters," Dad said.

"When you see Jesse, tell him not to forget his swimsuit and be back here by three o'clock," Mom said over the sizzle of the skillet.

"No problem," I said looking out the window over the kitchen sink just in time to catch Jesse coming across the backyard. There went those butterflies again… I went through the laundry room and lifted up some towels on top of the dryer. Bill's tape-recorder from the other night sat underneath. I remembered Bill had laid it there when we came back from

Little Deer's, so I had slipped it under some clean towels. I was sure Bud wouldn't mind if Jesse and I used it. Probably wouldn't even miss it. Jesse had said he could use one for our plan. Wasn't sure exactly what he had in mind, but here it was nonetheless.

The morning was already hotter than a firecracker, I discovered as I met Jesse outside. "Whoo whee, it's sweltering out here," I said.

"Yeh, if we weren't going swimming over at your friends place later, I'd be in the spring today for sure," he said wiping sweat from his forehead. "I see you borrowed Bill's tape-recorder."

"Well, I didn't exactly borrow it. I just sort of took it off the dryer where they left it," I told him nervously.

Seeing my hesitation, Jesse said, "Don't worry, it will be fine. We'll get it back in one piece, I promise." He smiled that smile that made it hard to worry about anything.

"We'd better get going," Jesse said.

We were both curious as to what Little Deer wanted this morning. Jesse said he had a couple of the bushel baskets hid out in the woods for us to put the things in we needed for later. "How we going to get them out to your place without Jasper and Earl seeing us, or maybe your momma?" I wanted to know.

"Jasper and Earl left earlier this morning to take some of their fresh moonshine over to Astor and Ocala," Jesse said. "Those boys at the fish camp are good customers. I saw them loading their barrels in the back of Jasper's pickup when I first got up this morning. They won't be back until suppertime. Then they'll be getting the next batch ready for the Pepper Pot. There's going to be some real celebrating out at that little hole in the wall tonight."

The morning sun beat down hard as we walked. I thought my sneakers might melt in their tracks because the sand beneath them was burning hot. Thankfully, a canopy of moss covered oaks and thick, leafy Kudzu vine hanging from the tops of the pines shaded our path leading to Little Deer's.

"What do you suppose Little Deer needed that was so important this morning, Jesse?" I asked kicking at a fat June bug wiggling across the sand.

"Remember I told you my Momma was acting peculiar lately? Well, she was up and gone soon as Jasper left this morning, had a batch of fresh blueberry muffins in her tote bag. Remember Little Deer saying how she and my momma loved them so.?"

"Yeh," I said.

"Well, I'll bet you my Momma is out at her place right now, the two of them sitting there laughing and eating blueberry muffins."

"You think so, Jesse? That would be great. But what if Jasper catches her?" I said.

"After tonight, maybe she can come and go and do whatever she pleases, and not have to sneak around, worrying about Jasper Tate anymore," he said.

Jesse and I kept walking and as we made our way into the bright sunshine of the clearing, a shadow swept overhead. Gazing upward and following its shadowy path, the Peregrine Falcon soared high above us. I imagined its sharp eye already set on its next victim, a small rabbit or squirrel. "Jesse, I'll bet that's the same falcon we saw eating out of Little Deer's hand. Look how its wingspan spreads over a good yard. He's certainly a fierce one."

"I can't wait to get up there and fly like that someday in my jet plane," Jesse said standing back and watching the majestic bird. "Look, it's diving down over by the swamp. I'll bet he just made some rabbit his dinner."

"Poor thing," I said just as the bird, its wings tucked streamlined, shot across the treetops with its prey clasped in its sharp talons.

The baskets were just where Jesse had left them, stuffed between two cabbage palms. A troop of red ants were marching up the sides of them from a small ant hill. "Get off of there you red devils," I said shaking off the baskets.

"Jeez Cally, they're just ants," Jesse laughed.

"Just ants?... Why they're vicious little stinging marauders. Get into everything if you don't keep them sprayed or burnt out. Bud puts a little gasoline on the hills and lights them up. I hate them, their bites burn like fire. One day I was out with my Dad and Bud putting trash in our garbage pit out back. As I sat on the edge of the pit, poking the trash with a long stick, I thought I felt something crawling on me. I was horrified as I looked down to see I was covered with the little red buggers. It was just a matter of seconds. I commenced to screaming and swatting because they started biting. Mom heard me coming with Dad and Bud behind me. She stripped me down at the back door and Dad said to put me in the bathtub with some Epsom salts. I soaked in there until I was a wrinkled prune. Mom had to put calamine all over my legs. Kate said my legs looked like pink candy sticks."

"Well, you better move now or you'll have them all over you again," Jesse said as I looked down at the mound near my foot.

Jesse had a mop pail stuck inside one of the baskets. Said it was for some of that glowing mud at the swamp. He had some fishing line inside the pail. We gathered up the baskets. A gator croaked, sounding like a giant bullfrog along the canal. Swish, went the bushes, something scurrying through them caused us both to turn. Just as we did, out of the bushes came the big red dog, head down, panting hard. I'd not seen him in quite a while. I figured somebody must have shot or poisoned him for stealing their laundry, maybe even got snake bit. The crazy dog caught a glimpse of us and jerked and dodged moving like a house afire in the opposite direction. He had some pink colored silky thing between his teeth.

"He's up to his thievery again," Jesse laughed.

"Kate says he's a pervert," I told Jesse.

"He's a strange one, that's for sure. Probably got his own private collection of Playboy magazines stashed out here somewhere too," Jesse said.

"Jesse Tate!" I acted shocked. "You saw one of them magazines?"

"Why sure, I read them all the time. Jasper keeps them in the garage."

"You do not! You're just making that up. You're too young to read such things," I said blushing. "Don't tell nobody, but my brother Bud has one stuffed down in his nightstand in his room."

"How would you know Cally, you been sneaking around in your brother's drawers?"

"Have not! Just one time me and my friend Patty were looking for a comic book and we found it."

"Wait 'til I tell Bud," Jesse threatened.

"You wouldn't? Please don't tell Bud. I wasn't snooping," I said.

"Yeh not much," Jesse teased. I could feel my face getting hot.

"Well, anyway, you shouldn't be looking at that stuff. It ain't good for you," I told him.

"I'll decide what's good for me," Jesse said. "Don't go getting so prudish on me Cally Cummins. I'll bet Connie wouldn't be shocked."

That did it. I picked up a pine cone and tossed it at him. "Well, if you think Connie is so grown up and all then you can just get her to help you," I said, the green-eyed monster coming out of nowhere, but I couldn't stop it. "Why I wouldn't be surprised if one day she wasn't in one of them magazines," I said wishing immediately I hadn't said that about my friend. The guilt was fleeting. Jesse's comeback really burnt me.

"Oooh, now that's a thought," he smiled instinctively ducking waiting for another pine cone to come flying at him.

Fire was burning inside me now. I wanted to just smack him right then and there. Instead I stomped off ahead of him.

"Oh Cally, hold on," he said still laughing. "I was just kidding."

"Yeh, sure you were," I hollered as I started crossing the mucky swamp over the narrow bridge of sand and pine logs.

The fresh aroma of coffee surrounded the cottage. Coffee sure smells good, but it takes plenty of sugar and cream to make it drinkable. The big red dog had come to drop off his latest find and sat by the big black kettle scarfing down some leftovers Little Deer had left him. Voices and laughter lofted through the morning from inside the cottage. Jesse quickened his step. Without even knocking he opened the cottage door, walking right on in like he owned the place.

"Momma? I knew it. I knew this is where you been coming lately," he said as I ran in behind him.

Lila and Little Deer sat at the long table by the hearth, sipping their steaming coffee.

"What's going on?" Jesse asked the two women, both looking like the doggone cat that swallowed the canary.

"Come in! Come in," Little Deer welcomed us. "We were getting worried that you wouldn't make it."

"Why didn't you tell me you been coming out here? We could have come together," Jesse told his mother. "What if Jasper finds out where you been?"

"That's exactly why I didn't tell you. If Jasper asked you where I was, you didn't know and wouldn't have to lie for me. Jasper's good at telling if someone is lying to him or not," Lila said.

"Takes a liar to know one, I guess," Jesse smiled.

The door swung open causing Jesse and me to jump.

"Curtis Malcolm," Little Deer smiled. "I'm glad you made it back. You're right on time. Did you get the dolls delivered?" Curtis shook his head yes. Little Deer went over putting her arm around the timid man.

Jesse asked if somebody would please fill me and him in on what the big deal was this morning.

Lila spoke up, "Jesse, as you and Cally both know, Curtis, Little Deer and you and I, are all tied by our past. This is the place where I spent many wonderful days of my childhood, visiting Little Deer and meeting your real father and Curtis. It was our secret place, like it is yours and Cally's now. I learned about my Seminole heritage here." She got a real faraway look. "It seems all so very long ago," she sighed.

I could feel tears welling up inside my eyeballs and I squinted hard so as not to make a fool of myself. I looked over at Jesse, but his momma's talk had only made him bristle up. "You mean you came here everyday until Jasper Tate came into your life and bullied you and made you afraid for your life and Little Deer's, too."

"Jesse!" I scowled.

"Woo Woo Woo!" Curtis started up again like he done the other night. Just the pure mention of Jasper's name set him off. Little Deer tried to comfort him.

"Gosh almighty, I wish he'd stop that. It about makes me crazy!" Jesse said still agitated. Through the Woo Woo's he continued his tirade at his momma.

"Well, it's true Cally! She let him bully her and change everything she was, and now look at us."

It didn't seem right for Jesse to talk to his momma like that. She seemed so soft-spoken, almost fragile and the words flew out of my mouth in her defense. "Well, what in the Sam Hill was she supposed to do? She was pregnant..." I felt myself starting to blush. Little Deer had calmed Curtis, but I was just getting warmed up, and the words kept coming... "For Pete's sake Jesse, your Daddy was dead and from what you've told me, she had already lost her mother and father. She had nobody. It's hard for a girl in that condition and so young to raise a baby by herself. Why I think she did a very brave thing."

"Brave!" Jesse laughed.

"Yes, Jesse Tate, Brave! Why she could have just given you away or worse," I said remembering Lynn's and my talk in the science building at the College. "She'd done what she did and instead of running away she gave you life. You know Jasper Tate was just waiting for your daddy to be out of his way and he took advantage of the whole situation. She was weak, that's all." There I'd said it and the room was silent as a graveyard. Looking at Lila, she had little streams of tears flowing from her eyes.

"I'm sorry Miss Lila. I didn't mean to make you cry," I said feeling guilty as all get out now.

"You're a very wise little girl, Cally, but Jesse is right; I should have been stronger. I could have gone somewhere else and started over with my baby. I was afraid," Lila said, dabbing her tears and standing up straight as an arrow, "But no more, Jesse!" Lila stared Jesse square in the eyes, "No more! Jasper Tate isn't going to burden us anymore. I'm going to make some changes for you and me. We're going to get away from Jasper and start over like we should've then."

"Woo!" Curtis started up at the mention of Jasper Tate again. Seems Curtis understood a lot more than what was given credit to him. I wondered.

"How are you going to leave Jasper, Momma? He already told you if you ever tried to leave him he'd see you dead. I heard him tell you that one night when he was falling down drunk." Jesse told her.

"That was the moonshine talking, Jesse. You let me worry about all that. Little Deer and I will figure something out," Lila said giving Little Deer a hug.

"After tonight you may never have to worry about him again," Jesse mumbled under his breath, but not quite low enough, because Lila's Indian brown face turned slightly ash colored at his words. Looked just like Madame Rosemary's the night Lucas Cane paid us a visit. "What did you say?" Lila asked her son.

To keep from answering, Jesse acted disgusted at Curtis' wild display again. "What is with all this Woo Woo stuff?" He walked right up to Curtis grabbing him by the shoulders. "Get a grip on yourself, Curtis. Jasper Tate is nowhere around here. It's just a name."

"Jesse leave him be," Little Deer stepped in. "We discussed this the other night. He's done it ever since the fire and there's no stopping it."

"Well, I hate to say this, I mean he seems a good sort and all, but I'm beginning to think people are right when they say he's a little touched," Jesse said pointing to his head.

Little Deer came unwound. Her words flowed slowly with a controlled force, jaw drawn tight, just like old Foxy when he had to repeat himself. She spoke, "Don't ever go saying Curtis is that way! Just 'cause he gets a little upset at certain names…"

"A little upset," Jesse huffed.

Little Deer kept focused, raising her tone, "Just because he doesn't say much, he's not ignorant. He hears everything you say and understands most, and most important he gets his feelings hurt. Something happened to him that night of the fire, something that shouldn't happen to anyone. He was what them head doctors call traumatized. It put a fear in him that he chose to block. I know that somehow…" but then her words turned into a whisper, "Jasper Tate is right in the middle of it. You can see the fear in Curtis' eyes every time that devil is mentioned."

"Well, I seen that look in his brown eyes too, and I don't think what they're reflecting is fear so much as it is a powerful, burning hate. It's the look I seen in my momma's eyes every time Jasper pushes me around."

Lila had been listening quietly, her brow furrowed deep with thought. I was certain she had heard every word of Jesse's promise earlier about taking care of Jasper and now she spoke her mind. "Jesse, I know you're up to something. You been sneaking around the garage and hanging around Earl while Jasper is away. You even had Cally come over, knowing full well Jasper would skin you alive for it. What's going on in that head of yours?"

I turned my attentions to Curtis Malcolm while Jesse and his momma had words. Curtis didn't even seem to notice anyone was in the room except him. He'd walked over and filled an empty cup with coffee from the stove and was munching away on a piece of fry bread. What was going on in that little world of his, this very minute? Jesse and his momma were still going back and forth. Lila demanded to know what was so important about tonight. Jesse kept denying ever saying anything about tonight except that he was coming to the Boyd's and getting his fill of my mom's fried chicken and potato salad. Lila called him a scoundrel and said she'd figure him out. As their bantering continued, I sat down beside Curtis. I just sat, watching him as he ate, oblivious to what was going on around him. I wonder... I was itching to tell someone about Jesse's and my secret. I could tell Curtis Malcolm. Who would he tell? Besides, I figured he should know we were going to take Jasper to task and make him pay for whatever he'd done to ruin so many lives, including Curtis'. I'd never heard Curtis say much more than Caleb or Woo Woo anyway. Curtis just sat, sipping his coffee in a world of his own. Little Deer said he understood stuff. Maybe if I told him it might come as a comfort to him. So as the others went at one another, I decided to tell Curtis a story about a Fourth of July Celebration to end all celebrations...

"Cally!" Jesse's voice filled the cottage.

"What?" I said startled, realizing the quarreling in the room had halted. Little Deer, Lila, and Jesse stood staring at me and Curtis. The way Jesse was staring at me made me uncomfortable, like I was up to something. He couldn't have heard me, he was too busy trying to convince his mother he wasn't.

"Well, seems like you two are getting well acquainted," Little Deer smiled at me and then looking at Curtis she said, "Curtis, my goodness what were you two talking about, you look so serious." I smiled back sheepishly and looked at Jesse, then back at Curtis. Curtis' face was serious alright. He had that worried look, the one I sometimes saw in my mom's face when she'd tell Bud to drive careful before he'd go out.

"Well, no time for such serious faces today, Curtis," Little Deer thankfully changed the subject, because I could almost see Jesse's mind ticking, figuring out what I'd gone and done. "I know you and Cally have to leave in a while for your party, so we should get started. Come along."

Little Deer walked to the door, opening it, then standing back she waited for the rest of us to join her. Jesse shrugged and followed and so did we all.

A puff of gray smoke swirled from behind the cottage and the smell of firewood filled the air. "Oh, good Curtis, you did a lovely job of making our fire," Little Deer said as we rounded the cottage to see a campfire with a rotisserie of two forked oak limbs, and a small iron pot swinging over the flames.

"Are we having a Fourth of July cookout?" I asked.

Lila smiled and took my hand, "Come Cally, you are in for a special celebration. Come with me to the sacred fire and our little 'Festival of the Green Corn Feast.'"

A small picnic table was set up near the fire. Bowls and platters covered the tabletop. There was smell of fresh cedar in the air.

"What's the sacred fire for?" I whispered to Lila.

Lila just smiled and took two colored ribbons from her pocket, a red and a yellow one. Taking some strands of my hair in her hands she tied one on each side of my head, then took out blue and green ones and did the same to hers. Little Deer took something off the table; it was her sky blue bed-jacket. Putting it on, she draped her long black and silver braids over each shoulder. Holding her head high to the sky, she looked quite regal. Removing a small brown, worn leather pouch from the jacket pocket, Little Deer held it up with one hand, waving us toward her with the other. "Please come with me around the fire now. Jesse, you stand next to me, then your mother. Cally and Curtis you may join us as we circle the sacred fire. We did as we were told and as we gathered quietly Little Deer began to speak in an odd language; I took for granted it was Creek. As she spoke she pulled apart the gathered top of the leather pouch and removed some of its contents between her fingers. Circling the fire and continuing a chant in her native tongue she tossed whatever had been in the pouch into the flames. Little Deer stopped and Jesse nearly ran into her. Turning to Jesse, she spoke, this time in English. "Jesse, today we are re-enacting a true tradition of our people. Usually it is a grand festival with dancing and celebrating lasting three days, with all the members of the tribes coming together. It is called the Festival of the Green Corn. During that festival, young Seminole men of your age celebrate a rite of passage and are given their Indian name. Your mother and I are your only connection to our great past in this place, so we chose to honor you in the naming ceremony ourselves. We can do this because I, Little Deer being the only child of our tribe's healer, received his tribal bag. Normally it is given to the eldest son, but my father had no sons and the pouch was given to me when he passed." Little Deer held up the leather pouch. This tribal pouch is passed from generation to generation and the sacred fire is impossible without a sprinkling of its contents."

I was dying to ask what was in it. What magical potion did it contain; fairy dust, like Tinkerbelle's maybe? I guessed I'd better ask later. This was much too solemn, like church.

Lila took Jesse's hand, "Today my son, you will become a true Seminole. Because you are the grandson of a full-blooded Seminole of the Muskogee tribe of the Big Cypress Reservation and I am the daughter of the Seminole people you too have that birthright."

I could tell Jesse was a little overwhelmed by all this and hadn't expected anything more than a little Fourth of July get together. His face was scarlet and I was pretty sure it wasn't just this sweltering campfire that brought the color to his cheeks. Yet, in spite of his red-face, Jesse beamed with pride. He looked as proud as the peacocks over at Blue Springs with their fancy tail-feathers all spread out for everyone to gawk and take pictures of.

Little Deer asked, "Lila, daughter of Red Hawk, what name do you give your son?"

Lila smiled a smile that I knew came straight up from her heart. Turning to Jesse she said, "My son Jesse, will hereafter be known as Ochee Somoli Coo-wa, Little Wild Cat. Because you are like the panther, wise, strong, and brave, with a spirit that is wild and free."

"Lila, you will hereafter be known as Lila, mother of Little Wild Cat," Little Deer announced.

Jesse's grin spread pretty much from ear to ear, pleased with his new identity. It fit him perfectly. Little Deer held the leather pouch out to Jesse. He looked confused and I could see he didn't know what to do.

"Take this Ochee Somoli Coo-wa. I have no children, but your mother and father were like my own. You shall now be the keeper of the tribal bag," she said.

"Oh, no, Little Deer, I couldn't. It's yours. Your father gave it to you. You're very much alive," Jesse stammered.

"Yes, Jesse, but Little Deer is ahassee…" she told him. Seeing he did not understand, she said, "Ahassee…Old. I am an old woman and probably will never return to the Big Cypress. You can take it one day. Your mother will teach you what it means to be Seminole and one day you will go to the Festival of the Green Corn and be a part of our heritage."

My eyes were welling up something awful and I couldn't control the tears as they ran down my cheeks. Jesse had defeated old Jasper Tate right here around the sacred fire, in the middle of this swamp. He shed the burden of ever having thought he was the offspring of such a scoundrel. He was Jesse, Little Wild Cat, son of Lila and Grandson of Red Hawk, a true Seminole. They never surrendered and Jesse didn't have to either.

"Now let's have our feast," Little Deer gratefully announced. Exciting and as emotional as it all was I was about to self-combust from the heat of the day mixed with the flames of the sacred fire.

As we all sat around the picnic table, Little Deer removed the lid from the iron pot in the middle of the table, revealing a wonderful smelling, thick soup like substance. I found as I scooped up a steaming bite, it contained corn and some sort of meat that from the gamey taste probably was venison. It tasted like the stew Mom had made from the deer Bud brought down last fall. As Little Deer served everyone, she explained that the soup was part of the traditional festival. Besides the soup, there were all kinds of fresh vegetables from Little Deer's garden: tomatoes, cucumbers, and onions. When everyone was served, Little Deer asked us to bow our heads to give thanks to the Creator. I quickly put down my spoon and checked to see if anyone had noticed I'd already started. "Forgive me," I whispered and I felt Jesse nudge me.

Before bowing her head, Little Deer took in a deep breath and slowly released it, "Oh Creator, my senses tell me you are here among us."

"How does she know that?" I whispered to Lila, who sat next to me.

Lila raised her head slightly. "The aroma of Cedar hangs in the air. It is the breath of the one above."

Closing my eyes, and taking in a deep breath, "Yes," I said softly. I could smell it too.

I bowed my head as Little Deer began to pray in the Creek Language of the Seminole. When she was finished no one spoke a whole lot for the next few minutes. Everyone was too busy stuffing themselves with all the delicious ceremonial meal. Curtis was the first one finished. Boy, did he have an appetite. He stood up patting his stomach with great satisfaction, then gave out with a belch so loud I waited for his toes to come popping out of his mouth. There were a couple buckets of sand near the fire and Curtis retrieved them, dumping the sand over the flames, extinguishing them. Hallelujah! Now maybe I could really enjoy this fine feast. It was a good ten degrees cooler here under the shade of the oaks without that fire. Little Deer poured a dark red liquid from a green aluminum pitcher into matching green glasses, just like the yellow ones Mom got at the Jewel T store when she bought $20.00 twenty dollars worth of groceries. The liquid was sweet, some kind of berry drink and best of all, ice-cold. Lila held up her glass and made a toast, "From the Creator, and Sacred Fire comes life, and I am proud to have been the vessel that gave you that life my son." Then she spoke a word from the Creek language, "Ecenokkecis"

Jesse smiled, "Ecenokkecis," he said back to his mother.

Everyone heartily raised their glasses and said something in Creek. For lack of knowing what else to say, holding my glass high I chimed in, "Cheers!" The women laughed.

We finished our meal and Jesse told his mother and Little Deer how much he appreciated what they had done and that he was honored to be a part of a heritage as proud as the Seminole. We celebrated a little while longer, but the hour was getting late, so Jesse told Little Deer he and I really had to go, because we had to help get things ready for the Boyd's picnic. He lied. Before leaving, Jesse asked Little Deer if we could borrow her old wagon she kept for toting the vegetables from her garden. She agreed and the two of us left the others to bask in the glory of their celebration.

Colleen Affeld

23 CHAPTER

"I'm sure glad you borrowed this wagon, Jesse," I said as he and I scooped up a bunch of the swamp mud in the pail, placing it inside the wagon. "We'd have never carried all this stuff back to your place without it."

We maneuvered the wagon back across the log bridge.

"You sure Jasper won't be around?" I asked.

"Trust me Cally, when it involves his shine, Jasper will be occupied all day."

"Well, I'd sure hate to get back to the canal behind his garage and have him catch us," I said.

Stopping to catch our breath and wipe the sweat beads from our faces, I had to ask him, "Hey, how's it feel to be an honest to goodness Seminole Indian?" I was so proud of him. "Besides Little Deer and now Lila, and you, I've never known any real Indians. It's funny how in real life you're not anything like what I'd expected. I mean, like the ones on television or in the movies."

Jesse just looked at me like he couldn't believe I even said that.

"Well, really Jesse, Indians today are much more civilized, just regular people, not Miss Dulsey Mae Stoner's murdering' savages. We studied about the Seminole and their chief Osceola in school. That's when they were always fighting."

"Just trying to keep what was theirs, that's all," Jesse reminded me. And, it's Asen Yahola, not Osceola. It was the English that corrupted his real name. They couldn't pronounce it, so Osceola is what we read in our history books. My mom told me all about it. Asen was a ceremonial drink and yahola means, 'cry of the wolf.'"

"Well, maybe now that you're an official Seminole, maybe you can get them to change it," I told him.

Jesse just shook his head. "You know Cally, I've always been Seminole, but I just didn't know it. Now, it's official that's all. To answer your question though, mostly, I guess I just feel proud. I don't know quite how to explain it. I mean, I've been finding out all kinds of things I am lately and it's real strange. It's like I've had this whole different secret identity. I guess the best part is finding out that Jasper Tate ain't my real daddy."

I was curious about something Lila said back at the ceremony. "Jesse, what was that Indian word your mother said to you during the ceremony. It was something like, Ecenoke, or something such as that."

Jesse blushed. "She said, 'Ecenokkecis.' It means 'I love you.' She would say that to me from the time I was little."

Jesse went back to pulling the wagon. It wasn't sunburn turning his ears read so I dropped the subject and pushed. Trudging along past the Landing and Jasper Tate's aunts' houses I could see the magnolias where I'd waited on Jesse before. The sun beat mercilessly on us. The fragrant trees caste a wide circle of shade across the blistering, hot sand; they were a welcome oasis. The bubbling, crystal blue spring waters looked mighty inviting.

About to give in to the temptation of soaking my hot feet, Jesse stopped suddenly. "Someone's coming. Quick, help me get this thing off the road." He gave a jerk on the black handle nearly causing me to do a nose dive into the sand. Catching my balance and shoving as hard as I could we headed towards the cover of the magnolia and tall weeds.

"Ouch!" I said grabbing my foot after stepping into the thicket. "Gosh darn it Jesse!" A cluster of tiny round burrs stuck in my sock and now in my fingers as I tried to remove them. "Darn sand spurs!"

Seminole Landing

"Come on Cally, push! It might be Jasper," Jesse said.

Struck by fear, I painfully pushed the wagon until we had it safely behind the trees, ducking into the bushes. "Ouch," I whispered trying to pull one of the prickly things from my finger. A truck was coming slowly down the road, churning up a white cloud of dust and dirt. Through the dirty glass windshield sat Earl.

"I thought you said Earl was with Jasper," I said.

"Jasper must have sent him back for something," Jesse shushed me.

The truck passed and Jesse said to stay put, he'd be right back. Pulling something out of his pants pocket he tore off before I could say anything.

"Well that's just great," I said to nothing more than the magnolias. "Here I sit stickers in my foot and Lord only knows what kind of creatures crawling around in these bushes." Checking out the surrounding area, a buttercup, yellow butterfly flitted past and lit on some yellow tick weed. If I'd not seen it light I would have thought it to be part of the flowers, it blended in so. I ran my finger over my thumb. "I know there's a sticker in…Yow! I got it." A little speck of blood oozed from where the tiny thorn had implanted itself..

"Cally," Jesse said slipping back into the bushes, sending me off my haunches into the sand.

"Jeez, you scared me to death, Jesse," I said picking myself up.

"Shhhh!" he hushed me as the whir of an engine approached from his place. We ducked down and waited as Earl threw it into gear scattering sand and dust all over, speeding by like a bat out of H E double L.

"Now there goes a man on a mission," I said. "Sure didn't take you long. Where'd you take off to in such a hurry? He could've seen you, Jesse!"

"Relax, he didn't see anything. He was in too big a hurry. They must have forgotten a couple of orders. Earl was loading them up," Jesse said, a big grin on his face as he watched the dust trail settle Earl left behind.

"So, what did you do back there and why are you so smiley?" I asked.

"Just put a little something on the truck seat for Earl. A little blast from the past I found in one of Jasper's old Florida East Coast employee directories. By the way he took off out of here, I'd say it did the trick," Jesse said giving me the high sign. "Our plan is now officially in motion. We best be getting this stuff out back to the canal before my momma comes home."

I stood my ground. "Not before you tell me what sort of little something you put in that truck."

Jesse ignored me and started to pull the wagon, "Nothing much, just a little picture."

I stomped my foot inside the wagon to stop it. "What kind of picture?"

Jesse had that rascally grin that made it so darn hard to argue with him. "Just a nice mug shot of Lucas Cane standing in the railroad yard holding one of his lanterns is all," Jesse laughed, "Man, I'd give anything to have seen Earl's face when he laid eyes on it. Better yet to have known what he was thinking at that very moment."

This didn't make a whole lot of sense to me and I didn't see what was so great about it, and I said as much.

"Cally, don't you see? With any luck, Earl will take that picture straight to Jasper; at least that was my intention. It was pretty obvious Earl was all spooked at the thought of ghosts out here, now he's got a picture of one to stir him up a little more. He's sure to start in on Jasper about it. I want Earl to get the whole conversation started about Lucas Cane with Jasper before tonight. After the two of them get a little of that moonshine in them and commence to arguing about ghosts I'm hoping Earl starts flapping his gums about what really happened so long ago. Later, when they're back here and it's good and dark and they're good and drunk it might just all come out." Jesse picked up Bill's tape-recorder I'd taken from my house. "That's when I'll get it all right here, a confession."

"How are you going to do that without Jasper seeing you?" I asked.

"Just wait. All in good time, Cally," Jesse said as he began pulling the wagon again. I pushed with my good, sticker-less foot to get the back wheels over a gnarled up root sticking out of the ground. I sure hoped Jesse knew what he was doing.

The canal was dark and the water black as night, looking like too strong coffee. We parked the wagon between a fallen down scrub oak and some piles of dirt by a garbage pit. An old washing machine sat on its side, rusting away. Sorting through all the odds and ends in the wagon, fishing line, flashlights, tape recorder, and bucket of swamp mud, Jesse said we had everything we needed. Jesse took a roll of plastic from inside the wagon and spread it out placing it across our supplies. "Just in case the weathermen are actually right and it rains later," he said.

There was a burlap sack still in the wagon that I hadn't seen the contents of yet. "What you got in there?" I asked.

Jesse reached into the sack and pulled out two bright red sticks.

"That looks like dynamite!" I said. "Are you crazy? What the Sam Hill are you doing with those? You'll blow up the whole place, including us!" Expecting the whole sand cliff we were standing to explode and crumble into the canal, I stepped back.

Jesse threw down the sack, his eyes shooting daggers through me, "I ain't blowing up anything, Cally. What's the matter with you? Haven't you ever seen a flare? Besides, I ain't going to light them, you are!"

"I ain't doing no such thing, Jesse Tate. Why you're crazier than half-wit, Earl if you think I'm lighting up anything. Why, Mr. Wild Cat, I think your momma should have named you, Jesse, The Crazy Lunatic, if you think I'm even touching those things. I can't believe you ain't ever heard of what happened to poor old Mr. Allison."

"No, can't say I know the man," Jesse said patronizing me, with that darn smile on his face again. He was actually enjoying my ranting and raving.

"Well, you ain't ever going to know him neither," I told him. "Cause he's dead, blown to little tiny bits. He's got parts from the county road, clean over to the Landing most likely. I'll never forget it. I can still hear the explosion..."

It had been one of them moments in life that a kid likely never forgets, not even when they turned white haired and wrinkled, I guessed. I remembered it like it was yesterday.

Bud, Lynn, and Kate had left for school earlier and me and my mom were having poached eggs on toast, when all of a sudden, BOOM!! The whole house shook. Glasses and dishes inside the cupboard rattled and the rooster clock over the oven rocked on its nail. I'd just taken a bite of the runny, yellow yoke soaking into my toast. I can just taste it… Anyway, after the blast, I knew for sure right then, that those Russians had dropped the big one and it pretty well scared the life right out of me as I sputtered and choked on my breakfast. Mom slapped my back to stop my coughing. She stayed calm and took my hand leading me outside to look for any sign of the explosion. I told Mom we had better get back inside because the fallout would be coming soon. Mom, still gazing out over the field where our garden sits, said it wasn't a bomb that went off. She scanned the sky. "It's probably just one of those test pilots down at the Cape, breaking the sound barrier. They've been doing that a lot lately," she said. Then all at once she pointed to the south, "Look Cally, there's smoke coming up above the trees down near the Allison's farm." I looked in the direction mom pointed and sure enough little puffs of black smoke rose above the tops of the pines. I was relieved to see it didn't resemble a mushroom.

Sirens could be heard coming from downtown DeLeon. I asked Mom could we walk down the road a ways and see if we could get a better look.

"No, Cally," she said. "You need to get your things for school or you'll be late."

"Without even knowing what all the commotion is?" I pleaded. "Why I'd be good for nothing all day if I don't find out."

"My guess is Mr. Allison is blowing up some of the stumps in his pasture. Except…," she hesitated, "that one was a real doozy." Mom's expression was full of concern. She turned and scooted me back inside. "Tell you what, you get your things and I'll drive you over to the school this morning. Maybe we can see a little better down at the school road. The Allison's place is just across from there."

"Now you're talking," I thought running lickety split to get my things.

When me and Mom pulled into the school drive we could see the police and fire trucks parked along the fence surrounding the Allison's pasture. People were standing all along the fence line. Mr. Ellich, Bill's daddy was standing out front of his place talking to one of the policemen who was putting up some of those saw-horse looking things to block traffic. Stopping the car along the road Mom hollered over to Mr. Ellich, "William!"

Spotting us, Mr. Ellich came over to the car, but seeing me he lowered his voice so as to just speak to my mother.

Luckily there ain't anything wrong with my hearing.

"Allison, that darn fool, blew himself from here to Kingdom Come," he told Mom.

"Oh, Sweet Jesus," Mom gasped putting her hand to her mouth.

"He was blowing up stumps, like he's always done. Lord only knows why he just didn't hook some chain to his pick-up and pull them out," Mr. Ellich shook his head. "Fuse must have been either too short or too quick…I looked over one second and seen him, the next he was gone."

The poached eggs churned a million times over in my stomach and I thought I might be sick. By the bloodless color of Mom's complexion I thought she might join me. Funny, but all I could think of was to shut my eyes, because I didn't want to maybe see little pieces of Mr. Allison floating down onto the side of the road or draping from one of the trees like a piece of moss.

"Cally!" Jesse's voice brought me back to the here and now.

"Jesse Tate, there is no way I'm going to light no stick of dynamite or whatever you call that thing," I said before he could say another word.

Jesse just shook his head and mumbled, "We'll discuss it later." He just dismissed the whole thing. Just like that.

"You're right, we'll see Jesse Tate," I thought.

"I got to go," I told him kicking at the sand as I walked away, a pile of it seeping in and filling up my shoe. "Don't be late!" I hollered to him.

I was beginning to have doubts about Jesse's plan. We could be walking into a heck of a mess. Maybe I should tell Bud what was going on. He'd help us. I'd sure feel a lot safer if Bud was in on it. He wouldn't expect me to light those flares. I heard Jesse's warning as I walked home, "Don't go telling anybody else. You get too many people involved then it's all spoiled. Blow the whole thing sky high…"

"Yeh right, maybe myself too," I sputtered kicking at the sand again. Jesse could be stubborn as they come.

"Just do it the way I said, Cally or forget it. I don't need your help," I mimicked him.

He needed my help and he knew it. I'd stay quiet for now. So far the only one who knew was Curtis, a lot of good that would do.

24 CHAPTER

Mom and Dad were just about finished loading up the Galaxy's trunk with chicken and other good smelling stuff. I kicked off my sneakers and socks and put them next to me on the carport ledge where I sat waiting for Jesse. Where in the heck could he be anyway? Just as I was about to stick a hot foot in a cool spray from the sprinklers I spotted a skinny green chameleon peeking out at me from underneath Mom's bright red, Mr. Lincoln rosebush. Plop! A water droplet rolled off a green leaf landing on the tiny creature sending him leaping onto the cement block ledge, scurrying away onto the patio and out into the grass. Following his escape across the yard I saw Jesse's red T-shirt coming through the Sweet Laurel on the edge of the property.

"What took you so long?" I asked him as he dodged the sprinkler and sat down beside me on the ledge.

"Jasper came home earlier than we thought and made me help him and Earl unload some of his empty barrels and jugs from the truck," Jesse moaned. "I had to change my shirt because I didn't think I'd make too good an impression on your friends if I smelled like moonshine."

"Earl say anything while you were there about what he found in his truck?"

"No, but I could tell he and Jasper had been rippin' at one another because Jasper wasn't talking much, and what he did manage to say took a real nasty tone." Jesse flashed that million dollar smile and winked. "I'll tell you this much Cal, Earl was acting nervous and jerking his head around real squirrelly like. Looked like he half expected Lucas Cane to come floating out from the canal at any minute."

Hmmm, Jesse called me Cal. Bud usually was the only one who used that familiarity. I liked hearing Jesse say it.

Jesse was laughing, "The best part of the whole thing was when Jasper told Earl to go down by the creek and get a bucket of river water to pour in the radiator of the truck 'cause it was overheating. Earl started squawking about it and Jasper told him he was getting on his last nerve, and that it was broad daylight. He told Earl to get down there and do like he told him and quit letting his wild imagination make him act like a darned fool."

I had to laugh as Jesse did a pretty good imitation of Jasper Tate's gruff, alcohol- slurred voice. "I don't have time for none of your dang stupidity you half-witted, scaredy cat," Jesse sputtered out.

"I finished up what I had to do and left them standing there arguing like two crotchety old women," Jesse said. "I can't wait to see how Earl reacts later tonight when we get him going."

"He'll probably go over the edge," I said.

The smile had left Jesse's face when he turned to me now, "Cally, this has got to work. I owe it to my momma and Caleb Malcolm."

"Oh, Jesse, I hope for all our sakes it works," I whispered. "I'm getting a little nervous about the whole thing."

"Come on you two!" The sound of Dad's voice temporarily took away my fears.

The back door opened and Bud, Gloria, and my two sisters came out to join the rest of us. Kate had on her Jacqueline Kennedy sunglasses and carried her red, gold, and blue beach bag. She looked like one of those models in Mom's magazines. I had to admit she looked very classy, like Gloria. Kate didn't know it, but safely tucked under her things was my Indian doll Little Deer had made. Little Deer said it brought luck and if I ever needed it, it was tonight. The four of them headed over to Bud's Ford in the driveway.

"Hey! Where y'all going," I yelled. They had to come to the party. I wanted Bud there, just in case…

"Same place you're going Cally. You children are riding with Mom and Dad and we're riding with Bud," Kate said in a very annoying debutante voice, courtesy of one Miss Dulsey Mae Stoner, all the more reason to avoid those teas as long as possible.

"Kate, I only have so much room in here," Bud said looking at Kate's bag. We're only going for the evening, not a week."

I flashed Kate a big smart aleck grin and crawled in the backseat of Mom and Dad's car.

"Got your swimsuit, Jesse?" Mom asked as he crawled in beside me.

"Yes Ma'am, wrapped up right here," Jesse said holding out his rolled up towel.

As Dad started up the engine, I asked Jesse, "Can I tell them your news?"

Jesse looked confused then rolling his eyes, his face turned a little pink;, "I don't care. They probably won't be interested in all that anyway."

"Of course they will, Jesse, it's really so cool," I said nudging him.

"Well, you have to tell us now," Mom said turning around towards the backseat. "You've got our curiosity stirred up."

Jesse just sunk down in his seat real humble like, for Jesse. I guess he wasn't used to anybody paying much attention to anything he did. That is except his momma.

"Well, go ahead, you already started now, so you might as well finish," Jesse said. I swear I do believe he really did want me to tell them even if he acted like it was all just a big nothing.

Well, I was so proud of Jesse, once I started, I just kept rambling on so about Little Deer, Lila, and Curtis and how Jesse was a true pure blooded descendent of a real Seminole and how Little Deer's daddy was a Healer, or Medicine Man as we call them and how she waved the little leather bag and…

"Cally!" Dad yelled, "You're a talking machine and you're in a spin. You need to take it down a notch or two. Why don't you let Jesse tell us about it?"

Jesse looked surprised that anyone really cared and sat up kind of fiddling with his hands, then after an uncomfortable silence he began. Pride seemed to about burst from his very being as he told of the Green Corn Ceremony and how he had been honored with his Indian name of Ochee Somali Coo-wa.

Mom turned away wiping her eyes. "How proud your Mother must be, Jesse," Clearing her throat she added, "I mean...Ochee so... ...How do you say it?"

"It means Little Wild Cat," Jesse helped her out. "That's okay, Mrs. Cummins you can still call me Jesse," he smiled at her. I could see he was touched by her reaction.

"I think this would make for a terrific Sun News human interest story," Dad said. "It sure would be a lot more interesting than the latest cotillion Miss Stoner threw. What do you think Cally?" Dad winked at me in the rear-view mirror.

"No Sir!" Jesse panicked. "Jasper Tate would be furious if he knew about any of this. I can't ever tell anyone else," he said looking like a deer in the headlights.

"Sorry Jesse, I didn't think," Dad said. "I just think you should be very proud of what happened today and it's a shame you can't share it. It's just proof of the fine young man you're becoming. You know, you've done a great job out there in the garden. Don't worry; your secret is safe with us."

Jesse squirmed in the seat. He just couldn't stand much more praise. He just wasn't used to it. His cheeks were looking like I did when I had the Asian flu, all flushed and red. Dad turned on the radio and Jesse looked relieved he didn't have to talk anymore. As we sped along the boulevard across DeLeon, it looked like an advertisement for The Great American Way—little American flags lining the curbs, and the courthouse entrance draped in red, white, and blue banners. Along the boulevard, puffs of smoky barbecues, floated up over roof tops, their homes buzzing with families and friends playing badminton and volleyball. Laughter and soft screams of cool delight came from backyard swimming pools. Passing on by Aunt Ruth's and Miss Stoner's, the two elderly women sat on the white porch swing hung on Miss Stoner's front porch. Their hands slowly waved the cardboard fans from the First Methodist Church as they sat and read today's holiday edition of the Sun News, probably the society page with all the local gossip. Pure orneriness overtook me picturing Little Deer sitting with Lila on her front stoop wearing a silky blue bed-jacket.

Jesse stared out the car window, seemingly far, far away. Studying him I wondered what Patty would think when she first laid eyes on him. I knew she'd think he was just about the handsomest boy she ever did see around here. I couldn't disagree what with his tousled sun-kissed hair and tan skin framing that sly white-toothed grin of his. Of course, she wouldn't approve of his worldly ways or talk. I didn't care; that was all part of his charm. That's what made him so different from the boys at school. He must have felt my eyes on him because he turned away from the window and back at me. Glancing away, I could feel my face heat up in a bright red blush. I tried to think of something to say. "I just love the Fourth of July, don't you, Jesse?"

He turned back towards the open window. "Yeh, me too Cally," he answered his voice trailing off into the breeze. I thought I heard him say, "Independence Day."

Just past the city limit sign and the road leading out to where our friend Isaac lived along the river, the boulevard turned into a two-lane highway. It ran clean across the state from here to the Gulf of Mexico. Dad slowed down before the big draw bridge which spanned the St. John's and turned onto the Boyd's road. The channel was alive with holiday revelers as Johnson boat motors churned up the black water pulling skiers gliding behind streamlined boats.

"Won't be any good bass fishing today with all those yahoos out there stirring everything up," Dad said.

Mom reminded him that he needed to relax, that it was a holiday. "After supper when the fish are good and hungry you and Matt Boyd can fish off the dock," she said gently brushing his sideburns back.   "Yeh, until they start blasting off fireworks when it gets dark," he complained. My Dad didn't much care for fireworks. The loud popping explosions reminded him of the war. Mom had said that after he got back from someplace called

New Guinea in the Pacific, even the backfire from an automobile could send him under their bed. He lay there waiting for all H-E double L to break loose until he got good and woke up. That kind of explained why he took all that Red scare thing so serious and we ended up with a bomb shelter instead of a swimming pool. I was really starting to dislike them Red guys about as much as my Grandpa Cummins and President Kennedy did.

"Look at all those cars," Dad said. "What did they do, invite the whole town of DeLeon? I'll end up parking clear down at the Pepper Pot."

I caught a smile cross Jesse's lips. The first honest to goodness relaxed smile I'd seen from him since we got in the car. I wished Dad would hurry and find a spot. I was starving, smelling all that fried chicken wafting up from the trunk. Jesse must have smelled it too. "I'm starving, Mrs. Cummins. Good thing that fried chicken is in your trunk or there wouldn't be any left for the party," Jesse said pleasing my Mom no doubt.

Just as I figured, Patty's eyes just about popped when she saw Jesse. I could see she was impressed by his looks, but she immediately started sizing him up. She was giving him that, okay he looks real good, so there must be something wrong with him, kind off look. I'd already warned Jesse that the Boyd's and a lot of their company were Pentecostals and that just about anything a kid did was subject to damnation. So, Jesse didn't say much, but hello. It wasn't long before Mrs. Boyd and the other women started calling everyone to come and get it.

"It's about time," Jesse said. "Let's hurry up before your Mom's chicken and potato salad are gone."

"Behave, you ain't going to starve," I said, although my stomach was growling about as loud as the Coo-wa-chobee right now.

Jesse, Patty, and I couldn't fill our plates quick enough. We sat down across from Mrs. Boyd and a couple of women from their congregation. I noticed, Bud, and the others made a point of collecting their food and taking it back to a blanket on the lawn. Bud said Mrs. Boyd made him nervous, staring all the time, like she was waiting for his head to spin around or something.

Didn't take long for Jesse to dig in. "God, Mrs. Cummins, this is the best fried chicken I ever did eat."

Patty poked my ribs and I felt my last bite tighten in my stomach. Jesse took the Lord's name in vain, in front of all those Pentecostals. Lord, save the cabbage, he'd done it now. Patty was clearing her throat, I thought she was choking or something, but I knew it wasn't food that had her all in a tizzy. She'd found Jesse's Achilles. I was going to hear about it later. I just kept on eating like I didn't notice. Mom just smiled from down the table and said, "Why thank you Jesse, glad you're enjoying yourself. Glancing at my Dad I could tell by his boyish, stifled grin he was glad it was Jesse instead of him on the line here. Mrs. Boyd had finished chewing and I could just see her gears spinning as she delicately patted her lips with her napkin, and then removing it unveiled a self-righteous smile.

"Jesse...Tate, isn't it?" she started.

"Jesse sat up and looked straight at her, a lamb ready for the slaughter, "Yes, ma'am?"

"Tate. I believe I've heard that name somewhere. I just can't place your parents. What does you father do, Jesse?"

Jesse squirmed slightly on the bench.

Come on Jesse, I thought, you can handle this.

The picnic table had become very quiet, and I was really agitated at Mrs. Boyd. I had a feeling she knew exactly what Jesse's father or at least Jasper Tate did for a living by the way she was acting.

A smile that could melt butter like hot summer sun shot across Jesse's face, that charming, mischievous smile. Yes, Jesse knew exactly what to say. "My father is in the foodservice business," he said and took another bite of potato salad.

What? Foodservice, what was he thinking? I took a big gulp of Coca-Cola.

Mrs. Boyd wasn't satisfied. "What type of foodservice; restaurant or schools?"

"Beverage transport and delivery," he quipped back without missing a beat.

My Coke had not had a chance to make it down my throat as I began gasping in mid swallow, Coca-Cola shooting straight out my nostrils, down my chin and all over as I choked and sputtered. Jumping up from the table to a lot of "Oohs" and "Oh my's" echoing around the table, Patty pounded me on my back.

"Are you alright, dear?" Mom was standing up.

"She's fine, Kathryn," Dad pulled at her arm to sit back down.

Containing myself, I wiped myself dry with the napkins Patty grabbed from the table. Seems the whole unladylike display had caught the attention of Kate. I could hear her groaning clear across the yard. A lecture on etiquette was definitely in my near future. I couldn't believe it, but Jesse just kept on stuffing his face. He nearly caused me to choke to death and there he sat. Mrs. Boyd and her two friends had gotten up to go chit chat with the other guests. I could guess the topic of conversation. I could just feel the evil eyes on me now. Oh well, at least it stopped her inquisition. I seated myself back at the table. Jesse stopped eating long enough to turn to me giving me a quick wink.

"Thanks a lot," I said.

Being as most of my dinner was covered in Coca-Cola I picked up my plate and excused myself and went over to toss it all in the trash can. Patty was right behind me.

"You sure know how to clear a table, Cally," she said.

"Sorry, I can't help it if I choked," I told her.

"That Jesse is really something," Patty started.

Here we go; the same lecture I'd been hearing since we'd been friends.

"Did I hear him take the Lord's name in vain?"

I bristled. "I think he said gosh, Patty."

"No, I'm pretty sure it was God. Yeh, he said, "'God, Mrs. Cummins, this is the best fried chicken I ever did eat.' Besides, it doesn't matter, God or gosh, it's just not right to say. You better talk to him about it, Cally," Patty kept on until I thought I would explode.

"Don't start all that with me again, Patty. If you're so G-O-S-H darn worried about it you talk to him. I told you before, gosh is just gosh and anyway you just said exactly what Jesse did."

"Doesn't count, I was just telling you what he'd said and you better stop too before something bad happens. Remember the time at the cemetery on Halloween a couple years ago..."

"Alright, alright, you got me. I'm sorry," I said. You just couldn't win with her when it came to right or wrong, especially wrong. Jesse was walking towards us and I didn't want her to keep harping'. Fact was though, if she was right and something bad might happen because of it, I'd feel terrible. I didn't want to take chances, and mess up Jesse's plan.

"Bud wants us to come play some volleyball, Cally!" Jesse waved us over to the game about to begin. The afternoon moved into early evening quickly as we played and swam to cool off in the Boyd's pool. I caught Mrs. Boyd's watchful eye on Jesse several times during the course of the day. Mrs. Boyd could be very pretty if she would just let go of that stern disapproving expression she had on her face all the time. Kate said it took more muscles to frown than to smile and you could end up looking like a wrinkled up old prune if you didn't do more of the latter. I was afraid Mrs. Boyd was going to be old before her time.

The tangerine sun was beginning to fall across the St. John's, casting a warm glow behind the tops of the pines and cypress on the far bank. The sky to the west had turned a deep, purple orange. Maybe the weathermen were right about storms coming. I hoped not. It was still about an hour or so before the fireworks.

Patty and I had left the volleyball game to sit on the Boyd's boat dock and cool our feet in the river. Jesse had been back to the picnic table to grab a snack and was talking with Bud and Gloria. According to my watch, daylight would soon be fading. It was time. "How about a boat ride Patty?

Jesse's never been in your boat," I said getting up and moving down the dock towards the ski-boat.

"I don't know, Cally. It's going to be dark pretty soon. Besides I have to help clean up the nets and things from the games before the fireworks."

I didn't think this was going to be that big of a deal. "Well, how about me taking Jesse for a quick ride while you're doing that? Just up the river a little ways and back again. Your Daddy won't care. He let me take it out with Bud when you were down at Marathon Bible camp."

"That was with your brother," she said.

"Come on, Patty; just for a few minutes."

Suspicion showed all over her face, "Why are you so all fired up to take the boat Cally? What's going on? I know you, and I can see some scheme brewing behind those blue eyes," she said.

"I just wanted to show Jesse what a great boat you have. Give him a break Patty. Don't you think he deserves one after putting up with your mom's glaring at him the whole time he's been here?"

"She was not doing that," Patty protested.

"Well then she must have gotten too much sun that made her eyes all squinty every time she looks his way."

"Okay, alright, Cally. Go ahead, but just for a few minutes. You can't be out there after dark. My daddy would skin me alive if I let you." She'd barely finished and I took off to get Jesse. I stopped over at Kate's beach bag first. Digging out my Indian doll, I tucked it safely in my waistband, letting my shirt hang over.

"There's going to be some really big boomers tonight," Bud was saying to Gloria when I joined them. "Larry told me that Gary Oatman, the patrolman up at the U.D., said the county spared no expense this year. They'll see these clear over in Volusia County."

"I can't wait. I love fireworks," Gloria said.

"I sure hope they get them in before the storm gets here," Bud said, gazing up at the darkening sky. "I've got a couple of big Bertha's Bill bought for me when he and his Dad went up to Alabama last month, guaranteed to go a good hundred feet or more."

"Bud, aren't those against the law?" Kate squawked.

"Only if you get caught," Bud said. Realizing that wasn't a good answer for by- the- book Kate, so he told her, "Relax Kate, it'll be fine. We'll shoot them over the water. What could happen?"

Checking my watch again I interrupted. "Jesse, could you come with me to the boat dock?"

"What's going on down there?" Bud asked.

"Oh nothing, just wanted to show Jesse Patty's boat," I said.

"Cool, Gloria and I will come with you," Bud said grabbing her by the hand. "We can sit there and watch the fireworks."

Jesse grimaced.

I didn't handle that too well. I had better come up with something quick. I had it. "Bud, you don't want to sit down there. The skeeters are getting thick around the river. You wouldn't want Gloria to get all lumped up would you? We'll just be a couple minutes anyway. Why don't you guys find a good spot and me and Jesse will join you as soon as we're done."

"If I didn't know better I swear you were trying to ditch us, Cal," Bud said. He had a smirk all over his face that I didn't think I much liked. What exactly was it he thought he was insinuating with his eyebrows moving up and down at us.

"Very funny," I said grabbing Jesse's arm and pulling him along.

"Don't do anything I wouldn't do," Bud called as Gloria gave him a playful swat.

"Jeez Cally, why didn't you just blow the whole plan?" Jesse complained on the way to the dock.

"Hey, it wasn't my fault. You're the one wondering around over here instead of coming with me. Patty said we can take the boat for just a short spin, before it gets dark. We're wasting time arguing." I started running to the dock with Jesse right after me.

Reaching down to untie the rope from the post Patty's voice blasted, "Cally!"

I lost my footing and started grabbing hold of the splintering post to save me from tumbling to the dark water below. "Jeez o' Pete, Patty, you nearly made me fall in."

Patty stood her ground. "What do you think you're going to do, Cally? It's practically dark. You can't go taking the boat out now."

I heard some mumbling under Jesse's breath. Some unintelligible curse words by the tone of it as he threw his hands in the air and started walking back the other way.

"Pardon me," Patty called after him.

"Patty you'll ruin everything if you don't let us go now," I said angrily.

"Ruin what?"

I had to stay calm. We were so close I couldn't let her stubbornness keep Jesse from doing this. He'd probably never speak to me again. "Okay, if we can't take the boat ourselves, you come with us. But, Patty we have to do this! You don't understand!" I pleaded.

"Well, supposing you help me understand right now. I don't like the sound of this one bit. There's more going on here than just a spin in my Dad's boat. Fill me in now!"

I gave Jesse, who hadn't gone very far, my best pleading look. "Tell her Jesse! She's right. She should at least know what's going on."

I could see Jesse hadn't planned on Patty being so hard to deal with. He had no idea how strong she could be.

I decided to just do what I thought best being as Jesse wasn't budging any more than Patty. I tried in my most persuasive voice, "Patty, just please come with us right now before somebody comes down here and I will explain everything on the way. Please Patty. It could really be a matter of life and death."

Patty started laughing. I couldn't believe it. It was almost a hysterical laughter. I couldn't see what was so darn funny in this.

"Oh Cally, quit being so dramatic," she laughed at me. "Life and death; this is probably just more of that spirit ghost stuff, isn't it? You know you can just forget it if it is."

"Patty, just trust me! Please! I promise you're doing the right thing. It's not for me. It's Jesse. He needs your help." Jesse wasn't doing a doggone thing to help me out here. I gave him a come on and turn on your charm look. Amazingly he caught on. In his most irresistible boyish way he walked right up to her, and I could tell it was working as he reeled her right in, melting her with that smile and those baby blues. She was hooked.

"I really could use your help Patty. It would mean an awful lot to me," he said.

Patty tried to act like he hadn't gotten to her, but I knew he'd caught her, hook, line, and sinker.

"Fine, get in, but we need to hurry. I don't want to miss the fireworks," she said.

"There'll be plenty of that," I heard Jesse say under his breath getting in the boat and untying the dock ropes. Patty and I hopped aboard.

Patty pulled at the starter a couple of times and the engine gurgled, the propellers churning the black water. Luckily, everyone on shore were so busy, some playing volleyball, and others talking over one another so loud, there's no way they could hear the motor. As the exhaust hung in the evening air, Patty kept the boat at an idle, floating us along the seawall hugging the river bank. Darkness wasn't far away and the sparkling dark waters of earlier took on an eerie blackness. There was a welcome, cool dampness to the night air. Just past the lighted backyards along the bank, we glided underneath a canopy of hundred year old oaks, their gray moss beards dipping into the water. A disturbed white ibis startled me, flapping its broad wings as it lit out from the bank.

"Better cut the engine here," Jesse told Patty.

Up ahead, a stream of mustard yellow light, bouncing along the wind tossed white caps of the St. John's, revealed the Pepper Pot, hidden in the Pines. Its gaudy neon seemed out of place among the river and forest.

Patty cut the engine. Water lapping the sides of the boat, and the voices of a few inebriated fishermen were the only sounds to be heard.

"I don't think we should be down here. I'm not allowed," Patty said.

Jesse ignoring her took the oars and rowed us across the dimly lit river and back into the darkness beyond the Pepper Pot.

"Jesse, what if Jasper and Earl are already up there?" I said getting a little nervous now.

"I told you Cally, Jasper and Earl won't be at the Pepper Pot until it gets good and dark. They can't take the chance of being seen delivering their goods."

"Cally Cummins, I knew it!" Patty said loud enough to wake the dead.

"Shhh!" Jesse blasted back.

"Don't go Shhhn' me!" Patty stood up rocking the boat so hard I grabbed onto the side. "I just want Jesse to take a ride in your Daddy's boat Patty," she mocked me from earlier this evening. "Start talking, Cally!"

"For Christ sake tell her, Cally, we're running out of time," Jesse said, giving the boat a little shake back and forth causing Patty to flop back down on her seat.

"Hey!" she said.

"Okay, Okay! Look Patty it's like this," I began, Patty's eyes shooting daggers at me. This wasn't going to be easy. Jesse was not going to be any help in this at all. He was too keyed up. So, I gave Patty the quickest condensed version of the life and times of Jesse Tate Malcolm with as much of the plan as Jesse had filled me in on. All the while Patty's eyes kept getting wider and wider. I thought if anything hit her on the top of the head her eyes would just pop right out, like those little Pekinese dogs Mrs. Edwards used to have down the road. I talked and talked as fast and as thoroughly as possible so as not to give Patty a chance to butt in, or have time to think sensibly as usual and maybe turn the boat around. She just couldn't do that. "...So, that's how we ended up here in your boat and needing your help. We're counting on you Patty," I told her not believing she let me finish our saga without interrupting..

Jesse sat slumped down in his seat, holding his head the whole time I talked. When I finished he said, "Your dad is right on the money Cally, you are without a doubt, a talking machine. Now, can we get going or not?"

"What do you say, Patty?" I asked my dazed friend, her eyes practically glazed over with amazement trying to digest the whole story. I poked Jesse whispering, "Turn on a little more charm here would you?"

Jesse sighed and getting up climbed over my seat, kneeling down in front of Patty. Taking her hand in his he softly said, "Patty, if you help me out here, I'll be in your debt forever." Again, he flashed her that smile that just watching made my knees go weak. He didn't have to overdo it.

Patty took her hand back, pulling on the choke and cranking the engine over. "You don't have to be in my debt Jesse, but Cally will owe me big time," she said.

I couldn't believe my ears. Why Jesse Tate could be president some day. He was not only smart, but ten times better looking and more charming than JFK.

"I just want you to know Cally, I don't like this one bit," Patty got the last word in.

"Stop the motor, Patty," Jesse said after a while. Leaning over the front of the boat Jesse stuck an oar in to measure the depth.

It appeared to be pretty shallow. Jesse immediately began pulling the boat towards the landing beneath one of the limestone bluffs. It rose up a good fifteen feet at this part of the channel. Hopping over the side, and securing the rope to a thick root sticking out from above us, he scampered up the steep slope, lying down on the white sand at its peak. Returning excitedly Jesse said, "They're still up in the garage, Cally. Come on!" With that he ran back up the slope. Before joining him, I turned to my friend. "Listen Patty, at the first sign of any kind of trouble, head out of here as fast as you can and get Bud, you hear?" I started over the front of the boat.

"Cally Cummins if you think I'm sitting down here by myself you're crazier than the Woo Woo Man," she said.

"Hush Patty, he ain't crazy he's... oh, never mind." Even I couldn't explain all that right now. "Patty, you're safer here and we need you to go for help if things go wrong. You heard Jesse. Jasper and Earl are here. I got to go."

"I'm going to miss the fireworks Cally," Patty whined.

I took a deep breath and tried not to get so darn mad, after all she did go along with the whole plan. "We'll be back in time for the fireworks."

Jesse was already backing down the slope again, and having heard Patty's whining, he said, "If things go like I think they will, you'll see plenty of fireworks. Listen up Patty. We got two flares. Ignore the first, but if you see the second go for help."

"Jesse, I told you I ain't lighting no stupid flare," I said jumping into the ankle deep water and sinking over the tops of my sneakers into the bottom. "Oh Great," I said as the muddy river bottom sucked at my shoes. Sounded like the bathroom plunger when you stuck it to the floor.

"Don't be gone long or I'm warning you right now, I'm out of here," Patty huffed.

I gave my shoes one final jerk as the mud sucked and pulled, finally, freeing myself from the muck. Jesse had already disappeared over the slope and I strained my eyes to see where he'd headed. I spotted him under the big oak not far from the edge of the sand cliff. When I got there he was pulling the cover off the wagon with all our stuff in it. Leaves at my feet rustled as something slithered across the dirt and down the sand cliff.

"What was that?" I jumped back, imagining a nest of water moccasins under my feet.

"It's probably just a black snake. Relax Cally, your jumpier than a jackrabbit," Jesse said continuing with his inventory of our things.

My attention shifted to inside the garage and the dim light bulb hanging from the rafters. A head bobbed in front of the window pane. Well, they were in there alright. A coldness brushed up my arms as a breeze kicked up from across the river. Jesse dumped the flares from the burlap sack. I just stood perfectly still, hardly breathing.

"Cally, for crying out loud, I told you, they're not going to blow up. They're just flares," Jesse said bending down and picking one up, handing it to me. "Now take this one and this here lantern and climb up on that big coquina rock over there. Hang the lantern on that skinny limb sticking out over the rock."

"Why don't you just set the lantern on top of the rock?" I asked.

"Cally, we need the lantern up higher so as to be seen from that window," he said pointing towards the garage. "I want the lantern to dangle as if in mid air. The way the winds picking up it should be just about perfect."

Jesse took a match box from his pocket. Opening it he struck the flint and lit the wick of the lantern for me. I didn't argue and went to the rock,and crawled up the jagged slope of it, careful not to scratch up my legs and arms on the rough orange shell. Hanging the lantern, I jumped down before Earl or Jasper happened to see me from the garage. Jesse removed something else from his pocket and laid it down on the rock. Illuminated from the glow of light dangling above it was the lighter we'd seen at Little Deer's cottage.

"Okay, Cally, now take this pack of matches and the flare and hide back behind that tall Sable palm next to the rock. I'm going back to the wagon and get the tape recorder and that fishing line so I can string it. When I'm finished stringing the line, I'll hide over there behind them trees on the far side of the garage and make some noises. As soon as you see Jasper and Earl looking out that window over yonder you get behind this rock and light the flare. Make sure it's aimed straight up over the back of the rock, so they can't miss it; I want to bring attention to the lantern. That ought to be enough to bring them outside." Jesse was talking, but I felt like my head was spinning. My hands felt clammy and I was cold, though it was still at least eighty-five degrees out.

"Cally, are you okay?" Jesse stopped his instructions.

I had to be. I couldn't let him down now, even though I felt like running as fast as I could down that slope and joining Patty at the boat. "I'm fine," I sucked it up. "You okay?" I wondered if he was as scared as me. If he was he did a good job of hiding it.

"I'm okay, Cally," he smiled. Not a put-on Mr. Charm smile, just a real honest to goodness smile, from one friend to another.

"What are you going to do with that?" I asked him looking at the other flare in his hand.

"Cally, promise me, if you see this light up, get out. Go for help." Jesse looked as serious as I'd seen him all night.

"But, what about…" I said, but Jesse cut me off.

"No buts, Cally. Now go on, I'll be fine. Remember what I said."

Jesse ran off with the tape recorder and fishing line to the tall pines on the far side of the garage. I watched from behind the palm tree as he ran across the property stringing the fishing line from one of the pines. He didn't pull it up tight though. Jasper and Earl would be coming across the yard when all heck started breaking loose. Jesse would pull it when the time was right. I hoped it wouldn't be when Jasper was in hot pursuit of one of us. As I sat watching and waiting, a wind began swirling around me with a low howl, rushing through the wispy pine needles above. I had to be careful not to step back too far and go tumbling down the sand cliff behind me. Staring down into the black waters, it had become choppy, and the current ran swiftly. The tree line across the river was the only dividing line between blackness of sky and water. Again, a cold chill ran through me, like tiny fingers up my spine. Don't think, Cally. You think too much. I couldn't help myself. Here I sat in the darkness, my only light, the glow of the lantern that now was swaying hard enough to cause the hanger on top to clink with each movement. A sudden need to run seemed to overwhelm me, but fear of being seen kept me frozen in place. Relax Cally. You're not alone, Patty is behind you in the safety of the boat, and Jesse is not far away. It won't be long and half-wit Earl will be strung out with fear when Jasper makes him come back inside the garage. He'll flap those gums and Jesse will get it all on the tape-recorder from underneath the window. It would be a snap. Somehow I needed more convincing. A strange feeling crept through me. Was something watching me? I was now realizing how vulnerable I was to whatever night creatures might be out and about on an evening like this. I thought I heard a rumble off in the distance. Glancing from side to side, heat-lightning flashed towards the west.

A long mournful moaning sound began from somewhere behind me.

Whooo! Oohhh!!

Again, Whooo! Oohhh! My heart was racing.

"Jesse?" I whispered. No, it couldn't have been. It came from behind me, didn't it? Ooohhh! It came again. It was so blasted hard to tell where sounds came from at night, especially out here in the boonies. "What the...?" I started to panic, and then smiled getting a look at the side of the oak tree. Jesse must have done a little art work on the trunk with the river mud. The pale moon and lantern's glow lit up the swamp mud perfectly. The oak looked like one of them talking trees in *The Wizard of Oz* the swamp mud oozing down its bark from a misshapen mouth.

The window...I peeked around the tree catching movement inside the garage. Another moan came, but this time it had a familiarity to it. Jesse. Then there came another sound, an old witch's cackle and another moan. It too was near the garage, but moving towards me. A dimming moon had just enough milky light to highlight Jesse's blonde streaks as he ran ducking down behind some tall weeds. I relaxed. It must have been the wind before. Two heads appeared in the dingy glass peering from the garage. Jesse had gotten the two men's attention.

Oooh! Whoooo!

I held my breath. Slowly turning my eyes I strained them to see into the darkness across the channel behind me, where I thought the moan had come from again. My senses told me it hadn't come from Jesse, in the tall weeds this time, but definitely, from across the black river waters. Adrenaline flowed, pumping through my veins. All at once, men's voices were trailing through the night. Oh my Lord. I didn't light the flare. Matches...where were they? I tugged at my pants pocket sliding across behind the coquina rock. Sticking the flare into the soft sand, the fuse exposed, I found the matches. Pulling open the box, half the contents spilled to the ground. Grabbing one up I struck at the flint only to have the flame blown out by a sudden wind. The voices were getting closer. Again, I tried another. This time it snapped alive. Hands shaking, I reached for the fuse.

CRASH!

The hair raised on my arms and head. Realizing a bolt of lightning had struck too close for comfort was little relief, from the fear that I had just blown myself to smithereens with the flare. The lightning was ferocious. It appeared the whole woods exploded into bright flashing light. By the direction of the voices now, the lightning bolt had done a much better job than the unlit flare still sticking out of the sand could have ever done. It definitely drew the two men's attentions to the rock in front of me.

"Who's out there?" one of them called out.

Grabbing the flare and what matches I could, I eased myself over the sand cliff, rolling down the slope on the other side to the shoreline. I headed for Patty and the...

"Patty? Oh my Lord," I whispered.. Where was she? Did I misjudge where I was that badly? No, I'm sure this was the place. Patty and the boat were gone. My friend had deserted me. All that remained as I ran to the spot where we'd made shore was a slight indentation in the muck from a now vanished boat. Fear coursed through me as the two men's voices approached the rock. Panicking I spotted a thicket of cattails. Running to them as fast as my wobbly legs could carry me, another bolt of lightning crashed directly across the river with a crackling so loud and with such a rumble I thought the earth might split in two. My ears rang. The rumbling settling, Earl cried, "What's the matter with you Jasper? You look like you seen the devil himself." The men were at the rock now. Earl spoke again with amusement, "Why, it's just a lighter, Jasper. Probably used by whoever lit this lantern here. Maybe some kids out here drinking, celebrating the holiday that's all."

Earl sounded like he was trying to convince himself of these things.

Jasper's voice boomed almost as loud as the thunder. "That's my lighter, you crazy fool."

"How'd it get out here? You must have set it down while fishing. What's the big deal?"

"Shut up Earl," Jasper said. I heard footsteps coming down the slope. Afraid to look, yet having to, I watched Jasper Tate slide down onto the landing where the boat had been. Pacing back and forth and looking up and down the river he bent down picking something up from the shore.

"Oh my Lord," I reached at my waistband, the doll. A cool sweat poured from inside me. Jasper Tate held my Indian doll in his hands studying it in the dark. I thought my heart would jump clean out of my throat and into the river as Jasper looked up staring right at the cattails where I lay in the river muck. My good luck had run out. Closing my eyes again I placed a muddy hand over my mouth afraid I might scream.

CRASH!! I counted…one-one thousand, and two-one thousand, and three-one thousand. The thunder rumbled. The storm was a good three or four miles away. "Dear God, please don't let all this crashing and booming wake up a hungry gator," I said to myself. I felt like an appetizer sitting on one of Miss Stoner's party trays.

CRASH!

This jolt of lightning came mercifully closer than the last making Jasper bolt back up the slope towards the lit up rock. I didn't move a muscle until seeing the top of his cap disappear over the horizon of the cliff.

"Someone's playing tricks Earl," Jasper's voice carried through the night.

"How's that Jasper? Hey, what you got there Jasper? You're not playing with dolls are you?" Earl dared to make fun of Jasper.

"I found it over along the shore, you knit wit. Appears to be one of them souvenir Indian dolls," Jasper said.

Jasper held up the lighter to Earl. "This lighter is mine, but I ain't laid eyes on it since I lost it that night."

"What night's that?" Earl said.

"The night of the fire at the Malcolm's place," Jasper snapped back.

Here it comes. I knew it. I wondered if the tape-recorder could pick this up.

"Jasper!" Earl cried out. "Caleb Malcolm! Caleb Malcolm's come to get us!"

"Shut up you crazy fool! It ain't Malcolm, he died in that fire."

"Yeh, a fire we…"

"I said to shut your mouth," Jasper cut into Earl's words.

"If it ain't him then it's LUCAS CANE! Those stories are true. He is out here haunting, waiting for his chance to get revenge on you. I knew it," Earl cried.

"Not another crazy word, you hear!" Jasper hollered. "There ain't no such thing."

The wind howled and the cattails twisted and pounded flat against the mucky bottom. Ducking I tried to avoid their battering brown tails. "Ouch!" their tops felt like Foxy's ruler smacking me on my back and head so.

Aaeeeeee!! My heart leaped as the blood curdling, hellacious, screeching rang through the wind. The likes of I only imagined came from one of them Banshees live in those haunted castles of Ireland. We'd read about them at school. They were terrifying, ghostly creatures that could turn Dracula's black hair white and drain every drop of blood he'd sucked out of a body. I dare not look, but I had to. Whatever it was came from directly across the black waters. It wasn't Jesse. The wind picked up and a mist of river water spritzed my face. Ooooh, the most putrid odor of dead oily fish filled the wind and my stomach turned so I thought I might be sick.

"It's him!" Earl cried out.

What did Earl see that I didn't? A damp coolness lapped at my legs. The water seemed to be rising around me. I crawled through the cattails, trying not to think what I might be moving over. I needed to get out of this muck and to the safety of the tall weeds on higher ground. I needed to get further away from whatever made that awful sound. Looking to see if Jasper and Earl could see me, a stream of mud ran down my legs as I crawled to the weeds slipping behind them. I could just make out Jasper. Earl was nearly back to the garage.

"I'm going back inside, Jasper; you coming?" Earl called out.

Jasper's eyes looked all around, but he just stood there. Pulling a pack of cigarettes from his pocket he took one out and lit it with the lighter we had left on the rock.

"Still works," I thought I heard him say as he took a long drag on his smoke. Earl hadn't gone inside yet. He stopped just beyond where Jesse had strung the fishing line. Please don't let him see it.

Earl called out again, "Jasper, aren't you coming? Why don't you come back inside? We got work to do."

"What's your rush, Earl," Jasper taunted him. "What's the matter, you afraid of the dark?" Jasper was laughing now. What a bully he was.

"Go ahead and laugh Jasper, but something real strange is going on here. I don't think you should be laughing and making fun..." Earl's mouth slacked wide open, his head jutting forward and his eyes open, wide as he pointed behind Jasper. He seemed paralyzed, unable to budge.

This sent Jasper into a real fit of laughter now. I followed the direction of Earl's pointed finger. I figured it must've been Jesse's art work that had old Earl spooked so, but as I turned, a gasp of air was all I could manage as fear froze me in place. Blinking my eyes, hoping that the approaching storm was playing tricks on me, I could see it wasn't some mud covered oak had Earl going, and it definitely wasn't any trick of storms, mediums, or fakers neither. It was nothing of this world, for directly across the river I watched horrified as a dim light, swinging, held only by the howling winds, came gliding effortlessly across the channel towards the coquina rock, where a now extinguished lantern hung.

CRASH!

The lightning hit again across the river, its blast of electricity lit up the path of the eerie coming light. There was nothing around it, just a hazy glow. Splat! A large drop of rain landed on my head, nearly causing me to cry out. This last blast had sent Earl around the side of the garage headed for safety.

"Fool!" Jasper turned around. "What the?" he backed up slowly and the light moved over the rock toward him. "Lucas?" Jasper turned and lit back as fast as his feet could carry him towards the garage, throwing down my Indian Doll as he fled; my beautiful doll. The fishy smell was worse now, and my gag reflex took over. Nothing came, but my stomach heaved. "Jesse? Where was Jesse? Where was Patty?" I was alone… Alone with…I felt faint…LUCAS CANE! Little Deer said it was a folktale, crazy drunken fisherman tales, only I was sober as a Pentecostal preacher. A rustling came from the tall weeds where I had crawled from the cattails. "Jesse?" I turned. Two amber eyes peered out of the weeds. I had no breath. I was going to faint. Breathe, Cally… A high-pitched primal cry came from the amber glow. "Coo-wa-chobee!" I cried out to nothing but the wind.

Suddenly, just as quickly as it had come, the wind stopped, with a stillness that made my skin crawl. The putrid odor was gone too, just like that. I searched the top of the sand cliff for the coquina rock. Still blackness was all there was. A light rain fell now.

Kaboom!! Kaboom!!

My heart nearly jumped out my mouth. Looking back towards the Pepper Pot the sky was brilliant with red, white and blue explosions. Fireworks had begun. Great! I hoped Patty enjoyed the heck out of them, the nerve of her leaving me here to be taken by some ghoul or, snatched up in the ferocious jaws of the big cat. The big cat...Where'd it go? It was gone, vanished. Shadows bounced around inside the garage. Where was Jesse? "Darn it Jesse, you're supposed to be up under that window by now with the tape-recorder getting all that incriminating evidence we need," I said out loud. A shudder ran from my heart to my toes. I was really alone now, out here in this God forsaken place. Blast Patty anyway. How could she leave us out here? She was supposed to be my friend. She'd have been sorry if Jasper had discovered me hidden inside those cattails, and tossed me in the river at the mercy of the gators or Lucas Cane's spirit. I didn't care if we caught Jasper or not right now. I needed to get out of here. I needed to find Jesse. Panic and fear moved me now. I had to find Jesse and tell him what I'd heard. We had enough to tell the sheriff. We needed to leave this place right now... Walking quickly I passed by the dirt path Jasper Tate had chased Patty and I on, as we fled in her boat. I thought I might start to cry. "Get a grip Cally," I thought. Sticking close to the tree line across the back of the property Jesse was no where in sight. Something must have happened to him. Lord, what if he'd come up on a gator. My attention focused on the back of the garage as I ran, making sure the two men didn't come back outside.

"ACHH!" I cried, as a hand grasped my arm and another slapped over my mouth as I tried to cry out again.

"Cally!"

It was Bud, I realized as I felt the blood rush from my head and nearly dropped to my knees in a dead faint.

He released his hand.

"Bud, Oh Bud!" I hugged tightly to my brother."

"Man, you've really gone and done it now, Cally!" Kate's excited voice interrupted. Looking around, there stood my sisters and Gloria. By the looks on their faces I wasn't sure if Jasper Tate wouldn't have been better to tangle with right now. "Look at you? You're a sight," Kate scolded.

"You look like you been rode hard and put up wet," Lynn laughed. "You got mud all over yourself."

"What do you think you're doing, Cally?" Bud took over. "We thought you and Jesse were down near the docks with Patty."

Bang!

I jumped then realized it was just more of the fireworks that we were all missing now.

"Oh yeh,... Right Bud," I said. "Tell me; how about my friend Patty? She left us here to rot so she could get back to see her precious fireworks!" I complained.

"No, Cally, that's how we ended up here. She came and told me you and Jesse were in trouble and needed help. She even asked us not to go telling anybody else yet, because she wasn't sure if it was adult trouble or just kid trouble. She wasn't making a whole lot of sense. She at least had enough common sense to fill me in about Jasper Tate and what you and Jesse were up to. Cally, you can't tangle with people like him. You know that. He's a dangerous man."

"Well, she could've at least let me know what she was doing before she took off out of here," I snorted.

"Why? So you could argue with her, maybe all of you end up dead. She did you a favor and I, for one, am grateful," Bud said. "Where is Jesse anyway? Cally?"

I threw up my hands. "I don't know. He was supposed to wait in the bushes over on the other side of the garage for Jasper and Earl to go back inside, then take the tape-recorder and sneak up under that open window over there... OH NO! They shut the window Bud. We have to find Jesse. He's in trouble, I just know it."

"We need to find him and get on out of here before Mom and Dad realize we're all AWOL," Bud said.

I looked down the empty path, "How'd y'all get here anyhow?"

Bud nodded down the path, "My cars pulled in behind a bunch of cabbage palms back there. You can just make out the light of the garage between the palm fronds." Bud stood surveying the area and turning to my sisters and Gloria, he handed over the car keys to Kate. "Y'all go on back to the car and lock the doors," he told Kate. Reaching in his pocket he pulled out a pack of Winstons and pulled some matches from between the cellophane. "Here Kate, take these and if anything goes wrong here, get Big Bertha out of the trunk and light her up."

"Are you crazy? I am not lighting that thing!" Kate told him.

Gloria grabbed the matches from a shocked Kate's hands, "I will, Bud. You can count on it."

Kate just stood there dumbfounded.

"Go on now," Bud said. The girls ran back towards the car.

"You stay put right here half-pint," Bud told me as he stooped down to creep over to the window where Jesse was supposed to be.

"Yeh, right," I said and followed after him.

Bud stopped, turning around. "Cally, I said to stay back there."

"Bud, I don't want to stay by myself anymore." Looking down at my feet I realized I was standing on Jesse's fishing line. Bud was already under the closed window, so I crawled on my hands and knees over to him. One of us had to pull that fishing line.

"Bud," I whispered.

Bud turned a finger to his mouth, "Shhhh."

"But Bud, the fishing line…" I tried only to be shushed again. Muffled voices could be heard from inside the garage. Bud slowly raised himself up eye level with the window ledge and peered inside through the dirty panes of glass. He quickly ducked back down. The voices were loud and it appeared Jasper and Earl was in the middle of one big argument. Giant shadows of arms waving in fits of anger swirled across the wooden rafters inside. Bud raised himself up again and the two of us stood watching the show. Jasper grabbed up a wrench, hurling it across the garage where it came to a clanging halt against a gas can. Jabbing my side with his elbow

Bud nodded towards the other side of the garage near the old truck Earl had been working on earlier.

"Jesse, Oh my God," I gasped.

Bud hushed me.

"There curled up underneath a work bench sat Jesse with the tape recorder lying beside him. Jasper whirled around towards the window sending Bud and I back down to the ground. Jasper flew into another tirade of anger aimed at half-wit Earl.

Bud sat down in the tall grass wiping his hands across his face. "This is a fine mess. Man! Jesse is trapped inside with a killer and, as far as I can tell, the village idiot. Just how are we supposed to get him out of there, Cally?"

Bud was asking me? This wasn't good at all.

The fishing line, somebody had to pull it. I had a feeling we were going to need it. I took a deep breath, got up on my haunches and told my brother, "Stay here, I'll be right back."

"Cal…"

I ignored Bud and crawling at first, then moving to my feet I sprinted as fast as I could on the sides of my slushy wet, mud filled sneakers. Lynn told me it was an old Indian trick to walk on the sides of your feet. Said it made it easier for them to sneak up on the white man. With all the squishing and suctioning of my mud covered shoes I wasn't too sure. I'd seen Indians do it on the television westerns. I'd ask Little Deer next time I see her. A chill ran up my back—if I see her again. Which Pine was it? I should have gone back to the line and followed it to the tree? I had to start thinking clearer. Footprints with just the slightest curve of a Converse C pressed into the dirt at the base of one of the thicker Pines. I felt around the shaggy bark. "There," I said finding the string, grabbing the loose end, untying it from its slip knot. Pulling it taught as I could I double knotted it again around the tree. "There that ought to be good enough to knock them on their keisters." A warm breeze had picked up again coming off the river. With it came a faint, Whooo. Turning with a start, expecting to see Lucas Cane's fish eaten face in front of me, all I saw was blackness. Thunder rolled. We had to get moving.

CRASH!

Not again! I thought the lightning had moved on. The storm must be circling back again and sitting here under all these tall trees wasn't exactly where I wanted to be. A strong odor oozed up from the water, an earthy smell of worms after a summer rain. The odor grew stronger turning into that fishy, oily smell. Something dead! Then it struck me. I swallowed hard and took in a deep breath to keep from being sick. I don't know why I hadn't thought of it earlier. This was the anniversary of the terrible fire, the night the Malcolms perished at the hand of Jasper Tate, the eve of Lucas Cane's terrible fate.

WHOOOO!!

The howling crescendoed like the percussionist at the symphony orchestra we'd seen at the armory in fourth grade. Something told me to run as adrenaline made every nerve fiber in me come alive. Imagining some horrible, invisible being grabbing hold of me at any second, I dashed back across the yard careful of the fishing line that was drawn tight.

Bud, was standing peering through the glass again, and spun around as I grabbed hold of his shirt-tail. He raised his hand for silence. Rain began to fall gently. Bud held out his hand, "Great, that's just what we need. Son of a...," he muffled his words, "Cally, we need to think. I don't need you running off again, you hear?"

I whispered, "Bud did you happen to hear that howling coming from where I just was?"

"Probably just the wind," he said turning his attention back to inside what was going on in the garage.

"Bud, I thought maybe it was Jesse earlier when I heard it, but Jesse's inside the garage. Bud, do you believe that story about Lucas Cane haunting these woods along the river?"

Bud stepped back, "Cally, it's just the storm."

Crunch! A stick snapped loudly under his foot as he stepped forward again. Losing his balance, he bumped against the garage wall. We froze.

"Who's there?" A man's voice called from inside the garage.

Bud and I thinking we'd been discovered were about to run, when a commotion came from inside the garage.

Jasper yelled, "It's you! What the hell are you doing out here?" His voice was vicious and frightening.

Bud was at the window again. "They've discovered Jesse, Cally!" he said, terror written all across his face. I looked inside the smoky glass watching in horror as Jasper Tate jerked Jesse's arm so hard I waited for it to come pulling off. Jesse's face was tight and fearful.

"I can't believe it Bud, he must of showed himself to keep Jasper from coming outside and discovering me. Oh, Jesse," I whispered. Jasper shoved Jesse against the side of the garage with a thump, causing the window glass to shake hard enough to bust into a million pieces.

"He's been here all this time! He's heard everything," Earl bellowed turning on Jasper, "Now what? I can't believe this, after all this time!" Earl was rambling pacing back and forth like the Coo-wa-chobee. I noticed that Jesse had somehow managed to toss the recorder further under the work table before showing himself. Leaves crunched and the crack of twigs came from over near the woods. Bud and I both turned.

"Now what?" Bud said.

Again Jasper's voice rang out, drawing our attention back to the garage.

"You been a thorn in my side ever since you was born you little crumb snatcher. You're the one's been filling Earl here with your wild stories of ghosts and dead men coming back to get us. Where'd you hear all that? Was it your mother? I'll see her dead."

I could hear scuffling around and Jesse screamed, "Touch her and I'll kill you, so help me!"

"You won't be able to, you little...,"

Seminole Landing

"J.T. put that thing down. Come on man; you don't want to do this again!" Earl cried.

"I don't need you interfering Earl," Jasper shouted as Bud peered in the window again, but quickly crouched back down.

"Jasper's got a gun Cally, and he's got Jesse by the arm, pointing the gun on Earl. I rose up so as to see.

Again came Jasper's evil tongue, "I should of taken care of you along with Lucas, you dim wit," he said to Earl. "I'd be done with all of you once and for all. Dead men don't tell no tales. You heard that story before, boy?" he jerked Jesse tighter. "Better late than never, I say," he laughed an evil laugh and shoved Jesse towards the door and motioned Earl on with the gun.

"Come on Cally, hustle!" Bud grabbed hold of me and pulled me with him. Just then I spotted a red round stick lying at my feet, the flare. Jesse must have dropped it before going in the garage.

"Hold on Bud," I said bending down and picking the flare up just in time before Bud's strength won out and I flew across the yard with him towards where the girls were. Bud stopped in his tracks. Tall slender shadows rose up, towering over the trees. The men were coming from the direction we were headed. Bud quickly did an about face and pulled me with him the other way heading for the pine, over near the river's edge, the one with the other end of the fishing line tied to it. We ran along the edge of the sand cliff until we came to a low spot, sloping to the water. Flattening ourselves to the sandy slope we slid down just far enough not to be seen, peering over the cliff at the nightmare unfolding before us.

"Come on Gloria, light up the rocket," Bud said. The wind was whipping now, tossing white caps, their fine mist hitting me in the face.

"What is that?" Bud asked as he scrunched up his nose at the smell hanging in the air that I was all too familiar with. Closing my eyes, the pungent smell took me back to that frightful night around Madame Rosemary's séance table, just before Lucas Cane paid his visit.

"I hate to be the bearer of more bad news Bud, but that's the same smell me, Jesse, and Connie smelled at the mediums."

"I don't want to hear this now, Cally. We got no time for dead spirits, we got real, live problems to deal with," Bud said pointing to the activity coming around the back of the garage. Jasper still had a tight hold on Jesse and waved the gun at Earl who stumbled and fell as he tried to move away from Jasper.

"That's right Earl, move on over there by the canal," Jasper said wielding his power in his hand.

"Bud, he's bringing them over here. What do we do now?"

"Quick, slide on down and follow the water's edge around the point on the other side of the bluff."

I caught the interior light of Bud's car flash on for a second, and then darkness took over again.

"Come on Gloria," I said out loud. Just as I was about to ease on down the slope to the water, Earl, quick like a scalded dog, attempted to make his escape. Bud and I halted our decent down the slope and watched in horror as Jasper pushed Jesse to the ground to go after Earl. Jesse cried out in pain, hitting the ground with a sickening thud. He didn't move. Earl was moving fast and furious. "Come on, Come on," I watched. Wham! Earl's body flipped up in mid-air, right over the invisible trap we'd set for him. He fell flat on his face. I'd a laughed right out loud if I hadn't been so darn scared out of my wits for Jesse. Seeing what had happened to Earl, Jasper stopped. Earl was all contorted up in pain. Jasper went over and pulled Jesse up, dragging him along to where Earl now lay.

"Fool! You can't run from me!" Jasper shouted at Earl who lay there cowering in fear. Jasper sent Jesse tumbling to the ground again, this time beside Earl, cocking the trigger to his gun, which seemed to echo throughout the woods.

"Bud, we have to do something!" I cried. "Give me your matches."

Without a word, he took them from his shirt pocket and handed them over. The first strike lit up and sent sulfur burning my nose. I touched the flame to the flare, then throwing it as far into the air as I could, it lit up the sky, swoosh!

"What the...?" I heard Jasper shout. There came a commotion from the dark side of the garage where Bud and I'd heard the twig crack earlier.

"Hold it right there you son of the devil!" It was Lila Tate with a double barreled shotgun pointed straight at Jasper's back. Standing next to her was Curtis Malcolm, shuffleboard stick in hand, her great protector. Why he was puffed up like one of them wrestler men again. How did they know we were here...? Curtis. He understood...

Jasper turned facing Lila. She didn't flinch. "You shoot anybody and you're going to die," Lila told him. "Drop it, Jasper!" she ordered.

Ka-Boom!

"Good gosh, almighty," I said grabbing my brother's arm. The woods over near Bud's car lit up like one of them lightning bolts had been flashing around all night. Its trail shot straight over the pine tops and into the sky lighting up the whole darn river.

KaBLAM! Another flash came, but this one trailed off course and in a split second lit right into the garage roof, exploding dry shingles into a fiery blaze, and sending pieces flying everywhere.

"Yahoo! Gloria did it. She fired them up!" Bud yelled right out loud. No one seemed to hear him because of the deafening sounds of the blaze in front of us now.

In all of the mass confusion following the blast, Earl scrambled to his feet and ran to the woods. He was flat moving like a freight train.

Jesse wasn't moving. He was hurt. Jasper, snapping back to the problem at hand still had his gun on Jesse, obviously not threatened by Lila's warning.

"I swear you better drop that gun Jasper or I'm going to blow you into your next miserable life in hell," Lila screamed.

"Not before I blast your precious boy!" he taunted her by pointing the gun at Jesse then waving it back towards her and Curtis. If you don't drop that shotgun right now I'm going to put a bullet in Jesse here first then get rid of old Looney, Woo Woo there too," he dared her. "I'll put him with his brother!"

"No," Lila said, dropping her gun. "No!"

A flash of tan fur, slung low, sleek, and sly leaped from the cattails making a direct bee-line for an unsuspecting Jasper Tate. Jasper must have heard the cat approach. Dropping to his knees, pointing his gun he fired. The explosion caused the great cat to stumble slumping to the earth.

"HILIS HAYA! AIEEEEE!" a voice cried out to the night and the stars above, a sound as primal as that of the big cat. It was a fierce cry, the cry of a woman, a proud and strong Seminole woman, calling to the Good Maker, the Creator. Could it be?

A second explosion of gunfire exploded. My ears rang. I'd never forget that sound. It was the same sound I'd heard one other night, one of those other bad times I spoke of, when them Klansmen tried to hang our old friend, Isaac. It meant only death. I watched as the gun flew from Jasper's hands and he slumped to the ground next to the still Coo-wa-chobee.

In an instant the air filled with the dead fishy odor again, but hot; a pungent, fiery hot. It was as I imagined, only the hell fire of brimstone would smell like. The likes of what the Pentecostal Preacher talked about. The wind picked up, howling, unnatural and bone-chilling.

Aaa-WhOOO!! A loud enough to wake the dead kind of howling surrounded us. Time and everything in it seemed to be in slow motion, circling round on the wind, through the pines needles, swish, swish. Then everything stopped. In the silent stillness moved a strange light. Whoosh! It shot over top of Bud and I so fast it left a streak like one of them comets, a tiny ball of firelight, a flare or a…LANTERN…tossed across the darkness, trailing straight over the garage mixing with the fiery flame and smoke, then was gone. The nauseating dead smell was gone with it, replaced with the fresh hint of cedar filling the night air.

I drew a deep breath. "Rest in Peace, Lucas Cane."

"What did you say, Cal?"

"Cally, look," Bud said pointing towards the opposite corner of the garage from Lila.

"I knew it!" I said. Little Deer stood steady, and splendid, dressed in her rainbow, patchwork dress and blue silk jacket. In her hands she held the rifle that had hung over her hearth; it was now aimed at a fallen Jasper.

I thought I heard sirens coming from off in the distance.

"Did you see that? I can't believe it," Bud said as we both scrambled up the slope running to see if Jesse was alright.

"Little Deer," I called to the old woman who now was standing over Jasper Tate, making sure he didn't escape. The scene was chaotic, ablaze with firelight and crackling timber, echoing across the forest mixing with nature's own light show.

"He's still breathing," Lila said poking Jasper with the butt of her shotgun as Bud and I ran up behind the others, sobbing came from down on the ground. I made my way towards the sound and there lay Jesse sprawled over top the still cat.

"Coo-wa-chobee," I whispered. My heart felt as though it might break clean in two, right here on the spot. I ran to be by Jesse's side, my eyes filled so full I could hardly see. To my surprise, Jesse jerked back, knocking me so darn hard I fell backwards into the dirt. He took off towards the burning garage before anyone could stop him.

"Jesse!" I hollered after him. "Bud, stop him!"

Bud ran after Jesse just as two police cars came screaming through the woods, flashing red and blue lights, their sirens blasting. Headlights swept across the ground as they came to a halt. Surprisingly, Jasper was no longer face down in the dirt, but rose up now, his monstrous eyes glaring as he held a blood soaked arm. Little Deer had only wounded him. She was a crack-shot after all. She could have killed him. After all, Jasper Tate was evil for sure, no different than the rattler. He needed to be stopped from striking anymore, spreading his venom. Little Deer's goodness would let the law rid the world of this devil's creature, instead of her peace loving, father's gun. I wanted to run after Bud, but Lila caught my arm tightly when I started after him.

"No, Cally, your brother will find him."

"Cally!"

It was Kate, Lynn, and Gloria coming down the path as Sheriff Baines and his deputies stepped out of their squad cars.

The three ran to me and I swear I thought I'd suffocate with all the hugging and carrying on. Kate was crying, "Oh Cally, are you alright? Where'd Bud go?"

"Great job, Gloria," I hugged her.

Gloria stepped back, "It wasn't me Cally, it was Kate. She saw what was happening and was out of the car before I could get my door open."

I hugged Kate tight.

Sheriff Baines interrupted our hug fest. "What in the Sam Hill went on here tonight?"

"Arrest this man Sheriff. He's a murderer," Lila said.

"'She's crazy Sheriff. That wild old Indian woman's your murderer. She tried to kill me." Jasper held up his wounded arm, "See here, that savage did this. I'm the one shot here."

"Don't believe him Sheriff. He was about to shoot his buddy, Earl and he would have shot my boy, if we hadn't tried to stop him," Lila said. I couldn't hold back any longer, I'd heard Jasper as much admit to all his evil deeds, stepping forward I said, "Sheriff!"

Everyone's eyes fell on me including Jasper's dead, empty eyes. A chill ran through me. "Sheriff, Jasper Tate here is the one started the fire that killed the Malcolms years back and he killed Lucas Cane because he probably was going to tell what he knew."

Seminole Landing

"You little piss ant! You ain't got nothing on Jasper Tate," Jasper said. "That's where you're wrong, Jasper!"

It was Bud! Behind him was Jesse and they both were running like their lives depended on it.

"Everyone run! Get out of here!" Bud screamed.

"The mash is leaking out of the pipes and the whole place is going to blow!" Jesse hollered, running with the gosh darn tape-recorder under his arm. So that's why he ran back in there.

Everyone scattered. The sheriff made sure he had a tight grip on Jasper Tate as we all went every which way.

I tore out for the water's edge, over where we'd docked the Boyd's boat earlier and just as I was at the top of the sand cliff...KABLOOM!

All holy heck broke loose and someone was shoving me forward. I was falling head over heels down the sandy slope. It sounded like them Russians were bombing us and the sky was lit up like daylight. I landed face down in the river muck, my ears popping and ringing from the explosion. Warmth moved over me, hovering close.

"Cally? You hurt?" It was Jesse, shielding me from whatever debris may have come hurtling through the air. Looking up at him, his face was smudged with black soot. "Yeh, I think I'm alright, thanks to you and Bud, I'm still in one piece. Whatever got into you, Jesse? I can't believe you went back in there. You could have been blown to bits!"

Jesse sat down beside me, and all at once, gave me a big hug,

"We did it, Cally. We got Jasper Tate good. He can never hurt anyone or anything anymore. I don't know how momma, Little Deer, and Curtis knew to come here, but I'm sure glad they did. I knew my momma suspected something."

"It wasn't that Jesse. It was Curtis."

Jesse looked confused.

345

"Back at Little Deer's earlier today, when you and your momma were arguing, I told Curtis. I had to tell somebody. I was scared Jesse."

Then Jesse Tate did something I swear I'd never forget in all my life. He leaned over right then and there and kissed my cheek and softly said, "Ecenokkecis." Here I sat wet, covered in mud, and Jesse Tate kissed me and said I love you right in front of God and everything. The sky was ablaze in a fury of orange and red. People were yelling and chaos was all around us and I thought to myself, Cally Cummins, you've died and gone to heaven.

"Cally! Jesse!" Bud's voice called from the top of the slope.

"Over here, Bud!" Jesse called standing up and giving me a yank, pulling me to my feet. Seems heaven was fleeting.

"Bud!" I cried.

Jesse and I climbed up the slope to my brother. It had begun to rain hard and the downpour transformed the burning embers of the garage into bellowing black smoke. But even with the heavy rain the flames escaped, curling upward to the treetops. The heat was intense. The sheriff's cars had been joined by the volunteer fire department and all kinds of cars and people were milling around now.

"Look Bud, the sheriff has Jasper right where we wanted him," I said. Sheriff Baines shoved Jasper into the backseat of one of the squad cars, beside another man. The interior lights were bright enough to recognize Earl sitting on the far side of the seat.

Bud went up to one of the sheriff's deputies and asked how they caught Earl. The deputy shook his head smirking, "One of our other men seen him running like a crazy man just off the path, pretty near the Pepper Pot. Between being scared half to death by whatever went on here tonight and being half lit from that shine they made over there, it made it pretty easy to nab him. When the car lights hit him he looked like a dazed deer in the headlights."

A car slowly bounced along the path making its way until a sheriff's deputy stopped it. I heard a familiar and angry voice say, "That's my kids down there!"

"Dad," I gulped.

Bud grabbed my arm. "Come on, Cally. They must be frantic by now; time to face the music."

I didn't much care if my parents were mad or not, I was so relieved to see their faces as they got out of the car. Seeing their concern, guilt hung over me like the smoky haze. The next few minutes were pretty much a state of confusion and everyone talked over everyone else trying to explain what brought us all to this place in time. Condensed versions of murder, ghosts, moonshiners, fires, it was like the preview of coming attractions at the theatre in DeLeon. I stood huddled close to my mother, safe now; feeling like everything would be okay, no matter how much trouble I got into for getting myself and everyone else into another mess.

"Purr. Purr. Purrrrr."

"Shhh!" I ordered everyone around me.

"Cally!" Dad said.

"Listen!" I said stepping away from my mother's arms and moving towards the soft purring noise. It was coming from the smoky fog that now engulfed the one time garage and moonshine still.

"Purr! Purr!" The sound came closer.

Everyone stood silent...

"Purr, purr."

Jesse was beside me and took my hand. The downpour had turned into a light sprinkle. The two of us walked in the drizzle, in the direction of the sound. Approaching the smoky fog, Jesse's grip tightened and warm droplets of water began streaming down my cheeks, mixing with the light rain as a pair of golden, amber eyes burned through the fog. Moving slowly, limping slightly through the darkness, Curtis appeared, the Coo-wa-chobee draped across his strong arms. Jesse let go of my hand, running to his Uncle and the cat, wrapping himself around them crying out unashamedly. Little

Deer and Lila huddled close around the boy, the man, and the great cat.

The rest of us stood back, so as not to intrude.

"It's truly a miracle," Gloria said.

Spotting a bright piece of patchwork cloth draping down from underneath the Coowachobee; my doll was clutched safely in Curtis' hand.

"An old Indian woman's blessing, and good luck," I whispered to the night.

I could hear Sheriff Baines telling my dad they would be in touch if they needed any more information. He had Bill's tape-recorder with him as he climbed into his squad car.

"Let's get them out of here," the sheriff ordered his deputy, referring to the angry passengers in the backseat.

As we watched the last standing timbers of the garage tumble to the ashes below Bud said, "Man, I've never seen such an intense blaze, must have been the moonshine that accelerated it so."

"Fourteen years ago," Little Deer remembered, "I watched a house burn the same way. So intense, the firefighters couldn't do anything to save it or its occupants. They couldn't understand what would have burned so fast and so furious. It was pure moonshine. Jasper Tate knew."

"I'd like to hear more about that," a reporter from the Sun News walked up. He had been lurking around taking pictures in the excitement and jotting down notes while we were all telling what happened.

He snapped one more picture of Curtis, Jesse, Lila, Little Deer, and the Coo-wa-chobee just before a deputy grabbed him up by his suspenders and told him to get on out of there. "You got your picture, now leave them be. I'll tell you anything else you need to know," the deputy told him.

"Well, there goes tomorrow's headline," Bud said as the deputy and the reporter left us be.

"Now, everyone will know the truth about Jasper Tate," Jesse said.

Seminole Landing

Lila put her arms around her son. "Jesse, knowing how the papers love a juicy bunch of gossip they might also find out about how Jasper isn't your real daddy. I'm so sorry for any embarrassment that will fall upon you from this."

"Embarrassed," Jesse looked at his mother. "I don't care about all that. I'm glad Jasper Tate isn't my real father. I'm proud to be the son of Caleb Malcolm, an Air Force pilot. I'm glad that everyone will know that Curtis Malcolm isn't some crazy Loony Woo Woo man who killed his family. Why, he'll be a hero for helping to bring Jasper Tate to justice."

Lila held her son close.

What a glorious sight they were; what a picture it would make on the front page, the three of them standing with the great cat. With Jasper Tate finally taken away off to Raiford Prison, locked away where he couldn't hurt anybody again, Curtis, Jesse, and Lila were free spirits now. They were released from their burdensome life with Jasper Tate, free to come and go as they pleased like the Coo-wa-chobee in Curtis' arms. Nobody would go sticking their fancy noses up at Little Deer anymore. A big grin crossed my lips as I pictured Miss Dulsey Mae Stoner, sitting on her front porch swing, sipping her lemonade and reading her morning Sun News. She'd change her wicked talk about savages now when she saw Little Deer in her fine…Silky…Blue…, "Oh my Lord!" I erupted.

"Cally?" Jesse said. He had such a smile on his face. It glowed brighter than the firelight behind him. A true, proud Seminole brave. He'd defeated Jasper Tate and his mysterious past tonight. He never surrendered. It didn't matter none if I had to work all summer sweeping sidewalks or sit all starched and stuffy at the next ten cotillions Miss Stoner threw to pay for that jacket. My friend, Ochee Somali Coo-wa, Jesse, was free and he'd told me, "Ecenokkecis."

Colleen Affeld

ABOUT THE AUTHOR

Colleen Affeld currently lives in Indiana with her husband Keith. They have four children, Kerri, Jim, Wendy and Deanna. The Affeld's share a love of classic cars and spend Indiana's warmer months traveling with fellow car enthusiasts cruising the highways and byways in their '40 Chevy. Affeld, now retired, worked at Valparaiso University as an Administrative Assistant and Catering Coordinator for 32 years, and studied her craft of writing there. Born in Pennsylvania, but raised in central Florida, Affeld and her family return to both places as often as possible. She believes writing what you know makes for the most believable stories, hence the setting of the Sunshine State's cypress filled river banks and bubbling springs, conjuring up the tales of her youth's inspiration. Affeld has one other previously published novel, The Grey Ghost.

Made in the USA
Lexington, KY
30 March 2017